LAST ENGLISH HERO

By Gordon Anthony

ISBN-13: 978-1796565256

Prologue

The riders came from the south, clattering into the village on their large horses, the hooves throwing up billows of dust from the rutted earth of the roadway. They came at a canter, two dozen men wearing long coats of chainmail, each of them armed with lance, sword and shield, and the sound of their approach was like a rumble of thunder in the still, warm air of the summer's day.

Chickens squawked and flapped as they scattered out of the way, geese honked and pigs grunted in annoyance as they, too, hurried aside at the riders' approach.

The villagers who were working in the fields stopped their labours, standing very still as they watched the long train of horsemen, perhaps hoping that their immobility would render them invisible to the soldiers. Some of them uttered soft curses, others mumbled prayers, but all felt a sense of dread because they knew that soldiers always brought suffering and misery in their wake.

In the village itself, people hurried into their homes and closed their doors. Few Norman soldiers had ever passed through the village, but even the children knew what to expect when the armed patrols passed by, and nobody wished to attract the attention of the men who now ruled England through force of arms. So the villagers cowered inside their homes and prayed that the riders would simply continue on their way as they had always done before.

But these riders were in no hurry to pass through. They slowed to a trot when they reached the church, the only building in the village which was made of stone; they ambled past the graveyard where the local people had buried their dead for generations and, by the time they passed the smithy, the horses were moving only at walking pace. Then they arrived at the crossroads where they came to a halt, the horses stamping their feet and tossing their heads while the riders looked around, taking in their surroundings.

The leader, dark-haired and with saturnine features, was a large man who looked faintly ridiculous in his long coat of chainmail. In contrast to the lean hardness of his followers, his paunch made him appear ungainly in the saddle, as if he were more accustomed to sitting at table than on horseback. Below his iron helmet, his deep-set eyes glinted hungrily as he surveyed the village.

"So this is Bourne," he said with a satisfied smile. "It has potential."

His acquisitive gaze took in the well-built homes, the long stretches of farmland beyond the houses, the river meandering past the eastern side of the village, with ducks bobbing lazily on the smooth surface of the water.

"It would make an excellent base for you, Sir," observed the young knight who sat beside the leader. "It is close to the fenlands and within easy reach of Peterborough."

The leader nodded absently, removing a gauntlet and tilting up his helmet so that he could wipe beads of sweat from his forehead.

"It will do," he said laconically.

"The monks said the old Thane lived on the western side of the village," his younger companion remarked.

"Then let us see whether he has left us a comfortable dwellinghouse," smirked the leader as he adjusted his helmet and replaced his gauntlet before tugging his horse's head and setting off along the narrow, dusty road that led to the west.

Toki was awoken from his slumber by the sound of many horses. After a moment's initial confusion, he pushed himself out from under the covers and padded across to the window.

Even though it was mid-afternoon, the shutters were closed because he had wanted privacy. Now he gently eased one shutter open just far enough to allow him to peer down into the courtyard outside. The sight that met his bleary eyes froze him to the spot as a wave of shock and fear engulfed him.

"What is it?" Aelswith asked sleepily from the bed.

Toki stepped back from the window, his heart pounding in his chest. For a moment, his voice refused to come, his throat constricted by terror, but he managed a hoarse whisper when Aelswith repeated her question.

"Normans," he hissed.

The girl's face paled and she held a hand to her mouth to stifle her panic.

"What do they want?" she asked.

2

"I don't know," Toki hissed with an air of desperate panic. "But you had better leave, just to be on the safe side."

Aelswith needed no second invitation. She scrambled out from the bed, picking up her dress and hurriedly pulling it over her head, tugging frantically to let it fall and cover her nakedness.

Toki was also hurriedly dressing, pulling on his breeches and lacing up his shoes, then hastily shoving his head and arms into his tunic.

"Go out the back door," he told Aelswith. "Warn the other servants to stay out of sight."

He could see the fear on her face, but she nodded her understanding and made to the bedroom door while Toki steeled himself for a confrontation with the knights.

Aelswith opened the door but stopped and turned to face him. She reached out, took his head in her hands and kissed him fiercely.

"Be careful," she told him, her eyes already moist with tears.

"I will," he promised. "Now go."

He slapped her rump to hurry her along the corridor and down the wooden staircase which led to the house's great hall. She ran across the hall, then she dashed to the rear door and vanished outside.

Toki waited, allowing her time to reach the servants' outbuilding, then summoned his courage and headed down the stairs.

He could hear voices outside now, and recognised Wulfnoth's deep, suspicious tones demanding to know what the visitors wanted.

Toki feared he knew the answer, but he dreaded stepping out into the afternoon sun to meet the Normans.

Yet he had no choice. He might have been barely seventeen years old, but he was now the Thane. It was his duty to greet his guests.

Guests?

The thought horrified him. Normans were not guests; they were conquerors. Ever since the news of King Harold's death had reached the village, Toki had known this day would arrive. Bourne had been left unmolested for nearly two years but now, it seemed, the new rulers of England had taken notice of it at last.

3

Toki wanted to run away. He was not really a Thane; he had merely inherited the position after his father had marched away to that devastating confrontation at Hastings with so many of the men from the village.

Toki had been relieved when his father had ordered him to remain behind to take care of the estate. By framing his instructions as a command, the old Thane had ensured that nobody could make accusations of cowardice against his son. At fifteen years of age, Toki had been old enough to carry a sword and shield, but his father had known that the boy was no warrior. To save his son's reputation, the Thane had come up with the excuse that somebody needed to ensure that the estate was managed properly while the *fyrd* was away on campaign.

It was a decision which had probably saved Toki's life, because very few men had returned, and those who did brought the dreadful news that Asketil, a King's Thane, Lord of Bourne, had died alongside his King, leaving Toki as the only surviving member of the family.

Far away in London, a new King sat on the throne of England, but Bourne was a small place, nestled on the fringes of the Fens, and few travellers passed that way. King William, having seized control through brute force of arms, had far more important things to attend to than one tiny village, so Toki had simply stayed and the villagers, shocked by the loss of so many of their menfolk, had gradually returned to the drudgery of their daily lives. To Toki's astonishment, most of them had accepted that he was the new Thane, even though he had no idea how he ought to behave. The villagers did not need telling how to tend their crops or livestock, nor that the tithes must be collected and paid to the church. Toki had not even found it necessary to demand taxes because the villagers had brought him the Thane's share of the harvest and paid their dues in kind. So he had allowed people to get on with their lives while he had indulged himself by spending his time hunting, eating the best of foods and making love to Aelswith whenever the mood took him.

And now, on a warm, summer's day which had begun like any other, it seemed to him that it was all about to end.

Swallowing hard as he fought to find his courage, he walked across the empty hall, his footsteps sounding unnaturally loud as they echoed around the large chamber, and his eyes alighted on the sword that hung on the wall above the stone fireplace. For a brief moment, he wondered whether he should take the sword with him, but he decided it would be better to face the Normans unarmed. If he presented no threat, he hoped they would not harm him.

Taking a deep breath, he opened the inner doors and went into the tiny vestibule, blinking as he stepped into the bright sunlight that flooded in through the outer doors which stood wide open.

Wulfnoth stood outside the main doors, his long battle-axe gripped in both hands, his bulky frame blocking the entranceway as he stared belligerently up at the horsemen who had spread out across the wide courtyard in front of the house. Hearing Toki open the inner doors, Wulfnoth glanced quickly back over his shoulder, his expression one of deep concern.

"What is going on, Wulfnoth?" Toki asked in as pleasant and relaxed a tone as he could muster.

Even to himself, he sounded like a frightened boy, and he hoped his fear was not as evident as it felt.

"Buggered if I know, Lord," the surly housecarl said in answer to the question. "They don't seem to speak much English. All they say is they want to speak to the Thane."

"Well, I am here now," Toki responded as he stepped out of the house and took up position alongside Wulfnoth.

For some reason, the housecarl's bulky presence gave him confidence. It was, he knew, a misplaced reaction because even an experienced warrior like Wulfnoth could not face down the two dozen armoured knights who confronted him. Besides, Wulfnoth had returned from that awful catastrophe at Hastings with three fingers of his right hand missing. His grip on his battle-axe might appear firm, but Toki knew the housecarl could not hope to wield his weapon with anything like the skill he had formerly possessed.

Is this what we are reduced to? Toki wondered.

In his father's day, a dozen housecarls would have been at the Thane's command, yet now Wulfnoth was the only one who remained. He and two others had straggled back to the village in the aftermath of the defeat at Senlac Hill near Hastings, but one of the others had died of his wounds, and the third man had been so ashamed at outliving his Thane that he could not bear to face Toki every day. In despair, the man had gone off to join the outlaws who infested the forests and fens.

So Wulfnoth was now Toki's only ally. Yet the big warrior was facing the Normans as if their numbers could not daunt him, and his stolid stance gave Toki the strength he required.

Toki surveyed the riders, noting their armour and weapons, seeing the hard, cruel expressions on their faces. The smell of the horses was pungent in the warm air, their bulk intimidating as they crowded around the courtyard, snorting and tossing their heads, and stamping their hooves on the hard earth.

"I am Toki, son of Asketil," he announced, picking out the oldest of the knights, a plump, dark-eyed man who was scowling at him with obvious irritation.

The man said something in French to a younger knight beside him. This man leaned forwards over the neck of his horse and jabbed a gloved finger in Toki's direction.

"You are Thane?" he asked in heavily accented English.

"Yes," Toki confirmed.

The young man grinned malevolently as he said, "No longer."

Gesturing to the older man beside him, he went on, "This is Ivo de Taillebois, Sheriff of Lincolnshire. He rules here now. He requires this house."

"This is my home," Toki responded helplessly.

The young knight simply said, "No. You will leave now."

Toki felt helpless. There was nothing he could do in the face of such overwhelming odds. He had heard that the Normans were seizing land all across England and now he knew the tales were true.

There was a bitter taste in his mouth, but he knew he had no option except to give in to the demand.

He was about to acquiesce when Wulfnoth hefted his great battle-axe and growled, "Say the word, Lord, and I will cut this insolent cur's horse out from under him."

It was a foolish act of bravado, Toki knew. One housecarl could not defeat so many mounted men, yet Wulfnoth's willingness to die for him swelled his chest with pride and gave strength to his trembling knees.

But there had been too much death in Bourne recently.

Toki licked his lips and said softly, "No, Wulfnoth."

Wulfnoth did not relax his stance. The young Norman's eyes studied the big housecarl, lighting on his maimed hand.

"Where did you lose your fingers?" he asked sharply.

"Fighting my King's enemies," Wulfnoth growled belligerently.

"Your King is William, Duke of Normandy," the knight shot back. "I think you fought against him. Were you one of the rabble who opposed him at Hastings?"

Wulfnoth did not answer, but neither did he back down. He stood staring up at the clean-shaven Norman, his axe held across his chest.

The knight turned to the man he had named as Ivo de Taillebois and spoke in rapid French, his words bringing a malicious grin to the man's saturnine face.

The newly appointed Sheriff snorted a curt reply which the young knight interpreted.

"The Sheriff has named you outlaws," he told Toki and Wulfnoth. "You rebelled against your rightful King, so your lives and possessions are forfeit."

Even as he spoke, Ivo de Taillebois had signalled to some of the other riders. Several of them dismounted and drew their swords.

Toki felt his legs go weak as comprehension dawned on him. He could not move, could not speak, could not even utter a cry of despair.

Wulfnoth was made of stronger stuff. The housecarl immediately braced himself, raising his axe, but the young knight suddenly urged his horse forwards so that it buffeted the housecarl and knocked him off balance.

Wulfnoth staggered but managed to swing his axe in a clumsy arc which drove back two of the dismounted men who were coming for him. It gained him a brief moment of time, but his mauled hand could not hold the weapon properly. He was unable to haul the long-handled axe back quickly enough, and the Normans were on him in an instant, hacking at his body and driving him to the ground. The housecarl uttered one impotent cry of rage and despair before falling silent, while the Normans continued to slash at his blood-drenched corpse.

Toki looked on in horror, his mouth gaping, his voice lost beneath his terror. He was so petrified he did not even see the

Norman soldier who came up on his left and swept his heavy sword down on Toki's skull.

Ivo de Taillebois gave a weary sigh as he looked down at the blood-soaked corpses.

"Dispose of the bodies," he ordered, "but put their heads on poles at the crossroads. Then round up the servants and have a meal prepared. I am hungry."

He dismounted, handing the reins of his horse to one of his knights, then signalled to the young man who had acted as his interpreter.

"Come, Frederick, let us see what sort of residence we have inherited."

So saying, Ivo de Taillebois, Sheriff of Lincolnshire, strode into his new home.

Chapter 1

It was still dark when Edric awoke, only the dim glow from the embers of the forge providing any light. Pushing aside his thin woollen blanket, he struggled to his feet, felt around until he located his candle, then took it to the forge and held the wick to the dull, red heat until it burst into light. Carefully setting the candle down on a wooden work bench, he began the laborious task of scraping out the ashes from the forge and rebuilding the fire, keeping some of the glowing embers in a pot so that he could use them to relight the forge.

He was sweating by the time he had finished. It was always hot in the smithy and Edric's role was to ensure that it remained that way. Without the red hot fire, Uncle Ethelred could not work the iron, and without work, he could not earn a living.

Edric piled in some kindling, replaced some of the hot embers, and poked at the sticks until they caught. Slowly, he fed more sticks, then began adding lumps of charcoal until the fire was well ablaze and the heat was bringing beads of sweat to his face.

Once the fire was burning greedily, Edric ventured outside, noticing the pink glow on the eastern horizon which heralded the dawn. Now he shivered, the sweat on his body chilling him as the cold air struck him. It had been a tough winter which seemed reluctant to shake off its hold on the world, and spring was struggling to make its presence felt. Traces of frost sparkled on the grass, and the puddles which lay on the trodden earth of the smithy's back yard glistened with a thin skin of ice.

Edric went to the water barrel and, after stripping off his clothes, plunged his hands into its murky contents, exhaling sharply at the shock of the freezing water. Quickly, he splashed himself clean of sweat, feeling the goosebumps rise on his flesh.

Hurriedly, he towelled himself down with his old tunic, pausing only to examine the scar on his left thigh. It was still there, a white, jagged line set in a long dip where the flesh had been gouged. It would, he supposed, always be there; a reminder of what his Uncle Ethelred called his youthful folly.

Still shivering, he dressed himself again before scurrying back inside the smithy and feeding the fire once more. Then he tidied away his blanket and picked up a broom with which he swept the floor, shoving the gathered dust and detritus out the back door and into the yard.

He could hear the sounds of movement from within the house which stood behind the smithy and he could see candlelight leaching out from behind the shutters. Aunt Edith was up and would be preparing breakfast.

Edric replaced the broom, blew out his candle and went back outside, crossing the yard and entering the small shack which his aunt and uncle called home.

The interior of the house comprised a single room, with a small sleeping area curtained off at the far end. Close to the door was a heavy, wooden table, two high-backed wooden chairs and a couple of three-legged stools. The room was warm, heated by the fire over which Aunt Edith had hung a heavy pot. She greeted Edric with a smile as she stirred the contents with a long-handled, wooden spoon.

"It's another cold morning," Edric informed her.

"This will warm you up," she promised, nodding in the direction of her cooking pot. "Help yourself to bread and butter."

Edric perched his large frame on one of the stools, pausing only to acknowledge Aunt Edith's cat, Thorfinn, which purred as it padded around his feet. He bent to scratch it behind the ears before shooing it away and turning his attention to his breakfast.

It was Lent, a time of fasting, and breakfast should have consisted of little more than a bowl of warm milk, but Edric was not yet twenty-one years old, so he was not obliged to follow the Church's rules. His Uncle Ethelred also ignored the dictat, insisting that he could not carry out the arduous work in the smithy unless he had eaten a decent breakfast.

"I'll fast during the day," the surly smith insisted, "but I need some hot food inside me in the morning."

Lent had always struck Edric as a foolish notion. Most homes still had plenty of food left over from the previous year's harvest. It was the summer months where hunger could strike, as the supplies of salted meat, wheat, oats and barley ran low. Summer was often a time of enforced fasting, so it made no sense to Edric that they should abstain from food in the springtime.

Naturally, he kept such thoughts to himself, knowing he would only be given a lecture if he dared to voice his opinion. For the time being, he was determined to make the most of the food Aunt Edith provided.

Not that breakfast would be substantial. All the table bore was a loaf of dark bread and a slab of butter which Aunt Edith had warmed so that it could be spread. Taking his knife, Edric cut a thick slice of the bread which was still reasonably soft even though it had been baked the previous day. He coated it with the creamy butter and bit hungrily into it.

Aunt Edith brought him a bowl of steaming gruel.

"I've got some poached eggs as well," she told him as he picked up his spoon and delved into the thick, lumpy porridge.

"I see your appetite hasn't deserted you," Aunt Edith remarked. "It's no wonder you are so big."

"Working in the smithy helps," Edric replied between mouthfuls.

That was true. He had always been large for his age but now, nearly nineteen years old, his frame had bulked out and his muscles had been honed by several years of working for his uncle, the blacksmith.

Ethelred put in an appearance, emerging from behind the curtain around the bed, rubbing his stubbled chin and yawning expansively.

"Is the forge still lit?" he asked Edric curtly.

"Yes, Uncle."

Edric had grown accustomed to the question. It was the first thing his uncle said to him each morning.

"And the charcoal?" Ethelred enquired as he sat on one of the chairs and allowed his wife to present him with a bowl of gruel and some bread.

"Enough for a few more days," Edric answered as he chewed on another slice of bread. "But we could do with some more firewood and our stock of iron is running low."

Ethelred knew this already, but he gave a sour nod.

"I'll get more ore from the marsh dwellers," he grunted, referring to the lumps of bog ore which were often found under the swampy surface of the land bordering the fens. "As for fuel, you'd best go and gather some more wood this afternoon."

"I could go this morning," Edric suggested hopefully.

"No. I need you to take a delivery to the castle."

Edric nodded, concealing his distaste for the errand by taking a mouthful of poached egg. He had already scraped his bowl clean and he now devoured the egg in two mouthfuls before swallowing the last piece of his bread.

As soon as breakfast was over, Edric followed his uncle to the smithy and their day's work began. Edric unbolted and opened the front doors, allowing daylight and cool air inside, while Uncle Ethelred checked his tools and decided what needed to be done first.

The smithy was always busy these days, Edric reflected. The Normans often brought horses to be re-shod, and some of the soldiers even asked for new lance tips, stirrups, buckles, bridle bits or knives. They could obtain such things from London, of course, but Ethelred's smithy was close at hand and his work was of good quality, so many of the soldiers preferred to obtain what they needed from him. When the demand from the castle was added to the usual tasks of producing such items as ploughshares, cauldrons, axes, hammers and nails, Ethelred was as busy as he had ever been.

"Business has never been better," he would constantly tell Edric. "Whatever you think about the Normans, they'll make us wealthy yet."

Edric would nod whenever his uncle mentioned this. He did not like the Normans, nor the way they treated the local population, but his uncle was a man who prized his own welfare above that of others, and Edric had learned long ago that it was pointless to argue with him. Tempers would fray and then his uncle would threaten him with a beating unless he held his tongue. That was less of a threat these days, of course, since Edric was easily as big as his uncle and could probably match him in a wrestling contest. Ethelred's muscles bulged on his arms and chest, but long hours of pumping the forge's bellows and hammering at rods of iron had developed Edric's strength considerably.

Not that he was permitted to handle any of the valuable contract work, but his uncle had allowed him to produce many of the hundreds of nails the Normans had called for when constructing their castle around what had formerly been the Thane's house. Edric had also worked on knives and other smaller implements, developing his skills as a blacksmith under the ever-critical eyes of his uncle.

Edric laboriously refilled the water bucket which would be used to cool the hot metal, then stoked more charcoal into the forge and pumped the bellows until his uncle was satisfied that it was producing sufficient heat for his work.

The morning would be taken up by mundane work. A broken ploughshare needed repairing, the supply of horseshoes needed replenishing, and old Edmund had asked for a new axe head. In the afternoon, Edric knew, his uncle would work on a sword he was making. He had been labouring over it for weeks now, heating and cooling the iron, hammering long rods into a heavy, sharp blade. Edric had watched in fascination, asking questions as Ethelred sweated over the sword. He had soon realised that his uncle had never made a blade like this before.

"The Normans are always on the lookout for a good blade," Ethelred would insist. "This is an investment."

Edric was not so sure, but he held his tongue because he was intrigued by the process of turning base iron into a man-killing weapon. His uncle had promised him he could make the tang which would divide the blade from the hilt of the sword, where it would serve to protect the wielder's hand, but it would be some time yet before the work reached that stage.

For the moment, the routine work took up their time. Edric pumped the bellows, fed the forge, replenished the water from the barrel outside, and sweated in the heat of the forge, while Ethelred worked the metal, the sound of his hammer ringing loudly as he struck down to temper the iron on his anvil.

It was hard work, but Edric was used to it and did not complain. Still, he was grateful when a shadow darkened the open doorway as a potential customer appeared.

Ethelred stopped hammering and replaced his tools, wiping his hands on his stained leather apron as he greeted the newcomer. He was polite, but his face fell when he recognised who it was.

"Brother John," he sighed. "What can I do for you this fine morning?"

Brother John stepped inside the smithy, looking around appraisingly. He was a young man, in his mid-twenties, with close-cropped, dark hair and a boyish expression on his round, youthful face. As always, his blue eyes sparkled with vitality as he took in his surroundings.

"Oh, I was merely passing by," he said in a friendly voice. "I thought I might call in to see whether your good lady had any of her fine ale to sell."

Ethelred signalled to Edric but the young man was already on his way. The smithy, always warm thanks to the heat of the forge, was often a local gathering place for the villagers, so Aunt Edith had begun the custom of selling ale and pies to the visitors.

"I'm a blacksmith, not a tavern keeper," Ethelred would often grumble.

"It brings us in some extra pennies," Aunt Edith would respond cheerfully. "Besides, it's good to hear people chatting."

There was always plenty of chat when Brother John arrived. The young monk was an infrequent visitor to the village, for he spent his days wandering the countryside, stopping where the fancy took him, then moving on. If no local priest was available, he could sometimes be persuaded to offer prayers and counselling, and he had been known to baptise newborn infants, perform weddings and burials, but he rarely stayed in any one place long enough to undertake anything except the most basic of Church duties.

His principal role appeared to be the collection and dissemination of news. He was always hungry for gossip and enjoyed relaying what he had heard elsewhere. Edric particularly enjoyed his tales of London, a great city which, if Brother John was to be believed, was home to thousands of people. Edric suspected the monk might be exaggerating, but he liked to hear the tales nonetheless.

Edith soon arrived, bringing a flagon of ale and a plate of freshly baked eel pies which she presented to Brother John.

The monk grinned as he reached for one of the small, round, thickly crusted pastries.

"It is Lent," he remarked, "but one is permitted two collations each day. Join me, please."

Collations, Edric knew, were what the Church called small snacks which were permitted during Lent. One meal was allowed each day, provided it did not include meat, but solid food was allowed twice each day in addition to this meal, provided the two collations did not constitute a second meal. Aunt Edith had baked several small pies, so eating one would be allowed, since eel was a fish, not a forbidden meat.

Edric helped himself to a pie but his uncle muttered, "I have work to get on with," as he began arranging various items on his workbench.

Aunt Edith gave Brother John an apologetic smile, then invited him to tell them his news.

"We have not seen you since last summer," she reminded the young monk. "You must have lots of news from afar."

Brother John nodded, "I have news indeed. But first, tell me what has happened here since I last came this way."

"Nothing ever happens here," Edric muttered, earning himself a frown from his aunt and a slight smile from Brother John.

Aunt Edith said, "The main thing is that our poor priest died last month. We have sent to the abbey for a replacement, but none has come so far."

"That is sad news," Brother John responded solemnly. "What happens on Sundays if you have nobody to preach the gospel to you?"

"We gather in the church and pray," Aunt Edith told him. "Perhaps you could stay and preach to us this Sunday?"

Brother John gave a solemn shake of his head as he replied, "Sadly, I am not able to stay here that long. God willing, your new priest will have arrived by then."

"I hope so," Aunt Edith sighed, unable to conceal her disappointment.

Edric knew she would not be the only person who would feel regret at that news, because Brother John was a big favourite with the women of the village. His innocent good looks and natural charm had them fluttering around him whenever he visited, and even Aunt Edith was prone to acting in a girlish manner when Brother John spoke to her.

Edric liked Brother John but he could not help feeling a little jealous. Girls never flocked around him the way they did with the young monk, yet Brother John never appeared to notice the reaction he inspired. It seemed rather unfair to Edric because, although priests and bishops were not obliged to take vows of celibacy, most monks did follow the Church's recommended custom, and Brother John claimed that he, too, adhered to that particular practice.

15

Aunt Edith's face fell even further when Brother John went on, "Unfortunately, I should tell you that there is a new Abbot in Peterborough. I expect he will be extremely busy as he settles into his new role."

"He must send us a priest!" Aunt Edith exclaimed.

"Oh, I am sure he will. When he gets round to it."

"What can be more important than ministering to the souls of the people?" Aunt Edith persisted.

Brother John gave a slight shrug as he said, "Nothing, of course. I am sure Abbot Turold will find someone for you before very long."

"Turold?" Edric asked when he heard the unfamiliar name. "He is a Norman?"

"Naturally," Brother John replied with a sardonic smile. "The King does not appoint Englishmen to abbacies these days."

Edric felt his face flush but Brother John went on, "This particular Norman Abbot is, so I have heard, a rather belligerent fellow. They say the King has sent him here to help deal with the outlaws."

"A man of God should not be fighting," Aunt Edith frowned disapprovingly as she began to appreciate the monk's caution over when a new priest might arrive in the village.

Brother John smiled, "I fear Abbot Turold is a man of the world first and a man of God second."

"Then let us pray he sends us a new priest while he himself stays in Peterborough," Aunt Edith said fervently.

"Oh, I dare say he will pass this way soon enough," said Brother John. "But, if rumour is to be believed, he and Sheriff de Taillebois do not get on with one another."

Ethelred looked up from his work to say, "You should not be disrespectful to our betters, Brother."

"I can assure you I will always treat them with the respect they deserve," the monk replied with an easy smile.

Edric grinned, almost laughing aloud when Brother John winked at him as soon as Ethelred's back was turned. Edric's uncle had either not detected the sarcasm in the young monk's reply, or had chosen to ignore it.

The remark was typical of Brother John, who seemed to take delight in poking fun at his betters and in defying conventions. It was easier for him to do this, Edric supposed, because monks were not subject to civil law. If accused of a crime, they could appeal to be tried by the Church and would almost always be given a more lenient sentence than an ordinary person could expect. Not that Brother John ever actually broke the law as far as Edric knew, but the man often seemed on the verge of doing or saying something outrageous.

"What else have you heard, Brother?" Edric asked.

"Well, there are rumours of a Danish fleet harassing the eastern coast, although I have only heard these tales at second or third hand."

"The Danes are back?" Aunt Edith gasped. "Will they come here?"

"Who knows?" Brother John shrugged. "King Sweyn of Denmark has some claim to the English throne, but I doubt he is strong enough to wrest it from King William. I suspect the Danes will confine themselves to raiding as usual."

"They did more than raid three years ago," Edric muttered, the fingers of his left hand idly tracing the long line of the gash on his thigh.

"That was not the Danes," Brother John reminded him. "That was King Harald of the Norwegians."

Edric felt embarrassed at being corrected, but he merely shrugged. To him, one set of Northmen was much like another. They might claim to be Christians, but they had no qualms about plundering, raping and killing other Christians. Danes or Norwegians, they were all the same.

"What other news have you heard, then?" he asked the monk.

"Oh, no!" declared Brother John. "It is now your turn to tell me something of interest. What else has been happening here since my last visit?"

"Nothing very much," Edric shrugged.

Ethelred put in, "We work, we pay our tithes and we know our place."

"You have had no trouble with outlaws, then?" Brother John enquired.

"No," Edric told him quickly.

The look Brother John gave him told him that the monk knew he was not telling the truth. Edric briefly wondered whether it was a sin to lie to a man of God. It probably was, he decided, but

17

he had no desire to spread word of any outlawry which might bring yet more Normans to the area.

"No trouble at all?" the monk remarked doubtfully. "Then you are very fortunate."

"There was a little trouble a few weeks ago," Aunt Edith admitted. "We heard that one of the Sheriff's men was killed."

"Really? When and how?"

"We don't know the details," Ethelred said insistently, momentarily abandoning his task of noisily sorting through the items on his bench. "They say he was shot with an arrow when out chasing outlaws."

"How unfortunate," said Brother John with a sad shake of his head. "I shall pray for his soul."

"Pray the bandits are caught and hanged," Ethelred told him gruffly. "They bring nothing but trouble."

"Amen to that!" agreed Brother John cheerfully. "Well, I suppose it is now my turn again. Sadly, what I have to tell you brings me no pleasure."

"What has happened?" Aunt Edith asked, her face grave.

The monk sighed as he explained, "You know of the rebellion in the north last year?"

"Yes, we heard about that," Edric nodded. "You told us about it the last time you were here."

"Yes, I expect I did. Well, King William has suppressed the revolt."

"Good," stated Ethelred firmly. "We want no trouble. People need to get on with their lives and accept what God has decreed."

"Indeed," nodded Brother John. "On this occasion, however, it is King William who has decreed, and his orders have proved unhappy for the people of the North."

"What do you mean?" Edric asked him.

"I mean he has ravaged the land utterly," sighed Brother John. "His men killed all the livestock, burned all the crops and destroyed homes everywhere they went. The revolt was crushed and so, I fear, were the people. The land is laid waste and I have heard tell thousands have died because of famine."

Aunt Edith put a hand to her mouth and uttered a soft cry of horror, while Edric gasped, "A King should not treat his subjects like that!"

"They are rebels!" Ethelred snapped. "They deserve what comes to them."

"They were surely not all rebels," Edric insisted, his outrage fuelling his words.

"Indeed not," Brother John agreed. "But King William, in his wisdom, has seen fit to punish them anyway."

Edric was about to say more but his aunt placed a warning hand on his forearm and gave him a quick shake of her head. He glanced at his uncle, recognised the glowering anger in the blacksmith's flushed expression, and shrugged himself into silence, not wishing to spark another outburst.

Aunt Edith said, "I suppose the King must know what he is doing, but it is sad to hear of so many deaths."

"Thousands, so they say," Brother John murmured. Then he sat up, handed back his empty mug and rose to his feet. "I thank you for your hospitality, Mistress Edith. Now I must go to pay my respects to the Sheriff."

"I need to go to the castle as well," Edric told him. "I have things to deliver."

"Then I shall be delighted to accompany you," smiled Brother John.

Edric gave his uncle an expectant look. He had not been looking forward to visiting the castle, but having Brother John as a companion would make the short trip bearable.

Ethelred scowled but handed him a bag which contained the various items he had been sorting.

"Tell Master Frederick the price is ten pence," he told Edric. "I expect he will pay no more than seven, but get more if you can."

"What if he offers less?" Edric asked.

Uncle Ethelred's face twitched as he considered the conflict between his own desire for money and his subservient attitude to the Norman lords.

"Accept nothing less than six pence," he decided. "And hurry back."

Edric took off his leather apron, donned his cloak and picked up the heavy sack from the bench, the iron nails and tools it contained clanking noisily as he lifted it and slung it over his shoulder.

He grinned at Brother John.

"Shall we go, Brother?"

"Of course."

The two young men stepped out through the wide doors and into the street. The sun was doing its best to warm the chill air but a hint of winter still made itself evident in the cool, northerly breeze which pinched at their faces. Edric glanced down at Brother John's feet, noticing the monk wore sandals on his otherwise bare feet. He wondered whether the itinerant monk ever felt the cold. Brother John never wore anything except his thick, woollen robe which was loosely tied by a cheap cord around his waist, and Edric could not recall ever seeing him shod in anything other than cheap sandals. Apart from the wooden crucifix which hung around his neck and a small knapsack slung over one shoulder, Brother John had no possessions other than his robe, sandals and his faith in God.

Then, to Edric's surprise, he noticed that he was looking down on Brother John and could see the shaved tonsure on the crown of the man's head.

"What is so funny?" the monk asked with an amused smile.

"I just realised I am taller than you," Edric replied.

"I suspect that is because you were just a boy when we first met. I reached my full size some years ago, while you have continued to grow at what I must say is an alarming rate. You must be as big as your uncle by now."

"I suppose I am," Edric nodded.

"But not so fond of your Norman overlords as he is?" Brother John observed, his friendly tone taking any sting from the question.

"Uncle Ethelred is an old man," Edric replied cautiously. "He only wants to live his life in peace. He doesn't much care who runs things."

"And why should he?" Brother John laughed. "For those at the bottom of the heap, it does not matter whether those at the top are English, Danish or Norman. Taxes must still be paid."

Edric fell silent. For him, it was not a question of paying taxes, but the manner in which the people were treated. Life had been difficult enough when he was a boy, but now the Normans had laid their iron hands on the land and the people. Edric could see the injustice of many of the new laws, and he felt a sense of righteous outrage that nobody seemed prepared to stand up to the invaders.

Despite his youth, though, he had enough sense not to say such things when others might overhear, so he simply replied, "I would not say my uncle is at the bottom of the heap."

"Indeed not," Brother John agreed amiably. "But it was the principle I was referring to, not necessarily one individual's situation."

Edric had the feeling the monk was mocking him in some way, so he remained silent as they walked along Bourne's main street.

The village was quiet, most people either out in the fields or sheltering inside their homes from the cold wind. A couple of young children were struggling along with a bucket of water they had obviously collected from the stream, and the usual scattering of cats prowled the narrow lanes, but there were few other signs of life except the faint sound of women's voices from inside the tiny cottages.

Only two women had braved the chill to sit outside their doors so that they had better light by which to wield their spindles and distaffs to spin raw wool into long threads. Both of them gave Brother John a friendly smile as the two men passed. One called a cheerful greeting to which the young monk replied with a blessing. For some reason, this irritated Edric because few of the women in the village ever greeted him with such friendliness. He supposed it must be his fault for not being more outgoing, but he had always found it difficult to relax in the company of others, and he knew many of the villagers still regarded him as an overgrown boy rather than a man. He made a silent vow to try to be more outgoing in future, although he was not sure quite how he would accomplish that feat.

After a short while, the two young men reached the crossroads, where Brother John hesitated, stopping to take a look around. Bourne had once been a fairly prosperous place, yet there were few young men left alive, so the fields they could see beyond the collection of houses were now being worked by only a handful of older men and teenage boys who trudged along behind their oxen or mules, driving the heavy ploughs through the hard earth in order to prepare the ground for sowing.

Brother John's expression seemed pensive as he stared at the distant figures in the fields, and he seemed to be on the verge of making some comment, but he was distracted by the appearance of another person.

An elderly woman had stepped out of the door of her tiny cottage and come walking down towards the crossroads. Edric sighed when he saw her. He would have preferred to avoid her but it was too late.

The woman, who was pinch-faced and thin, wore a dark dress and had a shawl draped over her wispy, grey hair. She walked with brisk, confident steps, her head held high as if to proclaim an air of authority. She gave the two young men a scornful look as she passed.

"Looking for souls to save, Brother Monk?" she asked in a cracked, hoarse voice.

"Always, Mistress," Brother John replied.

"Then best start with the one standing beside you," the woman cackled. "He's a thief and a trouble-maker, no mistake."

Edric's cheeks flushed red but his tongue refused to work, and he stood as still as a statue until the old woman had passed him, turned to her left and headed eastwards towards the fields.

"A thief and a troublemaker, are you?" Brother John enquired once the old woman was out of earshot.

Edric lowered his gaze, staring at the rutted roadway as he mumbled, "I got in quite a few fights when I was a boy."

"So I believe. Your aunt often worried about your tendency to use your fists to settle an argument."

"I was just standing up for myself," Edric tried to explain.

He felt foolish, standing in the middle of the road, being compelled to confess his sins to a monk.

Brother John smiled as he said, "I know you only ever got into a fight when you felt you had been wronged. Or when somebody else had been wronged."

"You need to stand up to bullies," Edric murmured softly.

"A noble sentiment," Brother John remarked. "As long as one does not become a bully oneself."

"I never bullied anyone!" Edric protested, raising his head to hold the monk's gaze.

"I know," Brother John said soothingly. "But your frequent fighting perhaps explains why that old lady considers you a troublemaker. It does not, however, explain why she named you a thief."

Edric lowered his gaze again as he sighed, "She once caught me stealing an apple from a tree in her garden."

"Ah! Theft is a sin, as I am sure you know."

"I was given a beating by Uncle Ethelred," Edric admitted. "And that old witch has never let me forget it."

"A lifetime of penance for one apple does seem harsh," Brother John said with a smile. "I hope it was a tasty apple."

"It was rotten inside," Edric snorted. Then, recalling an expression he had heard his Aunt Edith utter at the time, he added, "Just like old Gytha there."

"The old woman? She is not well regarded, then?"

"Few people want anything to do with her," Edric informed him. "I think she is evil."

"How so?"

Edric sighed as he explained, "Last week, she accused her neighbour of stealing a leg of salted lamb she had been saving. The bones were found in his midden."

"Another theft?" Brother John frowned. "The lady seems to attract them."

"Except that Seaver didn't steal her meat," Edric explained with an aggrieved air. "He was out in the fields all day when he was supposed to have taken it. Plenty of people saw him."

Brother John frowned, "Then why did she accuse him?"

Scowling, Edric explained, "Seaver's wife died a couple of years ago. He's quite well off because he is a *sokeman* and owns his own land. But his two sons died at Hastings, and he has no children to inherit what he owns, so Gytha wanted to marry him."

"Ah!" said Brother John knowingly. "I think I understand. He refused her?"

"Wouldn't you? She's an ugly old spinster with a vicious tongue."

"And I suppose the alleged theft took place shortly after this refusal?"

"That's right. She complained to the Sheriff, who had Seaver submitted to Ordeal."

An expression of distaste flickered across Brother John's features. Trial by Ordeal was a common occurrence. The accused would have their hand plunged into boiling water. Bandages would

23

then be applied and the scalding wounds left for three or four weeks. Nobody was permitted to remove the wrappings until the Justice overseeing the case decided it was time to check how well they had healed. If the wounds were clean and healing well, the accused was obviously innocent since God had seen fit to cure him. If the wounds festered, he was guilty and would be subjected to whatever punishment the law decreed.

"Ordeal is an unpleasant thing to witness," Brother John admitted.

"It makes no sense to me," Edric complained. "In a case like that, there are plenty of people who can swear oaths to the truth of the matter, yet it is left to God to decide. It doesn't seem right."

"God is the ultimate arbiter," Brother John reminded him. "No man can claim greater authority."

"Yes, but if Seaver's wounds don't heal, he'll be punished for something he didn't do!"

"Perhaps he has committed other sins for which he should be punished," Brother John pointed out.

Edric felt his anger stirring again. He said, "I don't deny God's right to punish us. But the law is not God's law, is it? Men made that law."

Brother John treated him to a broad smile as he clapped him on the shoulder.

"You are very perceptive, my young friend. However, I suggest you keep such opinions to yourself. Such thoughts are dangerous, you know."

Edric sighed and nodded.

"I know. I am sorry."

"Feeling sympathy for the hurt of others is nothing to be sorry about," Brother John assured him. "I wish more people felt that way. However, as I say, it would be wise not to mention your thoughts to anyone else. Now, let us move on. We have tarried here too long. I must see the Sheriff, and you must deliver your goods. Distasteful as these tasks may be, we had best get them over with."

So saying, he turned and strode along the west road, forcing Edric to hurry after him.

"Why do you say the tasks are distasteful?" Edric asked as he caught up with the monk.

"Because dealing with Normans is never pleasant. They are a smug lot, especially since they took over this country."

Edric was shocked by the young monk's words. He had always known Brother John was disrespectful of authority, but he had not expected him to disparage the Normans so openly.

"I thought you were a Norman," he said warily.

"Me?" Brother John chuckled. "No, my young friend, I am an Angevin."

"A what?"

"I come from Anjou."

"Where's that?"

"It's in France, although I must confess that the Count of Anjou pays little attention to the King of France who is technically his overlord. It is to the south of the County of Maine."

Edric had only the vaguest idea of where any of these places were. All he knew for certain was that they were across the southern sea.

"I didn't know that," he said.

"There is no reason why you should," Brother John told him affably. "It is no secret, but it is not something I boast about. My heritage is very mixed, you see. I was born in Anjou, but my father was French and my mother half English."

"Is that why you came here?"

"Partly," Brother John said dismissively. "I came in search of a fortune and found God instead."

"Here? In England?"

"That is where I found him," the monk nodded, "although he is, of course, everywhere."

"Uncle Ethelred says he is on the side of the Normans," Edric sighed.

"It would be difficult to argue against that point of view," agreed Brother John. "I was here during the reign of King Edward, that most holy and pious ruler. I thought England was a land of peace and plenty, blessed by God, and that London was the most wonderful of all cities."

While Edric usually enjoyed listening to Brother John extolling the virtues of London, that fabled city remained as strange and mysterious as the lands across the sea. Edric was more concerned about matters closer to home, and those gave him little reason to be cheerful.

25

"I don't ever remember a time of peace," he observed dourly.

"Well, perhaps I exaggerate that aspect a little," Brother John grinned. "But it was a haven compared to life on the continent of Europe. Then, as you know, things changed when old King Edward died."

"I remember that," Edric nodded, his left hand again brushing against his maimed thigh.

"Now," Brother John continued, "I feel I cannot desert this land, despite what has happened over the past three years."

Edric was not sure how to respond. The thought that there was any alternative to staying had never occurred to him. He was worked so hard in the smithy that he rarely had an opportunity to travel anywhere else. Yet he supposed it was different for a man like Brother John who spent his life walking the length and breadth of the country. Perhaps that made the prospect of leaving England easier to contemplate.

"If you dislike the Normans so much, why are you visiting the Sheriff?" Edric ventured.

Brother John smiled, "Because, for all his faults, he provides a good table at dinner time, and I enjoyed my stay here last year. Besides, it is my duty to offer my respects to the local Lord."

Edric wondered what it would be like to eat at the Sheriff's table. He doubted whether he would be restricted to eating barley gruel and eel pie, but the chances of ever being invited to join that exalted company were so remote as to be not worth considering. In any case, he doubted whether he could stomach dining with a Norman lord whom he knew to be cruel and greedy.

Their conversation came to an end as they approached the castle, both of them falling silent as they neared the forbidding stronghold.

Edric eyed the place with bitterness. The Normans, so he had heard, had built many such castles, digging a great ditch and using the earth to create a high mound at one end of the enclosure. They would erect a solid palisade of wood all around the perimeter and build a high tower on top of the mound. The tower was a refuge, but the rest of the enclosure was where the Normans built their homes, stables, stores and kitchens. Such fortified places were, so everyone said, virtually impossible to take by storm without an army.

Here, in Bourne, the Sheriff had deviated from the usual pattern. The Thane's house was the most luxurious and comfortable for miles around, even possessing a stone chimney which wafted the smoke from the hearth fire up and outside instead of filling the hall. Behind the magnificent house were other buildings; the stables, cookhouse, bakery, stores and servants' quarters. With this ready-made home, Ivo de Taillebois had ordered his castle to be constructed around the existing buildings. The ditch had been dug, the palisade erected and a wooden tower placed atop the artificial mound which the workers had created behind the other buildings. It had taken weeks of work by the local inhabitants but the castle now protected the Sheriff and his men from any attack.

"The place wasn't quite finished when I was here last," Brother John observed. "They must have felled a lot of trees."

"They did," Edric confirmed. "But the forest is not far away. It kept Uncle Ethelred busy, too. We supplied all the nails, as well as extra axes, saws and hammers."

"Your uncle must have been very pleased," the monk smiled sardonically.

"Yes, he was."

"Then let us see the fruits of his labours," declared Brother John as he strode towards the open gateway.

There was a short roadway leading to the high gates, with the ditch leading away on either side. That trench, ten feet wide and six feet deep, was muddy and had a filthy puddle of water at the bottom, presenting an obstacle nobody could easily cross.

The timbers of the perimeter fence were strong and high, towering over the two young men as they tramped across the entrance path.

Two soldiers, each dressed in a mail tunic and wearing an iron-banded helmet, stood at the open gates.

Brother John addressed them in a loud, cheerful voice, speaking in Norman French. His words were spoken so rapidly that Edric, who had picked up a smattering of the language over the past months, could not understand them. Nor could he follow the reply one of the men gave, although he saw the mocking look the man gave him.

27

The guard waved them through without interrogation, and Brother John led the way.

"What did that fellow say?" Edric asked him.

"Nothing of importance," the monk assured him. "I told him I had come to see the Sheriff. I have news from Peterborough which he might find interesting."

"News of the new Abbot?" Edric guessed.

"That's right. Such news is valuable and will earn me my dinner this evening, as well as a bed for the night before I continue my travels."

"Where will you go next?"

"Wherever my feet take me," said Brother John. "I have a hankering to go north to see for myself whether the stories of the ravaging of the land are true. I might even go as far as Scotland."

"Why would you do that?" Edric asked in astonishment. "The Scots are savages. They are almost as bad as the Welsh."

Brother John laughed, "Have you ever met a Scotsman or a Welshman?"

"No," Edric admitted.

"Then how do you know they are savages?"

"Everybody says so," Edric assured him.

"And how do they know unless they have been to these places?" Brother John returned amiably.

Edric was not sure how to respond to that question, but the monk did not wait for an answer as he went on, "The Scots are Christians, like us. They speak a different language, to be sure, and no doubt they have different customs to us, but that does not make them savages. I expect they might feel the same about us."

"We are not savages!" Edric insisted.

"No? Perhaps there might be some people living in Northumbria who would disagree with that following the King's recent journey through their land. As for the Scots, many Englishmen have fled to King Malcolm's court, including Edgar the Atheling. Indeed, there are rumours that young Edgar's sister is to be married to Malcolm. If that is true, it hardly suggests he is a barbarian."

Edric felt naive and foolish in the face of Brother John's arguments. He supposed the monk probably knew more of the outside world than he did, but the man had an unsettling way of looking at things from an unorthodox perspective.

"Whatever the truth of it," Brother John went on, "I feel I should discover the facts for myself. Besides, a long walk like that should keep me out of Abbot Turold's way for a good few months."

Edric saw that the monk was grinning as he spoke, no doubt taking delight in mocking his superior. He hoped for Brother John's sake that nobody would inform the Abbot about his seditious comments.

By this time, they had crossed the main courtyard and reached the front doors of the great house. Brother John made to knock but Edric told him, "I need to go round the back. The Sheriff does not like me coming to his front door."

Brother John smiled and turned to him, making the sign of the cross in blessing.

"Then may the Lord watch over you, Edric Strong. I will be sure to call on you the next time I pass this way. I trust you will stay out of trouble until I return."

Edric detected a trace of concern and warning in the monk's words, but he was not sure how to respond. Feeling awkward, he mumbled a farewell and turned away, aware that Brother John had still not knocked on the door and must be watching him. He felt his back prickle at the knowledge and was relieved when he turned the corner and headed towards the rear of the house. He liked Brother John, but the man had a disturbing knack of unsettling his thoughts.

Edric shook his head, trying to dismiss their conversation from his mind. He had business to attend to now and he could not afford to be thinking about matters of justice, punishment or religion.

At the back of the house, the wide enclosure was busy, with servants chopping wood or grooming horses. He saw two young maids carrying pitchers of water or ale from one of the stores and heading towards the rear of the main house. He recognised one of them as Aelswith, a realisation which brought a flush of embarrassment to his cheeks.

She was about his own age and, he thought, the prettiest girl he had ever known. Even now, with her belly swollen by the child she carried, he thought she was beautiful. He wished he could find the courage to speak to her, but he had never been able to untie his tongue long enough to say anything more than a curt "Good morning".

Even that was beyond him now. Aelswith was chatting to her companion, a slightly older woman whose brown hair was tied back in a ponytail. Neither of them gave Edric more than a disinterested glance as they walked past him and went into the house.

That, Edric thought bitterly, summed up his relationship, or lack of it, with Aelswith. She had never taken any notice of him.

"Edric Strong?" a man's voice asked, interrupting his regrets. "What do you want?"

It was another servant. He was standing at the back door, regarding Edric with a supercilious expression. He was an older man, with greying hair and a pinched face. Dressed in black, he was the Sheriff's senior servant, responsible for the smooth running of the household. His name was Leland and he knew Edric well.

"I have brought the things Master Frederick ordered," Edric told him, lifting up the bag as evidence.

Unsmiling, Leland took the bag from Edric's hand, letting out a soft gasp as he felt the weight of it.

In his usual sneering tone, he said, "Wait here."

"The price is ten pennies," Edric called after Leland as the man turned away and walked into the house, leaving Edric standing outside the back door like a supplicant.

He waited, feeling dull and stupid, for what seemed an age. A few of the servants shot him an occasional glance but most were too preoccupied with their work to pay him a great deal of attention. Idly, he looked around at the buildings within the castle perimeter. The stables took up much of the space, stretching the length of the right hand side of the rear yard. They had been expanded since the Normans arrived because the soldiers had brought so many horses with them. Opposite the stables, the cookhouse, bakery, stores and servants' quarters lined the left side of the yard, while, at the far end of the open space was the great artificial mound on top of which stood a tall, wooden tower.

The tower intrigued him. There was only one small entrance which stood twelve feet above the ground. It was accessed by a ladder which could be drawn up so that anyone attacking the occupants could not break in without a great deal of difficulty. Since the tower stood atop a steep-sided mound which was itself within a ditch and high fence, Edric could not conceive of how anyone might be able to attack it in any event. Were the Normans so afraid that they felt the need to build such impregnable places of refuge, he wondered?

He did not see what they had to be afraid of. Nobody in the village ever offered any resistance to them, and the outlaws generally skulked in the forests and fens, never daring to venture anywhere near a Norman castle.

He caught sight of movement at the top of the great, square-sided turret and turned away, not wanting to attract the attention of the Norman sentry who was on watch. Instead, he looked up at the magnificent house which had once been home to Thane Asketil but was now the residence of Sheriff Ivo de Taillebois. It was a grand home, two storeys tall, with two bedrooms on the upper floor. The walls were solid oak, the thatch thick and well-laid. Edric wondered what it would be like to live in such a fine home, but the idea was almost too much for his imagination. Even a trained craftsman like a blacksmith could never aspire to such wealth.

He turned back to the door when he heard Leland return. The servant held out his hand, revealing a few silver coins.

"Master Frederick says the goods are worth eight pence," he said haughtily.

Edric stiffened.

"My uncle asked for ten," he argued.

"You can have eight," Leland told him brusquely. "Take it or leave it, as you please."

Edric frowned but held out his hand and accepted the coins. It occurred to him that Leland may well have kept a coin or two for himself, but there was no profit in making such an accusation. More likely the Norman had decided to pay the blacksmith less than he had asked because that was how the Normans generally behaved.

"Now be off with you!" Leland commanded peremptorily, gesturing to shoo Edric away.

Edric turned and began retracing his steps, feeling foolish. It irked him that Leland, an Englishman, should act that way towards him. It was bad enough that the Normans sneered at him, but having one of his own people do the same made him angry.

He left the castle hurriedly, ignoring the two guards who said something in their own language which was obviously disparaging but which he could not understand. He did not care. All he wanted was to get away from the place.

Uncle Ethelred was pleased with the price Edric had obtained.

"Eight pence is good," he affirmed.

"It's less than the work was worth," Edric muttered.

"We cannot set the prices," his uncle told him.

"You set prices for everyone else," Edric argued.

"That's different!" Uncle Ethelred snapped.

Which was, Edric knew, true enough. It was different because the Normans were in charge, so could dictate what they wanted, while the ordinary villagers must pay whatever price Ethelred demanded for his services.

"Now," Uncle Ethelred ordered, "go and gather some wood. Take the cart and fill it."

Edric picked up the long crook, a shaft of wood with a curved hook at one end. Crooks were normally used by shepherds to snare their sheep, but they were also very useful when gathering wood. It was illegal to chop wood from the forest, but it was permitted to gather loose wood which could be dragged down by a hook or a crook.

Leaving the smithy, Edric went into the back yard and pulled the cart from where it was stored at the side of the house. It was a small thing, with two wheels and a high-sided wooden storage area. In theory, it could be pulled by a donkey, but Uncle Ethelred did not own a donkey, so Edric grabbed hold of the two long strakes and pulled the cart himself. It was easy enough when the vehicle was empty, although he knew his return trip would be more difficult. Still, at least he would be out in the open air and not under his uncle's watchful eyes.

He headed north, leaving the village and hauling the cart to the fringes of the forest. It took him over an hour to reach the woodland, but that still left him the greater part of the afternoon to gather firewood.

He began by collecting fallen branches and throwing them into the cart. Dead wood was the best fuel because, even though the weather seemed determined to remain cold, the living trees were full of sap and their wood would sputter and crack on a fire.

Not that he had a great deal of choice. Their winter store of firewood was almost gone and the demands of the forge were insatiable. Uncle Ethelred would order charcoal from the village's charcoal burners, but wood was also required and most of the deadwood had been collected by the villagers over the winter months. Now, Edric would need to go deeper into the trees to find wood he could collect.

He did not mind this task. He used his long crook to tug at some low branches, managing to pull a couple free, tossing them into the cart. Once he got them home, he would use a hand axe to chop them into smaller, more manageable pieces, another chore which would keep him busy for quite some time. That was mindless, repetitive work which he enjoyed. He had made the axe head himself and he liked to imagine it was a proper battle-axe and the branches were Norman soldiers.

Now, though, he devoted his attention to gathering as much wood as he could find.

He was so engrossed in the work that he did not hear the two men approach until they were almost on him.

"Well, well. It's Edric Strong, isn't it?" a voice chuckled.

Edric spun round, crook in hand, ready to defend himself.

Two men faced him, both dressed in worn and dirty tunics of homespun cloth, with old boots on their feet and shabby hats on their heads. More importantly, though, each of them wore a sword and held a bow with arrows notched in readiness.

Edric sighed. He knew these men.

They were outlaws.

Chapter 2

The outlaws may have been shabbily dressed, but they looked healthy enough, and their hands were steady as they held their bows. Beneath the floppy hats they wore, Edric could see strands of their hair which confirmed their identities. One had straggly, ginger hair, while the other was so fair, his long locks were almost white.

"Siward White and Siward Red," Edric said, never taking his eyes from them. "What do you want with me?"

Siward White grinned as he addressed his companion.

"You see, Cousin? I told you he was a smart one. He knows who we are."

In response, Siward Red grunted, "Every sodding person for miles around knows who we are."

"What do you want with me?" Edric repeated, standing his ground.

He gripped the shaft of the long crook tightly, ready to launch an attack if they threatened him, but dreading to initiate a fight because he knew he could not reach them before they shot him with their arrows.

To his relief, Siward White smiled as he lowered his bow, pointing the arrow towards the damp earth.

"There is someone who wants to talk to you," he said.

"Who?" Edric asked suspiciously.

"Another cousin of ours. Will you come?"

"Why does he want to speak to me?" Edric challenged.

His initial shock had worn off, and he felt less afraid. He had nothing of value except the small cart, and he would not waste his life defending that if the Siwards tried to take it. Besides, although they were outlaws, the two Siwards were not known for acts of random violence. They had no qualms about attacking Normans, but they had never harmed any of the locals.

Unless you counted the occasional theft of a chicken or a suckling pig, Edric reflected. So their invitation puzzled him but also reassured him that they did not intend to do him any harm.

In answer to Edric's question, Siward White replied, "Not you specifically, my young friend. He wants to chat to someone who knows Bourne. You just happened to be the first person we came across. It's saved us quite a walk. So, will you come?"

Edric remained cautious, knowing it was a crime to associate with outlaws. He could be hanged if a Norman patrol saw him speaking to these men.

Yet their words intrigued him, and he wanted to learn more.

"Where is he?" he asked.

"In the forest. I shall take you to him."

"What if I don't want to speak to him?"

"Oh, don't be churlish, Edric. Our cousin asks a favour and will reward you for your time."

"I have wood to collect," Edric said, gesturing towards the cart.

Siward White thought for a moment, then gestured towards his red-haired cousin.

"Siward here will do that for you while we are gone," he said.

Siward Red scowled and rolled his eyes, but did not argue.

Edric remained unsure whether he could entirely trust them. He could sense a slight menace behind the men's apparent friendliness, yet it was a general air about them rather than a specific threat towards him. They were, after all, men who lived outside the law. That status was, Edric knew, a considerable downfall for them. He had never met either of them before, but he had heard plenty of stories about their former lives as well as their recent exploits. Cousins from families distantly related to Thane Asketil, they had lost their lands and possessions when the Normans seized control of England. Fleeing to the wilds of the forest and the fens, they had become outlaws. It was rumoured that it was they who had killed the Sheriff's soldier a few weeks earlier. Looking at them, Edric could quite believe it was true. Both men exuded an air of casual violence despite their veneer of friendliness.

"I need to be back at the village before nightfall," he told them.

"Then we had best set off now," said Siward White, taking Edric's words as agreement. "Come. Leave your crook for my cousin."

35

Edric did not like being told what to do. He briefly considered refusing, but the truth was that he wanted to know who the outlaws' mysterious cousin might be, and why he was so interested in events in Bourne.

With a shrug, he stepped to the cart and propped the crook against it.

"Make sure you fill the cart," he told Siward Red.

"Watch your mouth, boy!" the outlaw spat.

"Now, now, Cousin!" Siward white chided. "Edric is doing us a favour. We should do one for him in return."

"That's easy for you to say," Siward Red grumbled. "You're not the one who's going to spend the afternoon gathering firewood."

Siward White chuckled. Holding his notched bow in one hand, he signalled to Edric.

"Come, lad. We have a long way to go."

Edric followed the rangy outlaw deep into the forest, heading much further than he had ever ventured before. There were no paths that he could discern, but Siward appeared to be following a route known only to himself. The trees crowded together, the new undergrowth snagged at their legs, and the shadows deepened as the sky above was screened by the branches of the trees.

They stepped across a few narrow streams, scrambled round boulders, and dodged left and right between the trunks of large trees until Edric had lost all notion of where he was.

Siward White seemed disinclined to talk, but the silence began to grate on Edric's nerves, and his curiosity encouraged him to address a question to Siward's back.

"Who is this cousin of yours?"

The bandit did not bother to turn his head as he replied curtly, "You'll find out when you meet him."

Edric did not like this secrecy, but he had no option now except to follow Siward White. They were so deep in the forest it might take him days to find his own way back to the village. Frowning daggers at the outlaw's back, he continued the trek.

Siward set a fast pace, covering a lot of ground despite the uneven terrain. Edric judged they had been walking for over an hour before the outlaw finally slowed and held up one hand.

"Here we are," he announced.

It took a moment before Edric could make out what he was supposed to be looking at. There was a relatively open space, a small, sun-dappled clearing, in front of a steep, tree-covered slope which was around ten feet high. At first, he could make out nothing in particular but then realised he could smell woodsmoke and he noticed there was a small hut built against the embankment, its wooden walls covered by strands of ivy which helped it blend into the surrounding foliage and rendered it almost invisible.

"Home," Siward White informed him. "Or one of them, anyway."

"You live here?" Edric asked.

"We sometimes stay here for a short while," Siward answered. "We find it is wise not to remain in one place for any length of time. The Sheriff often attempts to trap us, you know."

He spoke lightly, as if his feud with Ivo de Taillebois were amusing, yet his words concealed the bitterness he must feel. At one time, both Siwards were men of rank who would have demanded Edric's respect because of their position in life. Now, they were merely outlaws, but Edric could not deny that he still respected them despite their fall in status. Men who were prepared to live in such reduced conditions because they opposed the Normans held a fascination for him in spite of their new reputation as thieves.

"Come inside," White invited, heading across the clearing towards what Edric could now see was the hut's tiny door.

As they drew near, that door swung open and a man came out, bending low to avoid bumping his head, then straightening as he watched them approach.

Edric saw this was a tall man with greying hair and a watchful, cautious air about him. He wore a tunic and trousers of good quality, although the rigours of living in the woods had left them looking a little rumpled. More than this, though, Edric also saw the sword the man held in his hand.

That gave Edric pause for thought. A sword was a valuable item which marked its wielder out as a man of some significance. Most Norman soldiers possessed swords, but they had been relatively rare among the English. As a rule, only the nobility, such as the two Siwards had once been, could afford to carry a sword.

"Greetings, Martin," said White. "I have found just the man we are looking for."

The tall man, Martin, nodded dourly as he stepped aside and swept up his left hand to invite them inside.

"The Lord is waiting," he informed them.

Edric had thought this older man was the cousin he had been brought to meet, but he now realised this was not the case. Martin was obviously the follower of a Lord, and it was that Lord who was waiting to see Edric.

But what sort of Lord would be skulking in a rustic shack deep in the wilderness of the forest?

The tiny hut was dark inside, only a sliver of daylight filtering in through one small window in a side wall, while a fire crackled in a ring of stones in the centre of the earth floor. As Edric's eyes adjusted to the gloom, he could see that there were three other people in the room. To his astonishment, two of them were women.

One sat huddled on a shabby, bracken-filled mattress which was squeezed into one corner of the hut. Her young face was tired and frightened. She wore plain clothes and had her hair tied up beneath a headscarf. She gave Edric only the faintest of glances before lowering her eyes.

The second woman was standing at the end of the room. She had obviously been looking out of the tiny window but now turned to look at Edric, positioned so that a narrow shaft of sunlight shone on her face, allowing him to see her vivacious features. She was in her twenties, he guessed, and had dark hair and flashing eyes which bored into him. She wore a long dress of bright red velvet with elaborately embroidered lace decorating the cuffs and collar, an outfit which was obviously unsuited to life in the forest, yet equally clearly the clothing of a rich woman. And even in the dingy lighting of the hut, Edric thought this particular rich woman was beautiful.

He wanted to look at her more closely, but it was the man in the room who seized his attention and forced Edric to turn towards him.

He was not a tall man, at least a head shorter than Edric, but he was stockily built, with broad shoulders and muscled arms. Those arms were bare since he wore a short-sleeved tunic of leather which was studded with rings of bright metal. Both forearms, Edric could see by the flickering light of the fire which played across the man's flesh, bore tattoos, although it was too dark for Edric to make out what they symbolised.

The man had long, fair hair which fell to his shoulders, and he wore a thick, drooping moustache of the type long favoured by the English aristocracy. At his side, Edric could not help but notice, was a sword with a jewelled pommel.

Siward White and Martin crowded in behind Edric, who was compelled to face the fair-haired young Lord across the fire. The man's icily blue eyes studied him intently.

"Who is this you have brought?" he asked White, his voice clearly revealing that he was an Englishman.

"His name is Edric," White explained. "He is the blacksmith's apprentice. In Bourne, they call him Edric Strong."

"I can see why," the Lord nodded appraisingly.

"He was wounded at Stamford Bridge," White recounted.

Edric blinked in surprise, wondering how White knew that. It was not a secret, but Edric had not thought anyone outside the village would have remembered his ill-fated adventure.

The Lord, too, raised his eyebrows in surprise.

"Really?" he asked Edric. "How old were you when that happened?"

"Nearly sixteen," he replied.

"You were training as a housecarl, perhaps?"

"No. I joined the *fyrd* when King Harold came marching north and called for the common folk to help defeat the Northmen."

"Good for you," the man nodded. "And you were wounded?"

The fingers of Edric's left hand brushed against his thigh as he nodded, "An axeman nearly killed me."

"So you did not march south to Hastings and the battle at Senlac Hill?"

"No. I was lucky to be able to get home after we defeated the Northmen," Edric admitted, finding it impossible not to answer the man's questions.

"And you live in Bourne?"

"Yes."

The tall man, Martin, prompted, "Yes, Lord."

Edric flushed, but the fair-haired warrior facing him waved a dismissive hand.

39

"I am no Lord here," he said. "My lands were taken from me years ago."

That remark intrigued Edric, and he decided to resolve the issue of the Lord's identity before asking any other questions.

"Then how should I address you?" he enquired.

"My name is Hereward," the man replied. "You may call me that."

"Then may I ask why you have brought me here, Hereward?"

Edric could sense some unspoken outrage from Martin, but he caught a glimpse of the dark-haired woman smiling at him, so he maintained his resolve not to be intimidated by anyone.

Hereward told him, "I want to know what happened in Bourne when the Normans arrived last year. Is it true they killed Toki Asketilsson?"

Edric pursed his lips as he nodded a silent confirmation.

"And they put his head on a pole?" Hereward continued.

"Yes."

"Did you see it happen?"

"I saw his head. Everyone saw it. Him and Wulfnoth."

"Wulfnoth?"

"His housecarl."

Hereward frowned, his jaw clenching, but he retained his composure and asked, "How many Normans are in Bourne?"

"The Sheriff has around two dozen men," Edric informed him. "But some are camped at Belsar's Hill."

"Where the old Roman fort is?" Hereward asked.

"That's right. It overlooks the southern approaches to the fens."

"How many are at Belsar's Hill?"

Edric shrugged, "Seven or eight, I think."

"So," Hereward mused, "perhaps sixteen or seventeen men in Bourne itself. How many man the gates of the fort there?"

"Always at least two," Edric told him.

"And I expect two more will be on duty in the tower," Hereward reflected. "They can keep watch on the surrounding area from up there."

Edric nodded, "Yes, I've sometimes seen them up there."

Hereward asked, "Have you ever been inside the castle?"

"A few times. I was there this morning."

"Describe the interior to me," Hereward said.

Edric took a moment to think, then described the layout of the castle buildings as well as he could remember, explaining that the Thane's house was the first building, with the stables, servant's quarters and stores laid out behind it.

"It is much the same as it was before," Siward White remarked. "All the Normans have done is put a ditch and palisade around your father's home and built a tower on top of a mound."

Hereward nodded in agreement, but Edric was already attempting to place the man from the few facts he had gleaned because the name now seemed faintly familiar. Thane Asketil had had two sons, he thought. But the older one had left England while Edric was still a boy. He vaguely recalled whispered rumours of a scandal of some sort, but the deeds of the Thane and his family had been of little interest to a young boy, so he could not be certain he had remembered correctly.

"You are Thane Asketil's son?" he ventured.

Hereward nodded, "And I want vengeance for my brother's death. Ivo de Taillebois owes me *weregild* or his life."

"He won't pay *weregild*," White asserted. "Normans never do. They kill Englishmen with impunity, while we are hanged if we kill one of them. They call it murder if a Norman is killed."

"Murder?" Hereward frowned.

"It's a new law," White explained. "If an Englishman kills another Englishman, it is manslaughter, and the victim's family is due *weregild* according to the old custom. But if a Norman is killed, they call it murder and they hang the killer."

"That's true," Edric agreed. Then he shot an accusatory look at White as he added, "And if they can't find the killer, the men who make up the local *tithings* are fined."

"That happens a lot, does it?" Hereward asked.

"Often enough that some men lose their land to the Sheriff because they cannot pay the fines."

That thought rankled with Edric. There were ten men in each *tithing*, each of them responsible for ensuring that the other nine men and their families obeyed the laws. In days past, if one man of a *tithing* committed a crime, the others were obliged to surrender him to the Shire Reeve for punishment. Now, the Saxon Shire Reeves had been replaced by Norman officials whose justice was savage and rapacious.

41

As a mere apprentice, Edric was not eligible to be a member of a *tithing*, but he knew how hard the fines had hit the villagers when outlaws had killed one of the Sheriff's men.

Hereward gave Siward White a rueful smile as he observed, "It seems you have caused some problems for our people, Cousin."

"I only kill Normans when I have no choice," Siward replied defensively. "I prefer to avoid them if I can."

Hereward nodded absently, dismissing the issue as his mind returned to the question of his younger brother's death.

"So what you are telling me is that Ivo de Taillebois will not pay me *weregild*? I suppose that means I will need to cut his head off and stick it on a pole at the crossroads."

The authoritative tone of his voice left Edric in little doubt that this was no idle threat. Hereward's eyes were cold and hard, revealing his determination to exact vengeance.

That was when the dark-haired woman spoke for the first time, saying, "You cannot simply march into his castle and challenge him."

Edric glanced at the woman, intrigued by her accent. She spoke slowly, as if English was not her mother tongue, and the accent sounded similar to the one he heard when Normans occasionally attempted to speak English. Was she a Norman, he wondered?

"I will need to think on this," Hereward admitted. "Perhaps I could catch him on the road somewhere."

Edric offered, "The Sheriff never goes anywhere without at least a dozen men to guard him."

"That's true," agreed White.

The woman said, "Why speak of killing him before trying more peaceful means? You could go to the Church and seek help. Your uncle is an Abbot, is he not?"

Hereward looked at her, frowned, then nodded.

"I suppose Uncle Brand might speak for me and demand recompense."

White gave a soft cough.

"I'm sorry, cousin" he said. "I thought you knew about your Uncle Brand."

"What about him?" Hereward asked sharply.

"He died last year," Siward explained. "I heard he caught a fever."

Hereward's jaw clenched tightly as he battled down his emotions. Then he made the sign of the cross and whispered, "May the Lord have mercy on his soul. So who is Abbot in Peterborough now?"

White shrugged, so Edric volunteered, "A Norman. His name is … Turold, I think. They say he prefers fighting to praying."

"Then I'll get no help from him," Hereward sighed.

He took a deep breath, then stepped around the fire and extended his right hand towards Edric.

"Thank you, lad. Your information has been helpful."

Edric shook the offered hand, feeling the firmness of Hereward's grip. Then, on impulse, he blurted, "I'd like to help you some more if I can. I want to fight the Normans."

"You would become an outlaw?" Hereward asked, his expression serious.

That made Edric pause. He had not considered the consequences of his offer, but a certainty took hold of him.

"If that is what it takes to rid England of the Normans, then yes."

He half expected Hereward to laugh at him, but the fair-haired Thane's son merely nodded.

"I thank you for the offer. I will let you know if I ever need you. For the moment, though, you can help me best by returning to your home and saying nothing of our meeting to anyone. Is that understood?"

"I can keep my mouth shut," Edric stated.

"Good. But keep your eyes and ears open. I may have need of them again."

"You can rely on me, Lord," Edric promised, giving Hereward the title he felt the man deserved.

"I am sure I can," Hereward smiled.

As he spoke, he reached into a pouch on his belt, extracting a small silver coin which he handed to Edric.

"For your trouble," he said.

"Thank you, Lord, but I need no payment. I am always ready to serve the cause of England."

"Take it anyway," Hereward told him. "And remember to say nothing of my presence here to anyone."

"I swear it," Edric promised.

Hereward smiled, "Then go with my thanks. I will send word if I have need of you."

Edric inclined his head in a swift bow, repeating the acknowledgement in the direction of the dark-haired young woman who stood at the window. Then he felt Siward White touch his arm to urge him outside.

He left the hut feeling bemused, half wondering whether it had all been a dream. His mind was whirling with thoughts of Normans, outlaws and bloody revenge; with visions of fighting off a horde of mail-clad soldiers as he defended a dark-haired woman who wore a red velvet dress. And of a Lord with icy blue eyes who dealt coins to his followers and death to his enemies.

"Come, boy!" White commanded. "We must hurry if you are to return home by nightfall."

So saying, the outlaw set off across the clearing.

Shaking off his bemusement, Edric hurried to catch up with him, his imagination giving way to thoughts of the questions he should have asked.

White glanced back over his shoulder and said, "You did well, boy. I thought you would."

"I could do more," Edric replied. "I have an axe."

"You'd need more than a wood axe if you were to fight the Normans," Siward chuckled.

"No. I have a battle-axe. It belonged to Wulfnoth. I took it after the Normans killed him."

"You did?"

"I hid it in the rafters of the smithy," Edric declared proudly. "I want to use it to kill Normans."

"Do you know how to wield a battle-axe?" White asked sceptically. "It takes years of training to do it properly."

"I practise at nights," Edric told him. "And I saw Wulfnoth use it at Stamford Bridge. He was the one who saved me when I was injured."

"So you want revenge for his death?" White asked, his tone becoming more serious.

"Yes," Edric insisted. "Let me join you."

"Not yet, lad," White told him. "At the moment, you are more valuable to us if you remain in Bourne."

Edric was not sure whether the outlaw had said this because it was true or because he wanted to deter Edric from becoming a brigand. Either way, he decided to heed the advice for the time being. For now, he had more questions.

"Who is the lady?" he asked.

"That was Torfrida, Hereward's wife. She was once a lady of the Court of the Countess of Flanders."

"Flanders? Where is that?"

"Across the sea. Near France."

"And she married Hereward?"

"That's right. He went to Flanders when he was exiled. Now he's back."

"He was exiled? Why?"

White shook his head as he replied, "You'd better ask him that. Nobody really knows the truth of it. But Hereward had a wild streak when he was younger. When he was about your age, he had a serious falling out with his father. It ended with King Edward banishing him. That's all I know. Martin Lightfoot might know more, but I doubt he'd tell."

"Martin is Hereward's servant?"

"Servant. Companion. Perhaps even a friend. He's been with Hereward for years. He even went into exile with him."

Edric nodded. That explained Martin's obvious devotion to Hereward.

"There was another woman in the hut," he remembered.

"Alice. She is Lady Torfrida's maid."

"Why have they come back?" Edric asked.

"You are full of questions, lad. But I suppose there is no harm in telling you as long as you keep your trap shut. Hereward doesn't want anyone to know he is here."

"Why not?"

"Work that out for yourself, boy."

Edric felt foolish. The answer was clear enough. If Hereward intended to kill Ivo de Taillebois, surprise would be his greatest weapon.

"So why have they come back?" he asked again.

"From what Torfrida told me, Hereward served under the Count of Flanders. Hereward is a fearsome fighter and knows how

45

to command an army. He won many victories for the old Count. But the Count died and his son does not like Hereward, so they came back to England."

"Why would a new Count not like a man who can win battles for him?" Edric frowned.

"Why do you think?" White retorted.

Edric considered the problem for a moment before guessing, "Jealousy?"

"Very good. I knew you were smart. Hereward defeated enemies who had beaten young Robert, so when Robert became Count, Hereward was not wanted at Court."

Edric could empathise with Hereward's plight. He often felt his Uncle Ethelred did not want him in the smithy.

He asked, "So what will Hereward do? About the Sheriff, I mean."

"I have no idea," White grinned. "But it will be something incredibly foolish. He is a great man, but he is stubborn and often too impulsive for his own good. Torfrida may be able to talk him out of doing something stupidly dramatic, but I wouldn't bet on it."

"Whatever he does, I want to help," Edric stated.

"I know, lad. He won't forget."

That was all the encouragement Edric could obtain from the rangy outlaw. Yet it was enough to convince him that a possible new future lay ahead for him. It would be a dangerous future, he knew, but it would surely be better than suffering his uncle's scorn and deferring to Norman bullies. The prospect of doing something – anything – to escape his life filled him with hope.

Some would no doubt say his decision was rash and foolish, the wild dreaming of a young man who was barely out of his childhood, but Edric knew why he had made the decision.

He had felt Hereward's power. The man had an air about him that spoke of determination and ability. He was, Edric realised, a man others would follow and Edric desperately wanted to be one of those followers, no matter where it led him.

Chapter 3

That night, Edric waited until he was certain his aunt and uncle must be asleep then, aided by the faint illumination from his candle and the glow of the open furnace, climbed onto the smithy's work bench. Carefully, he reached high up into the rafters, feeling around until he located the battle-axe he had concealed there. Taking extreme care not to lose his balance or knock anything over, he slowly lifted the great axe down, then carefully unwound the oily rags he had wrapped around it for protection.

The axe was a simple weapon, but brutally efficient at killing. The haft, around four feet long, was of smooth, polished ash which was strong yet light. It was shaped to fit comfortably in the hands, but it tapered near its upper end. This end was rammed through a ring of metal at the base of the great blade, which was forced down the haft until it fitted snugly, with bindings of leather cord helping to secure it in place.

The blade was narrow where it was attached to the ring, but it flared out gracefully in curving arcs until it came to sharp points at either end of the curved outer edge. This lethally sharp edge formed a convex curve which could deal a terrible slashing cut even if it did not dig itself deep into its target's flesh.

Wulfnoth had told Edric that this design gave the axe tremendous killing power because all the weight of the axe was concentrated on the outer edge of the blade. On the long march north to face the Norwegian invaders, the housecarl had claimed he could chop a man in half, or sever a horse's head, with a single blow. Young as he had been at the time, Edric had still not believed the big warrior until he had seen the dreadful weapons used in anger.

The housecarls, he recalled, had been awesome in their ferocity, swinging the great axes two-handed, whirling and smashing them, shattering shields, lopping off limbs and carving men into masses of bloody pulp. With their long hair and moustaches, dressed in chainmail and screaming battle cries as they wielded the axes two-handed, they had seemed to the frightened and impressionable young Edric to be like the heroes he had heard poets sing of.

Edric, armed with a spear and a wicker shield, had been dumbfounded by the sight of Wulfnoth and the other housecarls carving their way through the ranks of terrified Norwegians. The ghastly sight of dismembered limbs and trailing innards had made him feel sick, but he was also seized by a sense of tremendous excitement because the Norwegian king, Harald Hardrada, had come to conquer England, yet his army was being slaughtered by the power of the English axes.

As King Harold's army swept through and round the beleaguered Northmen, Edric had overcome his revulsion at the horror and had found himself desperate to contribute to the victory. Forgetting all the advice he had been given, he had rushed forwards to join the fight.

The men of the *fyrd* had made up the bulk of the King's army, but they were not trained warriors. They were mostly farmers, with a few artisans and tradesmen thrown in. They were armed with whatever weapon came to hand, including scythes and hand axes, but their role was to support the housecarls who would lead the fighting. In his youthful excitement, Edric had forgotten this and had charged recklessly into the fray.

The Norwegians were already beaten, but still fought on. They had won their own victory a few days earlier, smashing the forces of the Earls of Mercia and Northumbria, and they had been enjoying the fruits of that victory, unaware that King Harold had mustered an army and hurried north to confront them. They had been caught unprepared, without their armour and with barely enough time to form a shield wall before Harold had launched his army at them. Mounted housecarls had ridden around the flanks to surround the Norwegians, while others charged the shield wall on foot, smashing their way through the beleaguered Northmen.

Desperate to play a part in the victory, Edric had rushed up behind the housecarls who formed Thane Asketil's household warriors, and he had thrust his old spear at a Norwegian axeman who was duelling with Wulfnoth. In the press of bodies, with men yelling war cries, grunting with exertion, and screaming in pain, nobody had noticed Edric until his blade had lanced up to pierce the Northman's shoulder.

Edric had shouted in triumph, but his victory cry was premature. The Northman hardly seemed to notice the wound as he swivelled and swung his great axe down in retaliation.

Edric had barely had time to raise his shield, but even that had not been enough. It had deflected the blow sufficiently to prevent him being killed instantly, but the axe had sheared through the wicker before ploughing on to gouge into Edric's thigh.

The pain had been dreadful, and the force of the blow powerful enough to drive him to the ground. Looking back, he knew he had been fortunate that his shield had partly blocked the attack because he could have lost his leg entirely, an injury which would have seen him bleed to death in minutes.

Even so, he would have died had Wulfnoth not noticed him being knocked down. The big housecarl had swung his own battle-axe and smashed it into the Norwegian's ribs, killing the man before he could deliver a fatal blow to Edric.

"Get away from here, boy!" Wulfnoth had snarled as he returned to the fight.

Edric, though, had been unable to move. Blood was soaking his trousers, and the pain throbbing through his leg rendered him unable to do anything except moan in agony as tears flooded down his cheeks.

He was ashamed of those tears now but, at the time, there had been nothing he could do to stop them. He had lain there, sobbing with pain, believing he was going to die, until Wulfnoth found him again.

"You're a bloody fool, boy," the housecarl had told him. "But I'm glad you stuck that Viking. He was proving troublesome until you distracted him."

Then he had picked Edric up and carried him until he found one of the monks who had come to tend to the wounded.

"Have we won?" Edric had asked Wulfnoth between his gasps of pain.

"Aye, we've won. There are scarce any of them left."

Later, Edric was to learn that the Norwegian King, Hardrada, had been killed, as had Earl Tostig, King Harold's renegade brother who had joined forces with the Northmen. They had arrived in a fleet of three hundred ships, but so many had been slaughtered that only twenty-four ships had been needed to carry the survivors back across the sea to Norway.

It had been a magnificent victory, another example of King Harold's skill in warfare, yet it had proved to be their undoing. While Harold's army was massacring the Norwegians,

Duke William of Normandy had landed an army on the south coast of England and was ravaging the land as a foretaste of what he intended to do to the whole country unless the people submitted to him.

"We'll do the same to him as we did to these buggers," Wulfnoth had confidently assured Edric before the housecarl had joined King Harold on the long, exhausting trek to the south.

Of course, it had not happened that way. Tired and diminished in strength, the English army had withstood the Norman cavalry charges for an entire day before the enemy had eventually broken their line, killed King Harold, and scattered the remnants of the defending army.

Edric had only learned about the dreadful battle long after the event. Forced to remain near Stamford Bridge because of his wound, all his efforts were concentrated on regaining his health. The monks had tended his wound, stopping the bleeding and stitching up the long gash before providing him with a stick to help him learn to walk again.

"The wound is free of infection, thanks to God's grace," one of the monks had told him. "Your leg will never be pretty to look upon, but it should carry you well enough when the muscles heal."

It had taken several weeks before Edric had felt well enough to join a straggling group of other wounded men who were making their way back to their homes in the south. It was a long, slow and miserable trek because, by the time he returned to Bourne, England was in the hands of a new King.

A Norman King.

Edric stood in the dim light of the smithy, holding the great battle-axe he had retrieved when Wulfnoth's body had been dumped in the street by the Sheriff's soldiers. He had smuggled it into the smithy by detaching the blade from the haft and concealing it under his tunic. He had hidden the long, wooden shaft in the woodpile in the yard, sneaking it inside and re-attaching the blade late at night. Ever since then, he had taken it down each night and practised the swinging arcs he had seen Wulfnoth perform at Stamford Bridge.

"You hold it in a left-handed grip," Wulfnoth had told him one evening as he had sat nursing his own maimed hand while he recounted what had taken place at Senlac Hill. "That way, you can strike at your enemy's unshielded side."

He had allowed Edric to try a few swings and had told him how to keep the blade moving.

"When you are using two hands, you are unprotected when you raise the blade. The trick is to use its weight and momentum to keep it moving all the time. That way, you keep your opponent at a distance until you can deliver a killing blow."

After he returned from the defeat at Hastings, Wulfnoth's own grip had been too weak to wield the axe properly, but he had still refused to give it up.

"The Normans were terrified of it," he had told Edric. "They charged up that hill time and time again, but we drove them off every time. We nearly beat the bastards, but our line broke a few times when men disobeyed the King and left the hilltop to pursue the riders when they turned away. Some men thought we had beaten them, but all they were doing was falling back to regroup for another charge. When our lads ran after them, the Norman cavalry turned and slaughtered them."

Edric could only imagine how dreadful that conflict must have been. His own, brief adventure into battle had been nothing compared to the gruelling, day-long struggle on the blood-drenched slopes of Senlac Hill. Edric knew the power and strength of a horse, and was astonished that anyone could stand firm in the face of a mounted charge. It must be a terrifying experience, yet King Harold's men had done it time and time again.

"We fought as we'd never fought before," Wulfnoth had recalled. "We stood there all day, killing one after another as our own line thinned. They used lances and swords, and their archers showered us with arrows, but still we stood. Horses won't charge a solid line of men, and we were solid all day. Until the very end. When they broke through and killed the King, that was the end for us."

Edric remembered seeing King Harold, a short, stocky man with an air of authority and calm resolve. Wulfnoth claimed Harold was the best King England ever had, but Harold's reign had lasted less than a year. He had risked everything on that fateful day on Senlac Hill, and he had lost.

Wulfnoth had never really recovered from the shock of the defeat. He had survived when his King and his Thane were dead, and that was a shame he could hardly bear. Only a sense of loyalty to the Thane's son, Toki, had given him the strength to carry on.

"I should have died with the others," he had once muttered to Edric when he was drunk.

Then the Normans had come to Bourne and Wulfnoth had joined his companions in Heaven.

So Edric had inherited Wulfnoth's axe. He practised every night, keeping his feet apart, swinging the long haft in great figure-of-eight patterns, heaving it until he sweated and the muscles of his arms ached. As he did so, he imagined himself cutting down swathes of Norman soldiers, driving them out of England and back across the sea.

He longed to smash the blade into something; anything so long as he could test its power, but there was nothing in the smithy he dared strike. Uncle Ethelred would see the damage for certain, and Edric would lose the axe.

He supposed he could have used it for chopping firewood, but Wulfnoth had scowled when Edric had asked him whether he ever did that.

"It's a weapon, not a woodsman's tool," the housecarl had informed him gruffly.

"Then what do you practise on?" Edric had asked.

"Impudent boys who ask too many questions," Wulfnoth had replied with a grin.

"I'm serious," Edric had persisted.

"We use dead sheep or pigs," Wulfnoth had eventually informed him. "You practise chopping off their heads with one blow."

But Edric had no dead sheep or pigs to practise on, so he simply rehearsed swinging the blade until he grew too tired, when he would conceal the axe in the rafters and then try to sleep.

He followed the same routine on the night after he had encountered Hereward, except that this time he imagined he was killing Normans to prevent them molesting the Lady Torfrida. Then Hereward was telling him he was a hero, before asking, "Are you sure you wish to become an outlaw?"

Edric had been worried that he might change his mind once he returned to the safety and comfort of the smithy but, in his imagination, he saw himself giving the same response to Hereward's question.

52

"If that is what it takes," he whispered as he closed his eyes and fell asleep.

It was four days until Edric's resolve was put to the test. One of the intervening days was Sunday, when he was freed from his labours in the smithy and instead had to join his aunt and uncle in the little church where, in the absence of a priest, the villagers gathered to pray and sing communal hymns.

Sundays were a mixed blessing for Edric. On one hand, he was glad to be permitted a rest from his labours in the smithy but, on the other, he found the church gathering a tedious and rather pointless affair. Praying and singing psalms never seemed to make life any better for anyone in the village. As far as Edric could see, it was only the Normans, with their swords and horses, who were ever granted answers to their prayers.

Uncle Ethelred had been known to say that the victory of King William and his fellow marauders was plainly the will of God, and that ordinary English folk who felt they were being punished should take heed of the divine intervention.

"If we are being punished, it must be for our sins," he would declare righteously whenever anyone complained about the harshness of Norman rule. Quite what those sins were, he would never explain, simply falling back on righteous anger if anyone dared question him.

For his part, Edric had long given up openly grumbling about the Normans, yet he had no wish to sit in the house all day and listen to his uncle lecture him on why he should be content with his lot in life. So, after a meagre lunch of bread, eggs and salted pork, he went out for a walk.

"Where are you going?" Aunt Edith asked.

"Nowhere in particular," Edric replied. "I just want to go for a walk."

It was a wet, rainy day, overcast with grey clouds, but that did not deter him. Unlike most villagers who spent their working days in the fields, Edric was confined to the heat and physical labour of the smithy, so the chance to breathe some fresh air was welcome no matter the weather. Pulling the hood of his cloak over his head, he traced a route along the bank of the tiny stream which trickled slowly down the eastern edge of the village. He ventured as far as the fringes of the fens before slowly making his way home again. In truth, he had paid very little attention to his surroundings, his mind still full of wild imaginings of what it must be like to be an outlaw and fight the Normans.

Except, he realised, Siward White had admitted that they did not fight the Normans unless they had no alternative. The outlaws lived by hunting, and sometimes by stealing, but they rarely ambushed Norman soldiers because the consequences were so severe. That sort of life held far less appeal for Edric than taking up arms against the conquerors.

Yet that, too, was a foolish notion, he began to realise. If what Brother John had told him about Northumbria was true, the King's reaction to rebellion was to slaughter everyone and everything in the district that had dared stand up to him. The thought that his Aunt Edith might be punished because he had gone off to join a rebellion gave him second thoughts.

And yet, he mused, if nobody stood up to the bullies, what sort of country would they live in? He could see easily enough that the Normans took all the wealth and luxury for themselves while the ordinary people did all the hard work, scraping a living as best they could. The only Englishmen who thrived were those like his uncle Ethelred who willingly did the Normans' bidding. He supposed it had been little different in the days when Thane Asketil had lived in the great house, but it somehow felt as if the people had had more say in those days. They had rights and could make representations to the Shire Reeves if they felt any injustice had been done to them. Now, a complaint to the Norman Sheriff was just as likely to result in the complainant being punished. Lands were being stolen, punitive taxes imposed, and there was nothing the ordinary folk could do about it.

These thoughts troubled Edric. He wished he had somebody to confide in, but the only person he could think of was Brother John, and the young monk had left the village the day after Edric had spoken to him.

For all his thinking, Edric remained confused and frustrated, knowing he disliked the role his life had decreed for him, but knowing that none of the alternatives offered a better solution. So he resumed his daily routine, cleaning, sweeping, and helping create or mend tools, and shoeing two horses which were brought down from the castle.

Then, on the evening of the fourth day after he had encountered Hereward, just as the working day was coming to an end and the sky was beginning to turn dark, he heard the slow clopping of hooves and the rumble of iron-bound wheels.

The noise stopped outside the smithy, prompting Uncle Ethelred to put down his tools and walk to the open doors. Horses meant travellers, and travellers might mean business.

Edric followed his uncle, almost gasping aloud in amazement when he saw Hereward standing in the road, holding the bridle of a long-legged brown mare. Behind him was a small cart being pulled by a mule, with the tall figure of Martin leading the beast, and the Lady Torfrida and her maid sitting in the cart which also contained several large chests and bags.

Hereward's eyes scanned Edric but betrayed no recognition. Instead, the fair-haired young Lord addressed Ethelred.

"My horse needs a loose shoe fixed," he announced in an imperious tone, the voice of a Lord who expected instant obedience.

"That's no problem, my Lord," Ethelred replied with an obsequious nod of his head.

"I will leave her here with you," Hereward stated. "We will be staying at the castle tonight as guests of the Sheriff. Shoe the horse and keep her here overnight. I want her fed and watered. Then have your boy bring her up to the castle one hour before sunrise, since we will be leaving at first light."

"Of course, my Lord," Ethelred agreed.

Hereward produced two silver coins from a belt pouch and handed them over. Ethelred studied them, frowning as he did so. The coins were obviously foreign, but he quickly decided that silver was silver, so he shoved them into his own purse.

Edric was confused. Hereward's orders made no sense. There were stables at the castle where his horse could be fed and watered, yet he wanted the beast kept at the smithy. Edric immediately understood that there must be a reason for this, but Uncle Ethelred, lulled by the sight of silver coins and awed to deference by the sight of a Lord and Lady, did not think to question the commands.

As Hereward handed over the reins, he fixed Edric with his keen, blue eyes.

"Make sure you don't sleep in, boy. I want you to bring the horse one hour before sunrise. Do you understand?"

The shock of seeing Hereward and Torfrida had almost left Edric unable to speak, but he somehow managed to find his voice.

"Yes, Lord," he nodded, unaccountably feeling his cheeks flush. "I won't be late, Lord."

Uncle Ethelred put in, "I shall bring the horse myself, Lord."

"That will not be necessary," Hereward replied firmly. "You are a master blacksmith. There is no need for you to handle such a menial task. Let the boy do it. If he does, there will be another coin in it for you."

At the mention of a further reward, Uncle Ethelred bobbed his head eagerly.

"It shall be as you say, Lord."

Hereward nodded, "Take good care of the beast. She's an ugly looking thing, but she's got more speed and stamina than many thoroughbreds. Her name is Swallow."

"Swallow," Uncle Ethelred repeated. "Like the bird, Lord?"

Hereward's face split in a broad grin as he replied, "No, it's because she'll eat just about anything."

He laughed, then turned away, beckoning to Martin to follow him before looking back over his shoulder.

"Remember, boy! One hour before sunrise!"

So saying, he set off up the road towards the crossroads. Martin tugged the mule into motion and the wheels of the cart resumed their slow, squeaking progress. As it passed, Torfrida shot Edric a tight, nervous smile which brought a lump to his throat.

"What are you gawping at, lad?" his uncle demanded gruffly. "Here, hold the horse while I check its hooves."

Edric felt cold sweat on his face. He knew he must appear deathly pale. The shock of seeing Hereward so unexpectedly had stunned him. Worse, the Lord was going into the castle and taking Torfrida with him.

Edric could only guess at their reasons, and each guess filled him with dread.

Was Hereward going to attempt to murder the Sheriff in his sleep? Did he intend to fight the entire garrison on his own? What would happen to Lady Torfrida?

As he stood there, holding the mare while his uncle checked its hooves and located a loose shoe on the left hind leg, Edric could feel his heart pounding in his chest. Something was going to happen.

But what?

Torfrida forced herself to breathe slowly in an attempt to calm her nerves. The sight of Hereward walking calmly up the shadowy road, and Martin Lightfoot's stolid, dependable figure leading the mule, gave her some comfort, but she feared she had made a terrible mistake in persuading Hereward to heed her advice.

She had done her best to convince him to abandon his thoughts of revenge. She had pleaded, begged, and even shed tears, but he would not give up the idea.

"We came to England to find out what happened to your family," she had reminded him. "We have discovered that. It is a dreadful discovery, but there is nothing we can do about it. We should leave this country and find somewhere safer to live."

"I will not leave until Ivo de Taillebois is dead," Hereward insisted vehemently. "He killed my brother, and he owes me."

"And how do you propose to get into his castle?" she asked scornfully.

"It was my home once," he told her.

"It is not your home now," she pointed out.

"That does not matter. I must confront this Sheriff. I will demand *weregild* from him. If he does not pay, I will kill him. That is my right."

"Not according to King William," Torfrida pointed out. "Norman law applies here now."

"I am not a Norman!" he shouted. "And William is not my King!"

The ferocity of his outburst had appalled her, but she had always known he had a temper, so she had the strength to face him.

Her own anger was rising as she snapped, "All right! So, let us say you do somehow manage to get to him and kill him. What happens then? You will be hunted by the Normans until they catch you and hang you."

Hereward chopped a hand in the air to deny her argument as he shook his head.

"No. Once he is dead, we can leave. We can hide in the Fens for a few days, then take a boat and sail away."

Torfrida relaxed slightly as she asked, "Where to?"

He shrugged, "I don't know. Scotland, perhaps. They say Edgar the Atheling is there. Or Denmark. The Danes have always prized good warriors. Or we could go further. Anjou, perhaps. Or to one of the German kingdoms. Maybe even as far as Constantinople."

Torfrida nodded. It did not matter to her where they went. What mattered was that he had acknowledged the need to leave England.

"We could go now," she tried again. "There is no need for you to do this thing."

"Yes," he stated very firmly. "There is a great need."

Despite her certainty that he was making a very bad decision, Torfrida understood what lay behind Hereward's insistence. It was not only the desire for vengeance on Ivo de Taillebois that was driving him along this reckless path; there was another, deeper need.

Hereward had been in Flanders when Duke William of Normandy had raised an army in order to enforce his highly dubious claim to the throne of England. Hereward had been dismissive of William's chances, assuring everyone that there was no greater warrior in Christendom than Harold Godwinson, the former Earl of Wessex who had been elected to rule England on the death of old King Edward.

He had been so sure of this that he had not considered returning from exile on the death of the old King. That was mostly because Hereward's father was still alive, she knew, and there was bad blood between them, but new Kings often pardoned those who had been exiled by their predecessors. Hereward, though, had been content to remain in Flanders. He held a senior and very important position in the Count's household, and Flanders was Torfrida's home, so Hereward had seen no good reason to throw everything away for the sake of joining a fight which could only have one outcome.

Then word had reached the Court of Flanders that, against all expectation, Harold had been killed in battle and William had seized the throne of England, using threats of violence and destruction to force the Witan into electing him King.

The news had come as a dreadful shock, hitting Hereward hard. And Torfrida understood why.

"You wish you had been there at Hastings, don't you?" she had asked him gently. "You think you could have made a difference."

"I don't know," he had admitted. "All I know is that I did not raise a hand to help my countrymen. Now my father is dead, my lands stolen, and my brother slain by Ivo de Taillebois. I need to do something to avenge those things."

Torfrida knew him well enough to understand that he would not change his mind, so she said, "But you still have the problem of how you can get close enough to the Sheriff without throwing your own life away."

"I'll think of something," he shrugged.

Then she had told him how he might achieve what he desired, and it had been his turn to object.

"No!" he barked. "That is far too dangerous."

"It is the only way you can accomplish what you want. You know this. You are the clever tactician. If you can think of a better way to get inside the castle safely, tell me. If not, agree to my proposal. If you do not, I will leave you here and return to Flanders without you because I do not wish to see you die making some futile assault on a Norman castle."

That last threat had decided the matter. Hereward was not the sort to be bullied by a woman, but Torfrida knew he could not bear to lose her. So he had mulled the problem for hours before conceding that he could not think of a better plan.

And now they were approaching the castle. Beside Torfrida, Alice sniffed fretfully, her body trembling with fear. Torfrida sighed. She should have left the girl behind, but Alice was even more afraid of being abandoned than of being taken into what might become a battleground.

"It will not come to that, I hope," Torfrida had told the girl. "Hereward's fight is with the Sheriff. If the plan works, the rest of the Normans will be taken captive and tied up. There will be only one death."

That was her hope. Now she must play the part of a great Lady. She must show no doubt or uncertainty, betray no weakness. She knew how ladies of the court behaved, and now she must adopt that behaviour. She would help Hereward gain entrance to the castle, would present him with the opportunity to take his revenge, and then they would leave England and make a new life somewhere far away from this troubled land.

She hoped.

In the great hall of the main house, Ivo de Taillebois was sitting down to a dinner of baked trout served with a large helping of boiled vegetables. Lent might be a time of fasting, but de Taillebois enjoyed his food, so his only concession was to abstain from meat in the weeks before Easter. Fasting was not in his nature, so he insisted on plentiful servings.

He sat at the centre of a table which ran across most of the width of the hall. There were two other tables, one at either end of the top table, each placed at a right angle so that it ran down one side of the hall to create an open square. Servants scurried in and out, bearing platters of food which they served to de Taillebois and his knights. Flagons of ale and wine were delivered, and the mood in the large room was boisterous with the lively, boastful chatter of young soldiers.

The shutters had been drawn, candles lit, and a fire burned in the impressive stone fireplace which boasted a chimney, an invention de Taillebois had not thought to see in England, and of which he was inordinately proud even though he had merely inherited it from the former owner of the house.

This was what de Taillebois enjoyed about being Sheriff. He had a large home, a force of knights at his command, and plenty of good food.

His good mood was dented when Leland, his head servant, sidled up to whisper into his ear.

"There are people at the gates, my Lord. They request lodging for the night."

"People? What people? Who are they?"

"A foreign lady and her husband," Leland explained. "They are French, I think. At least, she spoke in French."

"A Lady?" de Taillebois enquired. "What sort of Lady would be wandering these benighted parts at night-time?"

"A young and rather beautiful one," Leland replied with a sly smile.

"She has her husband with her?"

"Yes, my Lord. And two servants.

"Just the four of them?"

"Yes, my Lord."

"She cannot be a very important personage with such a small retinue," de Taillebois mused.

"I could not say, my Lord," Leland replied. "But she is well dressed and speaks excellent French."

"And she is good looking?" de Taillebois enquired keenly.

"Very, my Lord."

Ivo de Taillebois grinned as his good humour returned.

"Then bring them in. Have the spare chamber prepared for them. And have extra plates of food brought in."

Leland scurried off and the two guests were soon brought into the hall. The servant, de Taillebois instantly realised, had been correct. The woman was very beautiful. Even in the dim candlelight, he could see the smooth flawlessness of her skin and admire the contours of her body beneath the dark dress she wore. Her black hair was covered by a tall hat of the style becoming popular on the continent, and she bore herself with impressive grace, apparently oblivious to the silence that had fallen over the room when she entered as every man's eyes studied her.

De Taillebois scuttled from his chair to greet her, kissing her hand formally and offering her the hospitality of his house.

"I am honoured to have you here, my Lady," he assured her.

The Lady introduced herself as Torfrida, while her husband, a taciturn and apparently moody individual, said his name was Flahert. De Taillebois virtually ignored the man; he had eyes only for the Lady Torfrida.

He escorted them to the top table, placing Torfrida on his left and her husband on his right, all three of them aware that every man in the room was watching them intently.

"We so rarely have guests," de Taillebois grinned. "The last was an itinerant monk who, although a man of God, was a most disagreeable person. It is such a pleasure to meet people of a refined background. You came from Flanders, did you say?"

He had half turned in his chair, facing Torfrida and ignoring her husband. He had decided that his aid, Frederick, could entertain the man while he himself concentrated on charming the wife.

"That is correct," she replied. "My husband was a member of the Count's Guard."

"I see," de Taillebois said with little interest. "So, what brings you to England?"

"My husband has a distant relative in Peterborough. We had news the old man was ill, so we came to pay our respects."

Ivo de Taillebois nodded, taking the opportunity to peer down the front of Torfrida's low-cut bodice.

"Have some wine," he invited, signalling to a serving girl, the pretty one who was several months pregnant, to pour for his guests.

Torfrida accepted a goblet but her husband placed his hand over the top of his own cup.

"I would prefer small beer," he told the girl.

This remark made de Taillebois swivel round in his chair.

"Small beer? That is a drink for women and young children," he chortled.

The stocky man's mouth twitched as he replied, "I find anything stronger upsets my stomach."

De Taillebois smirked, dismissing the man as a nonentity. He might be powerfully built, but he plainly had a poor constitution.

The serving girl was staring, apparently dumbfounded, her eyes fixed on the man's hand which still covered his goblet.

"Fetch some small beer!" de Taillebois snapped.

Leland, standing behind him, repeated the command in English, his voice impatient.

The girl blinked as if uncertain, then gathered her wits and managed to drag her eyes away from the Sheriff's guest. She turned and waddled slowly to a side table, returning with a pitcher of small beer.

As she poured, her eyes studied the face of the fair-haired guest, concentrating so hard that she almost spilled the drink.

"Have a care, girl!" de Taillebois barked.

"There has been no harm done," the man, Flahert, said evenly, picking up the goblet and sipping at the frothy liquid.

With a dismissive shrug, De Taillebois returned his attention to Torfrida. She, in turn, appeared curious to know about him. This suited him very well, since talking about himself was one of his principal hobbies.

"I am a good friend of King William," he informed her proudly. "I have known him since he was a young man. That is why he has seen fit to appoint me as Sheriff of Lincolnshire."

"That must be a very demanding role," Torfrida observed as she delicately chewed on her food.

"Indeed it is. In addition to all the usual matters such as judging legal disputes, keeping the peace in these regions is no easy task. The woods and marshes teem with outlaws."

"How awful!" Torfrida gasped.

"But we deal with them," de Taillebois assured her hurriedly. "These men you see here are highly trained soldiers. The enemy does not dare face us in open combat. They prefer skulking behind trees."

He looked around as he spoke, waving an expansive arm to take in his assembly of knights. In the flickering candlelight and deep shadows of the hall, few faces could be made out clearly, but he could see the men's eyes sparkling as they surreptitiously stole glances at Torfrida. Their patent jealousy filled him with a warm, contented glow.

"You must be a great soldier yourself," she remarked. "I mean, only a competent man could be appointed to lead such hardy soldiers."

Ivo de Taillebois grinned so widely the muscles around his mouth began to protest.

"I have seen my share of combat in the past," he said with mock modesty. "In fact, I was wounded at the Battle of Hastings."

"Indeed? Nothing too serious, I trust?"

"A broken arm," he explained. "I was attacking the English shield wall when one of their mad axemen stepped out and killed my horse with one blow. I managed to leap off and I killed him with my sword, but not before his axe smashed my shield and snapped my arm."

He held up his left forearm as if to display the still-shattered remains of the limb.

"It was very painful," he went on, "and it prevented me seeing the end of the battle, but I am pleased to be able to claim my part in winning that great victory for King William."

Torfrida's eyes were wide with admiration, firing de Taillebois's blood. He reached out to place his large hand on hers as he said, "I am sorry. We should not speak of such violent deeds. I hope you will forgive me. I am a simple soldier, not a courtier."

"I am accustomed to the ways of soldiers, my Lord," Torfrida smiled.

"Ah, yes. Your husband is one such, is he not?"

Her eyes appeared to him to hold a mischievous glint as she leaned close to whisper, "He is indeed, but he is not at all like you, my Lord."

Ivo de Taillebois grinned again. This woman, he thought, was incredible. He could feel a growing stiffness in his groin and he drained his goblet in an attempt to distract his carnal thoughts.

"This is a very fine home you have," Torfrida said to him.

"It belonged to a Saxon Thane," de Taillebois explained.

"What happened to him?" she asked idly.

"He died," de Taillebois replied casually.

"How convenient for you," she smiled.

"He was a traitor to King William," de Taillebois informed her. "Such men cannot be permitted to live. Once they rebel, they will never be obedient subjects. King William has discovered that the hard way. He has pardoned rebels before, and each time they simply begin another revolt after a few months. No, there is only one way to deal with such treasonous behaviour."

Torfrida nodded sombrely.

"I suppose that is true," she sighed.

The servants were clearing away the plates now. Normally, this was the time the soldiers played dice and drank more heavily. King William, de Taillebois knew, disapproved of such behaviour, but the King was a long way from Bourne and the Sheriff enjoyed such activities. He was, however, on the point of ordering a more restrained evening when Torfrida put a hand to her mouth to cover a yawn.

"I am sorry, my Lord," she said apologetically. "It has been a very long day. I think I must beg your permission to retire for the night."

De Taillebois felt a pang of regret at losing sight of her, but he could hardly refuse. Mustering his manners, he nodded, "Of course. I will have my servant light the way for you."

The woman and her surly husband rose to their feet, said their thanks, then followed Leland round the side of the hall and up the wooden staircase to the upper floor, the servant holding a brass candlestick to light their way.

Ivo de Taillebois watched them go, admiring the swish of Torfrida's long dress as she walked, noticing that his men were also studying her. He suspected some of the serving girls might find themselves summoned to share a sleeping pallet later.

Smirking, he turned to young Frederick, signalling to him to shuffle along to sit beside him.

"What a woman!" he breathed, unable to disguise the desire in his expression.

"She is very pretty," Frederick agreed, knowing it would be best not to display too much interest in the dark-haired Torfrida in case he aroused his lord's jealousy.

"So, what do you make of her husband?" de Taillebois enquired.

"He seems to know a thing or two about soldiering," Frederick replied. "I suspect that sword he carries is not merely for decoration."

"Really? I would not have thought that a man who drinks small beer could be much of a warrior."

Frederick shrugged, "He claims to have seen some action fighting for the Count of Flanders."

"He would say that, I suppose," de Taillebois said dismissively. "He is probably a braggart."

Frederick made no comment on the Sheriff's lack of self-awareness. Instead, he frowned, "There was something odd about his accent, though."

"He's from Flanders," de Taillebois snorted. "You can't expect them to speak properly."

"No," Frederick said with a shake of his head. "He speaks excellent French, but it sounded like the way an Englishman would speak it."

"An Englishman? That seems unlikely. Few of them speak French at all."

Frowning, Frederick pointed out, "But his wife said they were on their way to see a sick relative in Peterborough. So there is an English connection. Unless the relative is Flemish."

De Taillebois began to look a little less sure of himself. When he saw Leland returning down the stairs, he signalled to the servant to join them.

"What do you make of our guests?" he asked. "The man, I mean. What was his name again?"

"Flahert," Frederick reminded him.

"Yes, Flahert."

Leland's expression betrayed some uncertainty. He took a quick glance around the room, but the other knights had already begun playing dice or singing bawdy songs, while the servants had nearly finished clearing the tables. Nobody was paying much attention to their discussion, yet still Leland seemed unsure of himself.

"What is it?" de Taillebois asked gruffly.

Leland knew where he stood in the household. As a servant, albeit the head of the domestic staff, it was not his place to criticise his social betters. Yet Leland was a man who knew where his loyalties must lie if he were to retain his position. His status depended entirely on keeping the Sheriff happy.

Warily, he admitted, "There is something familiar about him, Lord. I cannot place it, but he troubles me."

The Sheriff gave a slow, pensive nod.

"We were just discussing the possibility that he might be an Englishman. Do you know of any Englishmen from these parts who travelled to Flanders?"

Leland shook his head, then paused as a thought struck him.

"I cannot say for sure, Lord. But Thane Asketil had an elder son who was exiled some years ago. I never knew the boy, but I heard he was an arrogant youth who was always causing trouble. He went to Scotland, I believe."

"Scotland?" de Taillebois scowled. "What has that to do with our guest?"

Leland sighed, "Well, Lord, I cannot be certain because the old Thane never spoke of his son, but I did hear a rumour that the boy had eventually travelled to Flanders."

De Taillebois sat very still, his thoughts whirling in his head.

After a long silence, he mused, "Have we allowed a fox into our henhouse, then?"

Leland hurriedly added, "I cannot be certain, Lord. Yet I did think he looked familiar. There is some resemblance to the old Thane, I think."

De Taillebois's face was growing flushed now, but he told the servant, "What else can you tell me about this Thane's son?"

Leland searched his memory, rubbing his chin as he did so.

"His name was Hereward, Lord. I have no idea what he looked like since I joined the Thane's service after the boy had been exiled. The only thing I recall is that he is reputed to have a tattoo on his arm. The image of a boar, I believe."

De Taillebois glanced at Frederick.

"Did you see any such tattoo?" he asked.

Frederick shook his head.

"He was wearing long sleeves. But a tattoo would prove nothing in any case. If he is English, he will probably have several tattoos. You know what they are like."

De Taillebois nodded, his face grave. What Frederick said was true. The English loved to decorate their bodies with tattoos of all sorts.

"Is there anything else you can tell me?" de Taillebois asked his servant.

"No, Lord. And I cannot be at all sure this man Flahert is not who he says he is."

With a curt wave of his hand, de Taillebois dismissed Leland who gratefully hurried away to the kitchens where he could resume his normal duty of chivvying the staff. Once he was gone, the two Normans sat quietly for a moment.

"What do I do?" de Taillebois wondered.

"Why not simply confront him?" Frederick suggested. "You could say he matches the description of a known renegade. Demand to see his arm. If there is a tattoo there, we can hang him as a rebel."

"Except that we do not know he is a rebel," de Taillebois frowned, his doubts making him indecisive. "Even if he is this Hereward fellow, he may have no interest in causing trouble. After all, he could have come back before King William took control. Why would he wait until now if he wished to stir things up?"

"If you are right, Lord, it does not explain why he would keep his identity secret," Frederick pointed out.

De Taillebois chewed his lip as he said, "Perhaps he didn't keep it a secret. Perhaps he really is who he claims to be."

"But if he is the former Thane's son, surely it is our duty to at least question him," Frederick suggested, knowing his overlord always required reminding of his priorities when a difficult decision had to be made.

Still de Taillebois prevaricated.

He admitted, "I do not wish to make myself look foolish by confronting a man who may be entirely innocent. If word of that reaches Peterborough, Abbot Turold will ensure a twisted version of events reaches the ear of the King."

Frederick understood the Sheriff's concern. There was bad feeling between de Taillebois and the new abbot in Peterborough. The young knight suspected the King had appointed Turold to his new post partly to ensure that the two local nobles kept a wary eye on one another. Each of them would certainly take great pleasure in informing the King of the other's indiscretions.

"Then do we simply let him go?" Frederick asked.

He studied his master, suddenly seeing a spark in the Sheriff's eye as a cunning look lit the man's features.

"You have an idea, Lord?"

De Taillebois grinned, "Indeed I do, Frederick. Oh, yes, an excellent idea."

He leaned closer, lowering his voice to a whisper as he spoke into Frederick's ear.

"They are leaving tomorrow, heading for Peterborough. But the roads are dangerous, as you know. There are brigands everywhere."

"Yes, Lord," Frederick agreed, wondering where this was leading.

"Choose four trusted men, Frederick. See to it that our guests meet an accident on the road."

Understanding began to dawn on the younger man.

"A fatal accident, Lord?"

"Yes. Make sure the man dies. And kill the servants. But bring the woman back to me. Unharmed. Do you understand?"

Frederick frowned as he said, "Is that not dangerous, Lord? She will know the truth of the matter."

"But who can she tell if she is held within this castle?" de Taillebois smirked. "And even if she does tell someone, who is going to believe her? I am the Sheriff. If I say bandits attacked her husband, then that is what happened. It will also give us an excuse to hang a few of the local renegades as punishment. Don't you agree?"

Frederick could tell that de Taillebois had made up his mind. It was a decision driven mostly by lust, he knew, but that scarcely mattered. The Sheriff was the law, and even if the Count of Flanders made enquiries, there was nothing he would be able to do in the face of an official response that bandits had murdered his subjects.

"It shall be as you say, Lord," he said. "Although there will be some risk in keeping the lady captive here. Word will get out sooner or later."

De Taillebois grinned, his mind made up by his desire.

"Well, if she proves too troublesome, then she can always meet an accident of her own. But not before I have had the pleasure of knowing her more intimately. Bring her to me, Frederick. I want her."

That, Frederick knew, was all the justification required. Ivo de Taillebois was a Norman; whatever he wanted, he would have. Frederick was unhappy at the prospect of holding a woman of Flanders captive, but such things were not uncommon. He doubted very much whether the Sheriff would carry out his threat to do away with the woman. More likely, if anyone protested that she was being held captive, de Taillebois would demand a ransom and then release her. The fact that he had murdered her husband and raped her would probably not concern anyone except the woman herself. And she, of course, counted for little.

"I will see your commands are obeyed, Lord," Frederick said with a slight bow.

"Excellent!" the Sheriff beamed.

Smiling contentedly, Ivo de Taillebois signalled to a serving girl to pour him more wine. He sat back, closing his eyes as he imagined what it would be like to take Torfrida to his bed.

A sudden alarming thought struck him, making him sit upright once more.

"I want my door guarded tonight, Frederick," he said in a low hiss. "If that man is who Leland thinks, he might have come here to assassinate me."

"I shall watch your door myself, Lord," Frederick promised.

Ivo de Taillebois relaxed again. Tomorrow, he thought, could not come soon enough.

Chapter 4

The servant had lit two candles but their feeble illumination could not dispel the shadows of the large room. Torfrida looked around, taking in the thick rugs on the floor, the well-padded armchairs, the heavy table by the front window, and the large bed. The room was fit for a prince, yet this was the guest room. Hereward's family, she realised for the first time, must have been very wealthy indeed.

Yet Hereward, whom she had expected to be distracted by the memories that returning to his old home must have evoked, seemed to have other concerns.

"That girl recognised me," he said in a low voice. "I don't know how, because she must have been a child when I left."

"Who is she?" Torfrida asked.

"I have no idea. I hope she keeps her mouth shut. But that servant who brought us up here was giving me odd looks as well."

"Do you think he recognised you?"

Hereward shrugged, "I don't see how. I've never seen him before."

"What will we do?" she asked in a nervous whisper.

"We stick to the plan. You should try to get some sleep."

He walked to the shutters of the window which looked out over the front yard. Slowly, he eased one of the shutters open far enough for him to peer into the night.

"I can make out the gates from here," he said with a satisfied nod.

He closed the shutter, moved to the bed and unbuckled his sword belt, propping the weapon against the wall beside the bed.

"You did well tonight," he told her. "That fat fool was besotted with you."

"He's disgusting!" she spat.

"He'll be dead in the morning," Hereward said diffidently. "Now, lie down and try to sleep."

He patted the bed beside where he lay, still fully clothed.

Torfrida could feel her heart thumping in her chest. She had managed to remain relatively calm during the meal. Ivo de Taillebois was such an idiot she had almost enjoyed secretly mocking him. Now, though, the danger of their predicament struck her forcibly as she imagined all the things that could go wrong with the plan. If the servant had recognised Hereward, or if the girl informed the Normans of his identity, there were more than a dozen armed men in the hall downstairs who could march up and seize or kill them with virtual impunity.

And even if the Normans did not suspect Hereward's true identity, the plan still relied on the young blacksmith, Edric.

Worry nagged at Torfrida's mind, making sleep impossible. Her plan had seemed so straightforward when she had first suggested it. Now, she realised, there were a myriad things that could go horribly wrong. She lay there, fretting over what the night would bring, then realised with astonishment that Hereward had somehow managed to fall asleep. She could hear his slow, steady breathing in the darkness, and she almost laughed at the absurdity. How could he sleep at a time like this?

She could still hear the sounds of laughter and revelry from below. That, at least, provided some reassurance that the Normans did not suspect them. She had no idea how long the sounds continued but, eventually, the noise faded away. The men must have been preparing to settle down for the night.

Then her heart thumped in her chest when she heard heavy footsteps coming up the stairs. She shook Hereward awake, hissing at him that the Normans were coming for them.

Hereward sat up, coming alert almost immediately. His hand felt for his sword, but the footsteps continued on their way, passing the door and moving further along the corridor.

"It's de Taillebois," Hereward whispered. "He's going to his own room. But there is someone with him."

Torfrida breathed a sigh of relief. It seemed they had escaped being discovered. And if de Taillebois had someone with him, that would deter Hereward from attempting to assassinate the Sheriff while he slept, and would force him to stick to his original plan. That was dangerous enough as it was, but at least it would mean Hereward would not need to face the Norman garrison on his own.

They could hear the sounds of movement through the wood and plaster wall which separated their room from the master bedroom. Then those noises ceased, and the house was still.

Hereward squeezed Torfrida's hand.

"Don't worry. This is going to work."

"As long as Edric plays his part," she replied softly.

"He will," Hereward assured her. "Now, I'm going to get some more sleep if I can. We have a big day tomorrow."

That, she thought, was an understatement. The following day would define the future course of their lives.

In the smithy, Edric had barely slept. Hereward had told him to be at the castle one hour before sunrise, but how could he tell that time accurately? He had no marked candle to burn away the hours. All he could do was try to count the passing of time in his head.

He had tended the horse once Uncle Ethelred had hammered home the loose horseshoe. It was an ugly beast, its legs seemingly out of proportion to its skinny body, and its mouth full of yellowing teeth. It was certainly not the sort of mount a fine Lord should be riding, but Edric knew that all the best horses were owned by the Normans. Perhaps, even in this region which had for centuries been famous for breeding the finest horses, an Englishman could only find a sorry-looking nag to ride.

Uncle Ethelred had grumbled about using some of their oats to feed the beast, complaining that he was not an ostler, but the silver coins were enough to keep his complaints to a mere muttering.

Not that Uncle Ethelred did any of the work after he had fitted the shoe. He had left everything to Edric, who had fed, watered and groomed the lanky beast, keeping himself occupied for fear of falling asleep.

In spite of his resolve to remain awake, he had eventually dozed off late into the night, waking with a start some hours later. He jumped up, cursing softly, checking his candle and breathing a sigh of relief when he saw that it had not burned down too far, confirming that he could not have slept very long, but even that short slumber had given him a fright. He dared not risk missing his appointed deadline.

He rubbed his face, trying to force wakefulness back into his body. Opening the back door, he stepped out into the chill air, checking that the horse was still tethered in the yard and also looking up to the sky for any indication of the time.

All he could tell was that it was still night. He could not even see the moon or stars because a layer of cloud masked them from sight. As he muttered an oath under his breath, he felt the first gentle drops of rain licking at his face and hands.

He exhaled loudly, cursing his predicament. Not only was he unsure of when he should take the horse to the castle, it seemed he would receive a soaking while carrying out his task.

He walked to where he had tethered the mare, patting its neck and asking softly, "Do you know what time it is?"

"Time you were getting ready," came a low voice from behind him.

Edric's heart leaped to his throat in fright as he whirled round, his sudden movement making the horse snort and shuffle her hooves.

"Who's there?" he hissed, keeping his voice as quiet as his alarm would allow.

"It's me, Siward White."

A shadow emerged from the path at the side of the smithy.

"What are you doing here?" Edric asked as his pulse began to return to something approaching normal.

"Making sure you are ready at the right time," the outlaw replied.

Edric could not make out the man's features in the darkness, but he suspected White was smiling.

"Saddle the horse," the outlaw told him. "And fetch your axe."

Edric hesitated, blinking in surprise.

"My axe?"

"You said you wanted to help. Hereward gathered a few lads together for this jaunt, but another man with an axe wouldn't go amiss."

"You want me to fight?" Edric gasped.

"Isn't that what you want?" White responded.

Edric swallowed nervously. The bravado he had displayed when he had first encountered Hereward seemed to have deserted him, and the enormity of taking up arms against the Normans now struck him as a daunting prospect.

Siward White said, "Look, lad, we need your help. With or without your axe, we need you to get the guards to open the gates. Our plan is to take them alive if we can. Hereward wants the Sheriff, not the others. Personally, I'd happily kill the lot of them, but Hereward promised Torfrida he would do his best not to start a full scale war. But that means the Normans will know you are with us. You'll be named outlaw whether you fight or not. So you might as well bring your axe because you won't be able to stay here after we're done."

The choice confronting him made Edric hesitate. For all his dreaming and imagining, this was suddenly very real. His decision would define the future course of his entire life. Yet, when it came to it, his decision was easily made.

"I'll fetch the axe," he said to Siward White.

He hurried inside the smithy, clambering up to lift the great weapon from its hiding place. Then he looked around, wondering whether he ought to take anything else with him. Not that he had any real possessions other than the clothes he wore. The threadbare blanket he slept under was of little value, and his only other possession was his cloak which he now fastened around his shoulders before taking up the axe, blowing out the candle and striding out to face his new future.

The two men led the horse down the path and out into the muddy street. The rain had become a constant drizzle which soon soaked them, yet Siward White insisted on moving slowly.

"We want as little noise as possible," he told Edric.

"You said you had others helping," Edric remarked. "Where are they?"

White replied, "Waiting at the castle. They've been sneaking up on the gates all night. They should be lying on the edge of the ditch by now."

"How many?" Edric asked.

"There are nine of us. Ten including you."

"You are going to storm the castle with ten men?"

"We're not going to storm it. We're going to get inside and capture the Normans while they are sleeping. Also, Hereward is already inside, and so is Martin Lightfoot. So that's twelve of us. It should be enough."

"So tell me how we are going to get inside."

"Isn't it obvious?" the outlaw asked. "They'll open the gate for you because they know you. Martin will have told them to expect you. All you need to do is stop for a moment so they can't close the gates again. Leave the rest to us."

"They'll get suspicious if I stop in the middle of the gate," Edric argued.

"Not if you stop to ask them a question."

"What sort of question?"

"It doesn't matter, does it? You don't speak French, and they don't speak English. All you need to do is keep the gates open and keep their attention on you."

Edric thought the plan sounded ludicrously optimistic, yet Siward White appeared confident it would succeed.

Then Edric thought of another problem.

"They'll see my axe," he pointed out.

"Not if you prop it against the outer wall of the castle," White told him. "You won't need it straight away. We'll deal with the guards at the gate. Then you pick up your axe and join the fun."

Edric wondered what sort of man would describe what they were about to attempt as fun. For his part, he could feel his legs begin to tremble at the prospect of a fight. Taking several deep breaths, he forced himself to continue walking, slowly making his way along the road, all the while conscious of the rain flattening his hair and trickling down his face. His mouth was dry, his palms sweating, and his heart was pounding like a pagan drum.

"You fought at Stamford Bridge," White murmured conversationally. "But have you ever killed a man before?"

"No," Edric admitted. "I stabbed a man with my spear, but it only wounded him."

White gave a low chuckle.

"You'll do fine, boy. But try to stay out of trouble. Carry your axe and look threatening, but keep clear if any fighting starts. Hopefully we'll take them by surprise and all you'll need to do is stand guard over some prisoners, but I don't want an untrained youngster facing a bunch of tough nuts if anything goes wrong."

Edric nodded thoughtfully, pleased that White was at least considering the prospect that things might go wrong, while he simultaneously dreaded how he would react if they did. He knew from his frequent visits to the castle that the Normans would not be easy to overcome in a fight, so he hoped the plan would work.

A plan which, he understood now, depended entirely upon him.

The pair turned at the crossroads, moving slowly because it was difficult to find their way in the rain and dark. Only the ruts on the trackway told them they were still on the road.

The horse clopped slowly behind them, Edric leading it by the reins, every splash and dull thud of its hooves seeming to Edric as if it were sounding his death knell.

But he was committed now. There was no turning back from this. He had given his oath to Hereward, and he had given his heart to Torfrida. He could not go back on his word.

As they neared the castle, he strained to see some sign of the other outlaws, but it was too dark and wet to make out anything except the black bulk of the fort's wooden ramparts.

Siward White, he noticed, had dropped back a little and was walking beside the horse in a sort of crouch.

"What are you doing?" Edric hissed nervously.

"Keeping out of sight of the men in the tower," the outlaw replied.

Edric doubted very much whether the men in the tower would be keeping a good watch on such a miserable night, but he took some comfort that White was taking precautions. Perhaps this mad plan might work after all.

As Edric turned into the approach to the gates, Siward White hissed a whispered reminder of his task, then silently slipped aside and lowered himself into the ditch, vanishing from sight in the wet gloom.

And then Edric was at the gates. Following White's instructions, he stepped to one side and propped his axe against the wooden palisade, peering into the murky gloom as he did so in an effort to locate the other men who were supposed to be lying in wait.

There was nothing to suggest the presence of anyone at all, let alone several outlaws, and Edric briefly wondered whether Siward White might be playing some sort of malicious trick on him.

He quickly dispelled that notion. Hereward and Torfrida were inside the castle. Nobody would play pranks with so much at stake.

It was time.

Taking a deep breath, Edric thumped on the gates with his fist, knowing that every blow signalled that he had become an outlaw and a rebel.

Inside the house, Hereward rose from the bed, fastened his sword belt in place, then made for the door, slowly feeling his way in the darkness.

"Be careful!" Torfrida whispered.

He had not realised she was awake, but he supposed she had found sleep difficult.

"I will," he promised as he slowly unlocked the door, wincing slightly at the sound of the large, iron key in the lock. Then he eased the door open and stepped out.

He had been fairly sure they would be placed in this room. The stairs from the ground floor ran up the right-hand side of the main hall, leading to a wide corridor at the back of the house's upper floor.

The corridor ran the length of the house, with two doors leading to the large sleeping chambers. If Hereward and Torfrida had been placed in the further room, he would have needed to creep past Ivo de Taillebois's room but, as Hereward had suspected, the Sheriff had taken that room for himself to take advantage of the warmth provided by the stone chimney which ran up the left-hand side of the building. The further room was also, Hereward recalled, furnished more luxuriantly than the chamber he and Torfrida had slept in.

So far, he reflected, everything was going as he had hoped.

He brushed the wall with the back of his hand until he felt his way to the staircase, moving cautiously to reduce the sound of his footsteps on the wooden floorboards.

Below him, he could make out the faint, dull glow of the dying fire, and hear the slow breathing of sleeping men. The long tables would have been pushed to the sides of the hall and pallets placed on the floor to provide mattresses for the soldiers.

What he needed to do now was descend the staircase without waking any of them.

He inched his way down, moving with deliberate slowness, testing each step as he went, and placing his feet near the outer edges of the wooden stairs to minimise the risk of loud creaks.

It seemed to take an age but, at last, he reached the ground floor. There was barely enough illumination for him to make out the doors, so he slowly crept to the front wall and felt around like a blind man until he located the handles. Scarcely daring to breathe, he eased one door open and squeezed through into the ante-chamber.

As he gently closed the inner door behind him, he breathed more easily. The hardest part was done. Now he stole to the main doors, felt for the locking bar, and lifted it out of its iron brackets, placing it to one side.

He exhaled a long, slow breath of relief, then turned in alarm as the inner door opened behind him.

"So it is true," said a voice in French. "You are the exiled Thane's son."

Hereward recognised the voice of Frederick, the young knight who had sat next to him at the table, discussing military tactics and weapons. He could make out the glint of a sword in the man's hand but it was still too dark to discern anything more than vague shapes in the shadows.

He wondered what Frederick would do. Hereward's sword was still in its scabbard, within easy enough reach, but to draw it now would leave him facing the entire garrison of the castle on his own. If he could stall for time, his cousins might reach the house before the other soldiers knew what was happening.

Frederick dashed that hope by raising his voice and calling, "To arms! We have a traitor here! To arms! And light some candles!"

From the main hall, Hereward could hear the groggy sounds of men waking from sleep, and could make out their questions as they came to full wakefulness.

He had no more time.

He swept his sword out of its scabbard, instantly swinging it in a furious arc to clash against Frederick's sword and knock it aside.

The young Norman may have been expecting some sort of attack, but Hereward was standing in deep shadow and launched his assault with such speed and ferocity that it caught Frederick completely off guard. Part of his attention was still on the men behind him as he called for them to come to his aid, and the viciousness of Hereward's sudden charge threw him off balance.

Hereward took full advantage, and the fight, such as it was, was over in an instant. All it took was one blow to knock the sword aside, a lunge forwards with one foot, and a reverse slash to hack at his opponent's neck.

Frederick fell with an agonised shout as blood sprayed from the awful wound. He staggered backwards, collapsing into the hall with a crash, leaving Hereward standing in the open entrance of the inner doors.

And facing fourteen armed men.

The little hatch in the gates opened, revealing a suspicious face which peered out at Edric. Curtly, the sentry asked something in French which Edric guessed was a demand to explain his presence.

He used the handful of French words he knew as he gesticulated at the beast behind him.

"The horse. It is for the Lord."

He heard the sentry mutter, then the hatch slammed shut and he thought he was going to be left standing outside in the rain, but he soon heard the sounds of effort as the locking beam was raised. A moment later, the gates slowly creaked open, revealing the shadowy silhouettes of two guards, each dressed in a chainmail tunic and iron helmet, and one of them holding a drawn sword in his right hand.

Edric took a tentative step forwards, hearing one of the guards say something to the other which brought a mocking laugh in response. Edric guessed the amusement was at his expense, and that knowledge spurred him into action. Tugging the horse behind him, he stepped further inside the entranceway, halting to face the two Normans so that they could not close the gates behind him.

He could see their outlines clearly enough in the damp gloom of the pre-dawn. A brazier stood behind them, the coals hissing in the rain but still casting an eerie, red light over the gateway. Beyond that was the small hut where the sentries could shelter from the elements, its door wide open, revealing the pale, flickering light of candles from within.

The man who had opened the gates gestured impatiently, signalling that Edric should keep moving, but Edric stood still, facing the two men.

"Where should I take the horse?" he asked them, looking from one to the other with what he hoped was an expression of docile innocence.

In response, the man with the sword flicked the blade to signal that Edric should move on, while the other man stepped towards the open gates, clearly indicating that Edric must move to allow him to close the barrier.

Edric's heart was hammering now. He remained still, telling the guards, "I don't speak French. Where am I supposed to take the horse?"

The swordsman spat a curse at him, reaching out with his left hand to seize the reins in order to tug the horse inside the fort. Edric refused to let go, earning himself another bout of angry French swear words.

Then, just as Edric felt he would have no option but to lead the horse away from the gates, he heard the sound of running feet from behind him. The Norman with the sword let go of the reins and whirled to see what was happening as his companion uttered a strangled gasp and went down under the weight of two dark figures who wrestled him to the ground.

The swordsman raised his weapon, opening his mouth to shout a warning cry, but Edric released his own hold on the mare's reins and lashed out with his fist, catching the man full in the mouth. The Norman stumbled backwards, blindly lashing out with his sword and forcing Edric to jump aside in order to avoid the wildly swinging blade. Then other men were surging past him and one of them swung a great axe which smashed into the guard's shoulder, shearing through his chainmail and shattering his collar bone. The guard's sword dropped from his hand as he fell to his knees, then his assailant kicked at him before swinging the axe again and decapitating him.

The mare was snorting in alarm as shadowy figures crowded into the castle entrance. Edric swept his arms out until he caught the reins again. He pulled the frightened beast close, speaking soothingly and patting its neck to calm it while men swarmed around him.

The horse snorted and tossed its mane, but it relaxed under Edric's firm grip.

Then Siward White tapped him on the shoulder and said urgently, "Well done, lad. Now move the horse out of the way. We need to shut the gates again."

Edric hesitated, glancing down at the huddled shapes of the Norman sentries.

"I thought you said you were going to take them alive?" he said.

"Accidents happen," Siward White replied with a casual shrug. "Now, move that bloody horse before the men in the tower notice that the gates are open."

Edric obediently tugged the mare towards the small guardhouse. Two of the outlaws had already barged inside to check that there were no more Normans. They ignored Edric as they came back into the rain, giving him the distinct impression that they considered him an outsider.

There was nowhere to tether the horse, so he let the reins drop to the ground, hoping the animal would not wander too far.

The gates were being pushed shut again. Edric darted towards them, saying, "Wait! I left my axe outside."

"Hurry, then!" came a gruff reply.

He slipped through the narrow gap, found his axe and hurried back inside. The gates were pushed shut, the locking beam dropped into place, and the outlaws gathered to hear Siward White's next commands.

"Right, lads, let's get up to the house. Quietly, now. Hereward should have opened the door for us."

Edric held his axe across his chest as he joined the group of rebels. He could make out no faces, did not recognise any of them other than the two Siwards, and he felt like the odd one out among these hard, brutal men who lived as brigands in the wilds.

Siward White placed a hand on the shoulder of a large, muscular axeman as he whispered further orders.

"Winter, you go round the back of the house. Don't let anyone escape out that way. Watch out for Martin. He should be there to meet you."

As the burly axeman grunted an acknowledgement, White turned to Edric.

"You go with Winter. Do as he says. Winter, take care of the lad."

Edric was not sure what sort of response was appropriate, but the axeman rumbled, "Stay close to me, boy. But keep out of my way if trouble starts."

Then they were moving, hurrying across the yard, making for the dark bulk of the house. As they reached it, the big man named Winter veered off and pounded along the side of the building, skirting past the stone chimney and rounding the far corner. Edric, his axe clasped tightly in both hands, followed him, not quite sure what he was doing, but revelling in the desperate excitement of the moment.

Winter slowed as he reached the back of the house. He did not speak, the first sign that he was even aware of Edric's presence being when he held out one arm to indicate that they should move more cautiously. They had taken only two more steps when a soft call came from the shadows near the door.

"King Harold!"

"King Harold!" Winter whispered in response. "Martin?"

"Yes. Did you have any trouble?"

"No. We killed both guards."

Martin did not appear troubled by this news. He asked, "Who's with you?"

"The boy," Winter told him.

"Edric?" Martin asked as he crept over to where Edric stood near the corner of the building.

"It's me," Edric confirmed, finding the words straining to leave his dry mouth.

"Come," Martin ordered, leading the way to the rear door of the house. Here, he stood to one side of the doorway, with his back to the wall, while Winter took up position on the other side of the entrance. Edric, feeling more than a little intimidated by Winter's gruffness, stood beside Martin.

"What do we do?" he asked in a low whisper.

"We wait," Martin replied softly.

"What if the guards in the tower see us?"

"They've not looked out for hours," Martin informed him. "I've been watching them."

Edric could not dismiss the idea that someone in the tower would surely peer out from time to time. If they did, would they be able to see the three men standing at the rear of the main house? It was still dark, but a faint lightening of the sky in the east warned him that dawn was not far off.

He tried to calm his breathing, tried to ignore the feeling that his legs had become jelly, tried to dismiss the tightening in his belly, but he could feel fear rising within him. The memory of what had happened to him at Stamford Bridge, when the Norse axeman had nearly killed him, was vivid in his imagination. What would happen if he had to fight a Norman?

Siward White had said they intended to capture the sleeping Normans, but two men had already died, and Edric suspected the outlaws would have little hesitation in dispatching the rest of the garrison.

He jumped in alarm when he heard the shouts from inside the house. There were urgent calls in French, the clash of steel on steel, then shouts of alarm and the thumping of many feet, accompanied by a hoarse cry of," King Harold!"

"Some bastard must have woken up," Winter observed. "We'd best get inside."

He turned, hefting his axe as he faced the door. Then he stepped back again because they could hear the sound of someone scrabbling to lift the locking bar. A moment later, the door was flung violently open and a figure dashed outside, only to trip over Winter's extended leg and fall sprawling to the ground.

Winter raised his axe, but Martin stopped him with a word as he leaped down to the prostrate figure on the ground.

"It's the servant!" he explained, "Leave him."

Edric wondered who Martin meant, but he had no time to ask because an explosion of noise billowed through the open doorway, the unmistakable sound of battle.

Then came the pounding of feet as more men hurtled out of the back door.

Everything happened so quickly that Edric could scarcely follow the sequence of events. One man crashed into Martin, both of them falling on top of the downed servant, all three men cursing in protest as they scrambled about in the darkness.

Winter spun on his heel, swinging his axe with graceful fluency to take the second Norman in the chest. Winter did not appear to have put much effort into the blow, but the Norman's body was hurled backwards to smash into the wall of the house, where he slumped down, his chest crushed to a bloody pulp.

Edric gaped in astonishment, then shook himself out of his stupor when he realised that the first Norman was rising to his feet, clutching a sword in his hand. The man was dazed and disoriented, but Martin was still entangled with the fallen servant, while Winter was facing the open doorway and had his back to the Norman.

Edric did not hesitate. All fear and doubt vanished as he lifted the axe over his left shoulder, just as Wulfnoth had taught him, and brought it down with all his massive strength.

The broad, curved blade chopped down through the Norman's shoulder, smashing bones and carving a deep gouge all the way into his chest cavity. The man collapsed, making a harsh, gurgling, rasping sound as he fell, dragging the axe with him.

Edric tugged, then yanked harder until the axe came free, the blade dripping blood and gore. He stared down in virtual disbelief at what he had done, then Martin was forcing himself to his feet and clapping him on the back.

"I owe you for that, lad. I must be getting too old for this sort of thing."

Edric, his eyes wide with excitement, gasped, "What do we do now?"

"We follow Winter's lead," Martin replied.

Winter had already vanished inside the house. Edric was about to follow him when he saw the servant scramble upright. He recognised the face of Leland, the haughty steward who had so often treated him with scorn.

Edric gave the man a wicked grin, his expression causing Leland's face to quail when he recognised who was facing him. Uttering a cry of terror, the servant turned and ran into the darkness of the castle enclosure.

"Forget him!" Martin snapped. "Get inside. Lord Hereward might need our help."

All of Edric's fears and doubts had vanished. Not waiting to consider what might face him, he charged through the open door into the short, narrow passage which led to the main hall. There were two doors in the passage, one on either side. Winter had already kicked one of them in, checked that the room behind it was empty of Normans, and was now smashing down the opposite door.

Beyond him, Edric could make out dancing shadows lit by ghostly fire, and he could hear the shouts and screams of battle. He wanted to rush into the hall, but realised that Winter was making sure nobody was hiding with the intention of coming out behind them. Unsure of what to do, Edric stood guard in the corridor.

Winter smashed down the door, roaring a challenge as he leaped inside, his axe held high.

The room was dark, but Winter soon reappeared, snarling a curse.

"It's a storeroom!" he spat. "Get into the hall and join the fight!"

Edric now found himself leading the charge into the main hall.

The door was open, so he ran through, growling an incoherent war cry, only to skid to a halt as he tried to make sense of the chaotic scene confronting him.

The dull light from the dying fire cast long shadows. A few candles had been lit but one of them had been knocked over and had set fire to a pile of blankets and a sleeping pallet, the flames already leaping high and illuminating a scene of horror.

Men were struggling, shouting and screaming as they hacked at one another. Edric could see several bodies lying on the floor, but could make little sense of the fighting itself.

Winter barged in behind him, bellowing a war cry.

"King Harold!"

His ferocious yell was enough to turn the tide. Hearing their enemy behind them, some of the surviving Normans broke and tried to flee. They charged at Edric as they made for the back door.

Edric reacted instinctively, sweeping his long axe in a wide arc at his nearest opponent. The man raised his sword to block the blow, but the axe smashed it from his hand, the power of the blow knocking the man off balance. Edric, too, stumbled as the axe continued its sweep. By the time he had dragged it back, the running man had shoved past him, stumbling as he lost his footing. Edric whirled, bringing the axe around in a desperate, clumsy swing which buried the blade into the back of the fleeing man's skull.

Edric staggered, still off balance, lurching as he hauled his axe back. He was breathing hard, his lungs gasping for air as he heaved himself upright, afraid that Winter and Martin might have been overwhelmed by the other Normans.

He need not have been concerned. Winter, fighting with deadly economy of movement, had killed two of the men who had run at him, and had injured the third who had then been finished off by Martin's long knife.

The fight was almost over, with only two Normans battling on, each of them surrounded by wild, half-crazed outlaws.

By the light of the flaming mattress, Edric saw Hereward, his long hair unkempt, his eyes blazing.

"Get out!" Hereward yelled, his voice cutting across the maelstrom of sound. "Everyone get out before the place burns down!"

"Take their weapons and armour!" Siward White shouted, pointing to the swords which lay scattered about the room and to where the Normans had bundled their chainmail tunics while they slept.

The outlaws stooped to grab up swords and chainmail, scurrying towards the rear exit, but Edric noticed that Hereward had not followed his own orders. Instead, he was running for the stairs.

Edric understood instantly.

Torfrida! She must be upstairs.

Edric dashed across the hall, weaving to avoid the tangled mass of fallen Normans, then raced after Hereward, thumping up the wooden staircase as fast as he could run. As he reached the upper floor, he became aware that someone else had followed him. Glancing back, he saw the tall figure of Martin Lightfoot. The older man's face was weary with strain but alive with concern.

"Torfrida!" Hereward yelled as he kicked open the first door.

"Hereward?" came her anxious voice in response.

"You need to get out. Quickly!"

Torfrida appeared in the doorway, her dark hair framing a pale face with large, frightened eyes.

"What happened?" she asked.

"Frederick wasn't sleeping. He woke the others. Now get out!"

Hastily, Hereward pushed her into Martin's arms.

"Get her outside!" he shouted.

"Where are you going?" Torfrida called as Martin wrapped an arm around her shoulders and bundled her towards the stairs.

"I have *weregild* to collect," Hereward replied darkly as he strode down the hall.

Edric, not wanting to leave Hereward unprotected, followed him.

Hereward reached the second door and pushed at it, twisting the handle.

"Locked!" he spat.

He kicked furiously at the thick wood, yelling as he did so.

"De Taillebois! You killed my brother! I am coming for you!"

The heavy oak door resisted his futile attempts to break it down. Several times he repeated his threats, shouting in French and in English. Then, frustrated, he stepped back, appearing to notice Edric for the first time. Breathing hard, he gestured to the door.

"Break it down!"

Bracing his legs, Edric swung his great axe, smashing at the wooden door, spraying splinters of wood as he hacked at the area around the lock. Four massive blows left the door mangled and hanging drunkenly on its hinges.

"Back!" Hereward ordered.

As Edric stood back, Hereward kicked the door open, letting it smash against the wall before leaping inside with his sword ready.

"Where are you, you bastard?" he roared.

But Ivo de Taillebois was not in the room. The shutters were open, admitting the cool, night air and showing how he had made his escape.

Hereward and Edric ran across the room, leaning out of the open window in time to see the Sheriff scrambling to his feet and limping hurriedly across the yard towards the castle gates. In the pale light of the pre-dawn, Edric saw that de Taillebois had dragged the mattress from his bed, shoved it out of the window and used it to break his fall. The effort had not been entirely successful, since he was limping heavily, but he had retained enough cunning to drag the straw-filled mattress away from beneath the window so that they could not emulate his escape.

Nevertheless, Edric made to clamber out of the window, but Hereward stopped him.

"You'll break your legs. Or worse. Come on! We can still catch him."

They dashed back to the door, along the corridor and down the stairs into a hall which was now burning fiercely as the flames spread. Edric was aware of corpses still littering the floor, of overturned chairs, stools and tables, of discarded weapons and clothing, of a writhing mass of dark smoke spreading through the room, but most of all, of the flames which were now licking around the front doors of the hall.

Siward White stood at the rear door, beckoning them urgently.

"This way!" he shouted.

Hereward ignored his cousin, instead risking the more hazardous route to the front doors. Edric, disregarding the danger, ran after him.

He hurdled a corpse, then leaped through the fiery doorway, flames licking at him, singeing his hair and scorching his skin, but he made it through the burning heat and into the small ante-chamber.

He followed Hereward out of the open doors and into the front yard where the two of them stumbled to a halt just in time to see Ivo de Taillebois mount the horse Edric had left by the guardhouse. The Sheriff had already swung one of the gates open and now kicked the mare into motion as he galloped away to safety.

"God curse you!" Hereward screamed in frustration as he watched his enemy escape.

Edric felt suddenly drained of energy. He could hardly believe what he had been through in the last few minutes. Ten of them had broken into a Norman castle, slaughtered the garrison, and set fire to the main house. Yet the one man they had come to kill had escaped them.

Chapter 5

Edric stood in the damp drizzle, listening to the crackle of flames from within the house, and glancing up at the leaden sky which, although there was no sign of the sun because of the obscuring clouds, was growing gradually lighter. Yet it was barely dawn, suggesting very little time had passed since the attack had begun. It had seemed to him to take an age, but it must have lasted only a few minutes.

The realisation of what they had done suddenly struck him. They had stormed a Norman stronghold and slaughtered their enemies. He had killed two men, cleaving them with his axe without a second thought, acting on pure instinct. He had not recognised the Normans in the darkness, but he realised that he had probably encountered those two men at some point during the past year. Should he feel guilty that he had taken the lives of men he knew? Perhaps he should, but he could not bring himself to feel anything other than relief that he had survived the dreadful fight in the dark confines of the hall. It had been brutal and fierce, but he had come through it, and it meant that he was no longer a blacksmith's apprentice; he was an outlaw warrior who had faced his foes and won.

Hereward, meanwhile, was staring at the open gateway, issuing a stream of angry invective against the fate that had robbed him of his revenge on Ivo de Taillebois. Then he uttered a long, slow sigh as he tried to gather his composure.

He turned towards Edric, giving him a brief nod of acknowledgement.

"Come on, lad. Let's see what everyone else is up to."

So saying, he strode off towards the corner of the burning house, heading towards the rear part of the castle's stockade. Edric followed, immensely proud that, of all the outlaws, he had been the only one who had stayed close to the Lord.

As they passed the house, giving the flaming building a wide berth, Siward White came running to meet them, with several outlaws at his back.

"What happened?" White demanded breathlessly as he came up to them.

"He got away!" Hereward snapped.

"How?"

"He jumped out the window and rode off on that bloody horse we left for him."

White frowned, unsure of how to react, but Edric could see the concern and disappointment on the faces of the other outlaws. They had thought they had won a great victory, yet Hereward's main aim had been thwarted, and his all too evident disappointment had a sobering effect on their good humour.

Yet Hereward did not dwell on his failure.

"He's gone," he stated, "and that's an end to it. Now we need to move quickly. He'll be on his way to Peterborough. We could have a small army of Norman knights here within a couple of hours, so let's get a move on."

White informed him, "There are a couple of Normans up in the tower. They've pulled up the ladder, so we can't get to them unless we burn the thing down."

Hereward raised his eyes to the skies.

"That won't work well in this weather," he decided. "No. Leave them. Set a couple of men to make sure they don't come out, but don't waste time trying to get to them."

"Winter and Ordgar are watching them," White informed him.

Hereward nodded, "Good. But I also want two men at the front gates."

White immediately signalled to two outlaws.

"Auti, Duti. You guard the gates."

The two lean, rangy men he had selected nodded and set off for the gates. As they passed Edric, he was astonished to see that they looked identical. Their faces were so alike, he could not tell them apart. He had heard of identical twins, but he had never encountered any before, and it was all he could do to prevent himself gawping at them. Like the other outlaws, though, Auti and Duti paid no attention to him.

Hereward was asking his cousin, "Did everyone get out of the house?"

The blond outlaw's mouth twitched in a slight grimace as he replied, "Murro and Guthrum were killed in the fight. Wulfric's got a gash on his arm, but he should be fine. Everyone else made it out."

Hereward uttered another soft curse.

91

"Two good men lost. And all for nothing."

"Not nothing," Siward White insisted. "We took the castle."

Hereward gave a sad shake of his head, then returned to the problem of what to do next.

"All right, let's take what we can and get out of here. Saddle all the horses and load as many supplies of food and weapons as you can."

He paused, frowning as another thought came to him.

"I'll bet that bugger de Taillebois had a money chest up in his bedroom."

"Too late to get it now," White observed with a wry grin, nodding towards the wooden walls of the house where flames were licking through the windows and smoke was beginning to rise into the dreary sky.

"The wet thatch will create a lot of smoke," Hereward nodded. "That will act as a beacon, so let's get a move on."

They hurried to the back of the house, maintaining a safe distance from the fire. When they reached the rear yard, White began issuing orders.

"Wulfric, you and Siward Red go and saddle the horses."

Wulfric, a dark-haired, long-legged character who had a bloody strip of cloth clumsily wrapped around his left arm, turned to go, but the red-haired Siward argued, "And what will you be doing, Cousin?"

White gave his namesake a scowl as he replied, "I'll be gathering up all the weapons and armour we dragged out of the house. Now go! You heard what Hereward said. The Normans could have a whole bunch of knights here before too long."

Red muttered something unintelligible but grudgingly followed Wulfric to the stables.

Satisfied, White turned to Edric.

"You know the servants," he said. "So go and talk to them. Tell them to collect as many supplies as they can and bring them out here. We want grain, salted meat and fish, honey, dried fruit, and anything else that will last. Understand?"

Edric nodded, "I'll see to it."

Bursting with pride at being given such an important task, he headed towards the long, low building which he knew was where the servants were quartered. As he approached, he saw that the door was slightly ajar, revealing an anxious face peering out through the narrow gap.

He straightened his back, swung his axe over his left shoulder the way he had seen Winter do, and marched purposefully to the door. He was a rebel, a warrior, and he would show the timid servants that he was worthy of their respect.

His determined mood lasted until the door swung fully open to reveal the plump, pregnant figure of Aelswith.

"Edric? Is that you?"

Edric stopped in his tracks, feeling his cheeks flush. Aelswith may have been several months into her term, but she was still beautiful in his eyes. Her slim face, with its high cheekbones, bright eyes and delicate nose, was framed by an old, shabby shawl she had draped over her head against the rain, but she still retained the power to render him speechless.

"Edric?" she asked again.

He coughed, cleared his throat and managed to say, "Yes, it is me."

She gave him a stern look, as if assessing him.

"I must speak to Thane Hereward," she announced. "Will you take me to him?"

Giving a resentful jerk of her head to indicate a slight figure behind her, she added scathingly, "This girl doesn't seem to understand English."

Looking beyond Aelswith, Edric recognised Torfrida's maid, Alice, who must have been given a bed in the servants' quarters. Alice's expression was even more nervous and miserable than he remembered, but the girl's face grew animated when she noticed something behind him and she dashed past him, crying out in French.

Edric turned to look back over his shoulder and saw that Hereward was standing near the stables, deep in a heated conversation with Torfrida, while Martin Lightfoot hovered protectively nearby.

Turning back to Aelswith, he told her, "I must speak to the servants first."

"Why?"

"We need supplies of food. We want grain and salted meat. And fish if there is any. Honey and dried fruit as well."

For an instant, he thought she was about to berate him for throwing in his lot with a band of outlaws but, after regarding him speculatively for a moment, she gave a decisive nod.

"Wait here," she told him. "I will arrange it."

Edric felt that he should insist on delivering the message himself, but Aelswith had spoken with such authority that he remained where he was while she disappeared inside the building. The rain continued to trickle down his neck and soak his long hair, but he could not will himself to move.

Aelswith reappeared moments later, with a handful of other servants, all of them women, nervously clustered behind her.

Waving her hand to hurry them on, she told them, "Go to the stores. Bring out what you can."

As the women scurried off towards the storehouse, Aelswith cocked her head at Edric.

"Now will you take me to speak to Lord Hereward?"

He was so tongue-tied, all he could do was nod his head, turn and walk across the yard to the stables.

The castle was, he realised, in chaos. To his right, the main house was well ablaze, a dark pall of smoke rising slowly into the wet sky as flames licked around the windows and timbers began to collapse into the blaze. Even at a distance of twenty yards, he could feel the heat on his skin.

Siward White was busily carrying bundles of chainmail armour towards the stables, heaving them inside for his cousin and Wulfric to load onto the horses, while Hereward and Torfrida appeared to be having an argument of some sort. Edric was reluctant to interrupt them, but Martin noticed him and said something which made Hereward turn.

"What is it, Edric?" he asked with a hint of impatience.

"Lord," Edric replied haltingly, "this is Aelswith. She wishes to speak with you."

Aelswith dutifully bobbed her head as she faced Hereward.

"You are the one who recognised me last night," he said in surprise.

"Yes, Lord."

"I am no Lord," he told her. "My name is Hereward."

"I know, Lord," she replied, insisting on using his title.

"How do you know?" he asked. "And how did you recognise me?"

"You have a scar on your right hand. I saw it when you placed your palm over your goblet."

Hereward raised his hand and glanced at the white scar which ran from the base of his little finger to his wrist.

"Lots of men have scars," he remarked.

"But not all men look like you, Lord," Aelswith responded.

"That doesn't explain how you know me."

"Your brother, Toki, often spoke of you. He told me he gave you that scar when you were teaching him how to use a sword and he accidentally cut you."

"You knew Toki?"

She nodded, placing a hand on her swollen belly.

"I am carrying his child," she said, her tone carrying a hint of defiance and challenge.

Hereward gaped at her, and Torfrida took a step forwards, her expression full of interest.

Hereward glanced at Edric.

"Does she speak truly?" he asked.

Edric's cheeks flushed again as he gulped, "She and Toki were … I mean, everyone knew."

Hereward nodded thoughtfully as he returned his attention to Aelswith.

"So what do you want from me?" he asked her.

"You must take me with you," she stated firmly.

"It is too dangerous," he replied instantly. "We are going into the Fens."

"To Ely?" the girl guessed.

Hereward's eyebrows arched in surprise, but Aelswith went on, "Where else can you go?"

"You are very astute," he nodded. "But it is still too difficult a journey for a woman in your condition."

"It would be better than staying here and becoming a Norman concubine," she retorted. "Do you want your niece or nephew to grow up as a Norman?"

Hereward hesitated, but Torfrida interjected, "She must come with us, Hereward. She is part of your family now."

Hereward frowned as he asked Aelswith, "Are you family? Did you marry Toki?"

She lowered her eyes as she shook her head.

"The priest died," she said in a low whisper. "There was nobody to marry us."

Edric shifted uncomfortably. Like everyone else in the village, he had known Toki had taken Aelswith to his bed, but whether the young Thane had ever had any intentions of marrying her was a different matter altogether. Thanes did not generally marry poor serving girls, no matter how beautiful they might be.

Aelswith said, "I will follow you whether you take me willingly or not. So will some of the others. There is nothing left for us in Bourne."

"She is right, Husband," Torfrida agreed. "I told you that you had started something you cannot control."

Aelswith, sensing she was going to get her own way, added, "There will be others in the village who will wish to join you."

Hereward's mouth twitched in a faint smile of resignation. Edric guessed that the Thane's argument with his wife would necessitate some sort of concession, and Aelswith provided that opportunity.

"Very well," Hereward sighed. "You may come with us. We will give you one of the horses. Edric, you will watch over her on the journey."

Edric's heart began to race, but he managed to maintain a serious expression as he nodded his acceptance of the task.

Hereward went on, "And you should go and speak to the other villagers. Tell them that anyone who wishes to come with us should be at the crossroads within the hour. They can only bring what they can carry. Is that understood?"

"Yes, Lord," Edric confirmed, feeling a thrill at being entrusted with this responsibility.

Torfrida again interrupted, saying, "It might be better if he did not go alone. Some of the villagers may not be happy about what we have done here."

Hereward sighed, "I suppose you are right, as usual. Very well. Edric, go and tell Winter he is to accompany you. The sight of him ought to scare off any troublemakers. You'll find him up near the tower."

Edric glanced at Aelswith and was rewarded with a broad smile which rooted him to the spot until Hereward barked, "Get a move on, lad! We must be away from here soon."

Edric bobbed his head and hurried off, heading deeper into the compound towards the great artificial mound which dominated the furthest part of the stockade.

Passing beyond the stables and workshops, he found Winter standing alongside another burly axeman, the two of them sheltering behind a small cart they had dragged to the foot of the steep-sided mound on top of which stood the castle's wooden keep. They had toppled the cart so that it lay on its side, providing them with a ready-made shield.

"Is that him?" the second man asked Winter as Edric approached them.

Winter gave a feral grin as he nodded, "That's him. Well met, Edric. Have you come to help me and Ordgar storm this place?"

He waved a meaty hand up at the tall, wooden tower which stood on top of the mound.

Edric stared up at the keep. He had never come this close to it before, and the sight fascinated him. He could see a dark doorway high on the wall facing them, and recognised this as the only entrance. With the ladder having been pulled up by the tower's occupants, there was no way of getting inside.

Arrow slits gaped on either side of the door. Edric realised this was why the two men were standing behind the cart.

"Have they shot at you?" he enquired.

Winter chuckled, "See, Ordgar? I told you he was a natural. He spotted that straight off."

Ordgar, a thickset, hairy man with a flourishing moustache, gave a sage nod.

"I reckon these buggers are horse soldiers," he intoned in a gravelly voice. "They ain't shot at us yet. Maybe they don't know how to use a bow, or maybe they're saving their arrows."

Edric asked, "How many of them are inside, do you think?"

"Three," Winter replied. "Two sentries and that servant who ran out of the back door last night."

"Leland? He's up there?"

"Is that his name?" Winter shrugged. "Older fellow with a face like a scared rabbit?"

"That sounds like him," Edric agreed. "Is he up there with the Normans?"

"That's what we reckon," Ordgar confirmed.

Edric frowned. He had not liked Leland, but he had thought the man might acknowledge his English heritage once he knew the Normans had been beaten. Instead, he had sought safety among the men who ruled his land through force of arms. Edric realised this was why Torfrida had been right to insist that he took someone with him when he went out to speak to the villagers. There would undoubtedly be others who would prefer to curry favour with the Normans than stand up to them.

His Uncle Ethelred, for one, he reflected grimly.

"Hereward says you and I are to go into the village," he told Winter. "I need to let them know what has happened and tell them they can come with us if they want to."

Winter snorted, but nodded his assent.

"You can handle two Normans and a servant, can't you?" he asked Ordgar.

The hairy axeman grinned, lifting his axe and patting the flat of the blade.

"Let them try to get out past me," he chuckled.

"All right, lad," said Winter. "Let's go and round up your people."

They made their way back through the compound, passing a line of horses which were being loaded with sacks and boxes of supplies under Siward White's watchful eye.

Aelswith was there, too. She gave Edric a smile as he passed, bringing another blush to his cheeks.

"Is that your girl?" Winter asked him as they steered a wide course around the burning house on their way to the front yard.

"No," Edric mumbled in response.

Winter shot him a crafty look and chuckled.

"You're sweet on her, though?"

Edric shook his head in denial, bringing another hearty laugh to the big man's lips.

"So whose brat is she carrying?"

"Thane Toki's," Edric told him, taking some delight in seeing the axeman's look of surprise.

Winter gave a soft whistle, then observed drily, "I'll bet Hereward is pleased about that."

Edric informed him, "He says she can come with us."

Winter shrugged, "Well, let's see who else wants to join the party."

The twins, Auti and Duti, were at the gates, each with a sword and axe. Edric could see no sign of the two guards who had been killed, but he guessed the twins had dragged them into the guardhouse to keep the entrance clear.

"A few folk have come out of their homes," Auti informed them. "They're keeping a safe distance away."

"Any sign of trouble?" Winter asked.

"No. Nothing."

"Pity," grumbled the huge axeman. "Come on, then, lad. This is your home, so you can do the talking. I'll just stand behind you and growl at anyone who starts anything."

"There won't be any trouble," Edric assured him.

Winter merely grunted as he stomped along the muddy road, picking a way between the puddles.

There was a small crowd of people at the crossroads, all of them peering nervously through the rain at the castle and the pillar of smoke which was seeping into the early morning sky. Some of the villagers hurried away when they saw two armed men marching towards them, but others recognised Edric and stood their ground.

As he drew nearer to them, Edric was glad Winter was with him. The outlaw was an imposing figure, broader and taller than Edric, who counted himself among the largest of the villagers. Winter walked with a calm confidence which gave Edric the strength to face the crowd.

"What's going on?" a man called as Edric and Winter reached the crossroads.

It was old Seaver, his arm still swathed in bandages from the ordeal he had undergone and for which his fate was still to be determined.

Edric looked at the anxious faces confronting him. He knew them all, had lived among them for most of his life, yet now they seemed almost like strangers to him. They were farmers and goatherds, not warriors.

"The castle has been taken," he told them. "The Sheriff has fled, but most of his men are dead."

A ripple of astonished gasps and concerned murmuring ran through the crowd until someone asked, "Taken? Taken by who?"

"Hereward, the son of Thane Asketil," Edric informed them. "He has come back and taken revenge for the death of his brother."

The men and women exchanged glances. They had all known and liked young Toki. His death had cast a pall over the village for weeks, but to learn that his older brother had returned and wrought devastation on the killers filled them with dread.

A woman's cracked voice called, "And now you will scurry away and hide like cowards and thieves!"

Heads turned to see who had spoken. Edric was not surprised to discover it was Gytha, the witch woman. She was standing near the back of the crowd, but he could see her plainly enough since the other villagers had begun to edge slowly away from her.

"You have become a rebel and an outlaw, Edric Strong," she went on, her right hand pointing an accusing finger at him. "You have brought death to this village and now you will run away."

Edric had always feared Gytha, but he sensed Winter stirring and drew confidence from the man's presence.

He said, "You cannot expect Lord Hereward to remain here to face a Norman army. That is what I have come to tell you. He is taking his men into the Fens. We are going to Ely. Anyone who wishes to join us is welcome. But you must be quick. We leave within the hour. If you wish to come with us, fetch what you can carry and return here."

Gytha snorted, "Only fools will join you, Edric Strong. You have earned nothing for yourself except an outlaw's death at the end of a rope."

She glared at him, then turned and stalked away, heading for her house.

Edric affected disdain, but he could not shake off a feeling of dread at being the subject of one of Gytha's curses. He glanced at the remaining villagers, wondering how they would react.

Seaver spat on the ground and growled, "Bloody witch! I'll come with you, young Edric. Don't go without me."

Others took heart from Seaver's determination, giving promises that they, too, would join the exodus. The crowd began to disperse as people hurried to gather belongings from their homes.

Or perhaps, Edric mused, to barricade themselves indoors until Hereward's gang had departed.

"Tell everyone!" Edric called after them. "Spread the word!"

In a small place like Bourne, it did not take long for the news to reach every home. It seemed only a few moments had passed before Edric saw the menacing figure of his uncle stomping towards him with Aunt Edith tagging reluctantly along behind him, a shawl draped over her head against the rain.

Winter whispered, "He looks like he might want a fight."

"I can handle him," Edric replied confidently.

"What's going on, boy?" Uncle Ethelred demanded angrily as he stormed up to Edric. "What are you doing with that axe?"

"I've been killing Normans," Edric told him.

"He's good at it, too," Winter put in.

Uncle Ethelred glared at the big outlaw. He seemed on the point of saying something harsh, but the sight of Winter's axe and the gleam in the outlaw's eye deterred him.

"So it is true!" he rasped. "Do you know what you have done?"

"I know perfectly well," Edric replied.

"Edric!" Aunt Edith gasped, tears filling her eyes. "Oh, Edric!"

"I always said you would come to a bad end, boy," Uncle Ethelred spat. "Well, good riddance to you. Go off with your outlaw friends. The King will have you hunted down and executed for this. You and all your new friends."

This outburst brought more tears to Aunt Edith's eyes. She sobbed into a handkerchief, turning away from Edric as if the sight of him were too much for her to bear.

"Hereward is our rightful Thane," he told his uncle. "I will follow him now, and I will fight until England has a proper King, not a foreign invader."

"You're a bloody fool, boy!" Uncle Ethelred rasped, echoing the words of Gytha the Witch. "Come, Edith! Let him go. We will not be tainted by his actions."

"You will grovel on your knees before the Normans, as usual?" Edric taunted, astonished at his own temerity.

Uncle Ethelred whirled, his fists bunching, but Edric grinned and hefted his axe across his chest.

"I am not a boy," he hissed. "I am a man. I am a warrior and what you can call a rebel if it pleases you, but at least I have the courage to stand up to the bullies who have taken our land from us."

His uncle glared balefully at him, but lowered his fists. He stood in the rain, staring at his nephew for a long moment, but Edric returned his stare without flinching. Eventually, Ethelred turned and stamped away, snarling at Aunt Edith to follow him. She gave Edric one last, tearful glance, then obediently followed her husband, her head bowed as if weighed down by despair.

Winter remarked, "That was a nice speech, lad. But you do realise he's right, don't you? We can't beat the Normans. They'll win in the end."

Edric was surprised to hear such pessimism from the big outlaw, but he did not care. Confronting and facing down his uncle had been the bravest thing he had ever done, and he felt it had indeed turned him into a man.

"That doesn't matter," he told Winter. "Whether we win or lose is not as important as the fact that we try."

Winter gave him an odd look, then nodded, "You're a thinker as well as a fighter, then?"

"I don't know about that," Edric shrugged. "I just know what I feel to be right."

"A man should always go with his gut feel," Winter agreed. "Me, I fight because it's all I know how to do."

"Will you teach me how to fight?" Edric asked him.

"You seemed to manage it fine earlier on," the outlaw told him. Then, with a smile, he added, "But you stick close to me and I'll show you what I can."

Edric grinned. At last, he truly felt as if he had been accepted into Hereward's gang.

Apart from Edric, there were seven men left in the gang. Before rallying to Hereward's call for men to help strike a blow against the Normans, all of them had been living as outlaws in the fens or forests. Their clothing was old and ragged, their skin ingrained with dirt, and their hair, beards and moustaches were unkempt, yet their weapons were well cared for, and Edric still felt slightly in awe of their obvious experience in matters of war.

He had already met or seen every one of them, so it did not take long for him to match names to their faces. There were the two Siwards, White and Red, Winter, Ordgar, the twins Auti and Duti, and a man named Wulfric who had such long legs that he was known as The Heron. There was also Martin Lightfoot who held the position of manservant to Hereward and the Lady Torfrida.

It was not, Edric reflected, much of a force to overthrow the Normans, but that simple fact could not persuade him he might have made a mistake in joining them. He was leaving Bourne for good and heading into the Fens where the Normans dare not follow. And he was going with Aelswith, a fact which filled him with equal measures of joy and anxiety. Joy because he had always wanted her friendship and respect; anxiety because he feared she would disdain him when she came to know him better.

They were almost ready. There had been another delay when the house had finally collapsed as the timber beams burned away and the thatched roof caved in, sending up great gouts of sparks with a hiss and roar which must have been heard all across the village. Once it had fallen in, however, the damp outer thatch and the continuing rain served to keep the fire in check, reducing it to a smoking, sizzling bonfire rather than a great conflagration.

Everyone stared at the burning ruin, and a few of the women retched when the faint aroma of burning meat reached their nostrils. Edric, who had been feeling hungry because he had not eaten since the previous evening, was now glad that his stomach was empty. Even so, he felt more than a little sick at the thought that so many bodies were burning inside the wreckage of the house.

"It always gets you the first time," Winter observed in a quiet voice. Then, to Edric's surprise, the big axeman crossed himself as he muttered a soft prayer.

"Two of our lads died in there," he explained when he saw Edric looking at him.

Edric felt slightly ashamed. He had not known the two dead outlaws and had given them little thought.

"Were they good friends of yours?" he asked.

Winter shrugged, "I only met them a couple of days ago, but they were comrades."

He did not seem inclined to say any more, so Edric turned his attention to Hereward, who was gazing grimly at the remains of the house. Edric realised the young Lord must have had many memories of the place where he had grown up. Now it was gone, even though it had been taken from him by circumstances long before the fire had destroyed it.

Hereward glanced up. For an instant, his eyes met Edric's across the yard. Edric could not tell what Hereward was thinking, but the Lord gave him a slight nod before raising an arm and declaring loudly, "Time to go!"

The nervous horses, now laden with supplies of food and weapons, were led around the blaze and out of the gates where Auti and Duti had added another grisly embellishment. In mockery of the symbol Ivo de Taillebois had employed to cow the villagers when he had first arrived, the heads of the two sentries had been placed on the rampart of the castle, one on either side of the gateway. It was a grim reminder of just how dangerous life would be for Hereward and his followers, for they knew the Normans would give no quarter to any rebel who fell into their hands.

Not that Edric cared. He had his axe slung over his left shoulder, while his right hand held the reins of a horse which bore Aelswith. He was leaving Bourne, leaving his uncle's constant complaints, and beginning a new life as a warrior. What more could he ask?

Hereward led them to the crossroads where around half of the villagers waited for him, each man, woman and child carrying a bundle of personal belongings. There were dogs among them, too, as well as a few chickens held in baskets, along with some goats and pigs who would be prodded into joining the procession.

Most of the villagers bowed low when they saw Hereward, acknowledging his status as their Thane, but the young lord insisted they should not treat him as anything other than the leader of a small war band.

"My lands and titles were taken from me years ago," he told them. "And now the Normans have stolen any chance I might have of regaining them. I am not your Thane."

He then spent a little time speaking to them individually, greeting them like old friends, but warning them that there was no turning back from their next steps. Most of their faces were grim and serious, but none of them changed their minds about accompanying him.

He grinned, "Then let us be off before this village is swarming with Normans."

With that, he turned his back on the village that had once been his home, and led them into the damp vastness of the Fens.

Chapter 6

Altruda lay in the darkness, savouring the warmth of the blankets which covered her naked body and the comfort of the down-filled mattress beneath her. She had no idea what time it was because the shuttered windows were concealed by thick, heavy drapes which blocked all light and muffled sound from outside. Something had woken her, but she was not yet sure what it might have been, so she lay very still and listened.

Beside her, she could hear the slow, rhythmic breathing and occasional snores of Abbot Turold. His presence was another reason for keeping still, she reflected. She had no doubt that, once awake, he would insist on making love to her again. She would permit it, of course, and would even pretend to enjoy it, even though she found the Abbot a rather repellent creature. He was old enough to be her father and, although he might once have been strong and well-honed, his body was beginning to succumb to his love of good food and comfort. His belly was no longer trim, his cheeks were slightly flabby, and the stink of his breath appalled her.

None of which would prevent her moaning in mock ecstasy when he entered her. Like all men, he would believe his potency would make her devoted to him when, in truth, it was she who was ensnaring him.

Altruda knew how to mould men's minds. Because she was a woman, they naturally viewed her as less intelligent and less rational than themselves. Yet all she generally needed to do in order to persuade them to do her bidding was whisper a few soft words or tease them with some gentle caresses and the promise of more intimate touches should they grant her desires.

Abbot Turold was no different, she knew. He was certainly not a man of God despite his title and position. What he wanted, Altruda had already recognised, were influence, power and wealth. The abbacy of Peterborough promised all those things. Not for nothing was it known as the Golden Borough. The abbey was rich in itself, owning vast tracts of land, and it was also home to significant amounts of treasure. A great deal of that belonged to the Church itself, but wealthy families, fearful of being robbed, often placed their valuables in churches or monasteries because nobody would dare to rob a house of God. Except the Danes, of course, although even most of that ferocious race had converted to Christianity and would baulk at desecrating a church.

Peterborough, with its large church and associated monastery, was one of the richest abbeys in England. Abbot Turold was determined to make it even richer. In the process, he would, naturally, enrich himself. He was a Norman, and England was now the Normans' plaything.

The man was also, Altruda had quickly realised, a braggart and a bully. The King had sent him here in order to quench the Abbot's thirst for war. The area abounded in rebels and bandits, the men the Church named "Silvatici", the "Men of the Woods". Abbot Turold had informed her that he intended to root out these rebels and execute every last one of them.

Not that she cared very much. Her reason for coming to Peterborough was altogether more important. The Abbot knew this, and she could have relied on the strength of the King's letter to make Turold do as she wished. But she had seen the lust in his eyes when they had met and she had known that, to ensure his cooperation, it would be best to satisfy his desires. That way, there would be no arguments when she needed to impose her will.

So she had slept in his bed pretending to enjoy his brutal lovemaking, and now she was awake, lying in the darkness and straining to discover what had roused her from sleep.

She could hear distant singing, the dissonant chanting of male voices, and knew that the monks were at prayer. Did that mean they were celebrating Matins, the dawn vigil, or was it later? Terce, perhaps? That would mean the time was after the third hour, nine of the clock. That was possible, she supposed. She did not normally sleep so late, but Abbot Turold had been quite demanding and had kept her awake for much of the night.

Then she heard the sound that must have woken her. It was a soft, tentative knock at the door.

"Lord Abbot?" a querulous and very frightened voice called softly, the sound barely audible through the thick oak timbers of the door.

Altruda stirred, pretending to be shifting her position, nudging Turold as she did so.

He mumbled, snorted, then slowly came awake.

"There is someone at the door," she whispered to him.

"What?" he muttered sleepily.

"The door. Somebody is knocking."

Reluctantly, he pushed himself up, cursing in a most un-Christian manner.

"This had better be good," he growled softly as he fumbled on the floor for his robe. "I'll have the idle swine flogged if he's woken me for nothing."

Altruda heard him pull the robe over his head, and listened to the flap of his sandals as he crossed the floor to the door, muttering oaths as he bumped into the end of the bed in the darkness. She heard him turn the key and then the door swung open, admitting a dazzling shaft of daylight from the outer corridor.

"What is it?" Abbot Turold barked.

"Lord Abbot," replied a quavering voice in response, "Ivo de Taillebois, Sheriff of Lincolnshire, is here. He says there is a rebellion."

Altruda came fully alert as she listened. She could not see the man who had brought the news because the Abbot's bulky frame blocked her view, but she did not need to see him to appreciate his fear.

Abbot Turold hesitated, then demanded, "Rebellion? What sort of rebellion?"

"The Sheriff says his castle has been taken and his knights massacred," the voice reported.

"God's Teeth!" exclaimed Turold. "Where is he now?"

"I have put him in your personal study, Lord Abbot."

"I'll be there soon," Turold said. "Have my breakfast delivered there."

"Yes, Lord Abbot."

"But open my curtains and let some light in here first."

He stepped away from the door, allowing Altruda to see a young man, a novice monk who acted as one of the Abbot's servants, enter the room. The novice drew back the drapes and pushed open the shutters, allowing light and fresh air into the room. He studiously ignored Altruda's presence in the bed, averting his eyes as if the very act of seeing her would offend him.

It probably would offend him, she thought mischievously.

"Shall I bring warm water, Lord Abbot?" the man asked nervously.

Turold shook his head.

"I will wash and shave later. Go and tell the Sheriff I will join him very shortly."

The novice gratefully hurried out, closing the door behind him. Once he was gone, Altruda pushed back the blankets and swung her legs out of the bed. Locating her clothes on the chair where she had placed them the previous evening, she dressed hurriedly, pulling on her white gown and adjusting the laces on the bodice so as to leave a small amount of flesh showing. That, she knew, would distract the abbot and his unexpected guest. Such distractions were useful because, as she had learned long before, a tantalising hint of female skin tended to loosen men's tongues.

While she dressed, Turold was doing the same, selecting a fresh robe from his wardrobe, all the time muttering angrily about de Taillebois's arrival.

"The man's a buffoon," he grunted sourly. "It's probably nothing more than a peasant uprising in his village."

"You think he is mistaken about his castle being stormed?" Altruda asked with an innocent air.

Turold merely grunted again as he hung a large, silver crucifix around his neck.

"If that is true, he's not only a buffoon, he's an incompetent buffoon," he snarled. "Wait here, my Lady. I will return once I have heard what he has to say."

"I wish to hear his story as well," she said simply. "It may have a bearing on my own mission."

Turold shot her a dark look, but did not argue. She was here at the King's express command, and Turold knew it. He would not dare refuse her.

She hastily combed and brushed her hair, applied some perfume, then accompanied the Abbot as he left his bedchamber and strode noisily down the stone-floored corridor to where the Sheriff was waiting for him.

In the Abbot's comfortably appointed study, Ivo de Taillebois was pacing up and down, clearly agitated. His hair was in disarray, his chin unshaven, his saturnine eyes wide with alarm and red-rimmed with tiredness. He was wearing an expensive-looking tunic and trousers, but had no cloak, and he had clearly dressed in a hurry because his fleshy fingers bore no rings.

Servants had delivered trays of food and drink, placing them on low tables which sat beside comfortable armchairs, but de Taillebois was in such a state of anxiety that he had made no effort to eat, although he had clearly consumed at least one cup of wine.

"Lord Abbot!" he blurted when Turold and Altruda entered the room.

He bustled towards them, hands outstretched in supplication.

"Sit down, man!" Abbot Turold snapped irritably. "And tell me what all this talk of rebellion is about."

The Sheriff's face fell, but he was so out of sorts that he did not object to the Abbot's unfriendly curtness. Obeying the command, he perched himself on one of the chairs, facing Turold and Altruda across a table bearing one of the trays of food.

The Abbot poured wine as he made the introductions.

"Sheriff, this is the Lady Altruda. She is here on a mission of the utmost importance to the King. My Lady, this is Ivo de Taillebois, Sheriff of Lincolnshire."

Altruda noticed the scorn in the Abbot's voice when he announced de Taillebois's title. There was clearly no love lost between these men, and it was plain that Turold held de Taillebois in some contempt.

Nevertheless, she smiled sweetly, telling de Taillebois she was pleased to make his acquaintance. He, in turn, let his gaze fall to her bosom where the laces of her bodice had fallen loose. He was in such a state of agitation that the sight barely seemed to distract him.

He displayed no inquisitiveness about her royal commission, but immediately began telling the story of what had happened to him the previous evening and in the early hours of that morning.

Altruda's heart quickened when he mentioned Hereward. Involuntarily, she placed a hand on her chest as if to quell the thumping beat within.

Her gesture did not escape the Abbot's notice.

"Is something amiss, my Lady?" Turold enquired.

"Perhaps," she said, recovering some of her poise. "Lord Sheriff, are you sure the man was Hereward, son of Asketil?"

"That is what I am trying to explain," de Taillebois blurted. "One of the servants thought it might be him, but we were

110

not sure. I intended to challenge him in the morning and compel him to show us whether he had a tattoo on his arm. The servant said that Hereward bears a drawing of a boar on his forearm."

"He does indeed," Altruda put in. "On his right arm. And he has the image of a bear on his left."

Both men looked at her in surprise.

"You know him, my Lady?" Turold asked.

"If it is indeed Hereward, I certainly do know him. He saved my life once."

"He did?" Turold asked, his eyebrows rising inquisitively.

"I will explain later," Altruda told him. "First, we must hear the Sheriff's tale to its end."

After downing another cup of wine, Ivo de Taillebois took up his story again.

"It turned out it was him," he said cautiously. "He attempted to murder me in the middle of the night. Fortunately for me, my men were alert and fought to protect me, but he was unstoppable. Our weapons could not harm him, and he slew everyone who faced him. In the end, I had no option but to flee. I had twisted my ankle in the fight, and I knew I could not beat him when so many others had failed."

He gave Turold a miserable, pleading look as he added, "You must send an army of knights to capture him, Lord Abbot."

Altruda interrupted the Abbot's response by asking, "Do you know why he tried to murder you, Lord Sheriff? It seems an odd thing for a guest to do."

De Taillebois shifted uneasily in his chair, then mumbled, "I had his brother executed for treason."

Altruda nodded, "I see. And Hereward had a woman with him, you said?"

"His wife," de Taillebois confirmed.

Altruda pondered that for a moment. Something did not add up here, but she needed more time to consider the Sheriff's story.

Seeking to elicit more information from the fat man, she asked, "You say your weapons could not harm him? How can that be?"

De Taillebois shook his head as he wrung his hands in distress.

"I do not know. But no man can defeat fifteen armed soldiers. Yet he did."

"Perhaps he had help?" Altruda suggested.

"A handful of peasants, perhaps," de Taillebois conceded grudgingly.

"Or perhaps he was enchanted?" Altruda teased.

De Taillebois brightened at that thought.

"Yes! The woman with him. His wife. She must have been a witch! How else could he have slaughtered my men?"

Altruda managed not to laugh at the Sheriff's foolish conviction. The man was indeed a buffoon, just as Turold had informed her.

The Abbot was more pragmatic. He asked her, "Tell me what you know of this man, my Lady. I have never heard of him."

Altruda composed herself, wondering how much of her own past she ought to reveal.

After some thought, she began, "It was several years ago, just after Hereward had been exiled. I was in Scotland, where I was due to marry one of their nobles."

She glossed over the events that had brought her to that position, wanting to keep some secrets to herself.

"I was only fourteen at the time," she recalled. "Hereward must have been nearly twenty years old. He was proud and boastful despite having been exiled by King Edward. He had come north in search of adventure, so he claimed."

"You said he saved your life," Abbot Turold reminded her.

"He did indeed. It was when a group of travelling entertainers arrived at the castle. They brought with them a dancing bear. It was kept in a cage in the main courtyard, but one morning it escaped. Nobody knows how it got out, but it was angry and it stormed around, attacking anyone it could reach. Most people ran, but I was too terrified to move. It had already killed one young boy by the time it noticed me, and I was unable to escape.

She paused, took a deep breath as if the memory still haunted her, then she went on, "That was when Hereward stepped in. He had a sword and shield, and he leaped between me and the bear. When everyone else had fled in panic, Hereward fought the beast and killed it. That is why he has the tattoo of a bear on his left arm."

112

Ivo de Taillebois regarded her with astonishment.

"Nobody can kill a bear single-handed," he declared disbelievingly.

"Hereward can," she assured him. "I saw him do it. He is quite formidable, my Lords."

She looked both men in the eye to show them that she spoke the truth, but she said no more about her first meetings with Hereward. Some things were best kept to herself, she decided. Yet the fact that he had returned to England twisted her emotions in a manner she had not expected. She prided herself on being able to maintain a calm, calculating outlook on life, never to allow emotions to influence her decisions. But learning that Hereward was back affected her far more than she would have thought possible.

Not only was he back, he had a wife.

And he had begun a rebellion.

"What else can you tell us about him?" Turold pressed.

She sighed, "I have heard various reports over the years. He did not linger in Scotland, but continued his wanderings. He is said to have travelled to Ireland, and then to Cornwall before crossing the Channel and reaching Flanders. I heard he had won many victories for the Count of Flanders, but I know no details of what he did there. All I can tell you is that you should be wary of facing him in battle."

"One man can be beaten easily enough!" Turold declared.

"Not if he is guarded by magic," de Taillebois insisted.

Altruda confined her response to a thin smile. The Sheriff's pathetic determination to cling to the excuse that Hereward had been aided by witchcraft had convinced her that de Taillebois was not telling the entire truth about what had happened during the night. She guessed that he was probably covering his own cowardice. From what she had seen of the fat Norman, he would not have survived had he genuinely faced Hereward in combat, and it was telling that de Taillebois had escaped while his knights had been slaughtered.

Abbot Turold made his decision.

"He may have the aid of witchcraft," he stated, "but I have the power of God behind me. I will lead my knights to Bourne and bring this rebel to justice. I'll soon have his head on a spike."

Altruda felt another unexpected wave of anxiety when she heard that vow.

She said, "If possible, my Lord Abbot, I would suggest you try to bring him back alive."

"Alive? He has rebelled against the King. He must die for that!"

Altruda was accustomed to thinking quickly. Her talent did not desert her now, even though she felt unusually flustered by her reaction to the news of Hereward's return.

She said, "I understand that it may not be possible, but I urge you to do all you can to capture him alive. He is, as I have explained, a follower of the Count of Flanders. We need to understand why he has come back and whether the Count is plotting against King William."

"You think this Hereward may be following the Count's orders?" Turold asked pensively.

"I do not know," Altruda admitted. "But there are, as you know, other interested parties who may be moving against our King. That is why I am here, after all. Perhaps the Count of Flanders has thrown in his lot with the Danes. I need to know. Capturing Hereward alive might answer those questions, while killing him might escalate what seems to have begun as a personal feud against our good Sheriff into a war with Flanders."

Abbot Turold did not seem convinced, but he gave a surly nod.

"Very well, my Lady. I shall heed your advice. I'll bring him back alive if I can."

Altruda nodded, "Thank you, Lord Abbot. I can ask no more of you than that."

Privately, she doubted whether Turold had the ability to capture a man like Hereward, but she felt an aching need to see the Englishman brought back in fetters. She wanted to see him crawl in front of her and beg for his life.

He was, after all, the only man who had ever refused her. For Altruda, that was an insult which demanded revenge.

Chapter 7

The Fens were a wilderness of reeds, marshes and waterways which appeared to change direction every time Edric glanced at them. The journey through the waterlogged wasteland was far worse than he could ever had dreamed. In the past, he had looked out across the wetlands, skirting around the edges and occasionally venturing a few yards into the tall reeds which often grew so high they towered over his head. Now, though, he was deep within the vast Fens and wishing fervently that the nightmare journey would end.

Wulfric, the Heron, was leading the long procession, probing the path with a long stick which was taller than he was, and stepping out as if he were confident of finding his way. The path he followed was invisible to everyone else, but Wulfric kept them clear of the deep bogs which could swallow a man in seconds, guiding them along narrow, reed-lined tracks which turned to a muddy quagmire as people and horses ploughed along in Wulfric's wake. Sometimes, the brigand would show off how he had earned his nickname by vaulting over narrow sections of boggy ground, planting his long pole in the ooze, then swinging himself over the obstacle. He would land with a flourish, turn and grin before repeating the trick, then finding an alternative path which the rest could follow without the need to leap over mud and dark water.

Wulfric may have been enjoying himself, but Edric was miserable. The cloying mud was often up to his ankles and occasionally much deeper. After twice plunging into muddy pits which reached up to his knees, he stopped to untie his boots and lace them together so that he could hang them around his neck. From then on, he plodded barefoot.

"I don't want to lose my boots," he told Winter when the big man laughed at him.

"Some folk will lose more than that, I reckon," Winter chuckled.

That, Edric privately admitted, was probably true. It was bad enough near the head of the column, but the path must be much worse for those at the rear who were trudging along a track which had been churned into a muddy morass by the passing of so many people and animals.

Edric glanced ahead. He knew that the twins, Auti and Duti, were following Wulfric, with Hereward next in line. Behind Hereward, Torfrida rode one of the horses which was weighed down with additional sacks of food supplies. Torfrida, Edric knew, had been forced to abandon the chests containing her clothes because they were too bulky and heavy to transport by hand, and there was no possibility of leading a cart through the Fens. What few belongings she had been able to bring were stuffed into two sacks which were being carried by her servant, Alice.

Edric felt sorry for Alice. The girl was barely seventeen, slightly built, and clearly terrified by the situation she found herself in. She trudged miserably along behind Torfrida's horse, the hem of her long skirts soaking wet and caked in mud, her shoulders bowed under the weight of the sacks she carried. Edric had helped her out of some boggy patches by grabbing her elbow, but the girl's only response was to regard him with frightened eyes and mutter something in French which he could not understand.

He still carried his axe over his left shoulder, feeling it grow heavier as the dull, wet day dragged on. His right hand led the reins of a horse on which Aelswith was perched, riding side-saddle and clinging on for grim life, sometimes uttering soft cries of pain when she was jolted as the horse lost its footing on the treacherous path.

Winter, calm and imperturbable, strode alongside the horse, using his free arm to support Aelswith when necessary.

Behind them came the rest of the villagers, along with their heavy packs and their animals. Pigs, goats and dogs floundered almost as much as the humans and at least one goat fell into a deep swamp, quickly vanishing from sight into the black depths of a murky pool.

At the rear, Edric knew, were Ordgar and the two Siwards, each of the cousins armed with a bow and a quiver of arrows. Their job was to fend off any pursuit, although Edric doubted whether any Norman would be insane enough to attempt to follow them into this desolate wasteland.

People lived in the Fens, he knew, but they travelled by boat whenever possible. The flat-bottomed vessels were propelled by long poles thrust into the water or by short paddles. Yet even

116

they were dangerous unless the occupants knew their way. The thick reeds and clumps of sedge grass grew so thick and tall that it was often impossible to see more than a few yards in any direction, and the streams within the Fens rarely kept to the same course for very long. Rains, floods and tides from the distant sea turned the waterways into an ever-changing maze.

"How long will it take to get there?" Edric heard Aelswith ask Winter.

"That depends on whether we take a direct route or go the long way round," the big man replied.

"Why would we go the long way round?" Aelswith asked.

"Because the direct route takes us near Belsar's Hill, and there are Normans camped there."

"So how long will it take if we go by the long route?"

"We should get there by tomorrow evening," Winter informed her before adding, "Or maybe the day after."

Edric's heart sank. Three days of tramping through this stinking quagmire with its treacherous footing and all-pervasive smell of rotting vegetation? The thought horrified him.

Aelswith must have felt the same but, after a long, contemplative silence, she began asking Winter more questions.

"If we are going to be travelling together for such a long time," she declared, "we may as well get to know one another better."

Edric heard Winter chuckle, "I am always keen to get to know pretty girls."

A flash of jealousy stabbed at Edric's heart, but Aelswith laughed, "I do not feel very pretty at the moment. I am wet, cold, covered in mud, and, unless you hadn't noticed, I am expecting a baby."

"Oh, I dare say some men will still find you pretty," Winter grinned.

Edric risked glancing back over his shoulder and saw that Winter was looking at him. The axeman gave him a broad wink, making Edric instantly return his attention to the path ahead.

Aelswith did not appear to notice the exchange. She asked, "Why do they call you Winter?"

"It's my name," the big man replied. "I had seven brothers and sisters, but they were all born in the summertime. I arrived in the middle of winter, so my father named me after the season."

"Where were you born? Near here?"

"No," he replied. "I am originally from Wessex. My father was a housecarl in the service of Earl Godwin. I followed him, and joined the household of Harold, who became Earl in his father's place."

"King Harold?" Aelswith asked. "You knew him?"

"I knew him well," Winter replied, his voice now more sombre. "I followed him as Earl and as King. He was a great man. The best ruler England ever had."

There was a pause as Aelswith considered how to pose her next question. Edric was certain she must be wondering the same as him, yet it was a difficult question to put to a man like Winter.

"Were you at Senlac Hill?" she asked eventually.

"Aye, I was there," Winter admitted gravely. "And I know what you are thinking. You are wondering how it is that I lived while my King died."

"I am sure it is not due to a lack of bravery on your part," Aelswith assured him.

Winter hawked and spat before giving his response.

"Harold was clever in war. He knew what we would face that day. He'd seen the Normans in battle before, and he knew they used horses while we would be on foot. We were crowded on that ridge, and we showed them a solid line. Harold knew they wouldn't break us as long as we stood firm. But many of the men were *fyrdmen*, not trained warriors, so he sent some of us among them, spreading us out so that we could bolster the line and keep the *fyrd* in place."

"So you weren't near the King?" Aelswith asked gently.

"I scarcely saw him all day," Winter replied. "I was too busy killing Normans. Then, when it all fell apart at the end of the day, I was too far from him to help when the Normans broke the line further along the ridge."

"So you came to Ely?" Aelswith prompted, knowing the account of the great defeat was difficult for the big warrior to recall.

"I didn't know what to do or where to go," Winter admitted. "One of the lads who got away with me was from these parts. I had nothing better to do, so I helped him get home. After that, I stayed."

"I'm glad you did," Aelswith told him.

Winter shook off his memories and asked, "What about you, lass? Where are your family?"

"Back in Bourne," Aelswith said, her voice harsh and unyielding. "They disowned me when I fell pregnant."

"Because you aren't wed?" Winter enquired.

"That's right."

"Parents can be foolish sometimes," Winter remarked. "So you've lived in Bourne all your life?"

"Yes."

"So you know young Edric pretty well?"

Edric was fairly sure the pair of them knew he could hear them, but he pretended to be lost in his own thoughts, refusing to turn round. Nonetheless, he listened intently as they discussed him.

"I've known him ever since he came to the village when his parents died," Aelswith told the axemen.

"How long is that?" Winter asked.

"Years ago. He was around seven or eight years old, I think."

"He wouldn't have been known as Edric Strong back then," Winter guessed.

"Oh, he was always a big lad. There were two other boys in the village who were called Edric, so they all had second names. Edric earned his early on."

Edric felt irritated that Aelswith was openly discussing him with a man she had only met that morning, but he was determined not to give either of them the satisfaction of knowing that their words were annoying him. Besides, Aelswith had always behaved as if Edric was nothing to her, so he was intrigued to hear what she might say next.

Aelswith surprised him even further when she said, "Edric has always stood up to bullies. He used to get into lots of fights when he first arrived, but they were mostly to defend anyone who was being picked on. The other boys soon learned to leave him alone because he was tougher than anyone else."

Edric felt his cheeks begin to burn again, and wished he could prevent that embarrassing response. He had not realised Aelswith had paid any attention to his youthful exploits, even though there were few secrets in a place as small as Bourne.

Idly, he reflected that none of the boys he had fought were left alive. The youngest of the Edrics had died of fever at the age of eleven, and the older had, like too many others, failed to return from Senlac Hill. Edric Strong no longer had any need of a second name, but it had stuck all the same.

Winter was now saying, "Well, he's still fighting the bullies, I suppose. Except now he's using an axe instead of his fists."

Aelswith fell silent, making Edric wonder what she was thinking. He was about to turn round to look at her when Winter spoke again.

"Don't look so concerned, lass. Edric has been charged with looking after you, and I've agreed to look after him. Whatever happens in the future, he won't stand alone."

This time, Edric could not help himself. He turned to look at the two of them. Winter grinned at him, winking again, but Aelswith looked away, brushing at her cheeks with the backs of her fingers as if to wipe away the rain. Or perhaps tears.

"Keep going, lad," Winter told him. "Only another two days to go."

They spent the night on an island, a hummock of damp grass which was only a few feet above the level of the surrounding waters. It was barely two hundred yards long and only around fifty yards wide, yet it was home to three families who lived in hovels of wood and reed thatch, and made their living by fishing in the streams and pools of the Fens. They had nothing to spare for the exhausted travellers except a small supply of firewood which was not nearly enough to warm everyone who needed it. All the villagers from Bourne could do was heat some of the food they had brought with them and then huddle on the ground in their wet clothes.

Aelswith sat, uncomplaining, with her back resting against one of the tiny shacks, spooning oatmeal porridge and salted beef from a small, wooden bowl, while Edric stood close to her, maintaining his promise to protect her but unable to summon the courage to actually speak to her.

She did speak to Torfrida, who made a point of going round everyone and talking to them to reassure them.

"I know it is a hard journey," she told them, "but it will be worth it. We will be safe when we reach Ely. There will be plenty of time to rest in comfort once we get there."

She had a special concern for Aelswith's health, solicitously enquiring about how she was bearing up.

"I will manage," Aelswith assured her. She placed a hand on her belly and winced as she added, "Although I could do without the baby kicking me quite so much."

"Rest as best you can," Torfrida told her. "The child will be fine as long as you do not do too much."

"Do you have children, my Lady?" Aelswith asked.

Torfrida gave a slow, sad shake of her head.

"No. I had a daughter, but she only lived for a few days."

"I am sorry," Aelswith said softly.

"It was God's will," Torfrida told her. "You need not fear. Your child will be strong and healthy, I am sure."

Edric, standing close by, felt embarrassed at hearing this conversation. Childbearing was not something he had ever considered, and it had not occurred to him that Aelswith's baby might be moving inside her. That must mean it was already alive, a thought which somehow disturbed him.

As for the child's chances of survival, Edric knew many children did not live beyond their fifth birthdays, and it seemed to him that God had a particularly strange way of expressing his divine will. Whatever the circumstances which had led to Aelswith's pregnancy, the unborn child had not been to blame. Nor, he guessed, had Torfrida's dead daughter committed any sin.

The Church, of course, insisted everybody was born sinful, but that did not seem right to Edric. He decided he would need to speak to Brother John about this when he next saw the wandering monk.

If he ever saw him again, that was. Ely was reputed to be safe, but Edric was under no illusions about the revenge the Normans would want for the attack on Bourne's castle.

First, though, they must reach Ely.

"Wulfric reckons we'll get there the day after tomorrow," Winter informed him. "We're not making very fast progress, you see."

"At least the rain has stopped," Edric shrugged.

"Always look on the bright side," Winter grinned.

The two men had edged away from Aelswith to give her a little privacy. Now they stood in the failing light, gazing out at the endless vista of swamp that surrounded the tiny island.

121

"Is Ely really safe?" Edric asked the axeman.

"As safe as anywhere in England," Winter replied. "There's no easy approach, so it has become a refuge for a lot of rebels. Siward Barn is there."

"Who is Siward Barn?" Edric asked.

"He's an old Thane from somewhere up North. I heard he was part of the last Earls' rebellion. He came here when the Earls submitted to The Bastard."

Edric had heard very little about the Earls' rebellion. All he knew was that two English Earls had attempted to seize control of northern England but had been swiftly crushed by William, the Norman King who was often referred to as "The Bastard" because of his illegitimate birth.

That made Edric wonder about Aelswith's child. It would be born out of wedlock, but that disadvantage did not appear to have harmed William. He had become Duke of Normandy, and was now King of England. God, Edric reflected, certainly did move in mysterious ways. Torfrida's child had died, Aelswith's parents had disowned her for falling pregnant while unmarried, but an illegitimate Duke's son had risen to rule the wealthiest kingdom in Christendom. It was all too confusing for Edric's baffled mind.

Winter, seemingly oblivious to Edric's distracted thoughts, continued his explanation.

"Old Siward has a few hundred men on the isle of Ely," he recounted. "Some of them are trained fighters, others are displaced farmers or tradesmen. All of them are rebels, that's for sure."

"I didn't realise there were so many of them," Edric said. "I'm surprised the Normans have left them in peace for so long."

Winter snorted, "The Bastard has plenty other problems to deal with. He's been ravaging the North, so they say, and the monks tell us that he's also having trouble in Normandy. Some of his neighbouring nobles are taking advantage of his absence. Added to which, Siward Barn has kept himself to himself. Maybe it's because his hands are so crippled with arthritis that he can't even hold a sword these days, or maybe he's just being canny, but he concentrates on keeping Ely safe and hardly ever ventures out. That's why I agreed to join Hereward's little gang. I am fed up sitting on my arse doing bugger all to stop the Normans. But, as for Ely, it is the least of The Bastard's worries."

"Won't that change now that we've destroyed the Sheriff's castle?" Edric asked.

Winter nodded, "Aye, lad. I dare say it will. But that's a problem for another day. We should rest now, because we've got another tough day ahead of us tomorrow. I'll take the first watch if you like. You try to get some sleep."

Edric did as Winter suggested, wrapping himself in his damp cloak and lying down a few yards from where Aelswith was restlessly sleeping. He soon learned why she was not resting soundly. The night was cold, making him shiver so much he could not sleep properly. To add to his discomfort, his leg was aching, as it always did after a long period of walking, especially when the weather was damp. Cold, wet and sore, he managed only a few fitful dozes before Winter woke him and ordered him to stand watch.

"What am I watching for?" Edric asked blearily.

"Anything that threatens us," Winter told him before laying himself down and appearing to instantly fall asleep.

That, Edric decided, was a warrior's trick he would need to learn.

The following day was a repetition of the first, a weary, trudging plod along muddy pathways which seemed to wind to and fro among the reeds, never following a straight route.

There was little talking because everyone was so tired and cold. Even the absence of rain and the occasional burst of warming sunlight from between the grey clouds did not improve the lot of the weary villagers. The ground remained boggy, the reeds still towered above them, water seeped into their boots and shoes, and now they were assailed by swarms of buzzing insects which whirred around them no matter how much they waved their arms to drive them away.

That was when Hereward showed his leadership qualities. He moved up and down the long, winding column of people and animals, encouraging them and telling them how well they were doing. He did not ride on horseback but ploughed through the mud and swamp on foot, showing them that he was enduring the same hardship as everyone else. His long hair was matted, his clothes and face spattered with mud, yet he remained outwardly cheerful and confident.

123

"Every step takes us closer to safety," he promised. "Keep moving and don't lose heart."

So the villagers ploughed on, squelching their way to safety. Only Torfrida and Aelswith were on horseback, the other animals being burdened with supplies of food, armour and weapons. Heavily laden, they often floundered in deep parts of the marsh and it took several men, and sometimes the strength of one of the other horses, to pull them free of the sucking, cloying morass.

"We could wear the chainmail coats," Edric suggested to Winter. "That would lighten the loads."

"Aye, we could," Winter agreed cheerfully. "But the horses would still struggle because they're a damned sight heavier than any man. Then there's the simple fact that it's dangerous to wear armour in this swamp. If you step off the path, you'll sink like a stone."

"Is that why you didn't wear chainmail when you came to Bourne?" Edric asked. "You must have a coat of it."

Winter's face crumpled in a sour grimace as he admitted, "No. I don't have a byrnie. I sold it."

"You sold it?"

"A man has to eat," Winter explained gruffly. "It's a long walk from Senlac Hill to Ely without food."

Edric tried to cheer the axeman up by saying, "You'll get another one now we've captured all those Norman ones."

"You think so?" Winter shot back. "You and I, my lad, may find it difficult to find one that fits. Not many of those Normans were the same build as us."

Edric frowned. He knew a byrnie was an expensive outfit, but he had hoped he might be able to persuade Hereward to award him one from the captured booty. Now, he realised, he might need to go without. For some reason, that thought depressed him.

"Cheer up, lad!" Winter told him. "All you need to do is find a big Norman and kill him. Then you can take his byrnie."

"You make it sound easy," Edric grumbled.

"You're a rebel now, lad. It's kill or be killed when you meet the Normans."

Glancing up, Edric noticed Aelswith watching him. Her face was pale and serious, as if the talk of further killing had upset her.

"The Normans won't come to Ely," he said lightly. "I probably won't need my axe, let alone a byrnie."

Winter, realising that Edric's words were directed at Aelswith, grunted, "Aye, well, you may be right at that."

It took them until the following morning to reach the promised sanctuary. Wulfric the Heron had led them in a wide arc around the large island so that they approached it from the eastern side, finding a spot where the water surrounding the isle was only thirty yards across. Wulfric called to some boatmen who began the long, slow process of ferrying the men, women and children across. The horses were unloaded, the baggage placed in the small boats and transported across the river, then the horses were led into the water, each one swimming to the island in the wake of one of the small vessels with a man sitting in the stern of the boat to hold the reins.

Edric stayed with Aelswith, but still found it difficult to talk to her. He disguised his shyness by putting his boots back on, shoving his wet feet into the wool-lined leather and fastening the sodden laces. Then he waited in silence until he was able to help Aelswith into one of the small boats. The touch of her hand and the grateful smile she gave him caused his cheeks to redden once more. Flushed and embarrassed, he sat beside her in the broad, flat-bottomed boat, not daring to look at her as the boatman slowly propelled them across the dark water.

"What will happen now?" Aelswith wondered aloud as they slowly traversed the dark water.

Edric could only shrug in response. He could see people beginning to gather on the far side, townsfolk from Ely, monks from the abbey, and men armed with spears, axes and swords, all of them hurrying to witness the arrival of Hereward's followers.

A substantial crowd had gathered by the time their boat bumped onto the grassy hithe, the landing place where the fishermen of Ely beached their boats. Edric was kept occupied with helping Aelswith step carefully ashore, then giving Winter a hand to unload the supplies which had accompanied their crossing.

He set one barrel of salted meat firmly on the ground and said to Aelswith, "Sit on that until we find out what's going to happen next."

It was, he guessed, the longest sentence he had ever spoken to her.

"Thank you, Edric," she said gratefully as she lowered herself onto the makeshift seat.

Winter grinned and winked at Edric as he heaved another couple of sacks onto the hithe.

When the boat was empty, the boatmen pushed off again, re-crossing the stream to collect the next group of passengers.

Wiping sweat from his brow, Edric paused to look around.

Hereward and Torfrida, he noticed, were speaking to a group of men which included a tall, stoop-shouldered, grey-haired monk and an even older man who wore a byrnie of chainmail and had a sword at his waist. They were too far away for Edric to hear what was being said, but the conversation, while animated, appeared friendly enough.

"That's Abbot Thurstan," Winter informed him in a sideways whisper. "He's a decent enough sort for a God-botherer. The old man in the armour is Siward Barn."

"I wonder what they are talking about?" Edric mused.

"We'll find out soon enough, lad. For the moment, take a rest. Oh, hello, here comes some food."

He was correct. Several monks were moving among the new arrivals, bearing loaves of bread and pitchers of ale which they were distributing to the thankful villagers. Winter grabbed a loaf from one monk, broke it into three chunks and handed a piece each to Edric and Aelswith.

"It'll taste as good as any bread you've ever eaten," he promised. "Food always tastes good after a long trek."

Edric bit into the dark bread and nodded. It was indeed excellent.

Winter gave him a nudge, simultaneously jerking his head in Aelswith's direction.

"Talk to her, lad," he whispered under his breath.

Edric, one hand resting on his axe, the other holding the bread, felt awkward once again, but he inched over to Aelswith and asked, "How are you feeling?"

"Tired," she replied. "But glad we are here."

She fell silent and Edric could think of nothing else to say. He was just beginning to feel uncomfortable when a voice from the crowd called his name.

126

"By all the Saints! It's Edric Strong! I might have known you'd get mixed up in the trouble."

Edric whirled, seeking out the person who had spoken. The hithe was crowded, with more people arriving all the time, but he heard a joyful laugh and picked out the round, cherubic face of the man who had spoken.

It was Brother John.

Chapter 8

"I thought you were going to the North?" Edric said to the smiling young monk.

"I am," Brother John beamed. "But I thought I would celebrate Easter at Ely first. God must have guided my footsteps, for it seems we are fated to cross paths. And I see you have a young lady with you."

Aelswith, clearly delighted to see a familiar face, made to stand, but Brother John gestured for her to remain seated.

"I saw you at the Sheriff's home, did I not?" the monk remarked.

"Yes," Aelswith nodded. "I was one of the kitchen staff."

"And now Edric has brought you here. I have heard a little of what has happened, but you two must tell me all about it. First, though, we will take you to the infirmary. It must have been an arduous journey for someone in your condition. Come, Edric, lend the lady your arm and we shall go to the monastery."

Edric looked around to find Winter, but the big axeman had wandered off to help Auti and Duti unload another boat which had bumped against the landing ground. With Brother John refusing to be denied, Edric had no option but to take Aelswith's arm and help her to her feet.

"I expect most of your companions will be housed in the town," Brother John explained as he eased a way through the throng. "But the infirmary is the best place to start. There's another of your village folk who needs attention, too. Where did he get to, I wonder?"

Brother John looked around, then nodded in satisfaction as he signalled to another man to join them. To Edric's surprise, it was old Seaver, his arm still wrapped in a bandage which was now a dirty brown colour and badly frayed.

"Brother Richard will tend to you," Brother John assured them. "He's a Norman, but he's a decent enough physician for all that."

"A Norman?" Edric gasped. "Here?"

"He's a monk first, and a Norman second," Brother John told him. "He has been here for a few years now. Since before the Conquest, anyway."

Edric was not happy at the prospect of allowing a Norman to attend Aelswith, but Brother John refused to hear his protests.

"Brother Richard is a fine physician," he repeated.

"I am not sick," Aelswith protested. "I am expecting a child."

"Ah," Brother John grinned, "but the infirmary is a place where you can be sure of finding some rest and perhaps some herbs to ease your aches and pains. It will be better than sitting on a barrel in the open while arrangements are made to find a more permanent place for you."

Aelswith seemed satisfied, so Edric did not voice any further complaints. Instead, he looked around at Ely as Brother John led them through the winding streets.

Edric had passed through a couple of large towns when he had marched north to his fateful encounter with a Norwegian axeman at Stamford Bridge, but Aelswith had never ventured out of Bourne, so she was amazed by what she saw, even though Ely was not a particularly grand place. It was, though, much larger than Bourne, with tall buildings and narrow streets which were filled with a riot of noise created by people, dogs, geese, donkeys and other semi-domesticated animals.

Their own presence did not attract a great deal of attention. Many of the townsfolk had already gone down to the hithe, but those who remained seemed to find the sight of a monk, a man carrying an axe, a pregnant woman and an elderly man with a bandaged arm as perfectly normal.

"So Hereward destroyed Ivo de Taillebois's castle, did he?" Brother John enquired as they slowly navigated through the narrow, meandering streets. "How did he manage to do that?"

Haltingly, Edric explained how he had been recruited to help the outlaws get into the castle. He glossed over his part in the fighting, merely saying that the outlaws had wanted to capture the Normans alive but that things had not gone as planned.

"So the soldiers were killed, but the Sheriff escaped?" Brother John asked.

"Yes. That's why Hereward brought us here."

"I dare say you would have needed to come here whether the Sheriff escaped or not," the monk observed. "I expect Abbot Turold would be seeking revenge either way."

"We'll be safe here, though," Edric said as if to reassure Aelswith.

"God grant that it be so," Brother John responded gravely. Then he brightened and gestured to a set of open gates within a long wooden wall as he added, "Here we are. Come, let us find the infirmary."

The high wall surrounded the sprawling abbey complex. Brother John led them through the unguarded gates into a broad, open area which was bordered by enough buildings to comprise a small village. As usual, most were constructed of wood with roofs of reed thatch, but there was a church with stone foundations and a circular stone tower. Edric caught sight of several monks going about their business, as well as a handful of men bearing weapons who appeared to be guarding some of the buildings. It was an odd combination in a place which was supposed to be devoted to the worship of God, but he had no time to contemplate what it might mean because Brother John was hurrying them across the hard-packed earth of the courtyard to a long, low building set some way apart from its neighbours. Edric gained the impression the monk was attempting to sneak them in without being challenged, but Brother John continued to sound confident and relaxed.

"Here is the infirmary," he told them as he guided them towards the door of the long house which stood near the exterior fence of the abbey complex.

He pushed the door open and called, "Brother Richard! I have some custom for you!"

Brother Richard was another relatively young man, no more than twenty-five years old. He was of average build, clean shaven, with dark hair cut in the usual tonsure, and hands which had long, delicate fingers.

His eyes widened when he saw Aelswith.

"I am a physician, Brother John, not a midwife!" he blurted.

"I know, Brother. But the lady has travelled a long way. She is in need of something to ease her discomfort while we find more appropriate lodgings for her."

Brother Richard scowled but gave a reluctant sigh.

"Very well. But she cannot lie on a cot in those filthy rags. Sit her down over there beside the fire, and I will mix a potion for her."

Brother John guided Aelswith to a wooden chair which stood beside a small, open fire at one side of the room. The fire heated a rectangular metal plate on which stood a couple of small pots. The room also housed Brother Richard's desk, chair and a large cabinet containing a wide variety of ointments, potions and herbs. There were also, Edric noticed, several large, leather-bound books neatly arranged on a high shelf above the desk. The only book Edric had ever seen before was the ancient, heavy bible in the village church, and he was astonished that any man, even a physician, could own so many.

The infirmary held a great many strange and novel things that he wanted to ask about, but Brother Richard gave no indication that he would be inclined to answer questions, so Edric contented himself with gazing around the room, trying to fathom the purpose of the arcane implements which filled the many shelves. Then, glancing to the far end of the room, he saw through an open door that there was another chamber beyond, a longer room with a row of narrow cots arranged against one wall. Only one bed appeared to be occupied by a thin figure which lay very still beneath a grey blanket. The infirmary, it seemed, was a place where the sick could find genuine rest. He supposed his original opinion of Brother Richard might have been unfair, since the man obviously cared for those who were unwell.

He watched as Aelswith gratefully sank onto the chair while Brother Richard poured warm water from one of the pots above the fire into a pewter beaker. The monk then went to his cabinet and located some herbs which he dropped into the water before stirring the mixture with a long-handled spoon.

"Drink this," the monk told Aelswith sharply. "It may make you feel a little drowsy, but it will ease any pains you may have."

Aelswith took the drink and sipped tentatively at it while Brother Richard cast a dark look in Edric's direction.

"Another fighting man?" he sighed. "I thought we had enough of them. I cannot understand why the Abbot permits them to stay within the abbey grounds."

Edric bridled at being talked about so openly, but bit his tongue, allowing Brother John to respond to the surly physician.

"Perhaps he feels they are necessary," Brother John said cheerfully. "These are dangerous times, Brother."

131

Brother Richard blew air down his nose but made no further comment on Edric's presence, preferring to ignore him. Instead, he focussed his attention on old Seaver, who had hung back near the door, clearly intimidated by his surroundings.

"And why is this fellow here?" Brother Richard enquired with barely disguised scorn.

"Ah, Seaver had a most unfortunate accident a few days ago," Brother John put in. "He was boiling a leg of lamb when he tripped and fell. His arm was badly scalded when he accidentally plunged it into the boiling water."

Brother Richard raised a sceptical eyebrow and seemed on the point of disputing Brother John's explanation, but Brother John hurriedly ushered Seaver towards him as he continued his invented tale.

"The bandage, as you can see, has become ragged and filthy during his sojourn in the Fens. Perhaps you could dress the wound properly, Brother?"

Brother Richard narrowed his eyes, but gave another sigh and gestured for Seaver to sit on the chair beside the desk.

Seaver's expression betrayed his horror at Brother John's lie, but the monk patted his cheek as he continued to talk.

"The poor fellow has been in considerable pain," he said. "I believe he may be in shock."

Brother Richard did not deign to respond. He merely picked up some scissors, took hold of Seaver's arm, and began to cut away the filthy bandage.

Edric shot Brother John an appalled look, but the gaze he received in return was one of pure innocence.

When the bandages came away, Brother Richard clucked his tongue and tutted loudly as he surveyed Seaver's forearm and clawed hand.

"That needs some salve," he muttered, fetching a small pot from his cabinet.

He spent some time gently cleansing the injury before smearing a greenish ointment onto Seaver's inflamed and wrinkled pink flesh, then wrapped a fresh linen bandage around the arm, tying it tightly with strips of cord.

"It appears to be free of infection," Brother Richard commented. "Let us pray it remains so, for the only option would be to amputate the limb."

Seaver's eyes widened in horror, but the monk continued, "However, I believe there is a good chance it will heal. Come back and see me in a few days and I will treat it again."

Seaver, still looking shocked, mumbled his thanks, then Brother John announced, "Thank you, Brother Richard. We shall leave you in peace now."

The four of them made their way out into the wide courtyard which was now filling up with people as the monks brought more of Hereward's group up to the abbey. Aelswith seemed calm, the drugs beginning to take effect, but Seaver was deathly pale.

Edric challenged Brother John on the old man's behalf.

"You lied to him!" he hissed.

"Did I? I would prefer to say that it was a small and wholly justified deception. Besides, Our Lord Jesus Christ urges us to aid those in need."

"But you lied to a man of God!" Edric insisted.

"That will be between me and the Lord," Brother John told him firmly. "And if any mortal man should accuse me of a sin, I shall simply say I misunderstood what you told me about the circumstances surrounding Seaver's injury. I am positive there was a leg of lamb and a pot of boiling water involved in the tale, but I may have mixed up the sequence of events."

Edric subsided into a sullen silence, so Brother John turned to Seaver.

"Don't fret, my friend. You were unjustly punished by the Sheriff. God must have thought so too, or he would not have sent you to meet me in this holy place where your wound can be treated."

"Are you sure, Brother?" Seaver mumbled uncertainly, his eyes lowered.

"Of course I am! All the same, though, I wouldn't let Brother Richard know what really happened. He might take a dim view of it. That would get me into trouble with the Abbot, and I'm sure you wouldn't like to see me being given penance for lying to a fellow monk, would you?"

Seaver shook his head uncertainly, but Aelswith giggled at Brother John's behaviour, and the old man relaxed a little.

"Now," said Brother John, "let us find out where you are to be housed. I shall do my modest best to find you lodgings within the abbey complex. That way, you can eat in the refectory. The food here is rather good, you know."

"Even during Lent?" Edric asked.

"Lent?" Brother John responded with surprise. "My dear Edric, today is Good Friday. This is Easter weekend. There will be prayers, processions and, I am delighted to say, a great deal of feasting."

Edric soon discovered that, for all his outward confidence, Brother John had little real influence within the abbey. He was, after all, only a mendicant priest who happened to be visiting the island. He did manage to attract the attention of Abbot Thurstan, but it was Torfrida who insisted on Aelswith being provided with a room next to the one she and Hereward had been allocated.

"She is family," Torfrida insisted.

The Abbot conceded the point when he learned that Aelswith was carrying Toki's child, although Hereward offered no support and scowled deeply at being reminded that he would be an uncle to Aelswith's illegitimate offspring.

Seaver, along with most of the villagers, was given lodgings within the town. The Church owned most of the land, so was able to insist on its tenants taking in lodgers. The villagers from Bourne had little coin to pay rent, but the Abbot assured them they would be put to work in order to pay for their keep.

"Everyone in Ely contributes to the wellbeing of all," he told them piously.

That rule did not appear to apply to the warriors. Siward Barn had a sizeable force of men, although few of them were based in Ely itself. Most were posted around the edges of the island where they had dug defensive earthworks to bolster the isle's security. A score of men remained in the abbey complex where they served as guards to Siward Barn. Hereward's gang were accorded the same privilege, so Edric found himself quartered in a dormitory with Winter and the others. Even the two Siwards, White and Red, were with them despite their noble birth.

"We are outlaws now," White shrugged with a smile. "We will make do with the same as the rest of you."

For Edric, it was not a case of making do. The dormitory may have been draughty and colder than the smithy where he usually slept, but the small cot he was allocated was far more comfortable than the floor where he was accustomed to sleeping.

Easter was, as Brother John had promised, taken up with prayers, processions, the singing of psalms and feasting. The warriors ate in the refectory, sitting alongside the monks, most of whom appeared quite at home with the fighting men. A few of the holy brothers made a point of ignoring the armed men whenever possible and only speaking to them if asked a direct question, but most treated them as welcome guests and were happy to share their mealtimes with them.

Apart from the Abbot's table, there was no set seating arrangement. Each man simply found a space at one of the long tables which filled the large hall. Hereward's gang sat together, although Hereward himself was given a seat at the top table beside Abbot Thurstan and Siward Barn.

Torfrida, being a woman, was not admitted to the refectory but, as she was a Lady, she was served in her own room. Edric discovered that Aelswith was permitted the same honour, mostly at Torfrida's insistence.

For his part, Edric tucked into the food, devouring everything he could lay his hands on, as did his companions.

"I think we have earned this," grinned Winter as he chomped on a cut of ham.

Edric could not argue. Coming to Ely seemed to him to have been an excellent idea. He had a soft bed, warm blankets, and plenty of food. What more could he have asked?

They soon began to settle into a routine. Over the course of the next few days, Brother John visited Aelswith regularly, ensuring that she was being properly cared for, and he made a point of maintaining close contact with the men of Hereward's gang. He generally sat among them at meal times, claiming they were the most interesting group among the diners. Edric, though, heard Siward White confide to his cousin that the other monks had little time for Brother John who, they suspected, served himself more than he served God.

Edric did not dare mention this to Brother John, but he did take the opportunity to raise the troubling subject of why young children died so often when they had committed no sin.

"Ah," Brother John sighed, "you would need to read the writings of the blessed Augustine of Hippo to answer that thorny question."

"I can't read," Edric told him.

"Then you have saved yourself some trouble," Brother John said in a low voice. "Augustine's works are very dull."

"But what does he say?" Edric pressed.

Brother John considered the question for a moment before saying, "Essentially, he asserts that each of us is born with the taint of original sin."

"So babies are born sinful?" Edric frowned. "That doesn't seem right to me."

Brother John fluttered a hand at him, urging silence.

"Keep those thoughts to yourself, my friend. Children are baptised in order to cleanse them of that sin. Yet men remain sinful and must seek to atone throughout their lives if they wish to be received into the kingdom of Heaven."

The monk put a finger to his mouth to indicate that Edric should remain silent. He leaned close, dropping his voice to a whisper.

"It would be best not to discuss such doubts as you have in this place, young Edric. Pelagius was excommunicated for expressing such heretical thoughts."

Edric had no idea who Pelagius might be, but he understood the warning. It was hardly the answer he had hoped for, but he took the monk's advice and kept his doubts to himself. He worried, though, that Aelswith's child might not be allowed baptism since its parents had not been married. If that happened, he knew, the child would never be permitted into Heaven. To Edric, that seemed a severe punishment for anyone to suffer. It was hardly the fault of the unborn child that Aelswith had caught Thane Toki's eye.

"Eat up," Brother John urged him. "The meals in this hall will revert to normal monkish fare once Easter is over."

Shaking off his glum mood, Edric took that advice too. He could not deny that the food was excellent. In addition to the usual fish and eels which were commonly eaten in the region, there were plates of roast goose and duck, dishes of eggs, boiled vegetables and selections of tiny pastries, along with mounds of freshly baked bread and pungent cheeses. He had never experienced food like it and succeeded in eating so much that he gave himself a severe bout of indigestion.

"That doesn't excuse you your duties," Siward White informed him with a wicked smile.

White was the acknowledged leader of their little band. He told the others that they must take turns to watch over Hereward and Torfrida.

"We are Hereward's men," he declared. "It is our duty to protect him."

"Protect him from what?" Ordgar wanted to know.

"From whatever might threaten him," Siward White responded.

The gang were now outfitted with byrnies of chainmail, although Edric and Winter could not find one to fit their bulky frames.

"There's a smithy in the town," White told them. "We'll have them make some new ones for you."

"I can't afford that," Edric admitted ruefully.

"We'll give him some of the swords and armour we captured in exchange," Siward White chuckled. "Go and see the master smith and place an order with him."

Edric had never seen his uncle manufacture a chainmail tunic, but he understood the process. It required the making of hundreds of small rings of metal which were individually stitched onto a leather undercoat so that the rings overlapped, providing strength while allowing the wearer to move without too much restriction. The armour was effective against swords, spears and arrows, especially when worn over a thick, padded undercoat of layered linen and wool. It could even reduce the impact of a battle-axe, although the victim would suffer broken bones if the axe was wielded with sufficient skill.

The problem with chainmail was the time it took to produce. Manufacturing the rings was delicate work, and attaching them to the leather coat individually took a great deal of patience and time. The Master Smith, though, encouraged by the sight of the swords and armour they offered, assured Edric and Winter that he could produce a byrnie for each of them within the month.

"I have lads making mail rings all the time," he informed them. "I'll get you measured up for size and we'll start making the coats immediately."

The smithy in Ely was much larger than the one Edric's uncle had worked. The master Smith had several assistants who were, he claimed, skilled at producing all sorts of implements, weapons and armour.

"Not that I object to adding to my stock with ready-made quality goods," he grinned as he examined the swords the two warriors had brought. "These are decent weapons. Are you sure you don't want to hang onto a couple for yourselves? They are worth more than the byrnies we will make for you."

Winter shook his head.

"My axe is all I need," he declared gruffly. "Swordplay takes years of practice."

Edric followed Winter's example. The truth was that he had been tempted to claim one of the swords for himself, but had decided against it because he still regarded the sword as the weapon of a nobleman. He had no wish to give anyone the impression that he had ideas above his station, so he emulated Winter and clung to his axe.

"You promised to teach me how to use it properly," he reminded the axeman.

"You've got the basic idea," Winter assured him. "You've also got the strength. What you need now is to develop your speed. It's a matter of practising every day."

Winter proved to be a good teacher, spending a great deal of time sparring with Edric and passing on advice. He showed Edric how to keep the blade oiled and sharp, and took him to a saddler's shop in the town where they exchanged some pilfered food for a set of leather slings on a strap which allowed Edric to hang the axe over his back.

"That'll save you carrying it all the time," Winter grinned.

Despite this new arrangement, Edric found that he still needed to carry his axe for much of the time. When he was not practising with Winter, he was one of the two men who always accompanied Hereward, or was posted on guard duty outside Torfrida's room. On those occasions, he sometimes managed to see Aelswith, who would emerge from her room to speak to him.

He cherished those moments, pleased to discover that he was now less shy in her company since she seemed happy to talk to him.

"They are very kind here," she explained. "The monks bring us food and that Brother Richard even came to make sure I was well. He's going to have one of the town's midwives visit me as well."

"I'm glad they are taking care of you," Edric told her.

"The Lady Torfrida is very kind and generous," Aelswith said. "She had this new gown made for me."

Edric had noticed the new dress. It was a sombre, dark blue in colour, with no frills or patterns, but it was clean and new, with no frayed edges, and it was broad enough to cover her rounded figure without appearing too tight. She also wore a new, white apron over the dress; another gift from Torfrida.

Edric's own garments were the ones he had worn in Bourne. They had been washed and patched, but he felt ragged next to Aelswith, although she was too preoccupied with her own new clothes to notice his shabby tunic and trousers.

"This dress is nice," she pouted, "but it's a bit shapeless. I wish the child would come soon. I am fed up of waddling around like a fat goose."

"How long will it be?" Edric asked.

"Another month at least," she sighed. "Maybe a bit longer."

"Then you should enjoy taking the time to rest," he suggested.

"Do you like it here, Edric?" she asked unexpectedly.

"Yes, I do. It's better than slaving away in the smithy all day."

"Even though you might need to fight the Normans?"

"There are no Normans here," he assured her.

That was what everyone said. The Normans could not reach Ely because of the surrounding marshes. Boats could sail upriver from the sea, but the navigable route was difficult and treacherous. Besides which, the boats could not bring enough men to storm the island. A large raiding party was the most the islanders needed to fear, and Siward Barn, the old warhorse, had made sure that all landing places were well defended.

All of which made Edric content, yet he soon detected that there was an unsettling tension in the air. Once Easter was over and life at the abbey had returned to something that passed for normal, Hereward and Siward Barn held conversations behind closed doors, while Torfrida and Hereward were often heard arguing in their room.

Edric was not the only one who noticed.

"What's going on?" Auti asked Siward White one evening when a few of the men were sitting in their dormitory.

White gave a slight shrug.

"I think Torfrida wants Hereward to keep his promise to leave England and find a refuge somewhere else."

Edric's heart sank when he heard that.

"Isn't this place as safe as anywhere?" he asked.

"As safe as anywhere in England," White agreed. "But Hereward promised he would leave once he'd taken his revenge on de Taillebois."

"Which he hasn't done yet," Red put in dourly.

"That's the problem," White agreed.

"The Lady still wants to leave?" Edric persisted.

White gave another shrug.

"Martin would know the details, but he's a close-mouthed old bugger. But yes, I reckon she does."

"But Hereward doesn't?" Edric guessed.

"He's quite mad, of course," White grinned. "He knows he's missed his chance of killing de Taillebois, so he might as well flee. His presence here brings danger for everyone on the island. You know what the Normans are like. When they eventually get round to coming after him, they won't spare anyone who has given him shelter."

Edric had not considered that outcome, and the thought worried him.

"So why does he want to stay?" he asked.

"Because he dreams of a free England," White replied.

Winter gave a snort of derision, but Wulfric said, "Others share that dream. Another dozen men arrived on the island this afternoon. They came to join Hereward's army, so they said."

"Then they'll be mightily pissed off if he leaves," Winter grunted.

"Them and all the others who have come over the past few days," Wulfric agreed. "I reckon well over a hundred have turned up since we got here. Word of what we did in Bourne is spreading, and men are coming to join the rebellion."

"There is no rebellion yet," White pointed out.

Edric had another question. He had not realised so many men had come to Ely in search of Hereward.

"Where are they all?" he asked. "I haven't seen any of them around here."

"Siward Barn's men have taken them in hand," White explained.

"But they came to join Hereward!" Edric protested.

"Barn is the senior Thane," White shrugged. "That's another thing which is causing some friction. He wants to sit tight and hope the Normans ignore us. Hereward wants to take the war to them."

"Now that sounds like a plan!" Winter growled cheerfully.

"Not much of one," White countered. "A few hundred of us can't defeat The Bastard's army."

Edric declared, "We should still fight them. We can attack them and then come back here where they can't follow us."

"I suspect that's what Hereward is thinking," White nodded. "But it won't be enough to overthrow The Bastard. We'd need a full rebellion for that."

"Perhaps that is what he is planning," Edric persisted, unwilling to admit to himself that Hereward might give up the fight.

"He hasn't confided in me," White admitted. "But you may be right. There are still some English earls who might join us."

"Edwin and Morcar?" Red scoffed derisively. "They've already rebelled twice, and both times they've surrendered as soon as The Bastard brought his army against them. I'm surprised he hasn't had them executed."

"They still command the *fyrd* of the North," White argued. "If Hereward led the army, we might have a chance of winning."

"And then what?" his cousin challenged. "Who would be King if we get rid of The Bastard?"

"Edgar the Atheling is in exile in Scotland," White replied.

"He's a boy!" Red spat. "And he's another bloody foreigner. He hadn't set foot in England until last year."

"He's the grandson of Edmund Ironside," White said calmly. "He's descended from King Ethelred. But it's up to the Witan to elect a new King. They might choose another nobleman."

Edric, to whom most of the names the two Siwards had mentioned meant very little, became suddenly interested, and blurted, "You mean Hereward?"

White laughed, "No, lad. Hereward is only a Thane's son, so there is no way the Witan would elect him."

"We could do a lot worse, though," Winter muttered.

"But, whatever happens, he'll stay in England?" Edric asked.

"I don't know, lad," White said gravely. "Siward Barn and Abbot Thurstan don't want a full scale war. But they have no long term plan except to hide among the marshes and hope The Bastard forgets about them. That's not much of a strategy either, if you ask me."

Red ventured, "If his wife wants him to leave, I reckon he'll go."

"And if he does?" Edric asked. "What happens to us?"

"That, my lad, is up to each of us to decide. We either go with him and take our chances of finding a new life across the sea, or we stay here and pray the Normans leave us in peace."

The conversation about the uncertain future unsettled Edric. He tried to chat to Winter about it, but the big axeman's attitude was that he was happy to go along with whatever Hereward decided.

For Edric, the thought of leaving England had never crossed his mind before then. Departing from Bourne had been an easy decision, but leaving the country was another matter entirely. Yet the future looked bleak if they were to stay.

He wished he could talk to Brother John, who had seen so much more of the world, but the young monk had gone on his way as soon as the Easter celebrations had ended. He had taken his pack, climbed aboard one of the small fishing boats, and set off on the next stage of his never-ending journey.

His departure had left Edric feeling a little deflated, and he noticed that Aelswith, too, missed the young monk's cheery presence.

"He is a kind man," she told Edric. "I hope he comes back soon."

"Me too," Edric agreed.

He hoped Brother John's leaving did not herald further departures. He had wanted nothing more than to be an accepted member of Hereward's gang, but now the prospect of that small group being dissolved left him feeling anxious about the future.

His glum mood persisted throughout the following day, and he spent most of the evening meal snatching glances at the top table in vain attempts to glean some indication of Hereward's intentions. The young Lord, though, gave nothing away. He engaged Abbot Thurstan and Siward Barn in conversation which appeared friendly enough, but Edric could not discern what it might mean for his future.

What would he do if Hereward decided to leave?

He did not know.

Then he heard the sound of hurried footsteps as the door of the refectory hall burst open and a flustered monk came hurrying in, skirting round the tables to the Abbot. When he reached Thurstan, he leaned down, his cheeks bright red as he whispered an urgent message into the Abbot's ear.

Old Thurstan sat up, the candlelight revealing a trace of alarm on his wrinkled face.

Everyone was watching him, knowing from his reaction that something dramatic had happened. Edric wondered whether the Normans had, after all, managed to send an army through the Fens.

Every man fell silent as Thurstan held up a hand and announced, "My brothers, we have a visitor. An emissary has come here from King Sweyn of Denmark. He has requested a public audience."

"The Danes are here!" gasped Winter, excitement flaring in his eyes.

Other men took up the cry, and everyone turned their necks to stare at the door.

Siward Barn suggested, "It would be better to speak to the man in private, Lord Abbot."

Hereward immediately countered, "If what he has to say is important, it is better everyone hears it from his own lips."

Thurstan hesitated, then nodded his consent.

"Show him in," he ordered the monk who had brought the message.

The man scurried out again, returning a few moments later with three men striding behind him. Two of them were huge, their bare arms rippling with muscles and decorated by arm rings of

143

copper and silver. They wore their hair long, and each of them carried a sword at his hip. Edric found their size impressive, but he realised they were only there to impress, for it was the third man, the one who wore a jerkin of leather over a white, linen shirt, with trousers of supple leather and sturdy calfskin boots, all topped by a fine cloak of dark blue wool, who was clearly the emissary.

His fair hair and beard were neatly combed, his fingers bedecked by rings, his expression almost haughty as he strode towards the top table, looking neither to left nor right. When he faced the Abbot, he gave a slight bow of his head while he clamped his left hand on the jewelled hilt of a sword which he bore at his left hip.

"My name is Ranald Sigtrygsson," he announced in a strong, confident voice. "I have come here at the command of my Lord, King Sweyn Estrithsson. He has come to England and wishes to know if there are any men here who would help him claim the throne from William, Duke of Normandy."

The hall erupted in a burst of acclamation as the warriors rose to their feet and shouted their approval. They stamped their feet, slammed their palms on the table and beat a rhythm that spoke of war. Even Edric, who had been raised to fear the Danish raiders who constantly harried the coastal towns and villages, was on his feet and grinning like an idiot. The excitement gripped some of the monks as well, with several standing and voicing their support.

Abbot Thurstan raised his hands, calling for calm.

When the noise subsided, he asked Sigtrygsson, "Is King Sweyn near here, then?"

"His fleet lies a little way up the coast," the emissary confirmed.

Siward Barn, his lined face serious, asked, "How many men does he have?"

"Enough," Ranald Sigtrygsson replied arrogantly. Then, seeing Siward Barn's expression darken, he added, "He has more than seventy ships."

"Around two thousand men, then?" Siward Barn asked.

Sigtrygsson nodded, "About that number."

"It's not enough!" Siward Barn declared.

"King Sweyn had hoped to find Englishmen who would join him," the emissary shot back. "Perhaps I have come to the wrong place. I had heard there were men here who opposed The Bastard."

Siward Barn scowled, some of the warriors called out that they were ready to help the Danish King, but Abbot Thurstan turned to Hereward, who had remained silent until then.

"What do you say, Hereward?" he asked.

Slowly, Hereward rose to his feet. With deliberate precision, he raised his right hand and pointed a finger directly at Ranald Sigtrygsson.

In a loud, sonorous voice, he announced, "I know this man. He is a liar. He cannot be trusted. We should give him a thrashing and then throw him out like a dog."

Edric could scarcely believe what he was hearing. For those few, brief moments when the Danish emissary had called for men to support King Sweyn, Edric had dared to believe that there was a way they could fight back against the Normans. Now, in four short sentences, Hereward had shattered those dreams.

The men around him clearly shared his shocked disbelief, for a deathly silence fell across the hall. The warriors had hoped that a Danish King had come to take the throne, just as Cnut the Great had done fifty years earlier. King Sweyn, a nephew of Cnut, at least had a valid, if distant, claim to the throne, and many Englishmen, particularly those who lived in the North and East, had Danish blood in their veins. They were the descendants of the Vikings who had overrun the old Saxon kingdoms, so a Danish King, while not ideal, was a better proposition than a French-speaking Norman.

But Hereward had named the emissary as a liar, so now the warriors and monks looked on in silence as they waited to see how the Dane would react.

Ranald Sigtrygsson stared at Hereward, his eyes hard, his jaw clenched tightly as he fought to maintain his temper in the face of the accusation that had been made against him.

He tilted his chin upwards in a signal of defiance and said, "And you, little man, are a braggart who dare not face a real man in a fair fight."

This brought an angry growl of protest from Hereward's men, and sharp intakes of breath from many others. Hereward silenced all protest by raising an arm and then stepping up onto the table. In one bound, he leaped down to confront Sigtrygsson.

The two men faced one another in grim silence. Edric found he was holding his breath. He had to force himself to gulp in air as he watched, knowing the only possible outcome to such exchanges of harsh words was a duel. He had never seen Hereward fight, although he had heard Winter and the others speak in awe of the young Lord's prowess, but Hereward, while broader in the chest and shoulders than the Dane, was shorter by half a head. Sigtrygsson was lean and tough-looking, and would have the greater reach.

Then, when everyone was expecting a challenge to be made, both men burst out laughing and stepped towards one another, flinging their arms around each other in a fierce embrace.

"I thought you were in Ireland!" Hereward exclaimed when they broke apart.

"I was," Sigtrygsson replied. "But I heard that my father had died, so I sailed back to Denmark to claim my inheritance. Unfortunately, by the time I got there, my brothers had divided everything among themselves and were not inclined to share. So I went to the King. He forced them to pay me my share of the inheritance, and then asked me to join his service, which I did gladly."

"So he really has come to take the throne of England?" Hereward asked.

"If he finds enough support," Sigtrygsson agreed.

Hereward grinned. Then, aware that everyone was staring at the two of them in disbelief, he announced, "This is my good friend, Ranald Sigtrygsson. I ask that you make him welcome among us."

Now there was laughter and more thumping of hands on the tables as the grand jest was applauded. Room was made for Sigtrygsson and his two companions, more food was called for, and the two young Lords engaged in reminiscences which everyone strained to overhear.

Edric and the rest of Hereward's gang were sitting at the next table, so were able to listen to the conversation without difficulty.

"How is your wife?" Hereward asked Ranald.

"She's as fat as three women now," the Dane laughed genially. "We have two fine sons and a daughter. They are still in Ireland."

Abbot Thurstan asked, "How is it that you know each other?"

Ranald took a slurp of ale before replying, "We met some years ago in Cornwall. I was attempting to free the daughter of a King who had been taken captive by a giant who had killed her father and seized the kingdom."

"A giant?" the Abbot asked doubtfully.

"A monstrously big man," Ranald confirmed. "Hereward agreed to help me fight him since the giant was twice as tall as a normal man and had killed everyone who ever challenged him."

"He wasn't that tall," Hereward interrupted. "I measured out the grave we buried him in. He was a little over seven feet tall."

Ranald sighed, "My friend, you never did learn how to tell a story properly, did you?"

"Seven feet is still a prodigious height," Abbot Thurstan commented.

"Indeed it is," Ranald agreed. "But Hereward soon cut him down to size. My Princess was rescued and, in order to repay the favour, I found a sea captain who agreed to take Hereward to Denmark."

"Denmark?" Thurstan asked. "I didn't know you had been there."

Hereward gave a shrug.

"I never got that far," he said. "The boat was caught in a storm and we were shipwrecked. Only a few survivors managed to struggle ashore. We found ourselves in Flanders, where I took service with the Count. I never did get to Denmark."

"But now," Ranald stated, "Denmark has come to you. King Sweyn has heard of your exploits and seeks your support."

"He has it!" Hereward declared.

At this, Siward Barn put in, "We still do not have enough men to defeat The Bastard."

"We will when others come to join King Sweyn," Hereward shot back.

Abbot Thurstan, caught between the two noblemen, wore a miserable expression.

He said, "I do not deny that a Danish King would be more welcome than a Norman one. King William is a harsh ruler, and a greedy one. But can he really be defeated? We are safe here where he cannot reach us."

"He will reach us eventually," Hereward retorted. "The Fens are a great barrier, and Ely is a safe refuge, but sitting here does us little good. The Bastard has all the wealth of the rest of England to sustain him and his army. If we wish to defeat him, we must march against him."

"We do not have enough men," Siward Barn reiterated dourly.

"Not yet," Hereward conceded. "But if we make attacks on the local Normans, other men will join us. We have a chance to light the flame of resistance."

His words brought a loud cheer from the men of his gang. Even some of Siward Barn's warriors thumped their hands on the table to indicate their approval.

Barn, realising he had lost the argument, lapsed into a sullen silence. Edric, watching from the next table, guessed that the two men had exchanged words over the matter on more than one occasion. Now, for the first time, Hereward had won the argument.

"Tomorrow," he declared to more applause, "We shall go and speak to King Sweyn."

The following morning, a delegation from Ely which included Hereward's gang boarded the longship which had brought Ranald Sigtrygsson to Ely. It was a long, sleek, shallow-draughted vessel which could cross oceans yet was also capable of rowing up any river which was more than a few feet deep, allowing the Danes to travel far inland along the many waterways of England.

The crew, wild-haired men with arms that were heavily muscled from years of rowing, propelled the ship downstream towards the sea with practised ease. They travelled slowly, for the river wound its way between high stands of reeds, and there were many mudbanks which could ensnare them. The steersman, a tall, fair-haired man with keen eyes, guided them expertly, while the rowers moved to and fro in a steady, almost hypnotic rhythm.

Hereward stood at the stern alongside Ranald Sigtrygsson, both of them in fine good humour, like young boys setting off on an adventure. Standing a little apart was old Siward Barn, dressed in his war gear but regarding his surroundings with grim distaste.

"Why has he come?" Edric asked Siward White.

"Because he needs to meet the Danish king," White replied. "Old Barn is no coward, lad, but he's been beaten by the Normans before, and he's naturally cautious. But to sit at home when a king calls for him would not be a sensible thing to do."

Edric nodded his understanding, glancing at the handful of warriors of Barn's guard who had accompanied the veteran Thane. Those men were keen to fight, yet subdued because they were pledged to their lord who disapproved of Hereward's rashness.

"He's a tired old man," White opined. "You can't really blame him, but he won't be able to turn his back on King Sweyn, and he knows it."

Edric had no desire to become embroiled in the politics of the matter. The affairs of kings and thanes were too lofty for a mere blacksmith's apprentice who had only recently taken up arms. Besides which, this voyage was an adventure for him as well. He had never been on a boat before. He kept looking around, fascinated by the longship and its crew, scarcely able to believe what he was experiencing. Everything seemed wonderful to him, from the creak of the oars to the gentle splashes as the long, wooden blades powered the sleek vessel down the river; from the tall mast with its broad, woollen sail which was now furled because there was no wind to speak of, to the impressive array of swords, axes and shields each crewman had close at hand.

Then there was the river itself, dark and menacing, yet now transformed into a roadway for the sailors. The reeds stood tall on either bank, herons flapped away as the boat approached, and Edric was entranced by it all.

"This is wonderful!" he whispered to Winter.

The big axeman snorted, "Give me dry land any day. The sea is a dangerous place."

"We are not on the sea," Edric told him. "This is a river."

"It's still water. It can drown you easily enough."

Auti laughed, "Winter can't swim. That's his problem."

"I can't swim either," Edric admitted.

"Then pray the boat doesn't fall apart under our feet," grumbled Winter.

The Danish ship did not fall apart. It delivered them to the mouth of the river and took them along the coast a short way to where dozens of other boats bobbed on the gentle waves like basking seals, and yet more ships lay beached on a long, sandy shoreline. Edric had not believed there could be so many ships in the entire world, let alone gathered here on the coast of England. He gaped in open-mouthed astonishment as their own vessel slowly edged between other dragon-headed longships.

"It's an impressive sight," Winter conceded grudgingly.

"King Sweyn's fleet!" Ranald Sigtrygsson announced unnecessarily.

Their boat coursed through the lapping waves and ground onto the sand. Then Ranald led Hereward, Siward Barn and their men to a spot near the hinterland where King Sweyn had made camp.

"Sweyn is a Dane but he was born in England," Siward White had informed the members of the gang. "He's a nephew of Cnut the Great, so show him proper respect."

Edric did his best to look like a veteran warrior as he ploughed his way across the beach with the others. Although he had seen King Harold on the long march north to the battle at Stamford Bridge, he had never really been close enough to the English King to see him properly. Now he came virtually face to face with the King of Denmark who sat beneath a wide awning, surrounded by his nobles and personal guards.

Sweyn, fifty years old, with greying hair and beard, was dressed in a shining coat of chainmail and bore a sword with a jewelled pommel. Another bright garnet stone gleamed at his throat, and he wore a gold ring on each of his fingers.

The nobles who clustered around him were equally finely dressed, their expressions welcoming, although the warriors who were tasked with protecting the king glowered suspiciously at Hereward and his men when they gathered in front of the monarch.

Grinning proudly, Ranald made the introductions, then King Sweyn called for ale to be served while he spoke to Hereward and Siward Barn.

The older man bowed his head in deference to the king, who congratulated him on keeping Ely safe from the Normans.

"I wanted to keep one part of England free," Barn replied gruffly.

150

"And you have done well," the king smiled. Then, turning to Hereward, he said, "As have you. I hear you have struck a significant blow against the Bastard."

"We killed a few Normans and ran off their Sheriff," Hereward confirmed modestly.

"It is a beginning," Sweyn nodded. "So tell me, what will it take if I wish to return England to the control of a Danish King?"

"More men than we have," Barn murmured.

The king frowned, but Hereward hurriedly put in, "We will find more men if we strike another blow. We must make an attack on an important site. We must let the entire nation know that we intend to oppose The Bastard. Then we should return to Ely where it will be difficult for the Normans to follow us. Their strength is in cavalry, but horses are no use in the marshes."

"I do not intend to become King of a marshland," Sweyn stated.

"That would be only a beginning, Lord King," Hereward assured him. "Ely would serve as our base, as well as acting as bait for The Bastard. If we defy him, he will have no option but to attempt to destroy us, but the terrain would be in our favour."

"So you suggest luring William into a trap?" Sweyn asked pointedly.

"That is exactly what I am proposing," Hereward agreed.

"Do you really think we can win? I can bring two thousand of my finest warriors but, as Siward Barn has pointed out, William can muster five times that number."

"Many Englishmen are coming to join us already," Hereward informed him. "When we make a dramatic strike against the Normans, others will come. But numbers are not everything. In the Fens, we can operate more easily than the Normans. We can wear them down until the time is right to destroy them."

"That may take a long time," Sweyn observed cautiously.

"Not if we undertake a raid that is so dramatic The Bastard dare not ignore it."

"I take it you have something in mind?" the King asked with a thin smile.

Hereward nodded, "From what I hear of The Bastard, he is a greedy, venal man. He prizes wealth above all else. The best way to hurt him is to steal some of his hoarded riches."

"And how do you propose we do that?" Sweyn enquired.

151

Hereward replied, "Much of the wealth of England is placed in churches. There is an abbey near here which contains vast quantities of holy relics, jewels and gold. Some of it once belonged to English families who placed it there for safe-keeping, some belongs to the Church, but most has been stolen by the Normans and taken there to add to their hoard."

"And you propose we should liberate this treasure?" Sweyn smiled, obviously tempted by the idea.

"Indeed I do," Hereward confirmed.

"Where is this place?" the King asked.

Edric knew the answer before Hereward gave it. There was only one abbey that matched the description he had given.

Hereward said, "Peterborough."

Chapter 9

Altruda was woken by the panicked shouting from outside her door and the thumping of fists on the thick oak.

"My Lady! Wake up! There is a fire!"

She hurriedly slipped from beneath the blankets and donned a robe before moving quickly to the door and unlocking it.

A short, plump, middle-aged monk stood there, his stance screaming anxiety and agitation, while his features displayed his intense relief that he had succeeded in waking her.

"A fire?" she asked.

"At the gates," the flustered cleric confirmed. "It is spreading all along the wall on the town side."

Even as he spoke, a sonorous bell began to ring, its booming urgency sounding the alarm.

Altruda frowned. The abbey's precinct was surrounded by a high, wooden wall, but many houses in the town backed onto the perimeter, as did the long building in which her room was located. If a fire had started in one of the houses outside the wall, it could easily spread to the abbey's buildings.

"What time is it?" she asked as she peered at a window behind the monk. As far as she could tell, the outside world was still wreathed in darkness.

"Nearly dawn," he told her before adding urgently, "Please, my Lady, leave your room and go to the abbey itself. It is made of stone and will keep you safe."

Altruda hesitated, wondering whether she should take the time to gather up some of her personal belongings, but she knew fire could spread quickly, so she grabbed up her cloak, wrapped it around her shoulders, and hastily followed the monk outside.

"The Sheriff is organising a bucket chain," the monk informed her as he held up a candle to light her way along the corridor and out into the courtyard.

The sun was beginning to lighten the sky as she stepped outside, allowing her to make out some shadowy details. Looking to her left, she was able to see a pillar of dark, oily smoke rising from the far side of the tall gates, and she could hear the crackle of flames from beyond the high wall even above the constant clamour of the church bell. A flickering glow of orange light told her that

153

the blaze was on the other side of the gates. That struck her as odd, because it suggested that the gates themselves had not fully caught fire. Yet flames were now licking through the thick timbers, so it would not be long before the blaze burned its way through.

"The abbey!" the monk urged her, tugging at her arm.

"I can find my way, thank you," she assured him as she gently shook off his grasp.

The monk flushed at her reproof, but bobbed his head in relief.

"I must help bring people out of the infirmary," he told her as he bustled away.

Altruda stood outside the building which housed the guest chambers. She had moved there after Easter, telling Abbot Turold that she required some privacy, and pointing out that it might not be wise for her to be seen to be sharing his bed every night.

"You are, after all, a man of God," she reminded him. "And we are not man and wife."

Nor ever will be, she privately added to herself.

Turold had not been pleased, but he had reluctantly agreed that she could move into one of the guest rooms which the abbey maintained for visiting dignitaries. That had been two weeks ago, she reflected. The Abbot was away on another of his excursions intended to track down the infamous Hereward, and she expected he would be as unsuccessful this time as on the two previous occasions when he had taken a patrol of mounted knights out into the countryside after receiving news of a rebel attack on a Norman garrison.

She had, she remembered with distaste, agreed to spend another night with Turold when he returned from his latest venture into the woods and marshes. That was not a prospect which held any great comfort for her, but she knew she must keep the Abbot on her side.

Idly, she wondered whether he might be too busy repairing his abbey to pester her. That was probably too much to hope for, but the fire seemed intent on causing a considerable amount of damage unless the monks and soldiers could bring it under control. So far, that appeared unlikely.

Around twenty men of the garrison, roused from sleep, were attempting to douse the inner sides of the burning gates with buckets of water which they were hauling up from the well that stood in the centre of the courtyard, but it was a long, slow process, and they had few buckets, so the water they were using to combat the flames which were licking through the timbers appeared to make little difference.

Other men were leading horses out of the stables and taking them to the far side of the courtyard. The horses, sensing the men's nervousness, snorted and whinnied skittishly as they were led to safety.

Off to Altruda's right, monks were carrying invalids out of the infirmary and struggling, bent-backed, to carry them to the safety of the stone-built abbey.

Altruda permitted herself a sly smile. It was called an abbey but it was, in truth, a small and rather insignificant church, with tiny windows and a round tower in the style of the Saxons. Turold, she knew, had plans to replace it with a much larger building which would be truly worthy of being called an abbey. Perhaps the fire would speed that process along, especially if it destroyed the houses which backed onto the abbey precinct. That would clear more space and allow Turold to indulge his ambitions for a vastly expanded abbey.

"My Lady!"

The shout jerked Altruda from her detachment. She looked across the courtyard to the doors of the church, where she saw Ivo de Taillebois, fat and grim-looking as ever. He was standing outside the church building, beckoning her over to him.

"In here!" he called.

Altruda began walking over to him, taking her time since the fire was nowhere near her and looked unlikely to reach anywhere close to her. The buildings along the outer perimeter of the abbey precinct might catch fire, but there was a wide, open space between those buildings and the abbey itself. She crossed that space now, following one of the paths of stone which criss-crossed the hard earth of the yard like shiny ribbons.

"What started it?" she asked de Taillebois when she reached him.

He gave a shrug as he replied, "I have no idea. Perhaps one of the peasants knocked over a candle. Some of the houses are on fire. It seems to have spread to our gates."

Altruda could see that the men with the buckets were fighting a losing battle against the flames which were now licking through the ancient timbers and climbing high around the gate posts.

"It appears the Abbot will need to pay for new gates," she observed lightly.

"He'll need to pay for a lot more than that if we don't put the fire out," de Taillebois scowled.

"Perhaps your men could get water more quickly from the river," Altruda suggested.

Following the line of her gaze, de Taillebois looked across to the far side of the precinct. Some sixty paces on the opposite side of the courtyard was another, smaller, set of gates which led out to the river bank. He nodded, marched to the well where two men were frantically hauling another bucket up from the depths, and began shouting orders, telling them to fetch water from the river.

Soldiers ran to obey. They sprinted across to the river entrance, lifted the locking bar and hauled the heavy gates open. Altruda watched them run outside, then blinked in surprise when she saw them come hurtling back only moments later. Frantically, they began struggling to heave the wooden doors shut once again.

"What are you doing?" Ivo de Taillebois roared at them.

One man turned, his face ashen with near panic.

"Northmen!" he shouted, his panicked cry cutting across the clamour in the yard. "There are longships coming up the river!"

Ivo de Taillebois gaped, his mouth hanging open in dumb surprise.

Altruda shook her head in disgust. The man was a fat fool, boastful and arrogant, and with little intellect. It was no wonder Abbot Turold despised him. For all his faults, Turold was at least a decisive leader. He might use fear and brutality as his preferred methods of imposing his will, but at least he did not stand around gawping like an idiot when decisions were needed.

Like the Abbot, Altruda had come to despise Ivo de Taillebois. Her scorn was fuelled by what the Abbot had told her of the Sheriff.

"He'll probably tell you how he was wounded at Hastings," the Abbot had warned her. "The story gathers embellishments each time he tells it. The truth is he was forced to join a charge much against his will. When he got near the English

156

line, he panicked, pulled too hard on the reins and his horse fell. He broke his arm in the fall and took no further part in the battle."

Altruda had laughed, "Are you serious, Lord Abbot?"

"I heard it from someone who was close by," Turold had confirmed. "De Taillebois is no soldier. He's just a jumped up cook."

"A cook?" Altruda had asked in wonderment.

Turold had smirked, "His father was a cook at the Duke's castle in Normandy. As I heard the story, de Taillebois was supposed to follow the trade, but he was a lazy boy, good for very little. But, one day when he was skulking away somewhere in order to avoid doing any work, he overheard two men discussing a plot to assassinate the young Duke."

"The Duke? You mean King William?"

"Yes. He had many enemies when he was younger. When he became Duke of Normandy, many people thought he would not last long. But he proved them all wrong, thanks to the grace of God."

"And de Taillebois helped foil a plot against him?"

"That's right. The boy's laziness served Duke William well. De Taillebois went to William with the tale of what he had overheard, the two men were seized, and de Taillebois was elevated to the rank of squire as a reward for his loyalty."

"So he is a favourite of the King?" Altruda had asked.

Turold had pulled a sour face as he answered, "King William grants him small favours, like the position as Sheriff, but he allows him little real power. Ivo is a useful idiot, but that's about as far as it goes. The King remains grateful to him for saving his life, but he has no real liking for the man."

Now, as she watched de Taillebois stand indecisively in the centre of the yard, Altruda could understand why de Taillebois was so derided by his fellow nobles. Despite the fear she could feel mounting inside her at the thought of Viking raiders coming to ransack the abbey, she almost laughed when the Sheriff turned his helpless gaze on her as if he were beseeching her for advice.

"To arms?" she suggested. "The Danes still need to break down the gates if they are to gain access to the abbey."

De Taillebois nodded, shaking off his indecision and shouting at his men to arm themselves. Some had already anticipated the command, running to their barracks to don armour and grab swords and shields. The task of tackling the burning gates on the town side was abandoned as fear of the Northmen spurred the soldiers into action.

Altruda was already devising her own plans.

"If they do manage to break through, we can barricade ourselves inside the church," she suggested.

"Yes!" de Taillebois agreed eagerly.

His left hand clutched at the hilt of his sword, his fingers clenching and unclenching nervously. He had no chainmail himself, having abandoned his armour when he had fled from his burning castle, but Altruda doubted whether he would have led the fight even if he had been wearing a byrnie.

Soon, his soldiers were rushing back out from the barracks, hastening to form a line inside the River Gate. One climbed to the top of the wall to gaze out at the river.

"Ten ships at least!" he called. "There may be more behind them!"

"Three or perhaps four hundred men," Altruda informed de Taillebois. "How many do you have?"

With a resigned wave of his hand, he indicated the small group of men who were hastily forming up in the courtyard.

"Thirty," he breathed, his voice betraying his fear.

Altruda began to share his anxiety. Three hundred men would take time to breach the thick wall of the abbey, but it was not a defensive rampart like a castle, merely a stout boundary. If the Danes broke through, their only hope was to bar the doors of the abbey itself and pray that they could hold out. But that course of action could easily see them trapped.

Altruda had no illusions about her fate should she be captured by the Danish warriors. She would be spared her life, but rape and captivity were ordeals she had no wish to experience.

"Is there any other way out of the precinct?" she asked de Taillebois, who was fidgeting with his sword and jumping from one foot to the other in his nervousness.

He looked at her blankly for a moment, then nodded, "There is another gate! At the far end of the church building."

Altruda nodded. Abbeys had been prime targets for raiders for generations, so the monks often provided themselves with an escape route.

"Will the Danes find it?" she asked him.

"It's a small door in the wall," he informed her. "I think it is screened by some trees on the outside."

"Then we have no need to panic just yet," she told him.

As if in agreement, the tolling bell ceased its ringing.

"That is a blessed relief!" Altruda sighed as the last echoes faded.

And then, almost as if the ceasing of the bell had been a signal, the gates on the town side finally succumbed to the flames and collapsed in a roar of fire and smoke, scattering fragments of timber and sending gouts of sparks dancing into the morning sky.

Everyone turned to look, many of them seeing a possible route to safety, but their hopes were immediately dashed when armed men leaped in through the blazing gap and began to form a shield wall as they created a bridgehead for the surge of men who followed them.

Altruda felt her stomach lurch. Now she understood why the fire had appeared to have started outside the gates. The raiders must have stacked wood and oil against the gate and set it alight. Fanned by the gentle breeze from the west, the fire had spread along the wall to the houses outside the abbey, but the fire had accomplished its main purpose, because the gates had crumbled and the raiders were now bursting through the fiery gap.

Then Altruda received another shock when she recognised one of the leading raiders.

"Hereward!" she gasped, her hand going to her mouth as her breath caught in her throat.

It was him! She recognised him immediately, even though he wore armour and an iron-bound helmet. He carried a shield painted with the image of a boar and a bear, and he wielded a shining sword in his right hand.

"It's him!" de Taillebois quailed.

The Norman soldiers in the courtyard were caught between the twin dangers of Hereward's English shield wall which was growing by the second, and the potential threat from the Danish ships approaching the River Gate, but the Englishmen were the immediate threat and defeating them gave the Normans the option of fleeing into the town before the Danes could breach the opposite wall.

"At them!" yelled one of the Normans, a senior veteran who had assumed control in the absence of any leadership from de Taillebois.

The Sheriff was appalled by the sight of men streaming in through the collapsed gates. They kicked smouldering chunks of wood aside, hefted their weapons and began to advance into the courtyard. There were several men in chainmail in the front rank, but others wearing only plain tunics or leather hauberks coming behind them. But there were not very many of them, perhaps twenty in all. They had gained a surprise, but they were outnumbered by the Normans who, if they could react quickly enough, could sweep them aside and open a route to safety.

"Kill them!" de Taillebois shouted, his voice high-pitched and frantic.

Altruda, watching in horrified fascination, nevertheless found a plan forming in her mind. There was so much happening so quickly, yet she was able to assimilate the fact of Hereward's presence and the simultaneous arrival of a Danish fleet. This was an opportunity she could not allow to pass, yet the course she needed to take was fraught with danger.

It was, though, the best plan she could devise at such short notice.

She seized de Taillebois's arm and hissed in his ear, giving rapid orders.

"Take me inside the church!" she commanded. "Pretend I am your prisoner!"

"What?" he gaped, unable to comprehend.

She heard the resounding clash as the Normans charged at the English raiders, heard the yells, the screams, and the harsh clang of metal on metal.

"Take me inside! Make it look as if you are dragging me against my will. Do it! Quickly."

She grabbed at his hand, placing it on her own arm, showing him what she needed him to do.

"Now!" she snapped, kicking his leg to encourage him.

De Taillebois was breathing rapidly, his eyes were wide with fear, but he eventually grasped her intent and made for the doors of the church building, pulling her behind him.

Altruda turned her head, waving her hand and pretending to struggle as she screamed, "Hereward! Save me!"

160

De Taillebois almost let her go until she hissed at him to continue the charade. She screamed again, caught a glimpse of Hereward's helmeted face in the shield wall and was satisfied that he had seen her.

"Inside! Quickly!" she told de Taillebois.

Then they were inside the church, with monks scurrying after them.

"Close the doors!" Altruda commanded.

"But there are brothers still outside!" one of the monks protested.

"Close the doors! Now! Altruda yelled. "The Danes are here for plunder, not to capture monks."

Ivo de Taillebois added his weight to her orders, screaming at the monks to close and bar the doors. They did so reluctantly, then hurried away. Some ran for the narrow doorway which led to the round, stone tower at the far end of the church, while others ducked into a low doorway which led outside and would take them to the abbey's hidden escape route.

"Wait!" Altruda told de Taillebois.

He turned, his breathing still fast and panicked, but she forced him to look at her.

"I want you to hit me," she told him. "Give me a black eye. Then get out of here."

The Sheriff blinked, uncomprehending, so she repeated her command.

"Hit me!" she hissed urgently as she raised her fingers to the side of her face. "Here! Make it good, because I don't want you to need to do it twice."

De Taillebois clenched his fist, but made no move.

"Why?" he frowned, not understanding.

"Because I want Hereward to believe I am here against my will. Now hurry! Hit me!"

Still de Taillebois hesitated, his gaze flicking uncertainly from her to the barred doors.

"Do it!" she told him furiously. "Hereward will be here soon."

That threat forced him into action. He took a deep breath, swung back his arm and then launched his fist at her face.

The blow was a good one, sending her staggering backwards to fall, sprawling, on the stone floor.

"My Lady?" De Taillebois gasped in a horrified voice.

Altruda shook her head, rubbing her hand against the throbbing pain beside her left eye. Her vision was blurred, tears of pain filling her eyes, but she was still in control of her other senses.

Looking up at the Sheriff, she barked, "Now get out! Tell the Abbot I will send messages when I can."

"Messages?" he frowned. "What do you mean?"

"I mean I am going to allow them to capture me. They will think me an ally. Now go!"

It was evident that de Taillebois had still not grasped the scale of her intentions, but he required no further invitation to escape danger. He turned and ran, bolting towards the church building's far door. From there, he could, with luck, sneak out of the far end of the precinct and be lost within the maze of the town's streets before the raiders located the hidden doorway.

Altruda watched him go, hoping she had made the right decision.

Yes, she resolved, this unexpected attack had presented her with an opportunity to complete the task King William had given her.

It was time to prepare herself.

She sat on the stone floor, nursing her bruised and swollen face. De Taillebois had at least performed that task adequately. For good measure, she twisted her cloak askew, then ripped the bodice of her dress before summoning tears so that her face would be streaked with pain and fear.

Then she waited.

For Hereward.

Chapter 10

It had taken some days to plan the raid on Peterborough. When he had heard what they were intending to do, Edric could scarcely believe it.

Hereward and his gang, accompanied by ten men from Siward Barn's war band, had taken four small, flat-bottomed fen boats to traverse the marshes. Ranald Sigtrygsson had also come with them, insisting that he wanted to fight alongside Hereward. He brought his two massive warriors with him, explaining that they had sworn to go wherever he went.

"Orm and Tostig will follow me even if I tell them to stay," he explained with his usual good humour. "And they are handy men in a fight."

Edric could well believe that. The two giant Vikings were even bigger than Winter, and looked as ferocious as any men Edric had ever seen.

Winter, although he would never have openly admitted it, was impressed by their new allies.

"It'll make a nice change to be fighting alongside Danes rather than against them," he grudgingly conceded.

The boats took them close to Peterborough, but they still needed to cross a wide tract of land on the last leg of the journey. To ensure that they were not detected, Hereward led them on a night trek, then found a small patch of woodland near the town where they could rest during the day.

"We'll go into the town tonight," he told the gang. "For now, stay quiet and rest while you can."

It was a long day, lying hidden in the woods. Hereward would not permit them to light fires, so they ate sparse meals from the provisions they had carried with them; hard boiled eggs, salted meat, cheese and dark bread.

Edric fidgeted nervously, feeling the need to pace up and down, but Winter ordered him to rest.

"The waiting is always the worst part," the axeman told him. "But stop fretting. You'll be fine when the action starts."

Hereward again displayed his leadership qualities by spending time talking to the men, making a special point of including Siward Barn's warriors in the discussions as he outlined the plan.

"Our role is to act as decoys," he told them. "King Sweyn's men will make the main attack, but it will take them time to break down the River Gate. We will give them that time by drawing the defenders away."

He went on to outline his plan, making sure each man understood the role he must play.

"Remember," he repeated several times, "our fight is not with the monks. I want none of them harmed. Nor should we injure any townsfolk. Our fight is against the Normans, and our main task is to relieve the Norman Abbot of the treasure he has hoarded. We will make better use of it."

"How many Normans will be in the abbey?" Edric asked him.

"Around thirty, I think. Abbot Turold is away and has half the garrison with him. He's running around the countryside chasing us, so I've heard."

That small joke brought a chuckle from the men lounging nearby, but Edric remained serious.

"But those who are left still outnumber us," he pointed out.

"True, but we have the element of surprise. Also, we need to give them the impression they can beat us. I want them to attack us."

"Why?"

"To allow the Danes to make the real attack without being observed," Hereward explained patiently.

Edric frowned as he said, "Yes, I understand that part. What I mean is, why don't we simply overwhelm the Normans with our attack, or even simply drive them out of the abbey? Why fight them at all?"

Siward White gave a soft chuckle as he said to Hereward, "I told you he was a thinker, Cousin."

Hereward regarded Edric with an intense look before saying, "We are at war. Our task is to kill the Normans. If we let them go, they will simply return in greater numbers. The more we can kill, the sooner England will be freed."

Edric could not help but hear the passion and conviction in Hereward's voice. It was so powerful it sent a chill down his spine. Still, he needed to ask another question.

"But why not let the Danes storm the abbey? There are a lot more of them than us."

"Because we must show that we are prepared to fight for our own country. King Sweyn seeks allies. We need to show him that we are prepared to fight alongside him."

Hereward stared into Edric's eyes for a long moment, then gave a wry smile as he added, "Finally, it is important that no monks are harmed. I know the Danes are Christians, but I also know how men behave when the bloodlust takes them. I want to be inside that compound before anyone else so that I can make sure nobody sheds the blood of a holy man."

Edric gave a nod to indicate his understanding, but he wondered whether Hereward's true reason might be that he was in search of glory. He confided his concern to Winter, who gave a soft laugh in response.

"Hereward already has all the glory he needs," he grinned. "No, lad, he just enjoys fighting."

Edric wondered how much that love of warfare had contributed to Hereward's decision to stay in England. Perhaps he was being unfair, but he knew that the Lady Torfrida had not been happy. The men who had stood guard outside her door had reported hearing loud arguments between her and Hereward, and Aelswith had confided to Edric that Torfrida was very upset by the change of plans.

"She wants to sail back to the continent," Aelswith had explained. "She says she will go anywhere else, but she doesn't want Hereward to die fighting for a lost cause."

"The cause isn't lost!" Edric had protested. "Not now that King Sweyn has come."

"That's what Hereward says," Aelswith had agreed. "The Danes have changed everything. And, deep down, I think the Lady knows Hereward will go to war wherever they end up, and that he will be miserable if he abandons the men who have come to join him."

She had smiled as she added, "Men like you, Edric."

It had been quite humbling to think that a Lord like Hereward, a Thane's son, might be concerned for someone as insignificant as Edric, yet he knew that Hereward was a man of contradictions. He might care for his men as individuals, yet he would not hesitate to place them in danger if it suited his plans.

It suited him now. As the day wore on and evening approached, Hereward went over the plan once again.

"Those of us with byrnies will go in first," he told them. We'll rush the gates as soon as they open them, then form a shield wall in the courtyard. I'll take the right flank. Ordgar and the two Siwards will be with me. Ranald, with Orm and Tostig, will guard the left flank. Those will be the most vulnerable places. If the Normans get round us, they will be able to surround us."

He did not need to explain the consequences should the Normans encircle them. Each man understood that would result in death for all of them. They also understood that, by placing himself on the right, Hereward would be in the place of greatest danger. Most men carried their shields on their left arm, leaving the right side exposed, so there was always a tendency for men in the battle line to slowly shift leftwards as they sought protection from their shield. The men on the right of the line needed to hold their position even though their right side was vulnerable to attack.

Continuing his explanation, Hereward jabbed a finger at Winter.

"You take charge of the men who don't have chainmail. Come in after us and gather behind the front line. You must support the armoured men. Fill any gaps and watch the flanks."

Winter growled, "I would prefer to fight in the front rank."

"I know," Hereward smiled. "But I need you to watch our backs. But don't fret. I expect there will be enough Normans to go around. You'll get your chance."

Then, to Edric's astonishment, Hereward looked directly at him and said, "You will act as Winter's second."

Edric blinked in amazement, and he heard a murmur from the other men.

One of Siward Barn's warriors, a thick-set, middle-aged man named Kenton who had a scarred cheek, grumbled, "Why would you give command to a boy?"

"Because I know my men, and he's best suited to the task," Hereward responded sharply. "Some of you may have more experience, but I've not fought alongside you before, so I appoint Edric to the task. Not that anything is going to happen to Winter, of course."

Winter grinned, "I might get bogged down and trapped among the bodies of all the Normans I'm going to kill."

166

Several men laughed at the boast, but Edric noticed that Kenton did not join in the amusement. Instead, he sat glowering at Winter and Edric, his lips moving as he muttered to himself.

Edric did not like the look of this man. He wore an old byrnie of chainmail which had some links missing, and his hair was unkempt, his moustache bushy and untamed. All of the men Siward Barn had allowed to come on this raid were tough-looking, violent men, but this man with the scarred cheek stood out even among that rough crowd. There was, Edric decided, something unsettling about the man's eyes. They seemed hard and cold, yet betrayed a hint of deviousness which Edric did not trust.

"Thane Barn has given us all the trouble-makers," Winter had confided to Edric when they had first met the warriors who would be joining them.

"Can we rely on them?" Edric had wondered.

"Oh, they'll fight all right," Winter had nodded. "I expect the problem will be keeping them in check."

Fortunately, it seemed Winter's fears were unfounded, for Hereward maintained strong discipline and made it plain that he would brook no disobedience. Not that Edric expected any real confrontation with the man named Kenton, for he would be in the front line because he had a byrnie, while Edric would be with Winter in the second rank. Still, the man's hostility was unsettling.

Having outlined his plan of battle, Hereward went on, "We know we are the best fighting men in England. Let's prove that. We must show the Danes how true Englishmen fight."

Ranald Sigtrygsson whispered something to his two companions, making both of the big men laugh.

When Hereward shot his friend a frown, Ranald smiled, "It seems we will have a competition, my friend. Orm and Tostig are keen to show you Englishmen how Danes can fight."

"Then, between us, we should be able to overcome these Normans easily enough," Hereward declared.

The words may have been trite, yet Hereward's strength of will made the men want to believe them and want to show him that his confidence in them was justified. They made no further protests, merely settling down to wait patiently for the command to launch the next phase of their raid.

At last, the sun dipped below the horizon and the trees around them became dark shadows. Yet Hereward insisted on waiting. The moon rose, pale and silvery, casting its ghostly light across the empty landscape, yet still they waited.

It was well past midnight when Hereward at last gave the order to move.

"No talking!" he commanded. "We go in single file. Stay close to the man in front of you. I don't want anyone getting lost. And make sure you bring your bundles of sticks."

Each man had gathered sticks from the copse. They carried these in addition to their weapons, because of Hereward's intention to use fire to help them breach the abbey's gates.

Carrying their bundles, they emerged from the copse and began the trek to the town, the moon and stars lighting their path. Occasionally, a man would trip over some unseen obstacle in the dark, but their long-snake-like procession reached Peterborough without serious mishap.

The town was a sprawling settlement, many buildings clustered close together around the abbey walls, with others more widely spaced on the outskirts to the north and west. These buildings had been constructed over many years, with little planning or forethought, creating narrow, winding streets of hard-packed earth which turned to mud in winter. It was, in short, a fairly typical English town.

Despite its name, Peterborough had never been a true *burh*, one of the fortified settlements created two centuries earlier by King Alfred in order to withstand the predations of his Danish foes. The defences had been built around the abbey but, with the homes and workshops of the townsfolk left unprotected. Nobody seemed to mind about this since there had been no direct threat to the town for many years. This meant that Hereward and his gang could approach the abbey precinct without hindrance. Provided nobody raised the alarm before they reached their objective, they should be able to catch the Normans completely unawares.

This was why Hereward had waited so long. All the houses were in complete darkness. The slow, steady tramp of their feet did not awake any of the sleeping townspeople, but a dog barked noisily as they passed along the first of the narrow streets near the abbey.

Edric's heart was pounding, fearing discovery, but none of the townspeople looked out to see what had prompted the barking, and the warriors moved on, soon reaching the abbey itself. There, they laid their bundles of sticks against the outside of the gates. Siward White poured oil over the kindling, then the entire gang retreated to the far side of the street where they hunkered down for another period of waiting.

To Edric, everything held an unreal quality. There were houses only a few yards away, full of sleeping, unsuspecting families, while twenty armed men crouched in the dirt waiting for the first signs of dawn to light the eastern sky. Soon, the whole town would be woken when the raid began. Until then, there was more interminable waiting.

Bats flitted overhead, and a cat came slinking along the side of the street. It stopped to stare at the men, then vanished silently into an alleyway between two of the houses. Had it not been for those two signs of life, Edric could have imagined that the town was utterly deserted.

It was different inside the abbey, where monks maintained vigils throughout the night. The faint sound of their chanting could be dimly heard, but Edric felt that only added to the unearthly feel of the night. The songs were ethereal, ghostly echoes muffled by distance, scarcely resembling human voices at all.

"This is a holy place we are attacking," he whispered to Winter. "What if God decides to punish us?"

Winter snorted, "The Danes have been ransacking churches for hundreds of years, lad. It doesn't seem to have done them much harm. Besides, you heard what Hereward said. The Normans have turned it from a church into a treasure house full of looted riches."

"Are you frightened, Boy?" a voice rumbled softly from behind them.

Edric twisted round to see the outline of Kenton, the scarred man who had objected to his appointment as Winter's second. The man thrust his head forward aggressively, challenging Edric with his scorn.

Winter remained silent, letting Edric know he must deal with this himself rather than rely on the big axeman's protection.

Keeping his voice low, he said, "I am not afraid of a fight, nor of any man. It is only God's vengeance I fear."

The man hissed belligerently, "Then let's wait and see how you fare when the Normans come for you."

"I've faced them before," Edric replied stiffly. "They don't scare me. Do they frighten you?"

Kenton uttered a low, rasping growl, but Winter cut in to end the argument before it could develop into a fight.

"All right! That's enough. We are supposed to be keeping quiet, so both of you shut your traps. Let your axes speak for you when we break into the compound."

Edric held Kenton's gaze for a moment before turning his back on him and settling down again. He heard the man mutter something before slowly easing his way further along the street.

"Stay calm, lad," Winter whispered in Edric's ear.

"I am," Edric nodded. "I just don't like bullies."

"Take it out on the Normans," Winter advised.

"I wish the waiting was over," Edric grumbled.

"It won't be long now," Winter assured him.

Time still seemed to drag but, when Edric had almost come to believe that the long night would never end, Hereward gave a signal to Siward White who immediately crossed the street, knelt down and struck sparks from a piece of flint until the kindling they had piled against the abbey gates caught fire. The oil ignited with a whoosh, and flames leaped up, casting a bright light and sending waves of heat across the street to where the warriors were now on their feet, readying themselves for the impending fight.

"That will soon get their attention," Hereward told them. "As soon as they open the gates to see what's happening, we charge in. Be ready."

The men tensed, gripping their weapons and offering softly whispered prayers, but the gates did not open. As they watched expectantly, the flames climbed higher, the crackling sound of the fire becoming louder, and a cloud of thick, oily smoke began to form.

The raiders watched in tense silence as the fire grew. It was only when the westerly breeze fanned the flames and caused them to leap up to the thatched roof of a nearby house that Hereward uttered a soft curse.

"Go and wake the people in there!" he barked at one of Barn's men. "Tell them to get out!"

The warrior dashed to the door of the house and began thumping his fist against the wood. By the time it was opened, the occupants had already realised there was a problem because the roof of their home was well ablaze. A child screamed in panic, then the family, a thin man, his wife and three young children, ran outside. Angrily, Hereward told them to wake their neighbours and clear the houses.

The children were sobbing, their mother vainly trying to soothe them, while her husband, still dressed in a long nightshirt, stared at the armed war band crowding the street.

His face paled and he seemed on the verge of panic until Hereward strode over to him and commanded, "Don't just stand there! Wake your neighbours and get them clear before the fire spreads any further!"

The man, visibly trembling, obeyed without protest, dashing to the next house in the row, thumping on the door and calling for the occupants to wake up.

Siward Red remarked grimly, "That ought to drag the monks away from their prayers. They're bound to notice us now."

In response, Ranald muttered, "I think we've overdone the fire a bit. Nobody's going to open those gates in case they find themselves in the middle of an inferno."

Edric was more concerned with the damage the fire was doing to the homes of innocent townsfolk.

"That wasn't supposed to happen!" he protested to Winter.

The axeman shrugged, "That's the problem with fire. It is its own master. You can never be sure what it is going to do."

What the fire was doing was spreading. The thick wood of the abbey's gates seemed almost reluctant to burn, yet the thatch and wood of the nearby houses caught light with astonishing ease as the breeze urged the flames along the row of dwellings which were so close together the fiery tongues could leap from one to the next with little difficulty.

"Forget the houses!" Hereward snapped at his men. "Our task is to get inside the abbey. If the Normans won't open the gates, the fire will soon do that for us."

His voice retained its confidence, but Edric could tell that the men were uneasy. The plan had been for the fire to merely serve as a means of getting the doors open, yet now there was a rage of flame confronting them. Even if the gates did burn, they would still need to pass through the blazing entrance.

171

As Siward Red had observed, the commotion had alerted the monks and soldiers inside the abbey. Edric could hear shouts of alarm from beyond the high, wooden wall, and then the church bell began to toll, the sound loud enough to be heard all across the town.

"I think we've lost the element of surprise," Winter muttered grimly.

Hereward still refused to panic. He drew his sword, settled his shield on his left arm and glowered at the gates as if willing them to collapse.

"It won't be long now," he insisted.

The fire was climbing, eating into the thick timbers of the twin doors, and the people inside were obviously afraid of opening them because of the spreading conflagration.

"Plans have a habit of going wrong," Winter chuckled.

Edric could see nothing to laugh about.

"What will we do?" he asked.

"Wait. We are here to distract attention from the river. The fire will do that."

Edric frowned, but knew there was nothing else they could do. He had placed his confidence in Hereward and that had seemed justified when the young Lord's plan had brought them this far. But things were beginning to go wrong now. Houses were burning, the townsfolk were waking up and shouting in alarm, and still the Normans had not opened the gates.

The sky turned pale grey, then pink fingers of light streaked the horizon, but still the fiery glow of the flames held their attention. There was panic among the townsfolk as people ran and shouted, some seeking to place distance between themselves and the fire, others yelling for water. Similar sounds were coming from within the abbey compound, yet all Hereward and his men could do was stand and watch.

The air was full of the smell of burning wood, of smoke and flying wisps of fiery straw which the breeze was whipping from the blazing rooftops. These tiny fragments of fire drifted onto other roofs, spreading the fire like ripples on a pond.

And still the gates remained shut.

"Open the sodding gates!" Siward Red blurted angrily.

He was in the front rank, dressed in chainmail and carrying a sword and a round shield. He looked every inch a warrior, yet, like the rest of them, he was helpless.

The gates, along with the wooden walls and the houses on either side of the abbey's entrance, were well ablaze. Flames writhed and crackled in a sheet of raging fire. The heat was so intense Edric could feel it on his face even though the width of the street separated him from the inferno. Smoke billowed into the sky, bending away to the east as the breeze continued to drive the fire.

Hereward cursed again, growling fiercely when he heard some of the shouts from within the abbey complex.

"They've spotted the ships!" he told them.

"What do we do?" Siward White asked.

Hereward merely shook his head and continued to stare at the fire. He knew they had made a serious mistake, but there was nothing any of them could do.

Then, without warning, the gates collapsed. The flames had consumed the lower sections where the fire had begun, and the upper parts, still burning, tumbled in a great shower of sparks, smoke, ash and flame.

"Inside!" Hereward yelled, pointing with his sword and then dashing towards the entrance.

"Jesus Christ Almighty!" Winter spat as Hereward ran towards the burning gateway. "He's mad!"

Then Ranald was running, and his two huge Northmen were pounding after him, all three of them shouting war cries.

"Come on!" Siward White shouted, and he, too, charged for the flames.

It was madness, it was insanity, yet the men followed their leaders and ran across the street, yelling to cover their fear.

Edric, clasping his axe across his chest, ran with the rest of them, not stopping to consider the foolishness of what they were attempting.

Ahead of him, he saw Hereward leap through the gap, braving the flames that licked at him from either side as he bounded over the burning remnants of the gates which were spread on the ground, still wreathed in fire.

"Clear the path!" Winter bellowed. "Use your axes!"

Several men had already braved the fiery leap through the gates, but there was so much burning debris that it was a dangerous and foolhardy act. Winter used his long axe to heave a chunk of burning wood to one side, yelling at others to do the same.

Edric braved the heat to shove blazing wood aside, then decided that his duty was to protect Hereward. He took a deep breath, ran a few paces, then jumped through the ring of fire which was all that remained of the gateway.

Flames licked at him, singeing his clothes, and the heat seared his hands and face. It reminded him of the mad leap he had made when he had followed Hereward in pursuit of Ivo de Taillebois, making him wonder whether he was fated to leap through fire every time he followed Hereward into battle.

Yet he was through in an instant, stumbling and almost landing on a chunk of burning, blackened wood.

But he was inside the courtyard, and he bellowed a wordless cry, both to shout his relief at having survived the fiery ordeal, and to issue a challenge to his enemies.

The armoured men who had braved the flames ahead of him were hurriedly forming a line of shields. Some of them, he noticed, had tendrils of smoke seeping from their boots and trousers where they had been singed by the flames.

But they were in the abbey precinct, their enemy were facing them, and Edric could feel the battle lust surging within him. The waiting was over, and the fight was about to begin.

The Normans came with a yell, holding their line so that they would strike the burgeoning English shield wall as one.

Hereward's men screamed their own challenge, and Edric joined the shout, raising his axe in a show of defiance. He was dimly aware that there was a great deal of commotion within the compound, yet his attention was concentrated on the armour-clad Normans who were charging at them. Everything else faded until he saw the giant figure of Tostig stagger backwards and topple over, the shaft of an arrow jutting from his throat.

"Beware archers!" Ranald yelled. "Keep your shields up!"

More arrows flickered across the compound. Nobody else in the front rank fell, but Edric ducked as an arrow flew over his head, and he heard a cry of pain from behind him.

There were only three archers. They had hastened to one side of the courtyard in order to shoot at the English line from an angle. Their fire was concentrated on the left flank, where Ranald stood, and they loosed their shafts as rapidly as they could. Most arrows thudded into shields, but some struck chainmail armour. This was where the myriad iron rings showed their value. The arrows had little real force, the bowmen only drawing their strings back as far as their chests in order to shoot more rapidly. The Englishmen who wore byrnies over thick coats of padded linen felt the impact of the arrows, but the points did not penetrate to their skin, leaving the men standing with feathered shafts protruding from their bodies but unharmed by the pointed tips.

The archers loosed several arrows each, but were soon compelled to stop shooting because the Norman soldiers had closed with Hereward's hastily assembled defensive line.

There was an almighty crash as the two sides met, shields slamming together and swords clashing with resounding echoes. Men shouted, grunted, heaved, slashed and cut, but both lines held steady.

Standing in the second rank, Edric was appalled by the ferocity of the fight taking place in front of him. The men were so close together they could smell the breath of their immediate opponent, see the look in their eyes and hear the ferocious yells that were intended to scare and confuse. It was brutal, close quarter fighting, with no holds barred, the aim simply to kill the man opposite by any means possible.

Edric hefted his axe, his eyes were darting all around, watching for any sign that the Normans might be breaking through or circling round the ends of the short line of warriors, then he sensed more men joining him, and he turned to see Winter, wreathed in smoke but grinning fiercely.

"Thought you'd start without me, did you?" he shouted happily.

More men were crowding in, adding bulk to the shield wall's depth, placing their shoulders against the backs of the men in the front rank so that the Normans could not force them backwards.

"Watch left!" Winter bellowed.

Edric saw that the Normans were circling around the end of the shield wall. Ranald Sigtrygsson was there, wielding his sword furiously, driving back one opponent but suddenly outnumbered. A sword lashed out, catching him on his right thigh and driving him to the ground. His armour had absorbed most of the blow's power, but the links of his chainmail had been sheared, and blood was seeping from a gash in his leg. The blow, delivered by a huge Norman, had been powerful enough to break bones, and Ranald dropped to the ground in agony.

Edric saw Orm, the second of Ranald's men, leap to protect his Lord, using his body to block a flurry of blows which came from several Normans. The Dane screamed in anger and pain, almost vanishing beneath the advancing Normans as he struggled to prevent them killing the injured Ranald.

Then Winter rushed in, leading several of Barn's men in a counter-charge, swinging his huge axe to smash the helmet and skull of one of the Normans.

Edric had made to follow, but realised that the surge of Normans on the left had attracted the attention of nearly all the men in the second rank. He took a glance to his right and saw that Hereward, too, was struggling to fend off an encircling move.

Hereward's skill with the sword was phenomenal, his speed and power keeping the men facing him at bay, but there were too many opponents for him to defeat them all. Beside him, Ordgar swung his axe to drive back the main Norman line, but two armoured soldiers had circled to Hereward's right and were closing in behind him.

Edric did not hesitate. Without a second thought, he left Winter and the others to deal with the attack on the left flank and ran at the two men who were threatening Hereward.

There was no time to be afraid; no time to think of anything other than protecting Hereward. Raising his axe in the left-handed grip as he had been taught, Edric launched himself at the two Normans, screaming a wordless challenge as he charged at them.

The men broke off their attempt to attack Hereward, turning to face the new threat. Lifting their kite-shaped shields, they held their swords ready as Edric stormed into them.

He smashed his axe down, forcing the first man to twist so that his shield would take the brunt of the blow. The heavy blade gouged into the wooden shield, spraying splinters and cracking the polished leather covering. The Norman gave a cry of pain as he stumbled backwards, unable to strike back because Edric's left-handed blow had forced him to turn his body in order to protect himself.

The second Norman was cannier. He waited until Edric had struck at his companion, then stepped forwards and lunged with his long sword, intending to gut Edric while the young Englishman was still attempting to haul his axe from the first man's shield.

Edric had expected the move. He leaped to his right, away from the attack, heaving with all his prodigious strength to drag his axe back. He swung it in a frantic attempt to block the sword, hearing the ringing clash as the two weapons met with an impact that sent a shiver through his arms.

He took another step backwards, regained his footing, and faced his enemy again. He was breathing hard, sweat dripped from him, yet he concentrated every fibre of his body on the fight. This was not like the battle at Bourne, where the enemy had been unarmoured and trying to break free; this was a desperate, bloody fight for victory, a life or death situation.

And the Norman was obviously a veteran. His companion was on the ground, feebly moaning as he nursed a broken wrist, the result of Edric's shattering blow against his shield, but the second man gave a grin as he advanced.

He spoke to Edric, a sneering comment in French which Edric did not understand. What he did understand was the man's intention to charge at him with his shield, tempt Edric into another swing of his axe, then use his sword to end the fight.

The man came at him, rushing forwards in an attempt to catch him by surprise. But instead of swinging his axe, Edric dodged right again, taking himself further from the man's sword but making his own attack more difficult because the Norman's large shield protected the soldier's entire body.

Or almost his entire body.

Edric suddenly dropped into a crouch and swung his axe in a sweeping blow parallel to the ground, aiming for the Norman's ankles. The move caught the man by surprise, forcing him to jump aside, then Edric was up, using the momentum of his swing to propel himself at his opponent. The axe swept up, then down, driving at the Norman's right arm.

The Norman tried to block the attack with his sword, but the axe blow was delivered with such power that it swept the weapon aside as if it were a child's toy. The curved blade of the axe completed its arc, plunging into the man's upper arm, crushing his chainmail and gouging deep into his flesh.

Edric's momentum carried him into his adversary, and the two of them fell to the ground, the sword falling clear, the shield catching Edric a dizzying blow on the side of the head. But the Norman was too stunned to offer much resistance. His right arm was useless, his left arm trapped beneath his large shield which was held in place by Edric's bulk sprawling on top of him.

Desperate to end the fight, Edric seized his opportunity. He had lost his grip on his axe, but he grabbed at the man's neck with one hand, yanked off his iron-bound helmet with the other, and smashed the Norman's head against the ground several times, grunting with the effort as he put all his strength into each blow.

He heard bone splintering, and saw the man's eyes glaze over. Edric thumped his head one more time, then released his grip, looking around for his axe. It lay beside him, so he grabbed it as he lurched to his feet. Barely stopping to consider what he was doing, he swept it down, cutting off the head of the fallen soldier with one blow.

He stood, panting for breath, leaning on his axe as he stared down at the decapitated corpse, its blood pooling around the severed neck. Then he heard another shout behind him. He whirled in time to see Hereward despatch the first Norman who had faced Edric. The man had abandoned his shattered shield but had seized his sword and had been trying to strike at Edric's back.

Edric felt a cold sweat run through his entire body as he realised that he had been so intent on one adversary that he had forgotten about the other man. That mistake could have cost him his life. Luckily for him, Hereward had seen off his immediate opponents and had swung round in time to deal with the injured Norman.

"Well done, lad," Hereward grinned, flicking his blade to indicate the headless corpse at Edric's feet. "Now come and help me rescue a lady."

The fight was almost over. Edric had no idea how long it had taken, but the Normans were gradually falling back, clustering into a desperate ring of shields and swords as the English raiders pressed around them. He could see several bodies lying on the ground, and recognised that one of the fallen was Duti, his face half torn away by a savage sword cut.

There was no time to see who else had fallen, for Hereward was running towards the church building, so Edric chased after him.

His legs felt weak, his feet weighed down as if by lead, his arms barely able to hold his axe, yet Hereward's insistence gave him fresh strength as he followed the young Lord to the doors of the church.

"Smash the door down!" Hereward told him, gesturing at the solid oak of the tall doorway.

Edric took a deep breath, gathered his strength and dutifully swung his axe, smashing it into the thick wood. It barely made a dent. He tried again, burying the blade deep into the wood, then struck again, aiming for the same point.

"Keep going!" Hereward urged. "Help is coming."

The help arrived in the shape of Danish warriors who had broken down the River Gate and were now swarming into the courtyard, diving into every building in search of plunder. Most headed for the abbey itself because they knew this was where the greatest riches would be found.

"Break down the door!" Hereward told them.

The Danes needed no second invitation. More axemen joined Edric, their blades chopping great chunks of wood from the doors which, at last, began to show signs of crumbling under the relentless assault.

A gap appeared, splinters of wood flying free, then the furious blades carved the opening wider until the locking bar was visible. Edric stepped back, wiping sweat from his brow as he allowed the Danes to finish the task. They chopped and hacked until the wood shattered into a myriad of splinters. Then they shoved forwards and the door gave a squeal of protest as it swung inwards.

With a shout of triumph, the Danes surged into the gloomy interior of the church, with Hereward and Edric shoving in amongst them.

"Find de Taillebois!" Hereward shouted to Edric.

The interior of the church was gloomy, only a few rays of early morning light filtering down from the high, narrow windows.

Edric paused, blinking as he peered into the shadows. The Danish warriors, intent on plunder, jostled and shoved past him, shouting their ferocious war cries as they flooded the building like a tidal wave of murderous aggression.

He had wondered why Hereward had been so desperate to break into the church, but if de Taillebois was in here, he understood. Perhaps they had a second chance to exact revenge on the man who had killed Hereward's brother.

But where was the fat Sheriff? Edric could see no sign of him among the jubilant Danes who were sweeping along the length of the building, seizing silver candlesticks and hauling crucifixes from where they hung on the walls. The long, wooden benches were being overturned, and the leading Danes were already smashing at the door to the church tower with their axes, yelling encouragement to one another as they did so.

As Edric's eyes adjusted to the poor light, he took a few steps deeper into the interior, using his bulk to force a way through the seething mob that was ransacking the church.

A woman's scream stopped him in his tracks.

He whirled, seeing two Danes grabbing a young, brown-haired woman who was struggling to break free of their grasp. Edric had not expected to see a woman in the abbey, but he knew Hereward had given orders that no monks or townsfolk were to be harmed, so he hurried to the scene of the struggle without stopping to consider what he might need to do.

"Leave her!" he barked at the two men as he came up behind them.

One of them turned to look at him, then laughed, "Get lost, boy! We found her. She's ours."

"We are here to kill Normans and take the Abbot's stolen treasure, not to harm ordinary people!" Edric insisted.

"She's not ordinary!" chuckled the Dane.

Edric glanced at the woman who was still uselessly wrestling against the two men. Her long, brown hair was unkempt and swirled about her face, her cloak was askew and her pale dress torn at the shoulder, revealing a flash of smooth, creamy flesh. Above all, though, he could see the swelling on her face where a livid bruise was forming.

His anger against bullies rose like a tempest within him.

Brandishing his axe, he shouted at the men, "I said leave her!"

Both Danes turned to look at him now, although one of them maintained his hold on the woman's arms, pinning her in place. Both men were, Edric could tell, hard-bitten warriors, each armed with a sword. They were big, tough men, although not as broad in the shoulders as Edric.

The first man raised his sword menacingly, and Edric could see murder in his eyes as he glared at the interruption.

"Last chance, boy!" he hissed. "She's ours!"

Edric became aware of other men calling encouragement and he realised the confrontation had attracted a small audience which was crowding in close behind him. Still, he could not back down now, even though he was alone and outnumbered.

He held the Dane's stare, showing the man he was not afraid, but neither of them was prepared to make the first move.

Then the woman took advantage of the situation. The man holding her was standing in front of her but had turned his head to watch his companion deal with Edric. The woman shifted her balance, then kneed him in the groin with such savagery that he yelled aloud, letting go of her as he doubled over. The woman leaped free, and the other Northman instinctively twisted to see what had happened.

Edric did not hesitate. With his left hand, he swung the haft of his axe to knock the Dane's sword aside, then jabbed his right fist into the man's face, catching him full on the nose and mouth with a blow that was powerful enough to send him toppling backwards to fall over one of the wooden benches behind him.

Edric kept moving, spinning round to place himself between the woman and the crowd of Danes behind him, but he need not have worried. The Northmen were laughing and applauding, delighted at the entertainment he had provided.

Ever cautious, he planted his feet on the stone floor, backed away and held his axe ready to defend himself. Behind him, he could hear the woman moving close to his back, obviously seeking his protection.

The two Danes who had seized her were in no condition to continue the fight. One was on his back, his knees raised and his hands clutched to his groin while he gasped for breath, the other was sprawled among the benches, blood dripping from his smashed nose and split lips. Even so, Edric noticed that some of the other warriors were eyeing him curiously, as if weighing up whether it would be worth their while trying to steal the woman away from him.

Then Hereward arrived, sword in hand, his shield slung over his back, shoving through the crowd and barking at the Danes to move out of his way.

"Leave the lad alone or I'll have King Sweyn castrate the lot of you!" he shouted belligerently, pushing the warriors aside.

Some of the Danes recognised him. Edric heard them say his name as they tugged their companions away.

"There's plenty of loot for you all," Hereward told them. "Go and find some, but the woman is not to be harmed."

Then he reached past Edric to take the woman's arm as he ordered, "Let's get outside! Now!"

Edric barrelled out of the church with Hereward and the woman following closely. He stepped out into the courtyard and moved away from the door, aware that the entire abbey complex was in uproar as a melee of Northmen ran riot, looting and plundering every building. The fighting appeared to be over, but there were so many men rushing around that he could not see any sign of the rest of Hereward's gang.

He stopped, looking to Hereward for orders, but the Lord was now confronting the woman they had rescued.

"Where is de Taillebois?" Hereward demanded sharply. "He was with you!"

The woman, Edric could see, was young and very pretty, despite the bruise on her face. She was, though, obviously in distress, placing her hands over her face and sobbing softly.

"He ran away!" she blurted between her tears.

Hereward frowned, but persisted, "You called my name. How is it that you know me?"

"Oh, Hereward! Do you not remember me?" she almost wailed.

Then she threw her arms around him and clung tightly to his chest. With his sword in his right hand, Hereward clumsily placed his left arm around her to comfort her, but he was clearly at a loss to understand her words.

"It is me!" she sobbed. "It is Altruda! You must remember me! You saved my life once!"

182

Hereward stiffened, an odd look flashing across his face, then he gently eased her away and looked at her more closely.

"It is you," he said in a low voice, his tone wary. "What are you doing here? And why were you with de Taillebois?"

Altruda sniffed and wiped at her red-rimmed eyes. Her chest was heaving as she fought for breath. Edric thought she looked very vulnerable, and he could not understand Hereward's stern reaction to learning her identity.

"I was being sent north to marry a Norman lord," she explained. "I did not want to go, but he wants my lands, and the King commanded me to marry him. I only stopped here for a few days to rest before continuing my journey."

Then she reached out to clasp Hereward's free hand in both of hers.

She forced a tearful smile as she added, "And now you have rescued me from that fate. Ivo de Taillebois hit me when I tried to escape from him, but he was afraid of you and ran away. Now you must take me with you."

Hereward gave her an uncomfortable look as he said, "My men will protect you and keep you safe until we reach Ely. I will put you in the care of Abbot Thurstan."

"Oh, thank you!" Altruda exclaimed. "May the Lord God bless you!"

Then, before Hereward could say any more, she suddenly asked, "These are Danes with you, are they not?"

"Yes," he confirmed.

"And you mentioned King Sweyn. Is he here?"

Hereward glanced across the courtyard to the River Gate as he said, "He is on one of the ships. I expect he will arrive here any moment now. He'll want to make sure he gets his share of the treasure."

"You must take me to him!" Altruda stated with sudden insistence. "I must speak with him."

"Why?" Hereward wanted to know.

"Because I have rather a lot of gold in my personal possessions here. I would prefer not to lose it all to his Vikings."

"I suspect it may be too late for that," Hereward told her.

"Nevertheless, I must speak to King Sweyn. Take me to him."

Even Edric noticed that her voice had altered to a more commanding tone. It was as if the need to protect her wealth far outweighed the outrage and fear she had experienced only moments before.

Hereward regarded her with narrowed eyes, then shrugged.

"Very well. Come, Edric. Let us take the Lady Altruda to meet the King."

Bemused, Edric dutifully followed the couple as Hereward guided Altruda towards the River Gate. They met King Sweyn as he entered the abbey compound, a dozen warriors surrounding him as an escort.

Edric hung back, not wishing to intrude as Hereward led Altruda to meet the King. Sweyn, Edric could see, was instantly attracted to the young woman, as was every other man there. She was, he knew, extremely beautiful and he could not understand Hereward's aloof attitude towards her. Yet the young English Lord seemed glad to be rid of her, stepping away and leaving her with King Sweyn as soon as he could. He turned, signalling to Edric to accompany him.

"Let's find the rest of the lads," Hereward growled.

"What about the lady?" Edric asked.

"She's the King's problem now. He's welcome to her."

"Why?" Edric pressed. "Who is she?"

"She's a viper disguised as a woman," Hereward muttered darkly. "Take my advice, lad, and keep away from her if you know what's good for you."

Chapter 11

"Brother Richard is quite scandalised," Aelswith confided to Edric from the seat she had taken from her room and placed in the corridor so that she could talk to him while he stood guard outside Torfrida's room. "In fact, many of the monks are appalled by that woman you brought back from Peterborough."

"I didn't bring her back," Edric replied dourly. "She travelled with King Sweyn."

"But you rescued her," Aelswith protested. "That's what everyone is saying. You fought half a dozen Danes to save her from being ravished."

"There were only two of them," Edric informed her. "And one of them was not in any state to fight me."

Aelswith regarded him with a smile.

"You are too modest, Edric. Even fighting one Dane to protect a woman you do not know was a brave act."

Edric shrugged, never comfortable with praise. He had grown up hearing little but accusations and criticisms from his uncle, so he was not sure how to respond to Aelswith's kind words.

She went on, "The lady is sleeping with the King. Did you know that?"

"I think everyone knows it," Edric grunted.

"Is she very beautiful? I have only seen her from a distance."

"I suppose she is," he replied with a show of disinterest.

After a short pause, Aelswith told him, "At any other time, Edric Strong, I would complain because you are supposed to say that, however beautiful she might be, she is not as pretty as me."

Edric felt a flush of embarrassment and began to form a clumsy response, but Aelswith laughed and patted her belly as she added, "However, I do not feel very pretty at the moment. I wish the baby would come."

Edric gave her a weak smile as he ventured, "You are always pretty."

She laughed again as she said, "It is too late now, Edric. You will not win me over that way."

Edric had not believed he was attempting to win her over. He had become accustomed to her sitting and talking to him while he stood his turn at sentry outside the room Hereward shared with Torfrida. He was not sure whether she did the same with the other men of Hereward's gang, and he did not have the courage to ask either her or any of his companions. He told himself she probably spoke to all of them because she was evidently bored by her inability to venture far from her room.

One thing he had learned was that Aelswith was keen to talk. She wanted to know about everything that went on outside the abbey's walls.

She asked him, "Was the battle very fierce?"

"Yes," he nodded.

What else could he say? The memory of that vicious combat had haunted his dreams, reliving the mortal danger, and keeping alive visions of the blood-soaked ground and the gory sight of those who had not survived. He could not tell her about those things, so he adopted the curt, apparently uncaring attitude of his more experienced comrades.

Winter had told him, "You lived, lad, and you fought well. That's all that matters. Others died because they lacked skill or luck. There's no point in dwelling on it. Just keep faith in yourself and your axe."

But Aelswith wanted to know more.

"Your friend, Duti, was killed?"

"Yes. His brother is very upset."

That was one way of putting it, he thought. Auti, having shed tears over his twin's body, had found a monk who promised to give Duti a Christian burial, but Auti had withdrawn into a dark, sombre place somewhere inside his own head. He rarely spoke except to answer direct questions, and he would sit brooding for hours at a time.

"It sounds as if you were lucky he was the only one who died," Aelswith commented.

"Ranald Sitrygsson's two men were also killed," he told her. "And Ranald is badly hurt. I am surprised he survived the trip back here."

"Brother Richard is tending to him, though," Aelswith said.

186

"Him and the others," Edric nodded. "A couple of Siward Barn's men were wounded too. That's not counting Siward Red, who lost the little finger of his right hand."

He lapsed into silence, not wishing to say any more because the memory of what had happened in Peterborough still disturbed him. The fire had destroyed several homes, creating misery for the families who had lost everything. Worse, the fight in the courtyard had been brutal. Duti, along with two of Siward Barn's warriors and the big Danes, Orm and Tostig, had been killed before the Norman line crumbled. Edric had not witnessed the end of the fight and, when he learned what had happened, he was glad of it. Caught between the victorious Englishmen and the horde of Danes who had smashed down the River Gate and surged into the compound behind them, none of the Normans had survived.

"Did none of them try to surrender?" he had asked Winter.

"If they did, we weren't in the mood to take prisoners," the gruff axeman had shrugged. "It's like Hereward said, we were there to kill Normans. England won't be free until every last one of them is dead."

Edric had been disturbed by Winter's casual dismissal of the slaughter, but he kept his thoughts to himself. He was, after all, a novice at warfare, although he felt the savagery meted out to the Normans had been unnecessary. They had been beaten anyway, so why massacre them?

"They'd do the same to us, boy," Winter had told him gravely. "Be in no doubt about that."

That, Edric supposed, was true enough. Everyone had heard how brutal the Normans were. He had seen it for himself when the heads of Thane Toki and Wulfnoth had been placed on poles at the crossroads in Bourne. What bothered him was the thought that Norman brutality should be used to justify equal savagery on the part of the English. At the same time, he knew that following the church's stricture to turn the other cheek would not free England from Norman rule. Perhaps there was a middle way, but he had no idea what that might look like, nor how he might find it.

He shook off the memories as Aelswith continued, "At least you came back unharmed. And now you have your armour."

Edric nodded. He was delighted with the new set of chainmail that had been made for him. It fitted well, although he was surprised at how heavy it was. It was no wonder, he reflected, that men did not wear it all the time. Marching while wearing it would be exhausting. Even so, he wore his new byrnie whenever he could find an excuse. It was new, gleaming and impressive. He had also acquired a new pair of boots with iron bands set across the top of his feet and around the ankles to protect him from any low blow aimed at disabling him. Those boots had come from one of the Normans who had been slain at Peterborough. Winter had found them for him, along with a helmet.

"These look about your size, lad," Winter had beamed as he presented the looted items.

The boots were slightly too big, but Edric had stuffed a pad of linen into the toes and they fitted well enough. His helmet had a dent in one of the iron bands of its frame, but it was serviceable. Made of thick leather within the iron framework, it was lined with lambswool and fitted snugly. The only problem Edric had with it was that it was a typical Norman helmet, with its long, iron nose guard. It made him look too much like a Norman for his liking. To offset that image, he had found a discarded shield, a circle of iron-bounded ash, painted green and with an iron boss in its centre. He now wore that on his back, and had completed his outfit with a long, saw-toothed knife which hung from a broad, leather belt he wore around his waist.

"You do look like a soldier now," Aelswith had told him when she first saw his new attire. "Did you get any other reward from your share of the plunder?"

"A few silver pennies," he told her. "Hereward shared it out, but the Danes kept most of the treasure."

That, he knew, was a continuing source of tension. The Danes had loaded a great hoard of treasure on their ships. They had taken chests of gold and silver, ornaments and crucifixes, plates and goblets, tapestries and bolts of cloth. They had emptied the abbey's library, especially prizing the huge tomes which had jewel-encrusted covers; they had ransacked every room, picking them clean of anything of value, and they had seized the abbey's prized collection of holy relics.

They had taken so much that some of the monks, unwilling to abandon the treasures, had insisted on accompanying them, virtually giving themselves into slavery in order to stay close to the holy artefacts. Abbot Thurstan had been shocked at this, but King Sweyn had refused to surrender anything his men had taken, and the monks of Peterborough would not be parted from their sacred relics, so there was nothing Thurstan could do.

Hereward, too, was less than happy because he wanted the treasure to be used to pay the men who were already coming to Ely to join the rebellion, but King Sweyn seemed reluctant to part with anything more valuable than a few silver coins.

"That's kings for you," Winter had grumbled. "No matter how much gold they have, they always want more."

So the bulk of the riches remained on the Danish ships, as did the Lady Altruda. Her presence was the cause of a great deal of gossip, and Aelswith delighted in sharing what she had heard.

"Martin says Altruda was only a girl when she met Hereward," she told Edric.

"Martin told you about her?" Edric asked in surprise.

"Of course."

"He doesn't tell anyone else very much at all," Edric complained.

"He's not a gossip," Aelswith said tartly. "He only told me to warn me to stay away from her."

"Hereward told me the same thing," Edric frowned. "But he wouldn't say why."

Aelswith gave him a knowing smile. She glanced around, checking that the corridor was empty and that the door to Torfrida's room remained closed, then lowered her voice to tell him, "She was to be married to a Scottish Lord. Hereward saved her from a bear which had escaped from its cage. Martin says she then pursued Hereward and insisted she wanted to marry him."

"He turned her down?"

"She was already betrothed. But, funnily enough, her husband died shortly after they were wed. Or so Martin says."

Edric raised an eyebrow at her, but Aelswith merely smiled as she went on, "He also says he's heard she married an English Thane after that, but he died as well."

"She sounds unlucky, that's all," Edric ventured cautiously.

"No," Aelswith told him. "It is the Lady Torfrida who was unlucky."

"What do you mean?"

Leaning close so she could whisper her answer, Aelswith delighted in telling him, "Torfrida was betrothed three times, but each man died before the wedding."

"I didn't know that!" Edric exclaimed.

"She told me herself," Aelswith assured him with a self-satisfied nod. "She thought she was doomed to be a spinster because men began to regard her as cursed. But then she met Hereward when he arrived in Flanders."

"So both ladies had bad luck," Edric remarked.

"No," Aelswith insisted. "Torfrida never married any of the men. They all died in wars or due to accidents before they could marry her. But Altruda married both men, and both suffered mysterious deaths. And, because she married them, she inherited their lands. She is very wealthy, you know."

"Are you saying she murdered her husbands?" Edric gasped.

"I didn't say that," Aelswith said with a sly grin. "But it was very convenient for her. From the sound of it, the Norman Lord she was supposed to marry has had a lucky escape."

Edric chewed his lower lip for a moment, then said, "It sounds a bit odd. I mean, it could be like that story you heard about me fighting off a small army of Danes when there were only two of them. Maybe her husbands really did die naturally. It happens, you know. People die all the time."

"Perhaps you are right," Aelswith shrugged.

Then, unexpectedly, she gave a short, sharp gasp and clutched at her rounded stomach.

"What is it?" Edric asked. "Is the baby kicking you again?"

"No!" she hissed from between clenched teeth. "It's not kicking! I think it's coming!"

Edric froze. If a dozen Norman soldiers had been marching down the corridor, he would have known what to do, but he had no idea how to respond to the arrival of a baby.

"Get me to my bed!" Aelswith panted.

Edric was not supposed to desert his post, but he propped his axe against the wall, bent and helped Aelswith to her feet. Then he guided her into her small room where he eased her onto the narrow bed.

"What now?" he asked helplessly.

Aelswith's face was very pale, and she was breathing in short, frightened gasps.

"Fetch the midwife," she begged.

Edric ran back to the corridor, picked up his axe and, knowing he could not leave his post, banged his fist on the door to Hereward's room.

The door was opened by Alice, Torfrida's maid. She peered at him inquisitively, but could not seem to understand his urgent requests for her to help. It was only when Torfrida abandoned the embroidery she had been working on and came to see who was causing the commotion that Edric felt some sense of relief.

Torfrida immediately took charge. She sent Alice to fetch the midwife, coaching her how to tell the woman that a baby was coming. Then she went into Aelswith's room, closing the door and telling Edric to remain outside.

He stood, restless and anxious, then began pacing up and down. It seemed an age before Alice returned from the town, leading a middle-aged, stout woman with straggly hair who carried a large wicker basket under her arm. Both of the women vanished inside the room, leaving Edric to his pacing.

Alice was sent out on several errands, returning from each trip with bundles of blankets, towels or jugs of hot water. Edric tried to steal a glimpse inside the room whenever the door opened, but he was unable to see what was happening because the women made it very plain that he was not to intrude.

Nothing seemed to happen for a long time. Ordgar came to relieve him, but Edric stayed, sitting on the floor with his back against the stone wall while he waited for news.

"How long does it take a baby to come?" he asked Ordgar.

"As long as it takes," the big man replied unhelpfully.

"Maybe I should go in and see if I can help," Edric suggested half-heartedly.

"Best not," Ordgar advised.

Even when Aelswith let out the first of what turned out to be several loud screams, Ordgar held up a hand to prevent Edric bursting into the room.

"She won't thank you for it, boy," the axeman told him.

The afternoon crawled its way towards evening, and still Aelswith could be heard moaning and shouting from within the room. Edric was almost frantic with desire to burst in and discover what the women were doing to her.

Ordgar chuckled, "You'd think you were the father. Relax, lad. There's nothing you can do except wait."

So Edric waited and, at last, he heard the sound of an infant crying. He stood expectantly, but was compelled to wait for another seemingly interminable time before the door opened a crack and Torfrida slipped out.

"It's a girl," she said, giving them a weary smile. "Both of them are well."

Hereward arrived moments later, having spent most of the day with King Sweyn. He was in a sour mood and the news of the birth did not improve his humour.

"You have a niece," Torfrida told him.

"So the girl claims," Hereward scowled.

Despite his scepticism, he accompanied Edric when the midwife eventually agreed that they could see the child. They entered the room cautiously, not sure what to expect, but Aelswith was smiling, lying on the bed with her dark hair plastered damply about her face, looking tired yet happy. A small child, wrapped in blankets, lay on her chest, staring with wide, blue eyes at the dimly lit room.

"Isn't she beautiful?" Aelswith asked.

Hereward grunted agreement, but Edric could only nod foolishly.

Aelswith did not appear to notice. She said, "I shall call her Torfrida."

Hereward seemed about to protest, but his wife gripped his arm as she said, "I am honoured."

So now, Edric realised, there were two Torfridas in the world. Yet one was a fine lady and the other was the bastard daughter of a dead Thane, and he could not help wondering what sort of life the girl would have as she grew up.

"This calls for a celebration!" Winter declared when he heard the news. "Come on, lad. We'll get you royally drunk, just as if you were the child's real father."

"But I'm not!" Edric protested.

192

"You're probably the closest thing to a father the child will ever have," Winter told him. "But I fancy a drink or two anyway, so let's head into town and see what we can find."

He tried to rouse the others into joining them. Wulfric agreed, but Auti shook his head.

"I'll go and relieve Ordgar. He'll go with you."

Winter attempted to convince Auti to join them, but the lean outlaw insisted he was not in the mood, and could not be persuaded.

The two Siwards had been with Hereward all day and had been royally feasted by King Sweyn, so they declined Winter's invitation, but White gave Edric two silver pennies to buy pints of ale.

"Try not to get too drunk," he warned with a grin.

Edric had no real desire to get drunk at all, but he soon found himself dragged along by Winter's enthusiasm. With Ordgar and Wulfric in tow, they left the abbey and went into the town in search of a tavern.

There were only a handful of drinking establishments in Ely. Taverns were an unfamiliar concept to Edric. He knew his Aunt Edith had served food and ale to the villagers who gathered in the smithy during the long winter evenings, but some enterprising individuals had set up businesses where they did nothing else but serve ale and food. They were places where men could gather to talk, to drink, to sing, tell jokes, gamble and, more often than not, settle arguments with their fists. Or worse.

The tavern Winter led them to was close to the abbey, but its proximity was the only thing in its favour. Even in the fading light of evening, Edric could see that it was a sorry-looking place, with shabby thatch on its roof and old, rotting planks for walls.

He was not keen to see the inside of the place, but Winter told him, "The other inns are near the river, and will be full of Danes. Come on, we can at least sample the beer."

He led them inside, where Edric found the interior matched his expectations. The place was cramped, with small tables jammed close together, and wooden stools or benches for seats. The floor was carpeted with a layer of reeds and straw, the earthy fresh tang overwhelmed by the all-pervading stink of beer and sweat. A couple of mongrel dogs were padding around, scrounging scraps of food from the patrons or snapping up anything remotely edible which had been dropped on the floor.

Yet the room did not appear threatening. It was lively and noisy, laughter and conversation greeting them in a wave of sound when they stepped inside. Someone hidden in the crowd was picking out traditional tunes on a small flute or whistle, and others were clapping their hands or stamping their feet as they kept time.

There was a long, wooden table at the rear of the large room. By the light of several candles, Edric could see the innkeeper, a big, balding man, scooping ale into pewter mugs from barrels which were arrayed behind him. He was handing them to serving girls who delivered them to the tables.

Winter caught the eye of one of the girls and held up four fingers. Then he led his companions to a table set against one wall of the inn.

The drinks arrived. Edric fished in his purse for the coins, but Winter insisted on paying.

"This is our treat, lad. Here's to the health of young Torfrida! May she live a long and happy life!"

Wulfric added, "May she grow up to be as beautiful and as fortunate as her namesake!"

They drank the toast, but Edric could not help recalling what Aelswith had told him about Torfrida's luck. Perhaps things had turned out for the best in the end, but to have three men die after becoming betrothed to her did not strike him as good luck at all.

He tried to shake off his sour mood. He was relieved that the child had come at last and that Aelswith was well. He was old enough to know that childbirth was a dangerous time for any woman, an ordeal which many did not survive. But his relief was tempered by the residual anxiety he felt over the child's future and by his feeling that Winter had bullied him into coming to the tavern.

He sipped at his ale, pulling a face at the bitter taste, and took another look at his surroundings. The men around him were little more than dark shapes in the gloom, for the room had only a couple of tiny windows set up near the ceiling, and it was almost nightfall. Candles sat on the tables, silhouetting the figures who sat around them, and he was surprised to see that some among the crowd were women. They were engaged in lively conversation, a couple of them draping their arms around the necks of the men, or even sitting on their laps.

Winter laughed when he noticed Edric staring at one woman whose loose shift had slipped, revealing one of her breasts.

"There's a room through the back if you want to spend some time with one of them," the axeman chuckled.

"Best be careful," Ordgar added. "You can catch all sorts of things from those girls."

"That won't stop you!" Winter grinned. "You'll be through in that room before the night is out, I'll wager."

Ordgar gave a smirk as he admitted, "Aye, you're probably right."

"They are prostitutes?" Edric asked.

"Of course they are!" Winter confirmed. "You'll not find many respectable women in a place like this."

"Who wants to meet a respectable woman?" Ordgar laughed.

Edric felt young and foolish. The thought of having sex with a woman was tantalising, and it conjured images of the few women he knew; Aelswith and the Lady Altruda being prominent in his thoughts. But he had heard of the wickedness of prostitutes and how, in addition to scarring a man's soul with sin, they presented a more physical threat in the shape of the horrible diseases they spread. He was not entirely sure what these diseases entailed, but Brother John had once assured him that they were, indeed, to be avoided.

And yet Ordgar was prepared to risk paying one of the women. It made little sense to Edric.

He took another surreptitious glance around the room, noticing a few more women among the townsfolk and fishermen who made up most of the customers. Then he noticed that a few of the men were warriors from Siward Barn's contingent of guards.

Wulfric, who was sitting beside Edric and facing the room, nudged him and nodded towards a table on the opposite side of the inn.

"There's a familiar face," he said in a low voice.

It was Kenton, the big, scar-faced man who had been with them on the raid on Peterborough. He was sitting near the blazing fire, with several other men Edric recognised as being members of Barn's warriors. The man had clearly seen Edric and his companions coming into the tavern, for he was staring directly at them, his face set in a hard, belligerent expression. Edric wondered whether the man was about to start some trouble, but the warrior suddenly drained his mug, said something to his companions, then rose to his feet and walked out, with one of the other men tagging along behind him.

"Good riddance," muttered Winter.

Ordgar and Wulfric murmured their agreement. Edric had learned that, after the fight in Peterborough had ended, the men of Hereward's gang had spent their time helping their wounded comrades, while the scar-faced man had encouraged the rest of Barn's men to join in the looting, claiming that the Danes would steal everything if they were not quick enough to seize their own share.

"He left his own men bleeding on the ground to go in search of plunder," Ordgar growled. "And all he's doing is drinking it all away."

"Forget him," Edric told the others. "He's gone now."

But the scarred man's presence had dampened their good humour, and the four of them sat in contemplative silence for a while until Ordgar tried to lift the mood by telling some bawdy stories about the women he claimed to have known.

Edric laughed at the appropriate times, but it soon struck him that men like Ordgar and Winter had very different outlooks on life to those he held himself. For them, fighting was what they were trained for, and all they wanted in return was food, shelter, ale and women, along with someone to tell them who to fight and to reward them for doing so.

What he did share with them was a devotion to Hereward. The young Thane was, Edric had realised, a man of deep conviction who was not above holding a grudge. He disliked Altruda and distrusted Aelswith, and he hated the Normans with a passion. Yet he was brave, clever in war, and inspired great loyalty in his men. Edric could recognise his personal faults, yet he also saw that, if England was ever to be freed from Norman rule, it would be the single-minded resolve of men like Hereward who would bring about that freedom.

Edric was so lost in his own thoughts that he was barely listening to Winter and Ordgar exchanging stories. As he shook himself back to the present, he happened to notice a slim figure

196

enter the tavern through another door in the rear wall which he had not noticed before. The figure wore a cloak with the hood pulled up, casting the face into deep shadow, yet its stance caught his attention. Whoever it was, they stood for a moment, casting their gaze around the shadow-filled room, then seemed to fix on him. The cloaked figure moved, sidling between the tables and picking its way towards him.

Edric guessed it was one of the tavern's whores. He could make out no details, but the person was slightly built and not very tall, so he supposed it was a woman who had picked him out as a likely customer.

He looked away, taking another drink from his mug, but the figure came right up to their table and stood at his shoulder.

"Hello," chuckled Winter, "it looks as if you have an admirer, lad."

Wulfric and Ordgar laughed, but Edric shook his head, refusing to look up at the woman in the hope that she would take the hint and leave him alone.

"Is your name Edric Strong?" she asked, the voice confirming her gender.

She sounded young, a little anxious, yet also determined.

He looked up, seeing a pair of bright eyes staring at him from a pale but grimy face. Hints of a full head of hair peeked from beneath the hood of her cloak which she held wrapped around her slender body, but which revealed the swell of her breasts and the flare of her hips.

Her closeness made Edric feel distinctly uncomfortable. He imagined everyone in the room was looking at him, although the background conversation continued unabated.

"Is your name Edric Strong?" she asked again, more insistently this time.

"Yes," he nodded. "Why?"

"I must speak to you," she told him. "But not here. Come outside with me."

She gestured towards the door through which she had entered the tavern, but her words brought a gout of ribald laughter from Edric's companions.

"You'll need to be gentle with him, lass!" boomed Ordgar.

The girl gave an emphatic shake of her head as she stated, "I only want to talk. It is important."

Winter grabbed at an empty stool and dragged it over.

"Sit down and talk here, lass," he commanded.

The girl hesitated, then sat, her eyes flickering from one man to the next, her body tensed as if ready to flee at the slightest hint of danger.

"What is it you want to talk about?" Winter asked.

The girl ignored him, instead turning to Edric.

"Do you trust these men? Is it safe to speak in front of them?"

"Yes," he asserted. "They are my friends."

The girl relaxed slightly, then asked him, "Do you know a man named Kenton?"

"I know him," he replied. "He was in here a few moments ago."

"Aye, we all know him," Winter growled.

Still the girl kept her eyes on Edric. Now that she was close to him, he could see that she was young, perhaps only sixteen or seventeen years old. Her eyes were large and bright within an elfin face, and she had a determined air about her.

She lowered her voice so as not to be overheard, although the precaution was probably unnecessary because the men around the neighbouring table were busy playing, and gambling on, games of King's Table, the old Viking game of *Hnefatafl*. They were too preoccupied to pay much attention to Edric and his companions. Even so, Wulfric and Ordgar had to lean in close to hear what the girl was saying.

"You saw him leave, then?" she asked.

Edric nodded, "Yes."

"He has gone to find some Danes," she informed him. "They have offered silver to anyone who can deliver you to them."

Edric felt a chill run down his spine, but he forced himself to remain calm.

"Why?" he asked.

"Why do they want you?" she frowned. "I don't know. But if you are asking why Kenton has gone to fetch them, it is because he wants the silver, and he wants to see you hurt."

Wulfric observed, "It must be those two Danes you clobbered in Peterborough. They probably want their own back."

"I suppose so," Edric conceded. "But what has this fellow Kenton got against me?"

198

The girl gave a casual shrug as she replied, "It does not take much for him to dislike a person. And he rarely gives up the chance to earn money."

Edric nodded thoughtfully but Winter growled, "Then we thank you for the warning, lass. We can deal with them when they get here."

Edric held up a hand to calm things.

"Hereward does not want any trouble between us and the Danes," he reminded his friends.

"It's not our fault if they start it," Ordgar remarked grimly.

"But we will be to blame if we do not avoid trouble when we are warned beforehand," Edric told him.

The girl suddenly put in, "I do not want you to run away from this!"

Edric gave her a puzzled look as he asked, "Then what is it you want? Why are you telling us this?"

She pursed her lips for a moment before saying in a low, yet clear and icily cold voice, "I'm telling you because I want you to kill Kenton."

Chapter 12

The table became an oasis of silence in the din of the tavern. All four men stared at the girl as if doubting whether they had heard her correctly.

"You want us to kill the man named Kenton?" Edric asked softly.

She nodded, an emphatic jerk of her head, her eyes holding his gaze to reaffirm her resolve.

Slowly, he said, "I think you were right. This is not the place to talk of such things. Let us go outside."

He stood up, the girl following his lead. Ordgar slurped down the last of his ale, while Winter gave a low grumble before pushing his stool back and hauling himself to his feet.

Edric led the way out into the street. It was fully dark now, the moon's silvery light casting deep shadows along the narrow street. He looked around, seeking somewhere less public, but the girl moved to the corner of the inn, stopping at the entrance to a narrow, stinking alleyway which ran between the tavern and the neighbouring house.

"There is nobody around," she said. "We can talk here."

The four men gathered around her, Ordgar keeping a wary eye out for any signs of treachery, but the street was deserted, the only sounds coming from within the tavern, the only lights seeping out from behind the shutters of the buildings which lined the narrow street.

Edric kept his voice low as he said to the girl, "You said you want us to kill Kenton."

Winter growled, "It would be a pleasure."

Ordgar rumbled his agreement, but Edric gestured impatiently, waving at them to be quiet.

"We can't kill him," he told them firmly. "For one thing, he is one of Thane Barn's men. His death would cause trouble for Hereward. For another thing, we'd need to kill the Danes as well, and that is likely to anger King Sweyn. Not to mention the fact that, in a fight, one of us is likely to be hurt or killed too."

Wulfric murmured, "The boy's right."

"There's always a risk in a fight," Winter grumbled. "I'm not scared of that."

Edric ignored him. Turning his attention back to the girl, he said to her, "Tell me why you want him dead."

She appeared to be struggling with some strong emotion as she sought for words. Then, in a low, barely audible whisper, she stated, "If you don't kill him, I will."

She had clasped her hands together in front of her. Edric thought he could see a slight trembling in them, as if she had locked her fingers together to prevent them shaking uncontrollably. Instinctively, he reached out and placed his own large hand on her shoulder. She flinched at his touch, but he gave her a gentle squeeze of reassurance.

"I want to understand," he told her. "Why do you want us to kill him?"

She shook her head, lowering her gaze as if she could not offer any explanation he would understand.

He tried again, asking, "Then what is your name? You can tell us that, at least."

She lifted her head and stared at him. Her face was only dimly visible, but he thought he detected a reflection of the pale moonlight, as if her eyes were wet with tears.

"My name is Ylva," she informed him flatly.

"That's a Danish name," Wulfric observed.

Ylva nodded, "My family are from York."

"So what brought you to Ely?" Edric prompted gently.

She gave him a hard look, her lips set in a thin line while she weighed her response.

"We came south with Siward Barn," she said after some thought. "You see, Kenton is my father."

That revelation resulted in another silence until Edric asked, "So you want us to kill your own father? I'd like to know why."

She paused again, then whispered, "Because of what he does to me."

Edric frowned as he struggled to grasp her meaning, but Winter muttered, "What sort of thing does he do?"

"Must I spell it out for you?" Ylva retorted with a flash of anger. "I have had enough of it. I don't want him touching me again. Not ever! And if you won't help me, I will do it myself, or perhaps it would be simpler to kill myself."

Edric, appalled at the sudden vehemence in her tone, fluttered a hand to tell her to lower her voice.

Ordgar rasped, "A man who does that to his own daughter deserves to die."

"We are not going to fight him," Edric insisted. "I told you, that will only cause more trouble."

The girl stifled a cry of outrage, then made to walk away, but Edric flashed out a hand to grab her arm.

"Wait! I didn't say we wouldn't help you."

Ylva tried to shake off his grasp, but he held tight, urging her to listen to him. When she reluctantly gave up, he let out a long sigh.

He glanced around the street, making sure it remained empty.

"All right," he said softly, "let's all stay calm, shall we? I'm sure we can work something out."

"What are you thinking, lad?" Winter asked.

Edric was not sure what he was thinking, but he knew he needed to find a quick solution before Kenton returned with his Danish thugs.

He asked Ylva, "What about the rest of your family? Where are they?"

She had given up attempting to escape his grip on her arm, but she remained angry with him.

"My mother died years ago," she snapped. "I had two brothers, but one ran away before we came here, and the other followed my father into the Thane's service."

"So your brother won't help you?" Edric probed.

She shook her head.

"He's only thirteen years old, and he's terrified of our father."

The bitterness in her voice clawed at Edric's heart. He could not recall ever hearing such despair. Yet Ylva still retained enough control over her emotions to answer his questions without breaking down.

"Is there nobody else you can turn to?" he asked.

"No."

She said the word emphatically, letting him know that he was her last hope.

He wondered what it had cost her to seek him out and ask for his help. More than he could ever imagine, he supposed. Yet she was able to maintain a measure of composure despite the effort of will it must have taken for her to admit her dark secret.

Now she regarded him with a spark of scorn in her eyes.

"Well?" she asked. "If you are too afraid to fight him, what are you going to do?"

Edric could feel Winter's outrage at the accusation of cowardice, but he kept his own voice calm as he replied, "I did not say we are afraid to fight him, only that doing so would create more problems than it solves. There must be another way."

"What way?" she demanded impatiently. "If you do not kill him, he will certainly try to harm you, and he will carry on … doing what he does to me."

The plea in her voice was almost desperate, and it drove Edric to make a decision.

"All right. You must come with us."

She gaped at him, her eyes wide.

"What do you mean? Come where?"

"We will take you to the Lady Torfrida. She will protect you."

Winter let out a murmur of astonishment.

"We can't keep her hidden forever, lad. Not in the abbey."

"No, but we can keep her safe. If she is under Torfrida's protection, her father won't dare do anything."

"You don't know him!" Ylva gasped.

Winter agreed, "It'll cause a bucketload of trouble, boy."

"Less trouble than killing one of Barn's housecarls," Edric pointed out.

Wulfric put in, "The monks will give her sanctuary."

Ylva gave a snort of derision as she said, "My father is not above defiling holy places. The Church will not stop him if he puts his mind to something."

"Maybe not," Edric said. "But we can stop him. Come with us. I promise you will be safe."

Doubt and distrust flared in her expression, but he looked directly into her eyes and whispered, "We will not harm you, and neither will your father. I swear it."

"I have seen men break oaths before," she retorted.

"I keep my word," Edric asserted. "Will you not come with us?"

"To the abbey? Thane Barn is there. And my father spends most of his time there, too."

"But Hereward and Torfrida are there," Edric replied. "And so are we."

Ordgar rumbled, "It's the best choice you've got, lass. And if it doesn't work out, you can always kill yourself later."

Edric shot the big man a dark look, but Ylva's lips twitched in a faint smile and she gave a resigned nod.

"Very well. I will come with you."

Edric could not prevent himself from smiling but, as they began walking slowly towards the abbey precinct, Winter sighed, "We're in for a shitload of trouble. Mark my words."

They hurried back to the abbey, navigating through the deserted streets by moonlight, with Ylva surrounded by their protective bulk.

"Some celebration this turned out to be," grumbled Winter.

"You're enjoying yourself," Edric accused. "You like stirring up trouble."

"Me? I'm just along for the ride, boy. It's you who's causing trouble. How are you going to persuade Hereward this is a good idea? The Lady might be willing to help, but he's got Barn to consider."

"I'm not going to persuade him," Edric replied.

"You're not?"

"No. I'm going to persuade Siward White. He'll convince Hereward."

Wulfric laughed, "The boy's got brains, Winter. You must give him that. He's as sly as a fox. Hereward will listen to White."

"A fox who could have a whole pack of hounds on his tail before long," Winter grunted.

Despite Winter's pessimism, they reached the abbey without incident.

"Wait over by the chambers," Edric told the others. "I'll go and speak to White. Keep out of sight if you can."

He entered the dormitories where he found the two Siwards sitting on their bunks. Red had removed the bandage from his hand and was flexing his remaining fingers while examining the scarred and still livid stump of his little finger. White was slowly scraping a whetstone along the blade of his sword, sharpening the cutting edges.

Both men looked up when Edric entered the small room.

"You're back early," White commented. "Was the ale not to your liking?"

"It's not that," Edric told him. "We have a problem."

White laid down his sword and cocked his head slightly to one side.

"Tell me," he invited.

So Edric recounted the story about Ylva, Kenton and the Danes, finishing by explaining what he wanted to do.

Siward Red let out a derisory laugh when he had heard the story, but his cousin sat quietly for a moment before responding...

"I'm glad you didn't try to kill the man," he nodded gravely. "You're right about the trouble that would cause. Unless you'd done it without anyone knowing it was you, of course. That would have solved the problem."

"Too many people saw us with Ylva," Edric replied instantly.

"I suppose so," White agreed. "Very well, let's go and see if we can persuade Hereward to go along with your idea."

"He must," Edric insisted. "If he doesn't, Kenton will take the girl back, and then she'll either kill him or kill herself. We can't let that happen."

Red muttered, "Why not? It's no concern of ours."

"It is now," Edric retorted heatedly. "We are supposed to be Christians, are we not?"

Red glared at him, but White stood up, gesturing at his cousin to be silent.

"Come on, then," he said to Edric. "Let's go and see Hereward."

They met the others waiting in the shadows outside the long building which housed the rooms where visitors to the abbey were accommodated. White, not wanting a large delegation to invade Hereward's room, sent Ordgar and Wulfric back to the dormitory before leading the others inside.

The long corridor was already crowded. Auti was on duty outside Hereward's room, but other men stood watch further along the corridor. These were Danes, their presence letting Edric know that King Sweyn had returned to the abbey for the night. The Danish king normally spent the day on his longship which was moored on the river because these guest quarters were not overly spacious, but he often returned to the abbey in the evenings.

Other rooms had been allocated to Siward Barn and the king's senior Jarls, leaving no accommodation for any pilgrims who might have come to pay homage at the shrine of Saint Etheldreda, but kings and nobles always took priority over ordinary visitors.

Ylva stiffened and hesitated when she saw the heads of every man turn towards them, but Edric gently touched her elbow and encouraged her to follow Siward White who studiously ignored the stares of the sentries as he led the small group along the corridor towards Auti.

"I take it Hereward is here?" White asked.

"It's late," Auti told him. "I think they might be in bed."

"Then we'll get them up," White grinned.

He knocked on the door which was soon opened by the nervous figure of Alice, then a few moments later, they were ushered inside.

"What's going on?" Hereward demanded testily.

He and Torfrida were both in nightshirts but had wrapped cloaks around themselves. While Alice scurried around lighting candles, White explained what Edric had told him.

Hereward's eyes fixed on Ylva.

"Is this true?" he demanded.

Ylva, who still wore her hood over her head, answered simply, "Yes."

Edric shot a glance at Torfrida who immediately grasped his plea.

She said, "We must look after her. It is our Christian duty. The Abbot would say the same thing."

"Barn might not think so," Hereward muttered. "If this fellow, Kenton, complains to him that we have stolen his daughter, I'm not sure we can prevent him taking her back."

"Then I will kill myself," Ylva announced in a surprisingly strong voice.

Hereward frowned, but Torfrida said, "Let us see your face, my dear. There is no need to hide yourself from us. We will look after you."

Ylva reached up to pull down her hood, revealing a mane of dark, red-tinted hair and a thin, elfish face. She seemed very small and frail standing among so many big men, but she stood proud and defiant under their curious gazes.

"You could do with a bath, I think," Torfrida said. "And some new clothes. We shall arrange that. You can sleep in the next room, along with Aelswith and her baby."

She smiled warmly as she added, "And you need not fear anything. There is always a guard outside, as you saw when you arrived."

Ylva's voice almost cracked as she whispered, "Thank you, my Lady."

"Alice will look after you," Torfrida said, signalling to her maid. "A bath and some new clothes for our guest, Alice. And try not to wake the baby."

She gave Ylva an apologetic look as she added, "I hope you don't mind having a baby around?"

Ylva shrugged, "I've dealt with babies before."

Her remark struck Edric as odd, and he wanted to ask more, but Torfrida ushered the girl out of the room, placing her in the care of Alice.

Ylva shot Edric a pleading look as she left the room, so he told her, "I'll be outside in the corridor."

Ylva allowed herself to be led to the next room, leaving Edric to face Hereward's disapproval.

"I may not be able to protect her, lad. You do know that, don't you?"

"I gave her my word," Edric replied simply.

"Well, she'll be safe enough for tonight," Hereward sighed. "Tomorrow will bring what it will."

Edric kept his promise to remain in the corridor all night, sharing the watch with Wulfric and Winter, who each stood sentry for part of the night. Occasionally, he heard baby Torfrida crying and Aelswith speaking softly to soothe her, but he heard nothing at all from Ylva who remained inside the room as if afraid to leave its sanctuary.

When he considered the comings and goings in the corridor, even during the night, he reflected that she was perhaps right to remain hidden. Guards were relieved every few hours, the replacements trooping in noisily, and some of those men were Thane Barn's warriors, for the elderly Thane slept in a room only two doors down from Hereward. It occurred to Edric that Kenton himself might turn up to do a stint as sentry, and that thought worried him a great deal.

What would he do if Kenton was standing just along the corridor and knew that Ylva was inside Aelswith's room?

All of a sudden, Edric doubted that his plan would succeed in keeping the girl safe. Yet he had given his solemn oath to protect her, and he could think of no alternative plan.

Winter, who was taking the last watch of the night, told him, "You can't stand there all day and all night, lad. You'll need to sleep at some point. And we need to guard Hereward, not watch over stray waifs."

"I gave her my word," was all Edric could reply.

"Aye, well, you know we'll help as best we can. But it won't be easy."

"The Abbot will offer her sanctuary," Edric decided. "The Lady Torfrida will speak to him in the morning."

But the morning, when it came, brought news which altered everything.

It began just as dawn was breaking, when the door to King Sweyn's room opened and a woman stepped into the corridor. She walked swiftly past the guards, looking neither to left nor right as she headed for the exit. As she drew near to Edric, the candles set along the wall revealed that it was Altruda. He had hardly seen her since their return from Peterborough, and she did not appear to recognise him as she swept past and went out into the pale light of dawn.

"Kings get all the best bits," Winter grunted sourly as he watched Altruda depart. "He's probably been humping her all night."

The crude jibe struck at Edric, just as every mention of sex did, but he soon realised there was a reason Altruda had left, for the King's door opened again, and one of his guards hurried away. Soon, other Danes were arriving, entering the King's room and

208

hurrying back out again. Each of the Jarls was woken and spoken to, and all of them left soon afterwards.

"What's going on?" Edric wondered.

Then a Dane approached Winter and told him that the King desired to speak to Hereward. Frowning, Winter thumped on the door, relaying the message via Alice.

Hereward soon appeared, unshaven but dressed in his leather tunic and with his sword at his waist. His expression, already stern, became even more clouded when Siward Barn stepped out of his room. He, too, had been summoned to see the King.

"This doesn't bode well," Winter muttered under his breath as the two English Thanes gave one another curt greetings before entering the King's room at the far end of the long corridor.

Edric soon heard raised voices, for Hereward was shouting about something, but he could not make out the words, only that his Lord was arguing strenuously and losing his temper.

Then the King's door was flung open and Hereward stomped out, his face like thunder as he stalked back towards his own room.

"What's wrong?" Winter asked when Hereward reached them.

Hereward stopped, taking a deep, angry breath before giving them the news.

"The Danes are leaving," he spat. "King Sweyn is returning to Denmark."

Edric felt the shock of the words like a physical blow which sucked all the breath from his lungs and set his heart racing.

The Danes were leaving?

He could scarcely believe it. Yet it must be true. Every Jarl had already departed, no doubt heading for their ships to prepare for the long voyage.

The Danes were leaving, and that meant that the rebellion had failed.

It was over.

Chapter 13

Altruda felt a glow of satisfaction as she left the guest building and made her way across the abbey's courtyard to the infirmary. It had taken longer than she had hoped for her to persuade Sweyn Estrithsson to depart from England, but he had succumbed eventually. Men's minds usually softened once she had used her physical charms to bring them round to her way of thinking.

It had not been the most enjoyable of experiences for her. King Sweyn was old enough to be her father, and he had grown sons of his own, yet targeting one of the younger generation would have served little purpose. King Sweyn was a strong-minded individual who could easily overrule his sons. So Altruda had found it necessary to submit to the King's desire and feign enjoyment of their lovemaking. Not that Sweyn was as repulsive as Abbot Turold, but it had still taken all of her skill to mask her true feelings.

Of course, surrendering her body to the King was only the first part of the task. It helped ensure she could have very private conversations with him and that he would be inclined to listen to her but, on its own, it was not sufficient to ensure he would do as she wished. For that, she needed to use their time alone to advance her arguments.

This was where her true skill lay, but it had been one of her most challenging encounters. Sweyn was not a man to be easily swayed by a lover's plea. She had found it necessary to use all her political and persuasive skills on him.

"You cannot defeat King William," she had insisted as she had snuggled against his bare body in the narrow bed they had shared.

"Why not? He is a man, like every other man."

"He is not like other men," she assured him. "After all, consider that he defeated Harold Godwinson, who in turn had slain Harald Hardrada of Norway. And Hardrada, as you know only too well, was recognised as the foremost warrior in Christendom."

Sweyn had tensed when she said that. Harald Hardrada, King of Norway, had been his enemy for decades, and had usually managed to defeat Sweyn whenever they resorted to force of arms to settle any dispute. Hardrada's death at Stamford Bridge had been a double boon to Sweyn, for it removed his nemesis from Scandinavia and also opened the door for Sweyn's attempt to seize the crown of England.

Yet mention of Hardrada's name still rankled with King Sweyn, so Altruda quickly moved on, saying, "But that is not what I meant. The problem you face is that you do not have enough men. William had the blessing of the Pope for his invasion of England, and he gathered thousands of men from all across Europe. Many of them are still with him, and have been richly rewarded for the help they have provided him. None of them will gladly give up the wealth they have obtained."

"I may allow them to keep what they have," Sweyn argued.

"A promise which has value only if you defeat William. All his followers know he is savage in reprisal for disloyalty. If they refuse to help him and he should still drive you off, they know he will turn on them like a wolf falls on the lamb."

"You are assuming he can beat me in battle, my Lady," Sweyn pointed out.

Inwardly, Altruda sighed. Men, especially Kings, always had an inflated view of their own talents in warfare. She was tempted to remind Sweyn that he had suffered his share of military defeats in the past, but she held her tongue, smiled sweetly and tried a different approach.

"I know you are a mighty warrior, Lord King, but you must recognise that you do not have enough men to defeat William's army. He could bring ten thousand experienced soldiers against you."

"Hereward says more men are coming each day," the King countered.

"In ones and twos. You need thousands, not a few hundred. And there are few in England who will dare stand up to William now. Not after what he did in the North."

"There are still some Earls who might join me," Sweyn argued.

Altruda laughed, "Yes, I know. Edwin of Mercia and his brother, Morcar of Northumbria. They have rebelled twice already. And failed both times."

"Yet they still live," Sweyn pointed out.

"Only because William is concentrating on establishing firm control in the South. He has been unusually patient with Edwin and Morcar. But his patience will be broken should they rebel against him again. Besides, they support the claim of Edgar the Atheling to the throne. They cannot continue to do that if they were to decide to back you. Which they won't. They are not brave men, you know."

"Even so," Sweyn said as he twisted onto his side and propped himself up on one elbow to look at her, "Hereward's plan is a sound one. If we lure William into the marshes, we can destroy him no matter how many men he has."

Altruda exhaled a snort of air from her nose as she retorted, "Do you really believe you can conquer a kingdom by sitting here in Ely and hoping William marches against you? Please believe me, Lord King. I know William. He is more likely to surround the Fens and let you rot. And all the time you stay here, your kingdom in Denmark is without a ruler."

She could see from the faint flicker of irritation in his eyes that her remark had struck a nerve. Now she pressed her case, aiming to drive the point home.

"You gained a great deal of wealth from Peterborough," she reminded him. "And much of it was the gold I had brought to pay you as *Danegeld*. If you are sensible, you will take that and leave. If you stay, you could lose everything."

He gave a soft laugh.

"You seek to bribe me with what is already mine?" he asked scornfully.

"I seek to remind you that you would have had much leaner pickings had I not brought that gold to Peterborough for the express purpose of gifting it to you."

"You are playing with words, my Lady!" he told her. "However the gold came to be there, it is mine now. Perhaps I should ask William for more?"

"He will not pay any more," she assured him. "He only agreed to provide that sum because he has other matters he wishes to deal with first. And, of course, he wishes to remain on good terms with you."

"Of course he does," grinned Sweyn.

He reached out, placing a hand on her bare hip and caressing her flawless skin as he added, "And I wish to remain on good terms with you."

"As long as you leave England after tonight," she whispered, nibbling at his ear.

"And what of you?" he asked as he wrapped his arm around her waist and pulled her close. "Will I take you with me?"

"To Denmark? I think not, my Lord. Your wife would not approve, nor would the Church."

"I do not think they would approve of what we have been doing these past nights," he said as he rolled to lie on top of her.

Altruda smiled. She parted her legs and reached down with one hand to guide him. And to tease him.

"You may not need their approval," she told him softly. "But you need mine. I am an emissary from King William, not a prize to be taken as a concubine."

He stared down at her, his face suddenly grim in the candlelight, his hands planted on either side of her shoulders.

In a low, hoarse whisper, he asked, "Do you think you could stop me doing what I want with you?"

Smiling, she said, "At the moment, my Lord, I do not want to stop you."

So saying, she lay back and let him enter her, uttering a soft gasp of pleasure as she thrust her hips to meet his.

It was over quickly, for she knew how to encourage her lovers to reach their climax. Sweyn gasped, grunted, and rolled off of her, leaving her feeling deeply unsatisfied. As he dropped into a deep slumber, she wondered whether she might need to take recourse to the dagger she had concealed under the bed. If he did not agree to sail away, she would be forced to kill him. That would not only be an admission of failure on her part, it would present her with the major problem of escaping with her own life. She had made contingency plans, of course, but she was all too aware of the risk they entailed.

Yet how much longer could she delay? If he was still determined to fight King William when he awoke in the morning, killing him would be straightforward, but escaping would not. He would be missed very soon after daybreak. But waiting another day might prove even more dangerous. If he truly appreciated the threat she posed, he might easily have her placed aboard one of his ships in chains. For all her bravado, she knew she could not physically resist the use of brute force. Sweyn might take her back to Denmark to keep as a plaything, but the sea crossing presented him with the ideal opportunity to dispose of her. Simply throwing her overboard would be all he needed to do. Whether he was ruthless enough to do that was not something Altruda wished to put to the test. In his place, that is precisely what she would have done.

Did she dare wait to see whether her words had been effective?

In the end, she decided to take the chance of waiting. She had no qualms about murdering him if that was what was necessary, but she had other plans which depended upon her remaining in Ely. She had not anticipated Hereward's rebellion when she had first arrived in Peterborough, but she knew King William would value her assistance in crushing the revolt.

But pleasing King William was not her only reason for staying on the island. She also had plans of her own, and killing King Sweyn would ruin any chance of seeing those plans come to fruition.

So she left the knife where it was, closed her eyes and went to sleep.

When she awoke, she learned that she had made the right decision. King Sweyn was irritable, his mind clearly preoccupied, and he rounded on her when she asked what was wrong.

"Your threats are what is wrong!" he burst out. "I am a King! I have a claim to the throne of England, and you would deny me that claim."

"Not I," she told him firmly. "I am merely a messenger from King William. It is he who opposes you in this. And bear in mind, Lord King, that he has God's blessing, and the Pope's support. If you go against him, you risk excommunication."

There. She had said it. Her last gambit.

He stood, dressed in only his trousers, his bare chest rising and falling as he took in long breaths of the chilly morning air. He was silent for a long time, his eyes scanning her face for any sign that she might be bluffing.

But she was not bluffing, and he knew it. The whole world knew that the Pope had given William his support and blessing. That support had clearly gained God's favour, for nobody should have been able to sail across the Channel in autumn and defeat Harold Godwinson on his own turf. Yet William had done it, and Sweyn understood that God must have been on his side.

He gave a long, resigned sigh. Men he could fight, but God could not be defeated.

"Very well, my Lady. I have gained a great deal of wealth from this visit, but Denmark needs her King, so I will sail home."

Altruda managed to keep the glint of triumph from her expression as she said, "You have made a wise decision, Lord King. I shall send a letter to King William advising him of your decision. When will you be leaving?"

He gave a slight shake of his head at her persistence.

"This morning," he told her. "Now that I have made the decision, there is no point in delaying. It would only create friction with Hereward."

She nodded, "Again, I acknowledge your wisdom, Lord King."

Then she pushed aside the blankets and stretched her body for him to see as she extended one arm towards him.

"But have we no time for one last celebration of our mutual admiration?"

She smiled at him as she arched her body and, as she had known he would, he once again gave in to her.

Later, while King Sweyn was issuing his orders, Altruda was in the abbey's infirmary, wiping tears from her eyes as she sobbed to Brother Richard, complaining of the cruelty of men.

"I have been told my beauty is a gift from God," she sniffed. "But too often I think it is a curse. Men see me and want me. And I cannot prevent them having their way with me, no matter how much I protest."

Brother Richard was both appalled and embarrassed. His face was flushed and his breathing coming in short, rapid gasps as he made useless attempts to console her.

"Are you free of him now?" he asked anxiously. "The King, I mean. Will he leave you here?"

"Oh, yes. He has had enough of me. Now he discards me, but another man will come along before long, and the same thing will happen."

A frown of deep concern creased Brother Richard's face as he asked, "Are you worried that you might be with child?"

Altruda shook her head, disguising her amusement by lowering her face and letting her hair tumble around her features. How could she tell a man of the Church that she had taken precautions? The midwife who had visited the pregnant girl in Hereward's chambers had provided her with herbs and she had made judicial use of other, more physical methods to prevent the King's seed impregnating her. In the eyes of the Church, such deeds were officially regarded as sins, although many priests and monks took a more pragmatic view.

Brother Richard, she guessed, would be of a more traditional outlook, so she said, "I believe I may be barren. That is another curse the Lord has seen to place upon me."

"Do not blame the Lord so," Brother Richard entreated.

"What am I to do?" she asked imploringly.

He gave a helpless shrug, then suggested, "Perhaps you might find the solace and freedom from men's lust if you were to enter a nunnery?"

Again, Altruda almost burst out laughing at the suggestion. The very idea of her being a nun was ludicrous. Sleeping with men like Turold and Sweyn might be distasteful, but she still enjoyed the physical act of lovemaking too much to take a vow of chastity.

She managed to retain her miserable expression as she said weakly, "I was thinking more along the lines of finding a husband who could protect me from other men's depravities."

"Ah. I see."

"I think I should appeal to King William," she went on. "He did have a man picked out for me, but he was not my choice. Perhaps I could petition the King to help me find someone more to my liking."

"I suppose that is possible," Brother Richard commented, although he plainly had no idea of how the King's Court operated.

"Would you help me?" she asked, fluttering her eyelids at him.

"Me? How?"

"If I write a letter, could you deliver it for me?"

"A letter?" he blinked owlishly. "Me? Deliver a letter to the King?"

"Not to the King," she assured him. "To Abbot Turold in Peterborough. He has the ear of the King. If I wrote a letter, could you take it to Peterborough?"

Brother Richard looked uncertain as he replied, "It is difficult to travel through the fens."

Altruda widened her eyes in a look of surprise as she asked, "Was I misinformed, then? I was told that you often travel to Peterborough to replenish your stocks of herbs and medicines."

The young monk flushed, then admitted, "Yes, that is true. But I do not go there often."

"But you could do it?" she asked, adding a hint of anticipation to her voice.

"I suppose so," he sighed. "It will be more difficult now that Hereward and his rebels are here, but I expect it will still be possible to find a boatman to take me most of the way."

"That is wonderful!" Altruda exclaimed, shooting him a look of gratitude.

Regarding him earnestly, she implored, "But I must ask that you keep it a secret."

Her eyes flicked towards the door leading to the infirmary's ward. It was shut, and they were speaking in Brother Richard's native French, so there was little chance of anyone overhearing or understanding their conversation. As far as she knew, there were only three patients in the infirmary; two Englishmen and the Dane, Ranald Sigtrygsson, who would now face the choice of risking a long voyage while suffering from his recent wound, or being left behind. None of the three could speak French, she was sure.

Turning back to the monk, she begged, "Please, brother. Help a poor, defenceless woman find some solace and safety."

Brother Richard's face flushed crimson and he swallowed anxiously before nodding, "Very well, my Lady, I will take your letter."

"Thank you, Brother Richard. You are a good man."

She reached out to take his hands and brought them to her lips, gently brushing them with a soft kiss.

And with that brief touch, Brother Richard became her loyal slave.

She could not write the letter immediately. She told Brother Richard she would need a day or two to compose her thoughts and to set them out in a letter. In reality, she waited to ensure that the Danes really did sail away, then she sent a message to Hereward, asking him to meet her in the cloister.

He came reluctantly, and he was accompanied by two of his gang; the tall, handsome man with the very pale hair, and the big youth who had rescued her in the abbey at Peterborough. With their armour and weapons on display, their appearance was jarring in the peaceful quiet of the cloister. More importantly, Altruda had wanted some privacy for this conversation.

"I wanted to speak to you in private," she told Hereward, addressing him in French.

"And I want witnesses to what is said here," he told her gruffly. "So speak English."

Altruda gave a slow, thoughtful nod as she switched to her native tongue.

"Some of what I must say is very personal," she warned him. "Are you sure you want witnesses?"

"Even more sure now that I hear that," he asserted. "Don't worry. Siward and Edric can keep their tongues in check. That is why I brought them."

"Not because you feared a trap?" she asked.

"That too," he nodded.

"Here?" she asked, her delicate eyebrows arching in an expression of innocence, and her arms stretching out to take in the peaceful quadrangle of the cloister.

A less dangerous place could scarcely be imagined. The cloister consisted of a colonnaded walkway which framed a square garden of flowers. Gravel paths led into the garden from the four sides, meeting in a small, circular patch in the very centre. There, the two of them sat facing one another on stone benches, while Siward White and Edric Strong stood behind Hereward, looking stern and unfriendly, an odd emotion in the tiny sea of tranquillity that was the cloister.

There was nobody else to overhear them. The buildings which formed the outer edge of the colonnade contained the tiny cells where the monks slept at night, but those cramped rooms were empty now because the monks were either at prayer or going about their other duties.

Idly, Altruda wondered whether nuns were housed in similarly drab and spartan quarters. She supposed they were, because everyone who took holy orders seemed to revel in misery and discomfort.

Yet the garden itself was a pleasant place. The sun was shining, bathing the little square in warmth, and bees buzzed around the flowers, while a blackbird sat atop a roof and chirped as if to proclaim his ownership of the garden.

Altruda was aware of all these things, yet she was most aware of Hereward. She knew he was a proud man, given to stubbornness and well used to violence. But he was, or at least he had been, a man of honour. She doubted whether he would lie to her, but she also knew he was one of the very few who would be able to resist her physical charms.

She needed to be careful here, she knew. There was a great deal at stake, both for her and for King William. Hereward's natural intransigence would be reinforced by the departure of King Sweyn and his longships. Without the Danes, Hereward's plans had been thwarted, and she knew he would suspect her of complicity in the affair.

She was right to be concerned about his truculence.

Scowling deeply, he asked, "Why are we meeting here anyway? You now have a room in the guest chambers. You could have spoken to me there."

"With your wife nearby?" Altruda smiled. "That might seem improper."

Hereward regarded her with a hard expression.

"Then tell me what you want," he stated coldly. "And be quick about it."

Ignoring his demand for brevity, she began obliquely, asking, "How is your friend, Ranald Sigtrygsson?"

She already knew the answer, but she hoped this might be a way to get Hereward talking and perhaps to loosen his stiff manner.

"He recovers slowly," Hereward replied.

"He decided to remain here when the Danes left?"

"He wishes to return to his home in Ireland," Hereward explained. "But I am sure you did not ask me here in order to discuss Ranald."

"Not specifically," she admitted. "But we must speak of the Danes. Or rather, what their absence means for you."

"It makes our victory a bit harder," Hereward shrugged.

"Impossible would be a more accurate word," she remarked.

"Nothing is impossible," he retorted.

"That is mere pride talking," she said flatly. "Anyone with a brain knows you cannot hope to defeat King William. King Sweyn understood that, which is why he returned to Denmark."

"He returned to Denmark because you convinced him to do so," Hereward challenged.

Altruda shrugged, "I gave him my opinion. The decision was his. But that does not matter. What matters is that you cannot hope to defeat King William now."

"He is not my King," Hereward stated, repeating one of his favourite mantras.

"He is King of England whether you like it or not," Altruda replied. "And there are no other viable candidates."

"Edgar the Atheling is in Scotland," he told her.

"Where he ran with his tail between his legs after his last attempt to claim the kingship. Besides, he is little more than a boy. And he knows nothing of England."

"So you are saying we should accept The Bastard because there is nobody else who could rule?"

"That is precisely what I am saying," Altruda agreed. "Let us suppose, for the sake of argument, you were to defeat him and kill him. What would happen then?"

"The Witan would elect a new King," he stated immediately.

"And the Norman Lords who have been granted lands here? They will simply give up their holdings and sail away?"

"If they know what is good for them," he confirmed.

"Do not be foolish, Hereward!" she snapped. "You know they will not do that readily. Besides, William has sons. The eldest will claim the throne, and the barons will support him. You will achieve nothing except the certainty that the country will be riven by war for years to come."

"It is riven by war now," he countered.

This was the opening Altruda had been waiting for.

She said, "Not if you seek terms."

Hereward's posture stiffened, and she saw Siward White's eyes widen slightly when he heard her words.

"Why should I seek terms?" Hereward asked.

"Because, despite your bravado, you are not a fool, Hereward. You have led men in war before now. You must know your paltry few hundred cannot hope to beat the thousands of men King William has at his disposal."

Spreading her hands in a gesture of openness, she went on, "But there is a solution to your problem. I have some standing with the King. I could act as an intermediary and speak on your behalf. I am sure I could persuade him to grant you back the lands your father once owned or, if not, other holdings of at least equal value."

"You think I am doing this to become a wealthy Thane?" he bristled.

She answered, "I think you are doing it out of a misplaced sense of grievance against Ivo de Taillebois."

"Misplaced? He killed my brother."

"Then I shall ask the King for justice on your behalf. But that is only one issue. The main thing is that this rebellion of yours can only end one way. You will bring death and destruction down on everyone around you. Will you do that simply for your own pride?"

She had stung him, she knew, but he refused to concede that he might be in the wrong.

"If we fight," he insisted, "others will join us."

"No, they will not," she retorted. "King William has crushed all other opposition to his rule. You may be a great hero with a famous reputation, Hereward, but you stand alone. You are the last man among the English who dares oppose William. The odds are too great even for you. You must know you cannot win."

Before Hereward could protest, she continued, "But the situation is not hopeless. I had hoped we could help one another. I told you that I was to be married off to a Norman lord. I wish to avoid that fate. That is why I am here and why I will stay here for the time being. But if you were to submit to the King, he would undoubtedly place you highly. He knows your reputation. That would give you an opportunity to help me."

Hereward's eyes narrowed as he asked, "So now we come to it. In what way do you expect me to aid you?"

221

Altruda sighed, casting a glance at the two men who stood behind him.

"This is why I wished us to have this conversation in private," she told him.

"Tell me what you propose," he said icily.

Altruda could tell he was struggling to keep his anger under control. She had, she feared, underestimated his resolve to continue the fight. Nevertheless, she had no option but to continue.

Giving another soft sigh, she told him, "It is well known that your wife is not happy here. She does not agree with your rebellion, so I hear."

"That is between me and Torfrida!" Hereward snapped.

"But there is more you must hear," she went on. "If the King were to grant you land, you would need a wife who could be of help to you in the King's Court. Torfrida cannot do that because she has long been in the service of the Count of Flanders. She knows nothing of England. Besides, I hear rumours that many people believe she is a witch, or that she is cursed."

Hereward's eyes blazed angrily, and she saw his hands bunch into fists as he spat, "Those rumours are lies!"

"Yet they persist," she smiled, forcing herself to remain calm in the face of his mounting fury.

He growled, "And no doubt you would see to it that they continue to spread?"

"I cannot prevent people gossiping," she replied with an air of complete innocence.

"You are trying my patience, Lady," he rasped. "Tell me what you want so that we can end this farce."

She could tell from the hardness in his gaze that she was losing the argument, but she had no alternative now. She must finish her case.

She explained, "If Torfrida were to take holy orders and enter a nunnery, you would be free to marry someone who could provide you with the support you would need in order to rise high in the King's service."

Hereward stared at her for a long moment, then threw back his head and laughed aloud, the harsh sound echoing around the cloister like an accusation.

Altruda saw the change immediately. No longer angry, he now regarded her with an expression of mocking contempt.

He said, "So your game has not changed. You wanted to marry me when we first met in Scotland all those years ago. You still want that."

"And why not?" she snapped irritably, her mask of composure slipping under his disdainful gaze. "We are well suited, you and I. You are a great war leader, while I understand politics better than most men. If we were to combine our talents, we could achieve great things."

He shook his head as he told her, "But you do not understand me, my Lady."

Now it was Altruda's turn to feel a burning rage building inside her. She dared not look at either of his two guards in case embarrassment overwhelmed her.

"Do you not understand anything?" she demanded. "I offer you titles, lands, riches, and peace for you and all your friends. All it will take is for you to bend the knee to King William, pledge yourself to him, and then marry me. Everybody would benefit. Do not throw it all away on a useless gesture which can only lead to your destruction!"

"I pity you, Lady," he told her scornfully.

Then he stood up, looking down at her as he added, "We have nothing more to say to one another. And I will tell Torfrida what you have suggested. She may agree with you about submitting to The Bastard, but she will never agree to your price. Nor will I."

He turned, signalled to his two guards, and began walking away, his boots crunching on the gravel of the path which quartered the cloister's garden.

"Hereward!" she called, her voice echoing around the colonnade.

He stopped and turned to look back at her.

Altruda took a deep breath, fixing her eyes on him as she told him, "Twice you have refused me now. Be warned, there will be no third time. Instead, it will be you who will crawl on your knees and beg for my hand."

He stared back at her, both of his companions watching him closely.

He said, "I doubt that very much."

His words stung her, but worse was the fact that he smiled when he said it.

The three men strode out of the cloister. Only when the echo of their footsteps had faded did Altruda slam her palms down on her thighs in fury. Then she took a deep breath as she forced her mind to a state of calm. She had always known he would prove difficult. She should have known better than to expect him to surrender to her plan immediately. Yet, where Hereward was concerned, she found to her annoyance that she had no patience for persuasion. He had refused her, and she could not tolerate that. Nobody refused her, certainly not twice. She would keep her promise that there would not be a third time.

No, she decided, there was no chance of persuading Hereward to see sense. Instead, she must use a different tactic.

She would write her letter to King William, telling him how to overcome the rebels. She would watch as they fell, one by one, until only Hereward was left. Ely would be destroyed by fire and by the sword, and she would glory in its destruction.

Then, at the end, with his plans in ruin and his companions slain, Hereward would be forced to submit, both to King William and to her.

That was not wishful thinking, she told herself. That was a solemn vow.

Chapter 14

Edric's mind was a whirl of emotions as he followed Hereward out of the cloister. He had not understood why the young Thane had ordered him to attend the meeting, but he was even more bewildered now that he had heard Altruda's shocking proposal. Did she really believe Hereward would abandon Torfrida for personal gain? That idea alarmed Edric more than the Lady's suggestion that the rebellion stood no chance of victory.

Martin Lightfoot was waiting patiently outside the cloister. His presence reminded Edric of a question that had been bothering him, and he decided to ask Siward White as soon as they were alone. That intention was foiled when Hereward told Siward to find his cousin, Red, and to meet Hereward in his room. Then he signalled to Martin to wait while he pulled Edric to one side.

"Do you understand now what I meant about that woman?" Hereward asked him pointedly. "Do you see that she is devious and untrustworthy?"

Edric nodded, "I see that, Lord."

"Good. Because I suspect she may attempt to sway one of my men to betray me in some way. You are the youngest, so she might think you are the most vulnerable. Be on your guard around her, lad. Do you understand?"

Edric nodded again.

"Is that why you wanted me there today?"

Hereward grinned, "That's right. But also because I know you can be trusted not to speak a word of what passed in there. Not to anyone."

Edric acknowledged the compliment with a brief smile, then ventured, "May I ask a question, Lord?"

"Only if you stop calling me Lord," Hereward replied.

Edric ignored the admonition. He asked, "I understand now why you wanted me there. But why Siward White? Martin is the most close-mouthed man I've ever met. Why did you not have him with you as a witness?"

Hereward gave a thoughtful nod before answering, "I trust Martin with my life. He is my oldest and closest companion. But he is a manservant, while Siward is, or was, a nobleman. If details of what was discussed were ever to come out, his word would count for a lot more than Martin's. Or yours, come to that."

"Why would it be an issue?" Edric persisted.

"I have no idea whether it will be an issue or not," Hereward told him. "But I have learned that it is as well to take precautions when dealing with the Lady Altruda. And that means I will be having all my food tasted from now on, and so will Torfrida."

Edric gaped at him.

"You think she would resort to poison?"

"I have no idea what she might resort to. As I say, I will be taking precautions. Now, forget her. There are other things I need to tell you."

Edric wondered what was coming. Had he done something wrong? Was it Ylva who had created a bigger problem than he had expected?

But Hereward surprised him by saying, "I need to make changes to how we handle this war. There are new men joining us, as you know. Some are joining Siward Barn's war band, but others are my responsibility. I am going to place the two Siwards in charge of them, so they will be away from Ely most of the time. I need them to train the men and to ensure all the approaches to the island are guarded."

Hereward reached out to plant his hand on Edric's shoulder as he added, "So I want you to take command of what is left of the gang."

"Me?"

"That's right. You've got more brains than any of the others, and you make the right decisions."

"But the others are all older and more experienced than me!" Edric protested. "Any of them could beat me in a fight."

"I know that. But they couldn't out-think you when it comes to knowing when and where to fight. You've got a natural talent for it, lad. So, you are in charge of my personal bodyguard as of this moment."

"Who will tell the others?" Edric wondered.

"White is doing that now," Hereward grinned. "The lads will know it's the right decision. Don't let it go to your head, though."

"I won't," Edric promised, his mind buzzing with thoughts of how men like Winter and Ordgar would accept him as their commander.

"Good," nodded Hereward. "Then there is one last thing I need to say to you."

He fixed Edric with his steely gaze as he said softly but insistently, "You need to do something about that girl you rescued. She is in danger as long as she stays with us."

Edric sighed. He had known Hereward would raise the subject of Ylva sooner or later.

"What can I do?" he replied forlornly. "She will be in greater danger if her father gets hold of her."

Hereward shrugged, "It is up to you what you do. You could always try to persuade her to seek formal sanctuary. Abbot Thurstan told Torfrida that is the only way he can guarantee her safety."

Edric frowned, "She insists it is no guarantee. She believes her father would enter the church and drag her from the altar. But even if he does respect the sanctuary, it only lasts for a year and a day. After that, she will have the same problem."

"A year is a long time," Hereward observed.

"Too long for Ylva. She has no wish to spend her time by the altar along with the other refugees who have fled from justice."

"Then you must think of something else," Hereward told him bluntly.

"But what? Killing Kenton would only cause problems with Thane Barn, even if I was confident I could beat him in a fight, which I am not."

"Don't fight him!" Hereward warned sharply. "He's a killer, and I don't want to lose you."

"So what other choice is left?" Edric asked plaintively. "The Abbot told Torfrida that the law is quite clear. Ylva belongs to her father."

Hereward regarded Edric with a sympathetic expression as he said, "The only other thing I can suggest is that she leaves Ely and tries to make a new life for herself elsewhere."

"On her own?" Edric blurted.

"Well, you're not thinking of going with her, are you?"

Edric shook his head. In truth, the idea had briefly crossed his mind, but he barely knew Ylva, and he had too many ties in Ely

227

for him to consider giving them up for the sake of a girl he had only just met.

Hereward sighed, "Then she has no real choice. If she will not return to her father and will not seek sanctuary in the church, she must leave."

Then he gave a crooked smile as he added, "Unless you can think of a way to make her disappear."

Edric cocked his head to one side, arching his eyebrows as he asked a silent question.

Hereward told him, "In war, I have often found that it helps to let your enemy see what you want them to see."

"What are you suggesting, Lord?"

"I am suggesting you find your own solution. I can know nothing about it, because I may need to swear an oath in front of Siward Barn and the Abbot. But if the girl disappears, then our problem is solved."

He gave Edric a slap on the back, then gestured to Martin to join him, and headed towards the guest chambers where he was to meet the two Siwards.

As Edric watched him go, he tried to make sense of what Hereward had said. The solution, when it struck him, was simple in concept, yet difficult to accomplish.

But he had no choice. He must act quickly, or Ylva would find herself back in the clutches of her sadistic father.

The confrontation came the following morning. Edric was standing outside the door to Aelswith's room, dressed in his chainmail and holding his axe across his chest. He was the only guard, because Hereward was off with the Siward cousins, overseeing the training of the new volunteers, and Torfrida had taken Alice with her when she went into Ely to visit some of the villagers who had fled from Bourne. Wulfric and Auti had accompanied Torfrida, while Winter and Ordgar were with Hereward, so Edric, who should have been resting, was standing watch on his own.

Only a few of the rooms were occupied now. Ranald Sigtrygsson had been moved into the room on the far side of Hereward's chamber. The Dane could hobble a short distance with the aid of a pair of wooden crutches, but he was very weak and spent the bulk of his time lying in bed and cursing his fate. Further along, in the room which had once housed King Sweyn, Altruda had taken up residence.

She had passed Edric earlier as she left the building, pausing to speak to him.

"I expect Hereward told you to beware of me?" she asked in a polite, friendly voice.

Edric nodded warily, "He did, Lady."

"You need not fear me, Edric. That is your name, is it not?"

"It is."

"Well, Edric, I wish only to be your friend. Hereward is a proud man, but I do not wish to see you or any of your companions die simply to bolster his ego."

Edric did not respond, but she appeared not to notice.

Maintaining her friendly attitude, she said, "I never did thank you properly for rescuing me from those brutes in Peterborough. I must find a suitable reward for you."

"I want no reward, Lady," he told her stiffly.

"No," she smiled, "I expect you do not. You have a habit of rescuing ladies, I believe. You brought your pregnant girl from Bourne, and I understand you rescued another girl only the other day."

Edric said nothing, but he silently cursed. He should have known it would not be possible to keep Ylva's presence a secret for long. Too many people knew about her.

Altruda tilted her head to one side as she asked, "Is she in that room behind you? Is that why you are here?"

Edric gave another shake of his head as he replied, "No. She has gone."

"Then why are you here? Does the baby need a bodyguard?"

Edric fumbled for an answer, but could find none. He merely shrugged, bringing a knowing smile to Altruda's face.

"Well, it is your business where you stand, of course. Now, I must be going, but we shall speak again, Edric Strong. Be sure of that."

He watched her as she walked along the corridor to the outer door, and he wondered how anyone so beautiful could be so devious. He had seen at first hand how she attempted to manipulate people, and he believed Hereward was correct in asserting that she had been primarily responsible for the Danes abandoning the rebels. Yet she looked like an angel, and the contradiction she presented left Edric feeling confused. It was difficult to heed Hereward's warnings when she was so close and appeared so friendly and enticing, but he knew he must be wary of her. What did she really want from him, he wondered?

He was still pondering her motives when the outer door opened again, admitting a flash of sunlight into the corridor which was then blocked as a man stepped inside. Glancing up, Edric felt a shiver of fear when he recognised the bulky, scar-faced figure of Kenton.

It was bound to happen, he thought. He had expected it, yet that did not prevent him feeling a stab of nervousness over what was about to happen.

The housecarl had a companion, a boy of around twelve or thirteen years old. Edric guessed it must be his son, the brother Ylva had mentioned.

The boy hung back nervously as Kenton stomped along the corridor, his eyes fixed on Edric.

"Hand her back, boy!" Kenton rasped as he stopped two paces away.

"Hand who back?" Edric replied, affecting ignorance.

"You know damned well who!" Kenton barked. "You were seen taking her away from the tavern. And I hear your precious Lady has spoken to the Abbot. Which means you've got her in that room behind you. She's not anywhere else in the abbey. I've looked."

"She is not here," Edric said stiffly.

Kenton took a step closer and hissed, "Open the door now. I will take her back."

"She wants nothing to do with you," Edric retorted, gripping his axe tightly as he faced up to the brutish housecarl.

"I don't give a rat's arse what she wants. Nor what you want. She is mine, and I want her back. Now!"

"She is not here," Edric repeated. "I suggest you leave before you make a fool of yourself."

"You're the fool, boy!" Kenton spat.

The man was fast. Edric had both hands around the haft of his long axe, but the corridor was too narrow for the weapon to be used effectively. Kenton suddenly produced a dagger which was at Edric's throat before he had time to react.

"Open the fucking door or I'll slit your god-damned throat right here and now!"

Looking into the man's feral eyes, Edric realised that it was only the knowledge that murdering one of Hereward's men would have consequences which kept Kenton from killing him on the spot. Yet it would not take much for the savage housecarl to take the risk. After all, he had his son as a witness. They could both swear that Edric had started the fight.

Edric's shoulders slumped in a gesture of defeat. He felt pressure on his axe as Kenton placed his own hand on the haft.

"Give me the axe!" the housecarl ordered.

Reluctantly, Edric released his grip on the weapon. Kenton yanked it from him and tossed it aside, letting it clatter to the stone-paved floor. The sound of its fall echoed along the corridor, signalling Edric's humiliation.

"Now open the door," Kenton told him. "And no tricks. I'll fucking slice you if you try anything."

Edric did not try anything. He turned slowly, feeling the tip of Kenton's dagger prick the base of his neck once his back was to the man. He knocked on the door, rapping urgently.

He heard footsteps and the door opened a crack, revealing Aelswith's pale face.

"What is it?" she whispered in an aggrieved tone. "The baby is sleeping."

Kenton gave Edric a shove, forcing him into the door and knocking Aelswith backwards. She let out a cry of fear, almost falling as she slammed her back against the side wall of the small room.

Edric stumbled but managed to keep his balance, then felt Kenton shoving him again as the scar-faced man followed him into the chamber.

"Where is she?" Kenton demanded.

"She's not here!" Edric told him yet again.

Kenton could see that he was right. The room was too small for anyone to hide properly. Two narrow beds, a small table, a chest for personal belongings and a wooden crib for the sleeping baby were its only contents. Light came in through the paned window, revealing no other places where anyone could be hiding.

Kenton was furious. Despite the impossibility of Ylva being in the room, he checked under the beds, looked behind the door and even yanked open the chest containing Aelswith's sparse belongings.

"Where is she?" he demanded again, brandishing his knife in Aelswith's face. "What have you done with her?"

Aelswith did not panic. She had overcome her initial surprise and now showed her inner strength by standing up to the intruder.

"She is gone," she told him. "She said she could not stay, so she left."

"On her own? Where did she go?"

"I don't know where she went. She just said she needed to leave Ely."

Kenton whirled round, jabbing the tip of his dagger towards Edric's face.

"Where did you take her?"

"I wasn't here when she left," Edric said flatly. "I don't know where she is."

With a roar of anger, Kenton pushed Edric, hurling him against the wall. Then he lashed out with his left fist, catching Edric on the cheek and snapping his head viciously. Edric thought the knife would come for him next, but the baby was woken by the noise and began to cry, its piercing, terrified wail snapping Kenton out of his rage.

"I'll find her, boy!" Kenton promised as he lashed out with his foot, kicking Edric's shin. "And when I do, I'll find out the truth. Then I'll come back and gut you."

He turned away, allowing Edric to see his son standing in the doorway, the boy's eyes dark and unreadable as he surveyed the scene. Then Kenton shoved the boy out and the two of them hurried away, the man uttering a stream of curses as he went.

Edric listened to their footsteps recede, then peered around the door to make sure they had left. Once he was sure they had gone, he retrieved his axe and returned to Aelswith.

"Are you all right?" he asked her.

Aelswith had picked up baby Torfrida and was holding her close, rocking her as she attempted to soothe the child's cries.

Aelswith's eyes blazed as she replied, "No thanks to you, Edric Strong. Why did you let him in?"

"He had a knife. Besides, he wouldn't have believed me unless he saw for himself."

"So where is Ylva?" she demanded. "I know you weren't here when she left, but you were behind her disappearance. I'm sure of that."

Edric gave her a brief smile as he admitted, "It's best nobody knows. But she's a long way from here by now."

Aelswith snorted in disgust.

"Well, I'm glad she's gone. She may have looked pretty enough once she was cleaned up, but she's a wild one. We are well rid of her."

Edric felt a little guilty because he had lied to Aelswith, but he knew he could not afford to tell anyone where Ylva had gone.

"You needn't bother about her any more," he said.

"I won't!" Aelswith declared.

Edric gave her an apologetic smile, then stepped out into the corridor, pulled the door shut, and resumed his sentry duty. Once alone, his face broadened into a wide smile. His plan, hastily conceived and urgently carried out, had worked.

Aelswith was right about one thing; Ylva had scrubbed up well. With her face cleaned of grime, her hair washed and combed, and dressed in a plain skirt and blouse which Alice had provided from among her own clothes, Ylva was more than pretty.

She was small, reminding Edric of a bird, but she possessed a surprisingly full figure for someone of such a delicate stature. It was, though, her mane of red-gold hair which was her most dazzling feature, tumbling around her shoulders in soft, natural waves.

That and her eyes. Set within a thin, elfin face, they were blue-green in colour, and very animated. Ylva might not be conventionally beautiful, but she was striking, grabbing the attention with every move she made.

Edric had been momentarily tongue-tied when he had first seen her properly but, with Hereward's warning ringing in his mind, he had overcome his instinctive bashfulness and hurried to talk to her. Either by fortuitous circumstance, or perhaps through Hereward's design, he found her alone in the room she shared with Aelswith.

"She's gone into town with the Lady Torfrida," Ylva explained, adding with a nervous smile, "I think she wanted to get away from me for a while."

Edric had dismissed her comment because they had other, more important matters to discuss.

"I need to get you away from here," he had told her, his words coming out in a rush as he tried to explain the plan he had devised.

Ylva was plainly terrified by the thought that her father might find her, and she nervously rubbed her hands together while she listened to Edric outlining his plan.

"Do you really think it will work?" she had asked.

"It's better than waiting here for your father to come and get you," Edric had told her.

"Yes," she had sighed. "You are right. Very well, I will trust you, Edric Strong."

So, that evening, when most people were in the refectory, Ylva had told Aelswith that she was leaving Ely because she was too afraid to stay. She had simply walked out, explaining to Ordgar, who was guarding the corridor, that she was going to answer a call of nature.

As soon as she stepped outside, she found that luck was with her. The fine weather of the morning had turned grey and cloudy as the afternoon progressed. Now a fine but persistent drizzle fell from a leaden sky which was turning the evening prematurely dark and encouraging most people to stay indoors. In such weather, nobody would look twice at a figure wearing a hooded cloak.

With her features concealed by her hood, Ylva hurried through the deserted abbey precinct to the rear of the infirmary where Edric was anxiously waiting for her. He greeted her with a warm smile but put his finger to his lips to warn her to be quiet. Then he led her to a small gate in the precinct's wall. He lifted the latch, eased the gate open and they both squeezed through, finding themselves on a small, grassy hithe where a handful of fen boats were moored on a dark stream.

Edric had first stumbled across this place by accident several days earlier when he had been prowling around outside the infirmary while Hereward visited his injured friend, Ranald. He had subsequently learned that this concealed gate was used by the monks when they wished to leave the abbey unobserved. That desire for secrecy now served Edric and Ylva well. Stealth was what they needed, and the miserable weather aided them for it meant they had a perfect excuse to keep their hoods over their heads.

Edric, dressed only in shirt, tunic, trousers and cloak, still found that he was sweating as he helped Ylva clamber aboard one of the boats. He glanced nervously at the gate, dreading to see it swing open to reveal the figure of Ylva's father, but nobody seemed to have seen them leave, and the gate remained firmly shut.

Ylva sat on one of the boat's wooden benches while he untied the mooring rope and pushed the flat-bottomed punt away from the river bank. He stood at the rear of the vessel, grasping the long pole boatmen used for propelling the boats along the waterways of the Fenland.

"Do you know how to use that?" Ylva asked as he clumsily eased the boat out into the stream.

"Not really. I've seen it done."

It was a lot harder than it looked, and he was afraid of losing his balance and falling into the deep water, but he eventually managed to coax the boat into motion, driving it erratically along the narrow waterway which curled lazily around the perimeter of the abbey precinct.

It was an eerie journey, the already palpable air of tension amplified by the transition from the normally bustling abbey and monastery to the quiet seclusion of the river. There was barely a sound to be heard apart from Edric's laboured breathing and the constant hiss of the rain which created small ripples on the water as if a million tiny insects were dancing on the smooth surface.

Tall reeds marked the further side of the channel, although there was no river bank to speak of. On their right, a grove of willows and alders marked the nearer bank. Edric knew that the town of Ely clung to the edge of the water just beyond that grove. Not wanting to be seen if he could help it, he steered the boat close to the drooping branches of the willows.

Ylva momentarily broke his concentration by saying, "Your woman does not like me."

"What?"

"Aelswith. She does not like me."

"She hardly knows you. And she is not my woman."

"She thinks she is," Ylva stated. "Or, at least, she thinks you are hers to command."

"She is a friend, nothing more," Edric insisted.

Ylva gave a soft chuckle as she observed, "That's not what your face tells me when you are near her."

Edric could not think of a suitable response to her accusation, but Ylva carried on regardless.

"You should be careful of her," she warned. "She is a schemer."

"No she's not!" Edric protested.

"She'll use you if you are not careful," Ylva told him.

Edric scowled, "Never mind that. You need to worry about yourself. Now, keep your hood up and stay close to me."

They had not needed to travel far. Edric guided the boat towards another muddy, boggy stretch of land close to the first homes of the town itself. They stepped out, their feet squelching in the soft ground, and he pulled the boat ashore before leading Ylva towards the town.

"The rain should keep most people indoors," he whispered.

Ylva nodded, but signalled for him to stop.

"You should hold my hand," she told him as she extended an arm towards him.

"What?"

"You look as if you are up to no good, skulking around like this. Here, take my hand and walk slowly, as if we are lovers out for a stroll."

Edric hesitated, but Ylva placed her hand in his, stepped close to him and eased him into motion.

"Keep talking," she instructed. "Make it look as if this is perfectly innocent."

Edric did his best to follow her advice, but his hand felt clammy as he held hers, and he could think of nothing to say.

"Tell me again where we are going," she prompted. "You explained it all so quickly the first time."

Edric sighed, then leaned down towards her so that she could hear him over the patter of the rain on their hoods.

"We are going to the home of a potter. His name is Cecil, and his wife is called Garyn. They have six children, and Garyn is expecting again."

"Poor woman," Ylva remarked softly.

"She likes children," Edric assured her.

"She is fortunate so many have survived," Ylva said, her voice betraying more than a hint of bitterness.

"Some are still quite young," Edric replied, knowing that the first five years of life were the most dangerous.

Ylva was silent for a moment, then said, "I had a baby once."

Edric was so startled that he stopped dead in his tracks, staring at her. She frowned as she tugged him back into motion.

"Keep walking and talking," she scolded. Then, with a sigh, she added, "I'm sorry. I don't know why I said that. I didn't mean to tell you. I was going to keep it a secret, but I suppose you ought to know."

"What happened?" he asked.

She shrugged, "It was a boy. He died after only three days. He was very small when he was born, and he would not take my milk."

Edric could hear the sorrow in her words, the desperate, lonely sadness of her memories.

"How old were you?" he asked cautiously.

He could not see her face because of the hood she wore, but he could tell that she was staring straight ahead, not looking at him as she told her story.

"Fourteen," she informed him in a voice that betrayed a sense of almost unimaginable loss and sorrow. "And yes, before you ask, Kenton was the father."

Edric felt his legs go weak. She had hinted at Kenton's depravity, but he had not wanted to think about the precise details of what the man's wickedness involved.

"So now you know why I hate him," she said. "I'm glad I've told you, but please keep it a secret."

"If that is what you want," he mumbled.

"It is. Now, tell me about this man who will pretend to be my grandfather."

Edric was still reeling from her revelation, but he gathered his wits enough to say, "His name is Seaver. He is from Bourne, my own village. He was quite well off, but his wife died a few years ago, and he has no children."

"He must have a family if I am to be his granddaughter," Ylva observed.

This was the ruse Edric had devised. Ylva would take on a new identity and hide under the protection of a normal family. Seaver had found lodgings with Cecil, a florid-faced, cheerful man who earned a precarious living as a potter. He and his growing family lived near the southern edge of the town. Cecil's home was crowded, but he had hoped to supplement his income by taking in a lodger. Seaver, who had brought a stash of silver coins with him when he fled Bourne, had instead helped the potter by paying for additional rooms to be built on the back of the building which housed Cecil's workshop and home. He had promised that Ylva would be given one of those new rooms and that he would play the part of her grandfather.

"Yes, you are right," Edric admitted in response to Ylva's comment about Seaver's invented family. "The story is that his daughter married a man from York. Both of them died in the recent troubles up there, so you have come south looking for him. When you reached Bourne, you learned he had come here. You bumped into me, asked if I knew where he might be found, and I've brought you to him."

"Do you really think I can hide from my father in a place as small as Ely?" she asked.

"I don't see why not. It's a busy town now, with all the extra people having arrived. Nobody will ask too many questions. There are lots of newcomers now. Still, you'd best try to stay out of sight as much as you can. And you'd better think about cutting your hair."

She gave him a look of dismay before nodding her reluctant agreement.

"I'll wear a headscarf as well," she decided. "And I'd better use a new name, hadn't I?"

"That is a good idea," Edric nodded.

"Jetta," she said immediately. "I've always liked that name."

"Then you are now Jetta," Edric agreed.

"What about you? Will I see you again?"

238

He hesitated. There was something in her voice and the sidelong look she gave him which added a plea to the question.

"Not very often," he said gently. "I expect your father will follow me once he learns you are not being kept in Aelswith's room. I don't want to lead him to you."

She gave a slight nod, lowering her eyes to the ground.

"I understand," she said softly.

"I'll think of some way to keep in touch," he promised.

"It would still be easier if you killed my father," she asserted.

"I know. But Hereward has told me not to fight him."

"You don't need to face him in a fair fight," she retorted. "Just surprise him, slit his throat and dump his body somewhere."

"I can't do that," he told her.

Ylva sighed, "I know. Perhaps that's why I like you. Most warriors wouldn't think twice about murdering someone who threatened them."

"Maybe I'm not a real warrior."

"That's not what your friends say. They tell me you are a great fighter."

Edric was embarrassed to hear this, so he quickly changed the subject.

"Seaver is a good man," he told her. "And he owes me a favour. He'll look after you."

The light was fading fast now, but they were almost there. They had seen very few people since the rain was keeping the streets clear, as well as turning them to mud, but the few townsfolk they had passed had paid them no attention.

But now that their short journey was almost over, Edric felt a pang of regret. He realised he had enjoyed their brief time together. It was a new experience for him to walk anywhere holding hands with a pretty girl while talking about their lives in such an open, uninhibited way.

Then he felt guilty because he knew Aelswith was sitting in her room back at the abbey, and he felt he should not be enjoying the company of another woman. It had always been Aelswith who had been the object of his secret desires, and he could not shake off the feeling that he was somehow betraying her trust in him.

His emotions were confused even further once they reached the potter's home in a narrow back street near the southern edge of the town. Edric knocked on the door and waited, but Ylva suddenly reached up, pulled his face down, stood on the tips of her toes and planted a kiss on his lips.

"Thank you for what you have done for me," she whispered once the kiss had ended. "Whatever happens, I will always be your friend."

Edric stood agape, but was rescued when the door opened and Seaver himself greeted them with a warm smile and a grandfatherly hug for Ylva.

"Come in out of the rain!" he invited, hesitating slightly as he looked at the slim figure in front of him.

"Jetta," Ylva whispered. "My name is Jetta."

"Welcome, Jetta. My very own granddaughter!"

He gave Edric a broad wink as he said this, grinning all over his weathered face.

"Take good care of her," Edric told the old man.

"I will."

"You'd best go inside," Edric advised. "I need to get back before I'm missed."

"Yes," Seaver nodded. "Come, lass, you must meet Cecil and his family. They will make you welcome."

Ylva shot one last look at Edric, who gave her a quick smile in return. Then Seaver was leading her into the house and closing the door, leaving Edric alone in the damp, muddy lane.

He stood staring at the door for a moment, not fully understanding why the parting had left him experiencing a sense of loss. Then, with a shake of his head, he hunched his shoulders against the drizzle and trudged back down the narrow street, heading for the boat.

Chapter 15

William, Duke of Normandy and King of England, was a big man with short-cropped, red hair and piercing eyes. Ivo de Taillebois knew him well, so he delivered his message with some trepidation, for it was never certain how William would react to any situation. He was a man of direct action and strong opinions who had grown up trusting nobody. That trait remained with him. Inheriting the rule of Normandy while still in his teens, he had learned to take bold, decisive action against anyone who opposed him, and had displayed a ruthlessness which often scared even those who knew him best.

Ivo de Taillebois had hurried to London as soon as Altruda's message reached Peterborough. Abbot Turold would have preferred to deliver the report himself, but his presence was required in Peterborough where he was devising great plans for the rebuilding of the entire abbey and monastery. There was also the not insignificant matter of Hereward and the rebels in Ely to deal with. Altruda had given them an insight into how they might end the rebellion, but it required the king's approval and assistance, so de Taillebois had galloped to London to present their case to their monarch.

He had found William in the palace at Westminster, a collection of buildings arrayed on Thorney Island, close to the abbey and monastery which had been built by Edward, the last legitimate King of England. Edward, whom some were now calling a saint and others naming, "The Confessor" because of his piety, had built the abbey and the palace as a statement of his own power. William had now assumed control, seizing that power for himself.

De Taillebois understood that power and wealth were the driving forces which guided William's actions. The Duke of Normandy had taken control of England through brutal suppression of opposition and by threatening or bribing the nobles and Church officials. Bishops and other landowners were terrified of losing their wealth, yet William had decreed that everything in England belonged to him. Every field, every stream, every woodland, hill and valley; every hamlet, village or town was his to do with as he pleased. He could depose bishops and appoint his own favourites to replace them; he could remove noblemen and have their estates granted to the men who had joined his crusade to remove Harold Godwinson from the throne.

William's authority knew no bounds and he was using that power to enrich himself at every opportunity. Bishops who held land for the Church were compelled to pay extortionate sums simply to retain control of land they already owned, and their new tenure was always subject to the King's right to confiscate the land on a whim.

His whims were infamous. Nobles who offered him vast sums in order to be awarded a grant of land could find themselves suddenly replaced by another man who had offered more money. For William, everything was up for sale, and yet he still insisted that the land ultimately belonged to him and that his grants could be revoked at any time.

His dictatorial approach to kingship was typical of the man, yet nobody dared oppose him. He was King by right of conquest and by divine favour. To oppose him was to go against God's will. So said the bishops, because William instructed them to spread this message on pain of being removed from office, and so his control remained absolute and unchallenged.

Yet William, de Taillebois knew, was secretly insecure. He had lived his life in fear of being overthrown, imprisoned or assassinated. That fear drove him to excess in everything he did.

De Taillebois could understand that fear as few others did, for he felt it himself. He had risen to a position of authority thanks to having gained William's confidence, yet he knew only too well that the King could easily remove him and cast him into penury. Or worse.

The King's insecurity manifested itself in several ways. The most ludicrous, in de Taillebois's opinion, was his habit of parading around his court wearing a jewel-encrusted crown and long, ermine-lined robes in order to impress his nobles with his majesty.

Majesty. That was the word William wanted to burn into the minds of his subjects. It was also the title by which he insisted on being addressed. De Taillebois instinctively understood the reasons for these open displays of supposed superiority, and he played up to them for all he was worth.

"Your Majesty," he reported as he grovelled before William's throne, "I have the honour to present to you the Lady Altruda's news from Ely. King Sweyn and the Danish fleet have left England. The Danish King did not dare challenge your right to the kingship of England."

A murmur ran around the court when the nobles heard this news, but William's stern gaze did not betray any joy at hearing it. He stared down at de Taillebois from the vantage of his ornate throne, his expression forbidding.

"What of the other rebels?" he demanded. "The ones who burned your castle and killed your men?"

De Taillebois swallowed nervously. He had anticipated this question and rehearsed his answer, yet he still felt nervous as he explained, "The Lady Altruda is on Ely herself. She has sent word that there are fewer than five hundred rebels on the island, and they are split in their opinions as to what to do next. Some wish to do no more than hold what they have, while others seek to stir up trouble in the hope of attracting support from elsewhere."

"From elsewhere?" William rasped. "From where? Who will dare join them?"

"I doubt that anyone would be foolish enough to give them aid," de Taillebois replied smoothly. "But that does not mean the rebels themselves do not labour under the delusion that they can succeed."

William snorted, but asked, "What else does the Lady Altruda say?"

"She has informed us that the easiest approach to the island is at its southern edge, at a place called Aldreth. There, the river is at its narrowest. She says this is where the rebels most fear an attack."

"So they will have fortified it, will they not?" William demanded.

"Indeed, Your Majesty. But their rampart is of earth and sticks. If we had enough men, we could overwhelm them and crush the rebellion."

William sat back, his hands resting on the arms of his gilded throne. A faint smile twitched around his lips, the first sign of any real emotion.

He said, "So now we come to the nub of your reason for being here. You want men. Is that right?"

Ivo de Taillebois gave a wan smile as he stuttered, "Yes, Your Majesty. We, that is Abbot Turold and myself, humbly ask that you provide us with a force sufficient to cross the river and destroy the rebels."

"Turold is keen to fight, I presume?"

De Taillebois thought he detected a sliver of scorn in the King's tone, but he decided now was not the time to denigrate the man he would need to work alongside.

He said, "The Abbot is as keen as ever, Your Majesty. He wants only to destroy those who would dare rebel against you."

"I'm sure he does," William murmured. Then, fixing de Taillebois with a challenging stare, he demanded, "But you must cross the river? How? From what I hear, the Fens are a maze of streams and channels. How would you get enough boats there to force a landing in sufficient strength?"

De Taillebois knew William would identify this problem. The King, for all his many faults, was well versed in warfare. Fortunately, Abbot Turold had taken the time to read Altruda's letter aloud in full, so de Taillebois had an answer.

"The Lady Altruda suggests we could build a bridge, Your Majesty."

"A bridge?"

"So the Lady suggests. The river's current at Aldreth is not strong. The water is deep, but less wide than in other places."

William nodded slowly, "Yes, I suppose that might work."

"The Lady Altruda is very perceptive and highly talented, Your Majesty. Abbot Turold trusts her judgement implicitly."

"I know the Lady's talents," William retorted curtly.

De Taillebois bowed his head, but he knew he had planted the idea. If he or Turold had suggested building a bridge to the island, William would probably have raised objections. The fact that the proposal came from Altruda made a difference. She might be a woman, but she possessed an ability to identify and resolve problems which few men could match.

William considered his response for a short time before making his decision.

He said, "I must return to Normandy. I would like to settle this rebellion personally, but I cannot afford to remain in England while my home is threatened by my rivals. So, de Taillebois, I will follow the Lady's advice. I will provide fifteen hundred men, and you will build the bridge. Tell Abbot Turold I want the revolt crushed. Absolutely crushed, do you hear?"

The king's face grew hard and his voice rose almost to the level of a shout as he finished his sentence, accompanying his words with the thump of a clenched fist on the arm of his throne.

De Taillebois bent almost double as he bowed low.

"It shall be as you say, Your Majesty. We shall wipe them out."

He did not mention the one odd thing in Altruda's letter. For some reason, she had asked that the rebel leader, Hereward, be taken alive. She had not explained her motive, and de Taillebois did not care. For his part, he wanted Hereward done away with, because the man was out for vengeance against him, and he would not be safe until the Englishman was dead.

And now he had King William's blessing to slaughter every last one of the rebels. Including Hereward.

That, de Taillebois decided, was something to look forward to. By summer's end, the revolt would be over and Hereward would be dead.

Then there was the matter of Torfrida, the dark-haired, voluptuous witch who had been the cause of de Taillebois's downfall. She, he decided, deserved a special fate, one that he would be only too happy to oversee.

"You will be mine," he whispered to himself as he imagined what he would do to her.

First, though, the island of Ely needed to be taken by storm. He would allow Abbot Turold the glory of directing that assault, then he would move in once victory was assured. There was, after all, no sense in placing himself in danger. That was the last thing he wanted.

But when the fighting was over, he would march in and take Hereward's wife into captivity. She would be his reward.

And all it would require was an army of fifteen hundred soldiers and the building of a bridge.

On the island of Ely, Altruda found it necessary to be patient. Brother Richard had delivered her letter, but it would be some time before she would know whether William had approved her plan.

In the meantime, she laid the groundwork for other eventualities. Brother Richard was already a willing accomplice.

His Norman upbringing made him a natural ally, for he hated the fact that the abbey was swarming with armed rebels.

"This is a place of worship and contemplation," he complained to Altruda. "It is not meant to be an armed camp."

"Perhaps there is a resolution," she suggested.

"What sort of resolution?" he frowned. "Abbot Thurstan supports the rebels."

"There may be a way to bring about a peaceful conclusion to this sad situation," she told him. "If I can find such a solution, can I count on your help?"

"Of course you can," he confirmed eagerly. "But how can you do that?"

"I do not know yet," she lied. "But I may need you to carry more letters for me. Would you be prepared to do that?"

He did not hesitate to agree, swearing to keep her liaison with Abbot Turold a secret.

"Thank you, Brother Richard. But please be patient. These things often take a great deal of time."

He had given his word, and she had rewarded him by kissing his hands and praising his loyalty.

But Brother Richard would play only a small part in her plan. If the rebellion was to be put down, she needed other means of creating division among the rebels.

With that in mind, her next target was Thane Siward Barn.

The old warrior regarded her with some suspicion when he granted her an audience in his private chamber.

"Hereward warned me against speaking to you," he informed her gruffly.

"Hereward and I have had our differences in the past," she replied smoothly. "He is a stubborn man and will not listen to reason."

"He is certainly stubborn," Barn agreed. "But he is not a fool. He is a fine leader of men in combat."

"I do not dispute that," Altruda replied. "But, even with his skill, you cannot win. This is what I told him, but he refused to listen to me. You, on the other hand, are a man of intelligence. You must know this rebellion is ultimately doomed."

Barn stared at her, his old, lined face as impassive as a stone. Then he said softly, "I know we cannot defeat The Bastard unless we have help. But that does not mean I am prepared to lay down my arms and surrender to him. I am an Englishman, and he is a foreign invader who has stolen the crown."

"Oh, I agree with you!" Altruda insisted passionately. "I wish there was some way to defeat him. But we must face reality, my Lord. Without the Danes, there is no hope of success. Nobody else will dare join your uprising. In the end, no matter how brave you are, King William will take Ely by storm."

Barn let out a long sigh before nodding, "I know that, my Lady. Yet Hereward tells me you were the one who persuaded King Sweyn to sail back to Denmark."

Altruda saw the harsh glint of accusation and suspicion in the old man's eyes, and she knew she must play her part well if she were to have any chance of convincing him.

"That is not true!" she protested, putting her hands to her eyes as if to hold back tears. "Sweyn took me as a prize from Peterborough and then discarded me when he made up his mind to return home. You can have no idea how degrading that is for me, my Lord. I was powerless to prevent him treating me like a common concubine. I certainly had no influence over him, nor did I have anything to do with his decision to leave. He simply decided that the treasures he had seized from the abbey were sufficient reward, so he made up his mind to go home with what he had rather than risk a battle he was not confident of winning. That is the truth of it, my Lord. You must believe me!"

Barn seemed embarrassed by her display of emotion and the alleged treatment she had suffered at the hands of King Sweyn, which was precisely the reaction she had hoped for. Once he was off balance, she pressed home her advantage.

"I have seen the brutality of war, my Lord," she told him. "I have learned at first hand how innocents suffer. I wish to prevent anyone else going through what I went through. I do not want to see any more men slain or women violated, nor holy places defiled, nor monks dragged off in captivity. There must be another way; a solution which would prevent more bloodshed."

Barn's expression had softened under the passion of her speech, and he was less hostile as he asked, "What way is that?"

"Exile," she said carefully. "Many Englishmen have fled abroad. We could take a ship and sail away."

"And go where?" he snorted.

"Anywhere. Flanders, one of the German kingdoms, France, or perhaps as far as Constantinople. There are many rulers who would welcome a strong man like yourself."

Regarding her coolly, he said, "You said, 'we'. Does that mean you intend to go into exile yourself?"

"Naturally," Altruda lied. "Provided I can find a nobleman who is prepared to protect me."

She could see that he understood her unspoken compliment. She was telling him that he was a man of honour whom she could trust. It was a subtle piece of flattery to which even an old man like Barn would be susceptible.

"And what of my men?" Barn retorted. "I would need more than one ship to transport them all."

Altruda bowed her head and shrugged, "It was merely an idea, my Lord. I am only a simple woman who does not understand these things. But surely you could find ships from somewhere? And exile would be better than a useless death, would it not?"

She studied him, looking for signs that her words had sparked some doubt in his mind, but Barn was an old warrior, set in his ways and as hard as nails. To her annoyance, he wrecked her hopes when he shook his head.

"England is my home," he told her defiantly. "I will not abandon my country or my men, no matter what."

"I admire your courage and conviction," she nodded, holding back the frustration she felt. "Then at least you might try to prevent Hereward stirring up more trouble than is necessary. Ely is a haven, but he will only draw more Normans here if he persists in making his raids."

Barn nodded, "I know that, my Lady. But Hereward is his own man, and I cannot control him."

He straightened in his chair as he said, "Now, I think we have said enough. I appreciate your concerns, my Lady, but do not doubt my commitment to remaining free of the Normans."

Altruda smiled, "I understand, my Lord."

"Then I will bid you farewell," he said. "Unless there is anything else you wish to discuss?"

"There is one more thing, my Lord."

"And what is that?"

"I am here alone, as you know. I would greatly appreciate some protection. A woman alone is always vulnerable, even in a holy place, when she is surrounded by so many men who are accustomed to violence and war."

"You are safe from my men," Barn assured her. "None of them would dare do anything to you."

"I know that, my Lord. But Hereward's men are less disciplined than your own warriors. I intend to hire a maid, but I was hoping you might appoint one of your men to be my protector."

Barn looked doubtful, but asked, "One man?"

"Is that too much to ask? I know it is probably unnecessary, but I would feel much safer knowing I had someone close at hand. Will you not grant that small favour to a weak and defenceless woman, my Lord?"

Barn waved a resigned hand in submission to her request.

"Very well. I can give you one man."

Altruda suspected he had agreed so that he could end the discussion quickly, but that did not matter to her. She was getting what she wanted, so she rewarded him with a dazzling smile.

"Thank you, my Lord. There is one man in particular I have noticed who would seem ideal."

"Oh? Who is that?"

"I believe his name is Kenton."

"Kenton?" Barn frowned, clearly taken by surprise. "He is a dangerous man, my Lady. Very dangerous indeed."

"Which is why his presence would deter anyone else from attempting to …" she hesitated, allowing him to mentally complete her sentence.

Still he objected, saying, "I think you would be making a mistake, my Lady. Kenton is not a man I would trust in any matter other than warfare."

"Nevertheless," Altruda persisted. "You see, he has a grudge against Hereward's gang, so he would make an ideal protector for me."

Barn gave in, shaking his head but allowing her what she wanted.

"Very well," he sighed. "If that is your wish, I shall instruct Kenton to attend you."

Altruda showered thanks on the old man. Her visit had been less successful than she had hoped, but there was still time to work on the old fool.

And now she would have the assistance of a man who hated Hereward and his gang.

Kenton brought a boy with him, a sullen, timid lad of around twelve years of age. The boy hung back, remaining near the door, while Kenton stood leering at Altruda.

"The Thane said I was to be your guard," he said with a swagger.

"That is correct," Altruda confirmed, sitting facing him with as much composure as she could muster. She was all too aware of the man's brute strength and air of menace, yet she could not afford to betray any hint that she feared him.

"Let us be clear, Kenton," she told him. "I require your presence as a safeguard against anyone who might seek to prevent me going about my business. In turn, I can help you. But that is as far as our relationship will go. Do you understand?"

He smirked at her, his tongue flicking out to lick his lips.

"Whatever you say, my Lady," he said with little sincerity.

"My business will affect you, too," she went on.

"How?" he demanded, a frown furrowing his brow.

"By saving your sorry life when King William arrives with his army."

That surprised him. He said, "We are safe enough here."

"Not for much longer, I expect," she countered. "The King, as you may have heard, is savage in his reprisals against those who oppose him. I have good reason to believe he will soon turn his attention towards Ely. When that happens, those who defy him will suffer. Mutilation is the least you can expect. Would you be happy to have your eyes put out? Or to lose a hand or a foot?"

She could see that Kenton was a man who would respond to threats, yet he was no coward.

He grunted, "The Bastard will need to get to us first. That's near impossible."

"The King is not a man to be dissuaded by difficulties," she told him. "Sooner or later, Ely will be under his control. When that happens, only those who can prove they were not against him have any hope of being set free."

"You want me to turn traitor?" he demanded with a suspicious glare.

"I did not say that. I know you are sworn to serve Thane Barn. But he has spurned my advice and will not go into exile, so we must face the consequences of that decision. I seek a peaceful end to our predicament and, if you help me achieve that, I will have enough influence to ensure you do not suffer like the others. But if you decide you would prefer to take your chances, so be it."

"What influence would you have?" he asked, doubt clouding his features.

"I have many friends in high places," she replied. "The highest place of all, in fact."

"So you are a Norman spy?" he growled, shooting her an accusatory look.

"No, I want only what is best for England. I want peace. I want an end to this rebellion. I have friends in both camps, so I am well placed to bring about a peaceful resolution. That is what I will work for."

"And you want my help?"

"Not with that. I merely want you to act as my protector. There are some among Hereward's gang who might seek to do me some harm."

That caught his attention, as she had guessed it would.

She went on, "I want no confrontation between you and Hereward's men until I say so. Is that clear?"

"One of them stole my daughter," he protested.

"Edric Strong, I believe."

"That's him," Kenton agreed gruffly.

"Then we both have an interest in him."

"Yeah?" Kenton sneered. "What is your interest in him?"

"Not what you are thinking," she shot back. "No, Edric might yet provide me with a way to nullify Hereward."

Kenton's frown grew deeper as he asked, "how?"

"I do not yet know. But Edric is young, and less experienced than the other members of Hereward's gang. More importantly, he knows how to think. I may be able to use that against him."

"I don't understand," Kenton admitted with a surly shrug.

"Your understanding is not required. Your obedience is. I want Edric Strong left alive. Is that clear?"

"He stole my daughter!" Kenton blurted angrily.

"And, if he was clever, he sent her far away. There are boatmen who will carry people through the Fens for the right price. You know that."

The scar on Kenton's face seemed to burn with an inner fire, but he gave another angry nod.

"And yet," Altruda continued smoothly, "he might have been very clever and simply hidden her somewhere close at hand. After all, if he wanted to keep her safe, sending her out into the world on her own is hardly the most sensible course of action."

Kenton's eyes narrowed as he stared at her.

"You think she's still here? I've looked, but I can't find her."

"I have no idea where she is," Altruda admitted. "But Edric Strong may yet tell us where she can be found."

"Do you think you can get him to tell you?" Kenton scowled.

Instead of responding, Altruda suddenly changed the subject.

She said, "You have not introduced me to your son."

Kenton blinked, "What?"

"Your son. Introduce him to me."

Confused, Kenton turned to usher the boy forward. The lad stood in front of Altruda, trying to appear unafraid, but evidently nervous.

"This is Halfdan," Kenton said as he placed his hand on his son's shoulder. "Bow to the lady, Halfdan."

The boy bobbed his head in a perfunctory bow. His eyes, Altruda thought, looked dull and almost blank, like the eyes of a dead fish. There was no spark in them at all. He had, she guessed, been beaten so many times that all traces of vitality had left him. He and his clothing could have done with a decent wash, she thought, but her immediate concern was the task she had in mind for him.

"You are training him to be a warrior?" she asked Kenton.

Kenton grunted, "Trying. He's got no brains at all. And he's soft. He killed his first man when he was twelve, and blubbered like a baby for hours afterwards. But I'm toughening him up."

"I'm sure you are," Altruda smiled, wondering what dark deed had taken place for such a young boy to have killed a man.

Turning to Halfdan, she asked, "How old are you?"

The boy swallowed anxiously, clearly overawed, but Kenton put in, "He's fourteen."

Altruda's eyebrows arched. The boy was scrawny and looked barely older than twelve. Still, he should be capable of following her orders.

"Do you know the man called Edric Strong?" she asked him.

Halfdan gave a silent nod in response.

She told him, "I want you to watch him. Stay out of sight as much as you can, but try to know where he is at all times. If he should go into the town, follow him and see where he goes and who he speaks to. Can you do that?"

Again, Halfdan nodded.

"Speak up, boy!" Kenton barked, giving his son a slap on the back of the head.

"Yes, my Lady," Halfdan mumbled.

"Good," said Altruda. "And if, by any chance, you should discover the whereabouts of your sister, you will tell me first. Do you understand me?"

The sudden icy chill in her voice struck fear into the boy, who barely managed to mutter a reply.

"Yes, my Lady."

Altruda smiled again.

"Then we understand one another. Kenton, you will follow me at a respectful distance when I require you to accompany me. You will not take any action against any of Hereward's companions until I give you leave to do so. Halfdan, you will follow Edric Strong and keep me informed of everywhere he goes and everyone he talks to."

Father and son both nodded their understanding, one of them angry and bewildered, the other frightened.

Altruda told them, "Neither of you will breathe a word of anything I say or do. If you serve me to my satisfaction, I may just be able to save your sorry necks when King William arrives. Fail me, and you will suffer. Be in no doubt that the King will win in the end. Even Thane Barn acknowledges this. If you wish to survive, you will do as I say without question."

It was a small victory, but Altruda enjoyed wielding power. Kenton was experienced enough to know that she spoke the truth, and his desire to find his daughter would bind him to Altruda's wishes. Halfdan, a dull-witted, frightened boy, would do as she commanded because he knew no other way to act when given orders by a noblewoman.

So Edric Strong was safe from Kenton's wrath, which would leave Altruda free to pursue the next stage of her plan.

Chapter 16

For Edric, that summer was both the easiest and the most difficult he had ever experienced. It was easy because he was free from the strenuous labour of working in his uncle's forge, yet it was difficult because he had so many problems to contend with.

Being put in charge of Hereward's small personal guard involved anticipating the young Lord's moods and actions, and ensuring that at least two members of the group were able to accompany him wherever he went. This proved difficult since Hereward was a mercurial character who rushed from place to place, always on the move, always issuing orders and demanding perfection from the men under his command.

The two Siwards, Red and White, were busy training men and ensuring defences were constructed and guarded. Stockpiles of food and weapons were being created, and messengers appointed to carry word from one end of the island to the other.

Hereward insisted on inspecting everything. He never rested, from dawn till dusk, and it was tiring keeping up with him.

Then there was the additional problem that Torfrida refused to be confined to her room and would insist on going into the town to visit the various villagers who had fled from Bourne, checking to see how they were faring. A guard needed to be appointed to accompany her whenever she decided to venture out.

One unexpected thing her visits did solve was the problem of how Edric could keep in touch with Ylva.

Torfrida took him aside one afternoon when she returned to the abbey after having visited the town.

"I met Old Seaver today," she said with a knowing smile.

"How is he?" Edric asked, attempting to conceal his anxiety.

"He is well. He says he much prefers helping Cecil make and sell pots to labouring all day in the fields."

"That's good," Edric mumbled.

"And he has a granddaughter staying with him now," Torfrida said, her blue eyes pinning Edric to the spot.

"Oh?"

Torfrida leaned close, placing a reassuring hand on Edric's arm as she whispered, "She is well, Edric, and asked me to give you her thanks."

Edric sighed, "You recognised her?"

"Only when I spoke directly to her. You needn't worry. She is being careful. And I will not reveal her secret. But let me know if I can take any message back to her."

Edric hesitated, then said, "Tell her to remain watchful, my Lady."

"I will," Torfrida promised.

Once she had gone, Edric relaxed from the tension that had seized him. He looked around, wondering whether anyone had noticed their conversation, but there were only a couple of monks walking slowly across the compound and a young boy sitting with his back against the wall of the infirmary, his concentration on the task of whittling a stick with his knife. Edric recognised him as Kenton's son, and was happy for the lad since he seemed to have escaped the scar-faced housecarl's stern company and was often to be seen simply hanging around rather than trailing after his brute of a father.

Edric had expected more trouble from Kenton, but the scarred man had proved to be less of a problem than he had anticipated. The thuggish housecarl often glared at Edric but he never made any overtly threatening moves.

"He's scared of Thane Barn punishing him if he does anything," was Winter's verdict.

Winter, along with the others, had also proven to be less of a problem than Edric had feared. The four men accepted his position as their commander and appeared to take a perverse pride in the fact that their nominal leader was little more than a boy.

"You're the one with the brains," Winter assured him. "We'll do as you say, as long as you don't try to tell us how to fight."

"I wouldn't dream of it," Edric assured him.

In fact, he rarely told them to do anything. He merely asked them to carry out a task, or suggested they might want to perform a duty which needed doing, and they would nod and go about the job without question.

There were, though, other people who concerned Edric.

Aelswith seemed ill at ease. Her baby was growing strong, crying lustily and feeding well, yet motherhood did not seem to suit Aelswith, and she often complained about being tired. Edric would sometimes sit with her when his duties allowed, and would hold baby Torfrida, not quite sure what to do with the human bundle of frailty, nor how to deal with her unpredictable cries and smells.

"I never knew it would be so hard," Aelswith would complain when the baby kept her up half the night.

"You are managing fine," Edric assured her, smiling to cover his concern at the hollow look in her eyes and her air of perpetual exhaustion.

"You think so?" Aelswith retorted.

"Of course," he lied.

The truth was that she barely seemed to be coping with the demands that the child placed on her, yet she had no other tasks to occupy her. Unlike most women who had children, she was not required to run a household, to cook or to spin wool while caring for her baby.

Edric was worried about Aelswith, but his main concern was the Lady Altruda.

He could not ignore the noblewoman. He noticed that Kenton was often with her, and that added to his worries. He could not understand why she would want the scarred man anywhere near her, and their association made him even more wary of Altruda's motives.

Yet the lady would always make a point of stopping to speak to Edric whenever she saw him. She was always pleasant, always asking how he was getting on, what he was doing and promising to offer prayers for his continued good health.

"You need not worry about me, my Lady," he told her.

"Oh, but I worry about everyone on the island," she replied with an air of sadness. "The Normans will come soon, and we will all be in grave danger."

"Hereward will keep them away," Edric stated confidently. "And Saint Etheldreda will protect us."

Etheldreda was a minor saint whose tomb was located in the abbey. This was a convenient source of revenue for the monks since many pilgrims came to Ely for the express purpose of offering devotions at the tomb. According to Abbot Thurstan, the

257

blessed Saint had been the original founder of the monastery on Ely and had somehow remained a virgin despite being twice married. Edric thought that sounded unlikely, but the monks accepted the tale as true, and Hereward took advantage of the devotion the people of Ely held towards Etheldreda by insisting that every man in his service should swear loyalty to the Saint and to the cause of English freedom. It was a solemn oath which bound the defenders together, and even Thane Barn's men had sworn the pledge.

Edric had willingly given his oath, but he also recalled Winter's gruff advice after they had sworn on the Saint's tomb.

"Pray to the Saint for aid and good fortune," the big warrior had said. "But trust in your axe to keep you safe."

Altruda also had something to say about the efficacy of Etheldreda's powers.

"Do you know how Etheldreda died?" she asked Edric.

"No," he admitted, suspecting he might not like what he was about to hear.

"She died from a tumour on her neck," Altruda informed him. "It was considered divine punishment for her vanity, because she had often worn expensive necklaces."

Edric's eyes automatically shifted to the golden necklace Altruda wore, but she merely laughed as she fluttered a delicate hand at him.

"I do not claim to be a saint," she told him. "My point is that vanity can lead to one's downfall. Bear that in mind the next time Hereward tells you how easy it will be to defeat the Normans. Even with the protection of Saint Etheldreda."

Edric had no idea whether she was telling the truth about Etheldreda's fate. If Brother John had still been there, he would have asked him the truth of the matter, but it was not the sort of question he wanted to put to any of the other monks. Whether it was true or not, he did recognise that Altruda was attempting to undermine his loyalty to Hereward.

He could not let that go unanswered, so he said, "If God struck Etheldreda down, why is she a Saint? That makes no sense."

Altruda smiled, "Ah, Edric, it is always such a pleasure to talk to you. You are one of the few around here who uses his brain. But, to answer your question, I understand there were claims of miracles taking place near the Saint's tomb when she was first interred."

"Then I will put my faith in her power," he stated firmly.

"I wish I had your confidence," she said with a sigh. "The Saint may be powerful, but King William has God on his side."

"Hereward says he is not our King," Edric countered.

Altruda regarded him with a faintly patronising smile.

"I am afraid, Edric, that men do not decide who will be their King. God makes that decision for us."

"The Witan chooses the King," he argued.

"And the Witan, guided by God, chose William," she said. "We may not like it, but William is our King."

Edric was annoyed with himself for not being able to entirely hold his own with her. Once she was gone, he would sometimes think of things he could have said to refute her point of view, but she always seemed able to outwit him whenever they spoke.

To add to his predicament, Hereward had noticed Altruda's habit of approaching Edric, and he was not pleased.

"Watch her, lad," he warned. "She is not to be trusted. What does she say to you?"

"Only that she fears what will happen when King William … I mean, The Bastard, comes here."

To his surprise, Hereward's response was to laugh and clap him on the back.

"Oh, I hope he does come here," the young Thane declared cheerfully. "We shall teach him a lesson in how to fight."

The king did not come, but his soldiers did. Reports arrived of hundreds of men and horses ploughing their way through the swamps to a point opposite Aldreth on the southern tip of the island.

"They can't cross the river without boats," Hereward asserted when the English warriors assembled in the refectory to hear the news.

"They don't need boats," Siward Barn told him. "They are building a bridge."

That news stunned everyone who heard it. A bridge would take time to construct, but it would allow the Normans to flood across the water and charge home against the defenders in large numbers.

Hereward was the only man who did not appear concerned.

"A bridge?" he asked. "That is good news."

"Good news?" Barn retorted. "It's not what I'd call good news. Somehow, we must stop them."

"Stop them?" Hereward grinned. "On the contrary, my friend. We must help them."

The arrival of the Norman army galvanised the defenders into action. Hereward assumed command of the defences at Aldreth, asking Siward Barn to ensure that his men watched the other parts of the island in case the bridge was a feint to draw their attention away from the real attack.

"I don't think the Normans are that clever," he confided to his gang, "but this way, Barn is kept out of my hair and still feels he is doing something useful."

The change meant that Edric and the others left Ely and marched south to Aldreth. Only Wulfric remained behind to act as Torfrida's bodyguard.

Edric had been anxious about leaving only one man, but Hereward ordered Martin Lightfoot to remain in Ely as well, and Ranald Sigtrygsson, who was slowly recovering from his wound, promised to help with the watch duties.

"I can't walk far," the Danish nobleman declared, "but I can sit in the corridor on a stool and take a turn on watch."

Edric could tell that Ranald was desperate to help, so he readily agreed to the man's suggestion.

"Kill a few Normans for me," Ranald told him with a cheery smile.

"I'll do my best," Edric promised.

He was glad to get away from Ely. The mood among the monks had deteriorated, and many of the townsfolk were nervous about what was going to happen. They had believed that their marsh-girded island was impregnable, yet the Normans had arrived on the far side of the southern river from where they were threatening to overrun the defences. Altruda's dire warnings of the fate that awaited them did nothing to improve the mood in the monastery, but Edric's focus was now on helping Hereward fight off the threatened assault. Pausing only to ask Torfrida to reassure Ylva that she would be safe, he joined the rest of the gang and set off for the southern defences where they met up with the two Siwards.

"We've got nearly three hundred men now," White proudly informed them as he gestured to the armed men who manned the earth rampart which had been dug near the river bank.

"Against how many Normans?" Hereward asked.

White's face grew solemn as he admitted, "We reckon about fifteen hundred."

"Five to one?" Hereward grinned. "That's about fair, I think. One Englishman is worth five Normans any day."

His men chuckled, then laughed aloud when he added, "And he's worth ten if he's got Danish blood in him."

His words quickly spread among the defenders. Most of them could trace some Danish ancestry because Ely lay within the old Danelaw from the days when England had been divided between the areas ruled by Saxons and Danes. The country had been unified for two hundred years, but many men still took pride in their Danish blood.

"Right!" declared Hereward. "Let's take a look at what the bastards are doing."

Edric joined Hereward and Siward White when they scrambled up the ramparts to gaze out at the bridge the Normans were building. It was low, just above the surface of the water, and wide enough for half a dozen men to march side by side as they crossed.

"They are using local men to help build it," White explained.

Hereward nodded, "How many of our own lads are helping?"

"We've sent twenty who claim to know about carpentry," White grinned. "The Normans have hired them without asking any questions."

"Good. That should mean we'll always know what's going on over there. But we also need to make it look as if we are worried by the bridge. We need to make raids at night as if we are trying to stop them building it."

Edric plucked up the courage to ask, "Why do you want them to build the bridge? Shouldn't we really try to stop them?"

"There's no fun in that," Hereward replied with a grin.

"Oh, yes," sighed White as he rolled his eyes. "Making night raids across the river will be much more enjoyable."

Edric did not think the night raids were fun at all. Hereward insisted on leading the first attack, so Edric and the others squeezed into little boats which were paddled across the river in the dead of night. As he had feared, the Norman sentries were on the lookout for just such an attempt, and the alarm was soon raised. Arrows flickered through the darkness, most splashing harmlessly into the river but some thudding into shields or catching one of the attackers. One thumped into the low gunwale of Edric's boat, quivering wildly when it stuck its sharpened tip into the wood barely a hand's breadth from his foot.

"A miss is as good as a mile!" Winter told him cheerfully as the boat crawled its way across the dark water.

Edric swore softly, crouching lower behind his raised shield while the men who were paddling the boat grunted and sweated with exertion and the arrows continued to fly all around them.

At last, the boats thumped on the muddy bank and the English warriors sprang ashore, screaming their war cries, but the Normans were ready for them. For all the efforts of the raiders, the piecemeal attack was easily driven back.

Edric did not manage to strike a single blow. He was too busy trying to keep track of Hereward and watching his back. In the darkness, with men shouting, running and swearing, with the clash of weapons and the ever-present danger of being stabbed by an unseen enemy, the fight was a nightmare of shadows and noise.

Hereward slashed his sword at the line of Norman shields but could make no impression on their defence, so he soon shouted the command to withdraw.

Disheartened, the raiders straggled back to the island having lost three men killed and another seven wounded. In return, they had accomplished nothing at all.

Except, as Edric knew, to convince the Normans that the defenders were seriously attempting to disrupt the construction of the bridge. He was one of the few who knew that Hereward did not want to prevent the Normans completing the project. He did not know why, except that the young Thane was counting on the men who had infiltrated the workforce to accomplish some secret mission.

"What's he up to?" Ordgar asked Edric one evening as they sat around a fire frying fish for their supper.

"I don't know," Edric admitted. "All I know is that he wants us to make it look as if we are trying to stop them, but he really wants them to finish the bridge."

"He's mad!" Ordgar observed cheerfully.

Winter said, "No, he just wants a proper fight. He wants them to cross the bridge so he can kill them."

"That's a dangerous plan," Auti remarked dourly.

"Aye, but destroying the bridge still leaves hundreds of the buggers over there, and they'd just come up with some other plan. At least this way we know where they are going to attack, which means we can chop them into little pieces and send the survivors running for their lives."

Winter appeared confident in Hereward's ability to smash any attack, but Edric privately agreed with Auti that the plan was a dangerous one.

Hereward's attempts to convince the Normans he was serious about destroying the bridge continued. Some men who could swim were sent out at night with saws and axes to cut at the support piles which had been driven into the deep, muddy water. Their approach was disguised by yet another raid involving boats and fifty men whose task was to land downstream and make as much noise as possible. Siward Red led that diversion and came back satisfied that they had created some confusion among the Normans, although the men who returned with him appeared downcast and frustrated.

The night raids were hated by everyone. Crossing the river meant they were exposed and vulnerable when there was sufficient moonlight for the Normans to see them coming. When they reached the far bank, the fighting was a nightmare of blundering around, hacking at shadows, and accomplishing very little.

The next tactic they tried was to fire burning arrows across the river in the hope they would set light to the wooden bridge. The Normans had, though, foreseen this, and had kept men close at hand with buckets of water to extinguish the flames. The English archers managed to hit one of the Normans, but the fire did no damage to the bridge which slowly but inexorably crept closer every day.

"We could always shoot arrows at the men doing the building," Siward White suggested.

"Most of them are Englishmen," Hereward replied. "I don't want to kill our own folk."

"Even if they are helping the enemy?" White argued.

"Even then," Hereward nodded.

Not that there was much opportunity to shoot at the workers, for a row of Norman soldiers lined up on the end of the bridge each day, presenting a wall of shields to the island. Behind them, the workers dragged the heavy timbers which would form the piles, the thick beams which would support the planking of the bridge, and the long, planed planks which formed the top layer of the walkway.

Driving in the piles was the most difficult part of the work, but the Normans had gathered more than enough manpower and the sounds of heavy hammering went on all day. As the bridge crept past the middle of the river, they began doing the heavy work at night, setting candles and oil lamps to illuminate the area. Day by day, night by night, in rain and sunshine, the bridge grew in length.

"It won't be long now," White observed as he and Hereward studied the progress. "Only a few more days, I reckon."

Edric glanced at Hereward but could see no trace of concern on his young leader's face.

"Double the night watch," was Hereward's only comment. "They might try to surprise us."

On the southern side of the river, Ivo de Taillebois watched the progress with equal interest.

"Only a few more days now," he remarked.

Abbot Turold, dressed in a tunic of chainmail and carrying a great mace at his side, nodded sourly.

"It can't come soon enough," the Abbot growled. "I want this over with."

"As do I," de Taillebois agreed, allowing his thoughts to wander to the subject of Torfrida.

"Are the ramps ready?" Turold demanded.

"Oh, yes. The only problem I foresee is their weight."

"That's no problem," Turold told him. "We will advance slowly, carrying the ramps in front of us like enormous shields. Then, when we reach the far end of the bridge, we will drop them into place to complete the crossing."

This was Turold's idea. De Taillebois had been worried about how the final section of the bridge could be completed without interruption from the English defenders. Turold had spoken to the engineers among his small army and had devised a solution. Instead of building the bridge all the way across, the final section would consist of two heavy ramps of wood which would be dropped to span the final gap. Pointed stakes on the end of the ramps would be slotted into holes in the surface of the bridge to hold the ramps in place, and the Norman soldiers would swarm across, climb the ramparts and overwhelm the defenders.

"I want archers shooting at the wall to keep their heads down," Turold told de Taillebois. "And I want ladders following the first wave so we can climb the rampart."

"It's nearly ten feet high," de Taillebois pointed out.

"So make sure the ladders are long enough," Turold snapped. "Ten feet isn't all that high."

De Taillebois did not argue. In his opinion, a ten foot earthen wall was more than high enough when there were men on the top throwing rocks, spears and buckets of excrement down at the attackers. Fortunately, Turold did not expect de Taillebois to accompany the first wave of the assault.

"I want you on this side," the Abbot told him. "Get men across quickly. Don't let them shirk. Send them over at a run. As soon as we lower the ramps, we need to get as many men across the river as we can."

"It will be as you command, Lord Abbot," de Taillebois assured him.

Apparently satisfied, Turold led the way back to his tent where a servant poured goblets of wine for each of the noblemen.

As he lifted his cup to his lips, the Abbot remarked, "Lady Altruda sent another message. Her tame monk delivered it this afternoon."

"Oh? What does she say?"

"It is Hereward himself who faces us. She says he has around three hundred men. The rest of the defenders are scattered around the island guarding other approaches."

"Three hundred?" de Taillebois beamed. "Then our victory is assured."

"Indeed it is," Turold agreed.

Overcoming their mutual dislike, the two men clinked their goblets together as they drank a toast to their inevitable victory.

"Only a few more days," said Turold.

Edric watched with growing apprehension as the bridge inched nearer and nearer. There were several clashes, both by day and by night, as Hereward sent men out in boats to harass the Normans and to drive the workers back to the southern bank. Edric joined one raid but it was quickly over, the English warriors having only a few minutes to hack at the bridge's supports before they were driven back by the superior numbers of the Normans who came charging across the bridge.

Hereward seemed particularly shaken by that setback.

"That was too close," he murmured to himself as he frowned at the bridge. "We could have ruined everything."

Edric did not understand Hereward's concern, but he could not help noticing that there were no more attacks on the bridge other than a desultory loosing of arrows at the Normans who lined the near edge.

Watching the slow approach of the Norman construction, Edric could feel his stomach churning at the thought of the impending battle, and he became worried that he might turn tail like a coward when the fighting began.

Winter must have noticed his anxiety, for the big axeman asked him, "What's the worst that can happen?"

Edric almost laughed as he admitted, "They could kill us."

"Aye, there is that. But we'll all die one day. I always reckon it's how you live that's the most important thing."

"Standing up to bullies, you mean?"

"That's one way of putting it," Winter agreed. "Standing up for what you believe in is another."

"It's not so easy when you know what might happen to you, though, is it?" Edric challenged.

"No, but overcoming that fear is what makes you a man. Anyway, you're not the only one who's feeling a bit afraid."

"You're not scared, are you?" Edric asked in astonishment.

"Me?" Winter grinned. "No, lad. Fighting never did bother me. Ordgar says it's because I'm too stupid to be afraid. But most men feel scared before a battle. Take a look at how many of the lads are emptying their bowels more often than usual."

It was true. Edric had noticed men sneaking away hurriedly, or even dropping their trousers where they stood because the need was so urgent.

"Blood and shit are what war is all about," Winter observed jovially.

"And mud," put in Ordgar.

Edric gave a wan smile. Mud was certainly much in evidence. The earth wall they had dug along the bank of the river had a gentler slope on their side, with a wide step cut into the rear face so that the defenders could lean over the top of the rampart. That step had been partially lined with planks of wood and short strips of cut branches, but it was slick with mud, made additionally slippery by the constant tramping of feet and the frequent showers of rain that were such a feature of the English summer.

"It won't be long now," Winter said cheerily.

In fact, the attack came the following morning. The defenders were roused by the blowing of horns and urgent shouts. Scrambling up from where they had slept on the damp ground, they hurriedly pulled on their armour, grabbed weapons and shields, and ran to their allotted places on the wall.

Hereward ordered food to be handed out.

"We have a little time, I think," he announced as he stared across the river. "Get some bread into your bellies before the fun starts."

Edric chewed on a tasteless lump of dark bread while he studied the other side of the river. In the bright, clear light of dawn, he could plainly make out the Normans assembling in force, with some of them now lifting enormous blocks of wood, like the huge doors of a church, which they were setting up in front of their advance.

"Clever buggers!" observed Winter. "They're not going to try building the last section of the bridge. They're going to cross it using those things."

267

Norman archers drew up on the river bank on either side of the bridge. Soon, their arrows began to fly, arcing up into the air and tumbling all around the wall. Most fell short or looped too far to land behind the wall, but a few dropped around the defenders.

"Raise shields!" Hereward called, and the men lifted their round shields above their heads to protect themselves.

There were a handful of men armed with bows among the English defenders, but Hereward told them to save their arrows until the Normans were much closer. Edric thought this a strange command and shot Hereward a puzzled look, but received only a grin and a wink in response.

The Normans began to tramp onto the bridge, advancing slowly as the leading ranks sheltered behind the huge barriers they were carrying in front of them.

"That's no good," Hereward murmured. "They need to come faster than that."

Edric frowned, not understanding why Hereward was so desperate for the fight. He could not help but remember Altruda's warning about the effect of having too much pride, and Hereward seemed intent on allowing the Normans to come to close quarters. No more than half a dozen of them could march side by side as they crossed the bridge but, once allowed to reach the island, they could fan out and attack all along the line of the defensive earthwork, or they could gather in a huge column and punch a way through the very centre of Hereward's defence. Surely, Edric thought, it would be best to at least slow down their advance. Yet Hereward obviously wanted the opposite.

It made no sense to Edric, but his puzzlement turned to shock when Hereward suddenly announced, "They are coming too slowly. We need to make them hurry. White, you stay here. Edric, bring the rest of the lads."

So saying, he sheathed his sword, slung his shield on his back, and clambered over the rampart, slithering down the muddy embankment to the narrow strip of grass which lay between the earthwork and the river.

For a moment, nobody moved, then Edric shouted at the gang to follow, and led the way over the earth bank, slipping and sliding as he dropped to join Hereward.

Winter, Ordgar and Auti scrambled after them, cursing and grumbling as they slid down the steep slope.

"Right," said Hereward. "Shields and axes ready, boys. Let's encourage them to come and get us."

Winter uttered a feral cry of delight as he gripped his axe and stepped to the river's edge, the others joining him in a line, with Hereward at the centre.

"Shield wall," Hereward ordered as arrows hissed through the air around them.

Edric linked his large, round shield with Hereward's, while Winter did the same on Edric's right. Auti and Ordgar took up similar positions on Hereward's left.

Edric could contain himself no longer. He could not understand what Hereward was trying to achieve. The strip of land they were defending was barely twenty feet wide and offered no protection. If they stood here, they would need to face the entire Norman advance on their own because there was no easy way to climb back up the embankment.

"Why are we doing this?" he asked in a voice which came out of his lips as a hoarse rasp. "There are hundreds of them."

"And five of us," Hereward replied calmly. "You are right, it is a bit unfair. Maybe a couple of you should go back."

Edric laughed despite himself, as did the others.

Hereward, meanwhile, concentrated on the advancing Normans. More and more of them were crowding onto the bridge as the front ranks pushed the huge barricades ahead and tramped across the planking.

Hereward shouted something in French, the words a mystery to Edric but the tone clear. He was taunting them, encouraging them to come and fight him.

And they responded by pushing forwards more quickly, partially blocking the archers' view, which allowed the five men some respite.

"That's better!" Hereward breathed. "Stamp those feet, move those legs!"

Edric had never felt so terrified in all his young life, yet he stood his ground, holding his shield in the wall, gripping the long haft of his axe in his right hand and doing his best to appear ferocious. He could not see the leading Normans because the huge ramps still blocked his view, but the men behind were clearly visible and he could even make out the expressions on the faces of individual soldiers. The Normans were grinning, shouting obscenities at the English, and calling encouragement to one another as they pushed their way across the bridge. The great barricades were surging towards them now, the men holding them being pushed on by the press of numbers behind them.

"That's the way!" Hereward said approvingly. "Now, lads, time to offer up some prayers."

"Prayers?" Edric gulped, wishing Hereward had a better plan than relying on divine intervention.

Almost conversationally, Hereward asked his companions, "Do you know what happens when a column of marching men crosses a bridge?"

"They keep their feet dry," Ordgar suggested.

Hereward chuckled, "Apart from that."

He paused for a moment, then, receiving no answer, explained, "If they march in step, they create a vibration which causes the bridge to shake. It even happens on stone bridges. The Romans knew this, for their soldiers used to break step when crossing bridges."

Edric followed the reasoning but still could not reach the conclusion Hereward was obviously hoping for.

"You think they will shake themselves off the bridge?" he asked.

"Oh, I'm hoping for much more than that," Hereward replied. "They might not all march in step, but I want as many of them on the bridge as possible."

"Why?"

"What do you think our lads who joined the construction work were doing?"

"I thought they were spying for you," Edric answered, wondering whether Hereward was merely talking in order to distract their attention from the impending attack.

Hereward grinned, "No, Edric. They were sawing through support beams, fixing the struts with fewer nails than they needed, or even cutting the nails short so only the heads were left showing. That means it looks as if the beams are properly secured while, in fact, there is very little holding them in place."

Winter guffawed, "The bridge is going to collapse?"

"I bloody hope so!" Hereward chuckled.

Edric understood at last, but the bridge was crammed with Norman soldiers and still appeared as solid as ever, and the great ramps had almost reached the final gap.

He readied himself for the fight. The still, morning air was alive with sound. The tramp of Norman boots on the bridge, the hiss of arrows, the shouts in French and English being exchanged by the two sides. Above it all, Edric could hear his own breathing coming in great gasps.

Hereward remained an oasis of calm amidst the cacophony.

"All right," he called to his men. "When they lower those ramps, they'll come at us fast. So listen to me. As soon as they start to drop, we turn and run for the wall. I want no heroics. All we need to do is make them chase us. Do you hear me, Winter?"

Winter grunted in disapproval, as if he believed he could hold back the entire force of Normans on his own.

Then the waiting was over, because the ramps had reached the end of the bridge and begun to topple towards them as the Normans shoved them across the final gap. That space was around twenty feet wide, Edric guessed, and he wondered whether the ramps might fall short, but Hereward was already shouting at them to turn and run.

The line broke and the five men pounded towards the earth wall. Siward White had lowered ropes for them to clamber up, but the roar of the Norman soldiers filled the air and Edric heard the pounding of feet on wood as the enemy surged across the ramps and came in pursuit. With a sudden sense of dread, he realised they would have no time to climb the wall before they were cut down.

Hereward must have reached the same conclusion, for he yelled, "Turn and face them!"

Edric spun round, just in time to see a charging Norman raising his sword to strike at him. Instinctively, Edric raised his shield and crouched, but he also swung his long axe at the man. The weapon's reach was greater than the Norman's sword, especially when wielded in one hand. The huge, flaring blade went past the edge of the Norman's kite-shaped shield, allowing Edric to haul it away from his opponent. The Norman's sword smashed down on Edric's own shield with numbing power, and the two men crashed together as the Norman's momentum carried him into Edric. But Edric had pulled the man off balance. He now shoved forwards, ramming his shield into the man's body, knocking him over. Then, in one quick move, he slammed his axe down, carving deep into the man's chest, shattering chainmail links and gouging through the armour.

Another sword came from his right. He yanked his axe free, swinging wildly and knocking the blade away, then Hereward's sword flashed and Edric's opponent fell back, only to be pushed forwards, off balance, by the men crowding behind him.

Desperately, Edric swung his axe in an overhand arc, crashing the blade down onto the man's head, chopping clean through his helmet and burying itself deep in the Norman's skull in a shower of blood and brains.

Edric screamed, yelling his rage and fear, as he frantically tugged the axe free, fending off another attack with his shield, then thundering his axe into a Norman shield, splitting the wood and buckling the iron frame.

It could not last, of course. He was dimly aware of Hereward on his left, and Winter on his right, but five of them could not hold back the enormous surge of soldiers swarming across the bridge. Only the growing pile of dead and wounded men in front of them prevented the Normans from swamping them. Spears and arrows were showering down from the wall behind Hereward's gang, slowing the Normans who were flooding across the ramps, but there were so many attackers it was like trying to hold back the sea.

Then Winter gave a roar of defiance and hurled his shield into the face of the man in front of him, smashing the Norman's teeth and felling him instantly, creating a small space for Winter to move into. Grabbing his axe in both hands, he leaped forwards, swinging the long haft to left and right, shattering wood, armour and bones as he sent men tumbling like skittles.

For an instant, the Normans were horrified by the unexpected counter-attack, and Hereward took advantage, his sword licking out to take a man in the throat. Edric, too, advanced, stepping over a corpse to deliver another stunning blow which took off a Norman's sword hand at the wrist.

It was, he knew even as he took part, the last, desperate throw of the dice, a mad, futile attempt to take as many of the enemy with them as they could. It could only end one way, but he did not care. All he cared about was that, if Hereward was killed, the defenders on the wall would lose heart. Everyone he cared for would fall into Norman hands. Aelswith, Torfrida, Ylva and Seaver would never know how hard he had fought to defend them, nor how Hereward's pride had led him to this mad death.

Yet he fought on. He killed another man, then took a blow on his arm, his byrnie protecting him but the strike numbing his grip so that he almost dropped his axe.

He flung his shield up to block another sword, slipped on the mud, and almost fell. He blocked the blow, but heard a cracking sound as the willow of his shield split. One more strike would shatter it, and then he would be at the mercy of the Normans.

With a roar of defiance, he surged upwards, swinging his axe in blind rage, finding no target but driving back the men facing him.

And then, without warning, it happened.

There was a sound like thunder and again Edric heard the cracking of timbers, but this was far louder than the sound his shattered shield had made. This awful, ear-splitting noise was as if an entire forest had been felled at once. He heard screams and yells of panic to the accompaniment of loud splashes, and everyone stopped, standing as if expecting the wrath of God to strike them down at any moment.

Men forgot the fight as they blinked, turned and gaped in horror at the river.

Because the bridge had gone. One moment it had spanned the river, bearing hundreds of soldiers, the next moment it had vanished beneath the surface of the water, leaving only the surging of spreading waves to mark where it had been swallowed.

Stumps of piles stood in the water like isolated stepping stones, and shattered planks floated on the river's dark surface. One man could be seen clinging desperately to one of the piles, but he lost his grip and vanished, pulled beneath the water by the weight of his armour, leaving barely a splash to mark where he had been.

Hundreds of his companions had suffered the same fate. Encumbered by their armour, they had no chance of swimming, and had plunged into the water when the bridge collapsed under their weight.

Only a score or so remained alive on the near bank, but none of them showed any sign of wanting to continue the fight. They were all staring in disbelief at the river, as were the hundreds of Normans who remained on the far bank.

"Not before time," Hereward muttered wearily. "I thought the damned thing was never going to fall down."

Edric breathed a long sigh of relief. The fight was over, the battle ended and, against all expectation, he had survived.

He looked at the few remaining Normans who stood forlornly beside the river, their escape now cut off. One of them, he noticed, was a big man with a pot-belly who carried a large mace in his right hand. He was looking around wildly, as if seeking some escape route. He was obviously a man of rank, for he wore a silver crucifix on a gold chain around his neck.

Hereward called to him, "I suggest you surrender, my Lord. My men are keen to continue the fight, but I fear it would be too one-sided since you only outnumber us four to one now. Also, I have several hundred men up there on the wall behind us who would dearly love to kill a Norman."

"What terms do you offer?" the man growled angrily, as if unwilling to acknowledge that he was in no position to bargain.

"That depends on who you are," Hereward told him.

One of the huge ramps which had been trampled into the river bank now became dislodged and floated slowly away as if it were a symbol of the Norman defeat. The man with the mace glanced at it, scowled miserably, then faced Hereward again, his face flushed red with anger and frustration.

"I am Abbot Turold of Peterborough," he replied in a surly admission.

Hereward grinned, "Then I offer you these terms, Lord Abbot. Your men will be allowed to go free once they have surrendered their armour and weapons. You, however, will remain here as our guest."

"Your prisoner?"

"For the time being," Hereward nodded amiably.

Turold had no option, and everyone knew it. His men, who had been so confident of victory only a few minutes earlier, now wanted only to live. They had lost, and surrender was all that remained.

But the morning's surprises were not over. They were still waiting for Turold's response when another great shout went up from the Normans on the far side of the river. This time, it was not a shout of triumph but a wail of despair.

Edric saw men begin to run, the army dissolving into a rabble as they tried to flee from some unseen enemy.

Horns could be heard, their sharp blare faint yet triumphant as they called men to battle.

"What in God's name is happening now?" Auti wondered aloud.

Hereward turned, looking back to the top of the wall which was lined with armed men.

"What do you see?" he called up to Siward White.

White was grinning. He removed his helmet and ran his fingers through his blond hair as he shouted back, "You are not going to believe this, cousin, but I see a flag bearing a golden cross on a dark blue background."

For a moment, Hereward frowned in puzzlement, but then he began to laugh, delight beaming from his face as if his every prayer had been answered.

"What is it?" Edric asked.

"It's a bloody miracle," Ordgar chuckled. "That's what it is."

"A miracle?" Edric scowled. "What sort of miracle?"

"Do you not know?" Hereward responded, still smiling broadly. "That standard is the flag of Mercia. It seems others have come to join our rebellion at last."

He continued to laugh, and Edric joined in, his relief flooding his emotions. The men of Mercia, who had twice been defeated by the Normans and whom everyone thought were crushed, had once again risen up and come to join them.

It was indeed a miracle; even more unexpected than the collapse of the bridge. Men were shouting with glee, waving their weapons in salute, grinning like idiots as the full realisation struck them.

Yet still the wonders were not ended.

Siward White could scarcely be heard over the cheering as he shouted more news.

"I see the banners of Northumbria as well. All the men of the north have come!"

Edric could hardly believe what had happened. The Norman attack had been swallowed by the river, and the remaining Normans were fleeing before a vengeful horde of Mercians and Northumbrians who had attacked them from the rear.

So Edric laughed, and his companions laughed with him, because Saint Etheldreda had heard their prayers and answered them. The rebellion had survived, and the men of England were rising up to join them.

Ely was safe, and with Mercian and Northumbrian help, they would be able to free the whole of England from Norman rule.

To be continued ...

Edric Strong's story will continue in volume two, titled "Doomsday".

Author's Note and Acknowledgements

When I started writing this story it was intended to be a single volume. However, the more I delved into the history and legends surrounding Hereward, the longer the tale became. Eventually, I had to accept that the story would need to be split into two volumes, which led to needing to make a decision as to where the division should take place. I decided that the victory over the first Norman assault on Ely was the appropriate time since it was roughly half way through the first draft of the longer tale and it would allow me to end the story on a high note. My apologies to everyone who feels it leaves a lot of things hanging. It does. Hopefully that hasn't spoiled the overall story and will also encourage you to read the second volume.

As for Hereward, readers who are unfamiliar with his tale will note that he is never referred to by the name history tends to use. He was never called Hereward the Wake during his lifetime, and this addition to his name seems to stem from attempts by the Wake, or Wac, family to link themselves to him in an attempt to make them appear more English than their Norman descent would otherwise suggest. This sort of thing became fairly common in the centuries when England lost control of much of what is now France, and families descended from Normans tried to distance themselves from their ancestry.

The other main thing to note is that much of what is known about Hereward comes to us from accounts which are either legendary, semi-legendary or pseudo-history. It is almost impossible to distinguish fact from fiction, especially when some of the accounts flatly contradict each other. I have tried to include all of the known historical events with the main features from the other tales about Hereward, but the requirements of my own narrative have meant that some aspects have been slightly altered, others glossed over and a few minor ones omitted altogether. So if your favourite bit of

Hereward folklore does not appear in this or the second volume, I'm sorry.

Finally, I should mention the proliferation of Siwards in this story. One of the enduring tales of Hereward is the story of his "gang" which is, incidentally, one of the first uses of that word in English. Members of his gang are named, including his alleged cousins Siward Red and Siward White. Some accounts refer to them as Rufus and Blonde respectively, but since these are French versions, I felt it better to stick to the English names.

And then there is Siward Barn. He is a genuine historical figure who was on the Isle of Ely during the rebellion. Since I needed a character who would argue the case against antagonising the Normans, and since that character really had to be someone of noble rank in order to have sufficient status, I felt it was impossible to omit Siward Barn and create some other fictional character. So there are three Siwards in the story.

As for Edric Strong, he is entirely fictional but he will continue to play an important part in this retelling of the Hereward tale.

As always, I owe thanks to a team of friends and family who have provided feedback on the draft story and on the numerous typing errors I made. Moira Anthony, Stuart Anthony, Ian Dron, Stewart Fenton and Liz Wright provided an enormous amount of help and support. My thanks to them all.

GA

November, 2018

Other Books by Gordon Anthony

All titles are available in e-book format. Titles marked with an asterisk are also available in paperback.

In the Shadow of the Wall*
An Eye For An Eye*

Home Fires*
Hunting Icarus*

The Calgacus Series:
       World's End*
       The Centurions*
       Queen of Victory*
       Druids' Gold*
       Blood Ties*
       The High King*
       The Ghost War*
       Last Of The Free*

The Constantine Investigates Series:
       The Man in the Ironic Mask
       The Lady of Shall Not
       Gawain and the Green Nightshirt
       A Tale of One City
       49 Shades of Tartan

A Walk in the Dark (Charity booklet)

ABOUT THE AUTHOR

Born in Watford, Hertfordshire, in 1957, Gordon's family moved to Broughty Ferry in the early 1960s. Gordon attended Grove Academy, leaving in 1974 to work for Bank of Scotland. After a long but undistinguished career, he retired on medical grounds in 2008 without having received any huge bankers' bonuses.

Registered blind, Gordon had more time on his hands after retiring so, with the aid of special computer software, he returned to his hobby of writing and had his debut novel, "In the Shadow of the Wall" published in 2010. Gordon's books are now being read by a world-wide audience. As well as his historical adventure stories, he has ventured into crime fiction with some spoof murder mysteries in the "Constantine Investigates" series. He is also kept busy with speaking engagements, visiting libraries, schools and community groups to talk about his books.

In addition to his novels, Gordon devotes some of his time to raising funds for the RNIB. As well as visiting schools and social clubs to talk about his sight loss, he has self-published a charity booklet titled, "A Walk in the Dark", a humorous account of his experiences since losing his eyesight. The booklet is available free from Gordon's website www.gordonanthony.net . All Gordon asks is that readers make a donation to RNIB. This booklet can also be purchased from the Amazon Kindle Store. Gordon will donate all author royalties to RNIB.

Now completely blind, Gordon continues to write stories and, in his spare time, attempts to play the guitar and keyboard with varying degrees of success.

Gordon is married to Alaine. They have three children and one grandchild. The family lives in Livingston, West Lothian.

You can contact Gordon via his website or by sending an email to ga.author@sky.com

Printed in Poland
by Amazon Fulfillment
Poland Sp. z o.o., Wrocław

51477156R00159